DEAD ON ARRIVAL

DEAD
ON
ARRIVAL

A NOVEL

MATT RICHTEL

WILLIAM MORROW

An Imprint of HarperCollinsPublishers

DEAD ON ARRIVAL. Copyright © 2017 by Matt Richtel. All rights reserved. Printed in the United States of America. No part of this book may be used or reproduced in any manner whatsoever without written permission except in the case of brief quotations embodied in critical articles and reviews. For information, address HarperCollins Publishers, 195 Broadway, New York, NY 10007.

HarperCollins books may be purchased for educational, business, or sales promotional use. For information, please e-mail the Special Markets Department at SPsales@harpercollins.com.

FIRST EDITION

DESIGNED BY WILLIAM RUOTO

TITLE PAGE AND PART TITLE IMAGE © KEKYALYAYNEN/SHUTTERSTOCK

Library of Congress Cataloging-in-Publication Data has been applied for.

ISBN 978-0-06-244327-4

17 18 19 20 21   LSC   10 9 8 7 6 5 4 3 2 1

DEAD ON ARRIVAL

PROLOGUE

TARRY BLACK HORIZON. So dark, without contrast, it was as if they weren't moving at all. Flecks of condensation pecked the wide, arched windshield and disappeared.

Inside the cockpit swirled the pungent odor of nerves. Delta flight #194, the night's last inbound, and something wrong.

Captain Eleanor Hall stared into the flat Colorado sky and reached overhead to the instrument panel. She twisted the backlit rate knob a quarter turn left.

"Descend to Field Elevation Set. Anything on the radio, Jerry?"

"All I got is static."

"Not good . . ." She shook her head and clicked on the engine anti-ice. Then double-checked to see that the FASTEN SEATBELT sign was on. She glanced at the gauges. Just four miles out now, traveling 278 knots with 19 knots on the tail.

"The protocol's pretty clear."

First Officer Jerry Weathers put his mouth to the radio. "Hayden clearance, Delta one-nine-four ready to copy IFR."

In response, he got only static.

"Hayden, copy. This is Delta one-nine-four . . ."

Static.

"Okay," Pilot Hall said, looking for a steady voice.

"No, not okay. It's been ten minutes, Eleanor," Jerry said. Not a peep from anyone—local or distant—in ten thousand feet. "Definitely not okay."

Eleanor tensed. Jerry bordered on the officious even when things weren't going to shit. She went down her checklist. The protocol said you landed anyway. Communications systems could be finicky and, at a small airport like this, the regional control tower might actually be located a long way off, in Salt Lake City, maybe Denver, even Cheyenne. Still, it qualified as odd, in the least, the whole world having gone suddenly silent.

"Hayden, copy," Jerry said.

Static.

"We're in control of this, Jerry." She rubbed the slick perspiration of her palm on her blue pants.

At least the plane seemed to be responding, and landing instrumentation had come a long way. If a pilot could land on an aircraft carrier in World War II, two seasoned pilots and a whole lot of technology could surely touch down softly on an actual landing strip, even in the dark.

"Twenty-five hundred feet. You set the Nav?"

"Yep, for the third time. I got a good ident on the localizer. Must be a glitch at the comm tower. Doesn't explain why traffic is down everywhere."

"Stay with me, Jerry."

Eleanor listened to the wheels unfold—a sound that reminded her of a baby's hum.

"Landing gear down." Ordinarily, composure was her forte. It's why the airline used her for those corporate pep talks to new pilots, who could barely hide their displeasure at suffering a welcoming address. They were often military guys, not the kind of folks who relished a rah-rah speech unless it was before a bombing raid. They might've gotten a kick out of this: landing without communications, at night, at a tiny airport in the Colorado mountains outside Steamboat Springs.

Two miles, 214 knots, still the tailwind.

"What goes up must come down," she said.

"That's odd."

"Sorry, I just meant: We went up in the air. We gotta come down. This is good a time as any."

"No . . ."

"What? Fifteen hundred feet."

"Flaps 15," he announced. "Never mind—the other thing."

"Jerry?" She allowed herself to turn to her first officer and copilot. He was more than a head taller than her, thin and bordering on gangly. Long arms and legs. His elbows always seemed to be in the way. He hunched his neck in the way of someone uncomfortable with his height when he was in middle school and so took to shrinking in. Still, to those who didn't know him, he struck a pilot's confident pose. Eleanor knew him. This kind of pressure could get to him. It's why she had been pressing him on the communications.

"It's just . . . it's okay. When I pressed the foot brake, it was a little givey," he said.

"At one thousand. And now?"

"Less. I got this."

Less than a mile out, 150 knots.

"Final flaps?"

"At thirty. It's just . . . the instrument panel, did you see it—a second ago?"

"Jerry, I can see the ground, okay? We need to focus. The panel looks okay."

"It blinked."

"It looks fine to me. We're at five hundred."

"It blinked on and off. It . . ." He shook his head and didn't finish the thought.

She clicked on her headset and spoke. "Hayden traffic, this is Delta 194. We're in final, downwind from two."

More static.

The plane decelerated with that vacuum roar, touched down with three bumps, and raced into a taxi, the midsize jet speeding down the strip. Eleanor exhaled loudly, with enormous relief. Ahead and through the flight deck window on both sides, she could make out the tiny airport lit only by the hazy light from the nose.

"I think a drink is in order," Jerry said. "Or five."

Eleanor felt an urge to discourage him but decided to let Jerry have his fantasy that they might, at last, share cocktails at some hotel port of call.

"They put us at a lodge over by the mountain," he said.

She held her tongue. But it wasn't only because she didn't want to be presumptuous about Jerry's overture. It was the eerie nature of the airport. Unusually quiet, even for this time of night. In her left hand, she held the intercom to communicate to the passengers, and on her lips she held the words: *Welcome to Steamboat.*

But she couldn't get them out.

She pressed the button to talk and what came out was: "This is the captain. Please keep your seats for a moment; we're still . . . we're getting some unusual weather."

She depressed the button and stared out the window.

"What weather? Eleanor, what are you talking abou—"

He stopped fiddling with landing protocol. He looked over at her. "What are you . . ."

"Look."

She was mesmerized by the image in front of the plane.

"What the . . ."

"Oh my God."

PART I

STEAMBOAT

ONE

"D R. MARTIN?"

The voice came from the distance, echoed, died out. Lyle looked down at a square oak dinner table carved with names and initials he couldn't make out. Deep grooves etched inexpertly with a jagged blade. In the middle of the table stood an overstuffed burlap sack. It overflowed with fine white powder. Next to it, a small, clear plastic medicine cup.

Lyle picked up the cup with an unsteady hand, studied it, squinted to make out the dose at three tablespoons. Jammed it into the chalky substance in the sack. He lifted it to his lips, tried to drink, then swallow. Coughed, dust flew. It settled.

"Dr. Martin." Closer now. "Please. It's . . . it's vital."

The powder stirred, churned. Then became a flurry, a miniature tornado, a violent dust storm, swirling and pregnant over the bag. Lyle withdrew, shielded his eyes. The bag bulged, a shape emerged. Black and angular. Wings. Then snarling nostrils, spewed spittle, venom. A bat. Bright red eyes. It flapped furiously. Lifted, became airborne but only momentarily. The bat stalled, fluttered, straining upward as it got sucked back down and submerged into the ashy grave.

A nudge to Lyle's shoulder. "I . . . wait . . ." The plastic cup spilled from his hand.

He sucked in air, gulped, desperate to swallow. He shook his head. Another shoulder nudge, this one hitting its mark. Lyle willed his eyes open. He made out strands of red hair. *I'm dreaming,* he thought, managing, finally, a swallow. It, the dream, everything, has turned drug sour; too much diphenhydramine chasing too much insomnia.

He studied the hair—still from the beachhead of wakefulness.

"Melanie?" he whispered. The question was hardly out of his mouth before he knew the answer: no, not Melanie. Just someone with hair like hers, angry red. This woman was older than Melanie, not much of a resemblance at all. She blinked quickly. The clench of her jaw awoke Lyle.

Something was wrong.

"Are you Dr. Martin?"

He focused on the name tag on the woman's blue uniform. Stella. She leaned in, near his left ear. A flight attendant; he started to make sense of it. Full face, freckles, an animal smell—fear.

"May I have water?"

"They need a doctor," said the woman. She lowered her voice further. "In the flight deck. Dr. Martin. Lyle Martin?"

"How do you . . ."

"The manifest has all the names. Please, are you a medical doctor?"

He glanced around, saw eyes turned his direction. "Flight deck?"

"You were sleeping. On the way to Steamboat. I'm sorry to have awakened you."

Lyle unclasped his hands. He stretched his arms so that his fingers rested on his knees. He pressed fingertips into jeans, creating sensation. He needed to get his bearings. But, really, he could see this woman's desperation and it annoyed him. He sensed this infinitesimal delay in recognition would send a laser shot of annoyance, establish a pecking order. It was cruel and he didn't like that he was doing it and he couldn't help himself.

"Are you listening? Please."

"Yes, a doctor." More or less. Licensed, not practicing.

"Is someone sick?" asked the woman sitting next to Lyle. "Is that the problem?" She was slight, didn't take up the full width of even these tight quarters, with a mouth that looked to open little when she spoke.

"The pilot asked for a doctor," the flight attendant addressed the woman. "You know as much as I do from the announcement. I think everything is fine. Please keep the shades down.

"Can you join me, Dr. Martin?"

"Yes, right."

He stood, bumped his head on the overhead compartment, felt the eyes on him again, looked down. Focused on his right foot, the aged gray-and-maroon running shoe, and understood what it was that had caught his attention. His foot was stable. Not gently rocking as it would be in flight. No engine noise. Hadn't she said they were on the way to Steamboat? They'd landed?

He followed the flight attendant down the aisle. Around row 12, on the right, a woman with a shaking hand reached to open the shade.

"Please keep it down," the flight attendant chirped, her voice strained to the point of cracking.

"Why?" asked the woman. "Give me a break," someone else moaned.

"The pilot said it's to keep the temperature down. It's cold on the tarmac."

"So."

Tarmac, Lyle thought to himself. Maybe the pilot got sick and there was an emergency landing. Maybe they never took off. The woman in row 12, with thick arms—*probably diabetic,* Lyle thought—closed her shade. It set off another little annoyance. People are pliant on planes. *Powerless,* Lyle thought, *flying chattel.* He kept walking forward. The plane was neither full nor particularly big. One of the midsize deals, smaller even, less than three-dozen people. Cloth seats, a worn plane, but with those little screens mounted behind each one.

Lyle felt the eyes on him. Who, they must be wondering, was this man with the slight hitch in his gait, and light brown hair pasted to the side of his head from sleep? Still, even now, Lyle had the look of someone sturdy, even important, which he once had been.

"Please take your seat," the flight attendant urged a tall man as they threaded through four rows of first class.

"I need to get something from the overhead," the man protested. He wore noise-canceling headphones on his ears, and spoke a decibel too loudly.

"Take your seat. Just give us a few minutes." The flight attendant paused at the flight deck door and waited until Lyle caught up.

"I'm Stella. You're a doctor, doctor, right? Not a Ph.D. doctor."

"Both. Infectious disease, immunology. I'm not sure I can be of much help. We're on the ground?"

The woman nodded.

"In Steamboat?"

"Yes." But she half shrugged, noncommittal.

"Hang on." The flight attendant knocked on the flight deck door. A small slider window opened, giving way to an eye. The flight attendant explained she had the doctor, and the eye blinked. Lyle heard a woman's voice, faintly, say, "Step aside and let him in."

Lyle looked back at the planeload of passengers to see many of them craning into the aisle to glean his purpose.

He walked into the flight deck.

It was dark—outside, at least. Inside, the controls remained lit up, somewhat, a handful of red lights. The air hung, stale. Seated to his left in a tan chair, a woman, he thought, though her back was to him. She must be the pilot. To his right, facing him, sat the navigator or copilot or whatever. Between them, and overhead, a dense instrument panel that looked like the electrical version of wall-to-ceiling carpeting. In front of each pilot, two screens, each black. Between them, a big handle, which Lyle presumed to be the throttle. Other than that, it was Greek to him.

"I'm Lyle Martin."

"Eleanor Hall; the first officer is Jerry Weathers. You're a doctor."

"Yes." Thought: *Doctor*-ish. *Enough of one. Used to be.* Maybe that's why they kept asking him. To see if it was still true. "Is someone sick?"

Eleanor reached down to her right to the control panel and flipped a white switch.

Outside, there was an explosion of bright, the airplane's headlights. They illuminated a swath of pavement, the tarmac. A second later, she turned off the light. But the images were burned into Lyle's drug-tinged brain: a man in an orange jumpsuit, lying on the ground beside a luggage transporter; two other workers toppled upon each other; a desolate hangar to the right; and the clincher—inside the window of a small airport, a half-dozen would-be passengers or staff. Motionless.

"As near as we can tell," Eleanor said. "Everyone out there is dead."

TWO

LYLE HATED STABILITY and disruption in equal measure. When Melanie started putting sex appointments on their shared Google calendar, he skipped town for three days. And stayed awake for most of it. Niceties give him Olympic-caliber insomnia. He twice turned down speaking gigs that offered fifteen thousand dollars because the anticipation of the event left him ghost-walking until dawn. It wasn't the public-speaking part so much as the small talk afterward. It left him bobbing on the waves of inauthenticity, agitated, suffering fools, even ones not so foolish.

The vision outside the flight deck reminded him of one of the worst sleepless fits. The waking nightmares. A hole remained in his bedroom wall made with a broom handle attacking a waffle-size tarantula that wasn't there. Were these dead bodies for real? Were they dead?

"Was that . . ." Long pause.

"What it looks like," Eleanor said. "Bodies. Nothing moving out there."

"Jesus."

"No one answering distress calls. Nobody responding at all," the first officer chimed in.

"I didn't hear any shots," Lyle said. He figured he must've slept through it. Naturally, his mind would go to armed attack—terror or some heavily armed, local madman. Even Lyle, as isolated as he'd made himself the last few years, overheard or read the drumbeat of periodic, indiscriminate mass killings. Just days ago, a guy at the mall in Corpus Christi had mowed down shoppers and left a manifesto about how these "materialists" didn't understand the true spirit of Christmas.

"I don't think it's . . . a shooting." The pilot's voice sounded hoarse, phlegmy, halting. "Everything is calm."

"You said *everyone*. Everyone is dead."

"Everyone."

Lyle cleared his throat, started to get his footing. "How do you know this isn't an isolated thing—something at the airport?"

"I don't."

He looked outside, tried to. Not much to see, darkness and ghost outlines of the terminal, where he'd seen the bodies. "So why not just dock the plane?"

"We can't just pull up to a gate without help and, besides, I don't know how safe it is out there. Could be . . ." She shrugged. *Anything.*

He fell silent and realized he had no idea what they were asking of him. A medical opinion? Or some reassurance? Neither seemed realistic. He settled on a more primitive and frightening reason: they had no clue what was going on. They must have been sitting here for a while and had finally succumbed to getting outside input—from the doctor with hair matted against his forehead who had drugged himself to sleep.

"You can't get the police?"

"Like we said." Jerry's voice had an edge. Lyle got the impression the man didn't much want Lyle in the middle of this.

"You've sealed the vents." Lyle heard the scratch of sleep still thick in his throat.

"We're getting only recirculated. Mostly. The APU takes some from the outside." The pilot paused. "Auxiliary power. We used it briefly but decided against."

"We have flight deck oxygen. Discrete source, in the aft hold. Just below us," Jerry added.

"Are you . . ." Lyle tried to pick his words carefully but couldn't find suitably diplomatic ones. He asked, "Are you two feeling okay? Are you sick or is anyone on the plane feeling ill?"

"Not to our knowledge."

"I guess we're looking for a second set of eyes," the pilot said.

Lyle appreciated the frankness and its tone. But what good was he? He let himself tick down a list of options that might explain a handful of bodies inert here and no communications beyond the airport. The greatest likelihood was a terrorist attack, foreign or domestic. Nut job with a gun, or many of them.

After that, what?

Dirty bomb. One of those nasty things that leaves the buildings intact and kills all forms of life. He'd heard of it, but hardly could offer counsel.

Nuke.

So this was everywhere? Or the epicenter was near here? Small potatoes. In the middle of nowhere? Without fire? No.

His mind wandered further, drawing less from the literature than from more exotic theories. Nothing he'd ever read about resembled this.

Nerve agent, likelier than a nuke, given the modest evidence in front of him, maybe even likely. Sarin gas. It inhibits release or transfer of acetylcholine, a neurochemical that caused muscles to contract. In its absence, paralysis, asphyxiation. He'd heard about the Iranians' testing of a Zyclon B with hyperspeed effectiveness. It moved at the rate of data. A long shot but not as long as something organic, a virus, not very likely at all; nothing he knew about killed this quickly without killing the host so fast that the pathology couldn't spread. It's what made Ebola so, ultimately, self-destructive. When the CDC flew him into a Pakistani village, years earlier, after a *Washington Post* blog called him Young Dr. Pandemic, Lyle saw bodies akimbo much like the guy in the orange jumpsuit next to the luggage carrier, but in that case, with more signs of trauma, not, like this guy, just frozen in his tracks.

Bacteria. Forget it. The time between onset and death took, at its quickest, a day. Unless something had been gestating. But why only the people on the ground? Not in the plane?

He taught his last adjunct class at UCSF three years ago. Maybe there had been developments, diseases, stuff he hadn't kept up with, a superbug in the literature or lab. *It is flu season,* he thought. But no flu ever acted like this.

Could he be sleeping? Could this be a drug-induced hallucination, all the toxins in his brain and liver finally spilling over into madness? All this inside his mind. And this was going to be the trip that righted his ship.

"Say something," the pilot said.

"Food poisoning," he muttered.

"Seriously," said Jerry. Unclear if he was being sarcastic.

"Maslow's hierarchy. People gotta eat. You said no one is answering the communications?"

The pilot reached to the center console, unlatched a headset, brown leather strap across the top smudged from handling. He accepted them in his right hand, tentative.

"You have to put them on your ears."

They were tight—the pilot had a small head—and now he glanced at her as he widened the gadget's setting, catching her allure. Graceful, thin fingers on her right hand gripped tightly around a smaller throttle-type device, not the main throttle, next to her leg. Still couldn't see her face.

"Just static," he said.

She reached to the center console and turned a knob on the radio. New channel. More static. New channel. More static.

"The first two are the main air traffic control channels, the second two are backups. Nothing for nearly an hour."

"You've been sitting here an hour?"

No answer.

"How did you land?"

The copilot turned to Lyle. He looked a little bit like a fish—sloping forward, eyes bugging, and widened, wide lips. He said: "When the comms go down, you land."

Again, a slight edge. Defensive. Lyle decided not to wholly trust him but gave no indication. If Lyle had a true gift, it was mistrusting with great dignity, never with personal disdain. No one ever disliked Lyle for his healthy skepticism. Fact is, people liked Lyle, admired him, let him get away with his apparent non sequiturs and creative flights because they always sensed his goodness, even after he could no longer feel it himself.

"Mountains," Lyle said.

"What had you expected coming to Steamboat?"

What had he expected? Not much. A keynote address to a small conference and a chance to begin to make amends. Pay the bills again.

"Can you turn on the lights?"

"We don't want to bring attention to ourselves or continue to bring unwanted scrutiny from the passengers."

"Because?"

"Because I said so. Because it's obvious."

The pilot inhaled deeply. *Click.* In the five or so seconds during which lights flooded the tarmac, Lyle narrowed his focus from the macro—a small tarmac, such that it was, with one, two bodies lying on the ground to the desolate corporate jet parked to the left, painted red with the insignia "Corp Go," to the modest lounge in the single-story ranch-style airport frozen with bodies, to the dark maw of the hangar on the far right and, in the distance, wisps in the air, smoke?—to the micro—a single body, the man in the orange jumpsuit beside the luggage rack, frozen in time and space. Too far to discern anything. Other than: comatose or dead. No evidence of shrapnel wounds. No signs of explosion anywhere. But no movement since the last flood of light.

And mountains. They were in a valley.

Lights off. Just vapor trails of images. Then a fuzzy picture, inside his mind's eye, bodies on the corrugated roof shack off a dusty road in southern Tanzania. The images jolted Lyle, turned to static, faded.

"Looks like the Andes. Ski town, right?"

"Not in November. Mud town, now. Decent airport, though. Yampa Valley Airport, popularly known as Hayden."

"It's gun country."

"What?"

"People love their firearms here."

"We've been over this. Where's the blood?" the first officer asked.

Fair question. Why didn't anyone come to help? Where was the ambulance, the firefighters?

"Maybe he killed everyone in sight and flipped the power switch."

"Who?"

"Mr. Screw Loose. It's as good a working theory as any. Good reason to stay on the plane, I guess. What time is it?" Lyle asked.

"Here, just past one, in the morning."

"What's the temperature?"

"High thirties, but not trusting our gauges."

"You have electricity."

"Yes, sir."

Lyle squinted.

"Well?"

"We have fuel?"

"Yes."

Lyle looked at the pilot with a clear, unspoken question: *Then why not let's get the hell out of here?*

"Maybe enough. Probably. We've kept the engine running for the heat. No engine, no heat."

"But that burns fuel," said Jerry.

Lyle thought, *I slept through it*. He'd taken a Benadryl, or four. What you do when you can't get the good stuff. He rubbed his fingers together, creating sensation, assuring himself he's awake, sure now that he is.

"What kind of plane is this?"

"Do you know planes?"

"Not really."

"It's a 737, Boeing, two turbofan engines. But no communications and the electrical has been less than reliable. Some systems have gone offline. We have auxiliary power. I'm saving it. We take off, we risk coming straight down," the first officer said. "What we're asking is whether you've ever seen something like this—or read about it? That's the opinion we're interested in."

Lyle reached into his pocket, pulled out his phone. "May I?"

"It won't work. But be my guest."

He could look something up, but what exactly? It wasn't like he was going to go into PubMed and look up the symptom that everyone not on an airplane was dead. His phone came to life. No signal.

"Besides food poisoning," the pilot said with patience. Lyle liked the nuance in her voice, the control under pressure.

Lyle inched forward, as much as he could, before his knees hit the instrument panel. He put his phone down and peered into the night. Useful words and thoughts failed him.

"So in sum . . ." the first officer said.

"It's very hard to know from here. Looks to me like those people are either dead or quickly heading that direction."

"Why do you say that?"

"It's very cold."

There was a moment of silence.

"A storm is blowing in."

"How do you know?" Lyle asked. How could they see anything blowing in? No radar, presumably. But his interest was piqued; maybe the storm already came through, bringing something deadly, carried on the wind.

Jerry sighed. His meaning clear enough: *You might be a doctor but we're pilots.*

"What happens when you call someone, anyone?"

"It goes directly to voice mail or says all circuits are busy. We've been trying to find another human being for over an hour, just on the ground. I can barely contain the passengers."

"Won't they look for us, a plane that's off the radar?"

"One would think," the pilot said.

As Lyle took it in, he found his attention tugged to the dark horizon outside the plane.

"There," Lyle said.

"What?"

"The hangar. Movement."

THREE

DON'T SEE ANYTHING. It's too dark," said the pilot, turning to her second in command. "No need for that, Jerry."

Lyle saw the gun for the first time. It was holstered, sitting on the button-laden dash, beneath the copilot's sweaty palm. Lyle knew a bit about guns from the protection he sometimes got overseas and figured rightly it was a nine millimeter, standard issue for a licensed flight officer.

Jerry drummed his fingers on the gun. Lyle felt like the presence of the weapon should be telling him something but he wasn't sure what. It reminded him distantly of the meeting he had with the dean as things were spiraling downward. There was someone from the university's human relations department in the meeting, like a gun, just in case the dean needed to defend herself. *Lyle, your behavior belies the intellectual maturity of a . . .*

"Maybe I imagined it." Lyle sensed he didn't. But there was nothing there. Shades of black; even the grays were black, no reflections or shadows. "Why aren't the lights on out there?" Anywhere. He assured himself he saw something: a wisp, shape, vapor trail in an embodied form. Yet as he tried to see it again, he couldn't even make out the hangar.

"Some attacks disable electrical systems."

"So do some storms. Not unheard of."

"I'm not sure I can be of much help. I'm sorry," Lyle said. "Is there something specific you want from me?"

"We're grasping at straws," Eleanor said. Then, after a beat, she added, "I wanted to have something reasonable to say to them." It wasn't immediately clear who she was referring to but then, in the silence that followed, Lyle could hear the dull cacophony that swirled from outside the cabin. Voice stew starting to boil. "I wanted to make sure that we weren't missing something."

The pilot lifted the intercom. "I better say something."

She sat, lifted the intercom, pressed a button on the side with a sweaty-damp thumb. "Folks, I've got an update for you." Lyle almost laughed. She was using the same tone of voice they use when the gate's not ready or they need to deice the wings. He imagined what he'd next hear: *We've got a slight delay because everyone in the world is dead. Have some peanuts!*

"As you know, we've arrived safely at our destination in Colorado. Just outside Steamboat Springs. We are still working to fix our communications glitch." She stopped. Swiveled. Looked directly at Lyle for the first time. His first impression was that she was unwavering, and strikingly attractive but with slightly crooked front teeth, WASPy with a lemon twist, what his friends in college called light blue blood. He wanted to be on her team, could picture her painlessly climbing the company ladder, making only friends. "I'm going to come out and discuss all of this with you in person," she told the intercom, then took her thumb from the button on its side.

Just as she reached for the door, a rap of knuckles came from the other side, then a scratching sound.

"Hold on, Stella," Eleanor said through the door. "I'm coming." She cleared her throat, muttered something that sounded to Lyle like "No manual for this one."

To Jerry: "Only I get in here." To Lyle: "Would you mind joining me? Follow my lead. We're improvising, but with authority." Paused. "Got it?"

No answer required. She slid by Lyle to the flight deck door, glanced at him. "In your considered opinion, we're waiting to get some more information but there's no reason at all to panic."

"Yep. Been there, done that."

"Not that I expect you'll say anything."

Eleanor thought about what she'd say: *I'm Captain Eleanor Hall— the voice from the intercom. We're taking a cautious approach. Waiting for a position at the terminal. No reason for alarm.*

Another rap on the door and a woman's voice said, "Please."

"Okay, Stella." Eleanor opened the door.

She wasn't looking at Stella but a passenger.

"I'm coming out, I'd appreciate your—"

"They're all dead," the passenger said.

"What?"

The passenger, a short woman with short, bleach-blond hair beneath a gray-and-gold-colored knit hat, wobbled on her feet. She looked stunned and grabbed the side of the door. Eleanor glanced at Lyle, pursed her lips, and said to the passenger, "That's not at all clear. I've got a doctor here and there is evidence that people in the terminal may be ill or have some syndrome. I'm coming out to address that, and it's very important that we not spread rumors."

"What? Outside the plane?" the woman said. "No, I'm talking about . . . I'm saying that—"

It dawned on Eleanor and Lyle at the same time. They jointly pushed open the cockpit door all the way. They saw what she meant.

Row after row of passengers just like the man on the tarmac. Collapsed, tilted, crumpled, absent any signs of life.

"No, no," Eleanor said.

Lyle pulled on the arm of the passenger and yanked her inside the flight deck. He slammed shut the door.

"What the hell is going on?" Jerry said.

"It's in here."

FOUR

C OVER YOUR NOSE and mouth," Jerry said.

They all did it—Jerry, Eleanor, and the passenger—well, not Lyle. It wouldn't matter. Microbacteria or viruses would easily sneak through fabric or hands. He steadied himself against the wall and he whisked down a catalog of deadly invaders carried by air—the hantavirus and its many species: Puumala, Muleshoe, Black Creek Canal. Carried by rodents, defecated, dried and baked into dust, inhaled by humans. Inhaled. Delivered through the air. *There are horses up here, cows, presumably, lots of dry air.* Dried.

Where, he thought, was Melanie? And the baby. Got to be, what, three years old now and change? Safe, surely. Wherever they were.

"We have to get out of here," Jerry said.

"A spore, maybe, something that comes and goes," Lyle said, shrugging off the idea as quickly as it came, thinking aloud. Then he looked at the passenger. "What happened out there?"

"I . . ." Tears filled her eyes. "I came out of the bathroom."

"Where?"

"The back. Stop, stop, just tell me what's going on!" Freaked out, yes, but not entirely plaintive. Wavering between shock and what Lyle surmised as a basic inner strength. She looked distantly familiar and then he placed her; she'd been sitting next to him, sharing his aisle.

Eleanor stood and Lyle, without being aware of it, put out a gentle hand, trying to calm everyone. He made an equally subconscious decision to deliberately ask the passenger the most basic questions to steady her, so he could get as much information as possible before she imploded.

"We're trying to figure that out. You can help us. What's your name?"

She took a second to process it. "Alex."

"Alex?"

"Jenkins. It's a dream . . ."

"Alex, was there a noise? Before people got . . . sick. Was there a noise?"

"What kind of noise?"

"A scream," Eleanor said. "Was anyone in pain? I thought I heard voices."

"I was just going to the bathroom," she said. She brought a petite hand to the side of her face. Clear-painted fingernails had been gnawed. A nervous person, Lyle thought. Now trying to hold it together.

"And then you came out of the bathroom, and—"

"And I started to walk up the aisle and I noticed this guy was falling out of his seat—"

"Was in the process of falling, or had already fallen?"

"Cut this bullshit out!" Jerry said through the jacket he held to his mouth.

"Jerry . . ." said Eleanor.

"C'mon, we can play doctor later. We need to make a decision."

It was obvious what he meant. Stay or go.

Eleanor stood and walked to the door and stared out through the pinhole. "What about the cabin camera?" she said, sounding almost revelatory.

She'd completely forgotten. They had a hidden camera in the cabin that they rarely used; it felt gross, was how she put it. All the airlines had followed suit after JetBlue set the post-9/11 trend. Eleanor turned to Jerry, who fiddled with buttons in the middle instrument panel.

The screen in front of him flickered. It was a scene from a horror movie. A bird's-eye view of motionless passengers. They looked very much like soldiers felled midstep. Lyle took a step in the direction of the screen, not that there was much room to maneuver. He focused at random on one passenger, a man wearing a wool hat, form-fitting his skull, earphones protruding from the sides. His angular face tilted to the right, head almost on his shoulder. Lyle homed in further on the shoulders, pulled slightly back, not totally in repose. *What was it?* Lyle thought. He took a step closer, leaned in. *What is it about the guy?*

Then the image flickered. It went in and out. Jerry slapped the screen, willing it to life. But it flickered again, then went out.

"Does it record? Can you go back in time?" Alex asked. It was the first indication she wasn't too terrified to speak.

Jerry shook his head.

"Is this airtight? The cockpit?" asked Lyle.

"Flight deck," Jerry corrected him.

"Not the same thing?" Lyle regretted saying it immediately. Of course it was the same. This guy had to mark his territory.

Jerry continued. "And the answer is: the flight deck is more or less airtight. But it doesn't matter because we already opened the door, so whatever is out there is in here."

"Not necessarily," Lyle said, but it came across more as an internal monologue than dialogue.

"Please, I want to hear what the doctor has to say," Eleanor said, "and then I'll make a decision." Nothing subtle about her language; she, and she alone, called the shots.

Jerry tightened his hand on the gun.

"Did you notice if anyone was moving at all?" Lyle asked Alex.

She didn't answer right away.

"I didn't see anyone move," she finally said. "I didn't hear anything. I thought maybe everyone was asleep. After I saw the first guy, the one fallen over in the aisle, I saw another person folded forward, kind of, like how they tell you to put your face on your lap when you land. I probably wouldn't have thought anything of it but earlier this woman who was sitting in the middle of the plane had been saying she'd seen bodies—on the ground. She said she'd seen something . . ." Alex looked up and she was searching for a handrail. Lyle didn't want to fashion one yet; he wanted the information as undiluted as possible. "This woman said something about this country being out of control with guns and rage, and then someone else mentioned Wo Hop To, that gang that shot at the mayor's office, and an Asian man got really angry."

"Get to the point," Jerry said.

"Hold on," Lyle said. "Everyone was getting anxious?"

She nodded.

"We were scared."

On one level, of course, it was natural that people would speculate about armed attack or terrorism, especially if someone had seen a body. It was everywhere now, the violence, hardening people and accelerating a non-virtuous cycle: people wanted more police power, then feared government power and purchased more guns. Frustrated citizens hewed more tightly to views that, perversely, accelerated the trend further. More cops, more guns, more guns, more cops.

Everywhere now, in the news, the narrative had become the unzipping of civility, the hint of lawlessness, or a skepticism of the law, those who said it had become politicized. People had to prepare to defend themselves and their values. In the latest news, a group of heavily armed separatists in Oregon was daring law enforcement to come in and toss them off their compound on federal land. They'd taken a federal marshal hostage claiming him a spy and enemy combatant.

"I didn't hear any shots out there," Jerry said. "Did anyone have a gun?"

Alex shook her head in a way that said two things: *I don't think so* and *I don't know.*

"Maybe it's multipronged," Jerry said. He directed his comment only to Eleanor. "Guns and gas. Outside and in here."

"We've got no evidence anyone is atta—"

"Respectfully, Captain, let's not be naive here. This world has gone to absolute shit. It's a narco war zone south of the border, Arab teenagers run down innocent pedestrians in Jerusalem to say nothing of the rest of the Middle East, and it's bleeding onto our soil. You can't count on the cops. Hell, some are just hired guns of the government. Look at Oregon."

"Why here, Jerry, in Steamboat?"

"Why anywhere?" Jerry answered.

"Alex," Lyle said, "may I ask you a question?" He was looking at her square, very intensely.

She nodded.

"Is there anything you might be leaving out?" The way he said it was so graceful that only the most astute listener would hear the surgical challenge in it. Was she, he was in effect asking, telling the whole truth?

Eleanor picked up the subtlety and she blanched. This guy was good.

"Like what?" Alex asked, holding Lyle's gaze. "Help me remember. I want to help. I don't understand what's happening."

Lyle seemed satisfied.

"So speak, Doctor," Jerry said. "Give us your opinion so we can make a decision. Are these people sick or dead or what?" In the military, Jerry had admired this medic who made a decision and went with it, making decisiveness the highest priority.

Fair enough, Lyle thought, and he flashed briefly on an experience he'd had while doing his CDC work when he had visited the Jewish Quarter in Barcelona, where there had been a small outbreak of SARS. One of the patients was the young daughter of a Hasidic rabbi. She wasn't responding to any treatment. She was in agony, barely hanging on, having spent more than a week on the brink. Lyle recommended a new course of action. The rabbi called Lyle aside and, quietly, asked if he expected the treatment to do any good. "I can't be sure, Rabbi. We should try everything."

"Dr. Martin, may I ask you a question?"

Of course, Lyle had nodded.

"Do you know when to let go? When to stop fighting?"

Lyle had no ready answer to the questions or the rabbi's soft but probing brown eyes.

"When you start to pray," the rabbi said. "It doesn't matter if you're an agnostic or an atheist or a man of faith. You know, deep inside, when the better part of your treatment is hope rather than science."

Lyle had attempted, without success, to hold the rabbi's gaze.

As he stood now in the airplane, he tried to figure out if he was hoping or praying, applying science or faith. The answer rocked him: he wasn't sure where he stood on any of it anymore. He couldn't find his own center, let alone an answer for these people. All he could think was, *I want out. Out of here, this situation, this flight deck.*

"I'll need to examine them."

Eleanor made a clicking sound with her mouth, considering this.

"Do you want to turn the lights on again?" Lyle said, peering out the window.

Click went the lights.

"We've seen this," said Jerry.

"Like I said, the only way for me to know for sure is if I can examine them," Lyle interrupted. "Stating the obvious—repeating the obvious." He noticed his phone on the instrument panel and snagged it. He felt an urge to say, *I'll just take my phone and be on my way.* Maybe head back into the airplane and plop down and feel at home among people who were brain-dead or paralyzed or whatever they were. Is that what he was or was he just as terrified as everyone else and unable to tap into it because of the protective coating that had

enveloped him since Africa and everything that had happened with
Melanie?

He looked out through the right side of the window. Where he
thought he'd seen something. And, again, he imagined he saw movement in the pitch black with snow collecting on the window. Impossible, right? Or, maybe, that's why he looked in that direction in the
first place—because he'd picked up motion of some kind.

"What?" Eleanor asked.

"I'm not sure."

"Yeah, we get that." She waved him off—suddenly mistrusting
everything, Lyle too. "Is it colder in here?" She studied the cabin, like
a dog sensing something in the air. Then she realized what nagged at
her. The first observer's seat, the one behind the first officer's chair,
was folded up. It had been folded down earlier. On the floor below the
chair, a compartment door was ajar. She looked at her copilot. "You
didn't shut the door."

"What door?" asked Lyle. This piqued his interest.

"Earlier. Before you came in here, Jerry checked the main battery
and the oxygen."

"Was there anything . . ." Lyle looked for a word.

"Nothing strange," Jerry said.

Lyle nodded. Could the fact that they were getting some air seep-
age from the belly of the plane have spared them the syndrome?

"There's a case of champagne down there that looks like baggage
handlers commandeered and stowed it for their own use. It's nicely
chilled," Jerry said, trying for a joke.

"And?" Lyle said.

"And what?"

"Battery and oxygen. How are the levels?"

"Is that relevant?"

"Maybe."

"Tip-top."

Lyle now stared at Jerry until he thought it might raise a challenge and dropped his gaze. So this first officer was down in the hold, away from everyone else, and many people were dead? Or poisoned or something? Was that worthy of note?

Lyle wanted to keep the man talking.

"I agree with you," he said, looking at Jerry, "that we're running short on time. One question: How long can we keep this plane heated—in your estimation?"

"Like I said before, we're airtight-ish, which helps. Beyond that, it comes down to how much we want to run the engine, which costs fuel, obviously. What's your thinking?"

"Just, y'know, how long can these folks last if they're not dead—whether in here or out there. Snowy day. Night." He watched as a heavier snow flurry hit the windshield and stuck.

Eleanor shook her head. They were going to have to deal very soon with temperature and food.

"Open the champagne," Lyle said. "It'd warm everyone up, at least temporarily."

Eleanor blanched and Lyle tried to cover up his raw admission; he'd do anything for a drink right now.

"Sorry," Lyle said. "Anyhow, cold has its advantages, on a serious note. It can chill the nervous system, the brain, keep it alive."

"What's that have to do—"

"I'm not sure. I'm thinking aloud about the implications for us." He paused, then added, "And them."

"So."

"It slows the metabolic function. That can be useful."

"Hmph. I thought you just said that we wanted heat . . ." Eleanor's voice trailed into silence. It was so quiet Lyle could feel the flakes dusting the front window, melting, sticking, melting, sticking. Silence made a sound, that dull buzz you hear at a library that, in this case, no one seemed to want to break. Talk about a situation where there wasn't much useful to say. Lyle scanned the instrument panel, the gauges he didn't understand. He was looking for some logic to hold onto, a guidepost. He found only the memory of how he used to love the small-plane landings on makeshift strips in hidden parts of the world where he'd been called in to consult. Physics defying, he always felt it, the engines resisting gravity, commandeering it, that terrible moment before touchdown when it certainly seemed it might go either way. He loved the apparent confidence of the pilot and would try to draft on it. *If the pilot can land this metal hunk on this slab of dirt, then I can walk into the village and give death a good licking.*

"I'm decided," Captain Hall interrupted the silence.

"I'm going outside."

FIVE

UNTIL ELEVENTH GRADE in San Francisco, Eleanor had played baseball, not softball with the girls, but hard ball on the high school baseball team. *Helluva'n arm,* is what people would say about her. She got the nickname Jane Beam for her fastball. Then, her junior year, some jerk from Arvada High, her school's rival, had made it his personal mission to point out that girls didn't belong. He plunked her during her first at bat with a heater that would've broken a rib had she not turned in time. Furious, she dug in to take the guy's next pitch into the seats. She struck out.

She rushed the mound. Standing over the asshole pitcher, bat in hand, her teammates making a show of holding her back (but secretly wanting her to take a swing), she paused. She dropped the bat and she walked off the field. It had zero to do with being intimidated. It had to do with the fact that she'd really only liked the throwing part of baseball. She wanted to pitch. But that wasn't realistic; she lacked the arm to throw even another year. She knew, then and there, as she stomped off the field, that she didn't ever want to be in the position of defending an activity she didn't give a damn about. She wanted to do something affirmative.

Right now, she felt like she needed to do something and have it not be stupid or indefensible. Going outside was the least stupid thing she could think of.

"Of the two options, going back there"—she gestured with a jerk of her neck to the passenger area—"or going out there, my gut tells me that I'd rather be in a space that's not confined."

"You?"

"I'm the captain. At least we know that it's safe in here, for the time being."

"Why not all of us?"

"Because we need to hedge our bets."

"So you'll take one for the team," Jerry said. It was hard to tell if he was being generous or confrontational or maybe neither, just thinking aloud. "I don't think so. You're just going to slide down the window? I don't think so."

Eleanor clenched her jaw. Without her quite realizing it, Jerry's attitude reminded her why she was single. Men had no idea how to talk to her, not since Frank had died. Frank, the love of her life, his body never returned from a crevasse on Annapurna. That was years ago and Eleanor recovered and kept looking. But, in addition to Frank's memory, the challenges were manifest. She'd inherited a gorgeous house from her parents in a gorgeous San Francisco neighborhood and had self-sufficiency oozing from her pores and most men couldn't figure out their play, what they could give her. The harder they tried, the more she turned off.

Jerry embodied the worst of it. Internet dating had been a boon for him. The virtual medium paved over the nuances such that what translated to potential bedmates was: pilot and tall. He'd never had it so good. Eleanor privately named him the "Résumé Cowboy." He laid plenty of waitresses and aging midlevel marketing executives and started to believe his own profile hype. But they all caught on after a few dates, often the morning after. On some level, he understood that Eleanor's outright lack of romantic interest in him was telling him a truth about himself he hated. On the other hand, Eleanor did have a soft spot for Jerry, maybe the kind of affection she'd have had for a neighbor's dog. He was reliable, reliably Jerry.

"Through the cargo hold. I'll be able to get a radio, cell phone, get to the communications network. We need help."

"You have no idea what's out there—or who."

She chewed on this and he poured it on. "If it's terrorists or crazy people, they may just be waiting in the weeds. It'd be a suicide mission."

"We don't know there's anyone there. It seems . . . It seems like, I don't know, a syndrome, to borrow Dr. Martin's word."

She stood, turned left, facing away from Lyle and Jerry and opened the door to a head-high cabinet mounted beside the flight deck door. She pushed aside coordinate books, logs, thick books of technical jargon, looking for something behind them. One of the tomes fell out and hit her toe. "Shit!"

Lyle tensed. He recognized what was happening: Captain Hall was unreeling. In her shoes, who wouldn't? If he hadn't abandoned everything in the world he once cared about, he might be freaking, too.

He almost leaned over to pick up the book and realized it would be deeply patronizing. She yanked another couple of books onto the floor, her intensity laid bare.

"Eleanor . . ." Jerry said. He walked to the flight deck door. "Be practical. We're thirteen feet off the ground, even from the hold."

"Where's the medical kit—not the first aid kit, the one with more stuff?"

"Now you're planning to do field surgery?"

"Jerry, I don't like your tone."

"I'm not letting you go out there."

Eleanor turned. Instinctively, Lyle stepped backward. Eleanor looked like a Spanish bull turning on a circus clown. Fury. Then, just before she was about to say something, she zipped it up. Controlled again.

Alex gripped the wall of the door with a prurient fascination and horror. The tension on this flight deck threatened to blow these last survivors apart.

"Can anybody offer me better logic?" Eleanor asked.

She stood and looked at Lyle. He was a touch over six feet, just shy of tall, and she was only a few inches shorter and the quarters were so tight that he could smell the residue of mint on her breath.

"I think I should go," Lyle said.

Eleanor studied him for the briefest moment.

"An even worse idea," Jerry said.

"I have some experience—"

"In the apocalypse?"

Eleanor looked at Lyle, really studied him.

"What's your game, Dr. Martin?"

He shook his head, like *What do you mean?* But he sensed that she, rightly, understood he wanted off this boat.

As the pilot talked, Lyle noticed for the first time the way the first officer looked at his boss. It wasn't quite adoring but not far from it. He was absolutely letting her know that he was really listening, the way a man might on an early date. And Eleanor was using that by questioning the other man; *smart,* thought Lyle. *She's trying to keep together her alliances before this place turns into Lord of the Flies, or Lord of the Fliers.*

Lyle had a habit of watching people's reactions. In fact, he sometimes watched movies on silent and focused on how characters moved and gestured, what looked human and what looked forced. It was something he even encouraged med students to do to help them understand what is normal. He would tell his students that a good clinical exam could usually predict the outcome of a blood test.

What's your game, Dr. Martin?

Curiously, in another setting, that language might be the seeds of, if not attraction, flirtation, an invitation to fire back. It was the kind of thing Lyle could invite, even if he never fully realized that he had an allure or why. Most basically, he was attractive—even before his business card said doctor. He kept fit, rangy, by rowing a kayak on

Lake Merced, where he did hours of thinking, sometimes in pouring rain. He had a movie jaw and a full head of hair that showed no signs of abating. But mostly his magnetism owed to a set of dark brown eyes that had the rare quality of being able to paralyze both in groups and, more so, in intimate conversations. Melanie told him that most people communicated at a frequency that allowed them to captivate one or the other—individuals or groups—but that Lyle could do both. And, especially when he was in one-on-one settings, his potent gaze had the effect of causing people to stutter or even to go on the offensive, make jokes, keep it light. They would start the conversation with a defense mechanism.

"Jesus, we're digressing way off course." The pilot put her hands out, palms down, and pressed on the air. Like *Okay, let's get grounded here.* She's succeeded, though, in letting Lyle know his place on this doomed ship. "Would you mind checking for the medical stuff above the coats? I think that dimwit flight attendant from Montana left it there last time?"

Lyle wondered if Eleanor was toying with Jerry, creating another common enemy in some dimwit flight attendant from the past, pushing her agenda, using humor and authority, flirtation and fear. Or was Lyle misinterpreting? It filled him with dread. Human beings could be so manipulative, he thought. *I have to get out of here.* Lyle had an insatiable urge to find the drink cart and down two small plastic bottles —of anything, hell, even gin—and escape. He wasn't going to die on this airplane, asphyxiate, victimized at last by a syndrome he couldn't see, or, worse, hit by an errant bullet that Jerry fired at the captain to keep her from going down the hatch; or in a final dying cry of unrequited love.

Eleanor brought her hands to her head and rubbed her temples. "Jerry, is there an internal ladder—beneath the wheel bay?"

"Eleanor, please!"

"Check for an immune response," Lyle said suddenly.

He looked out the window, let all their eyes come to him.

"What are you talking about?"

"When you go out there," he said, "you're going to want to look for an immune system response. Even if they're dead, check for a muco-genic response, a pretty good indicator that T-cells have kicked in. If it's nerve gas, or something like that, you're likely to see . . ."

"What kind of doctor are you again?" Jerry asked.

"I.D.—infectious disease." Deliberate with the jargon. "Subspecialty in immunology."

"Where?"

"UCSF." There was an empty office there now where he used to hang his shingle. Lyle reached into his back pocket and pulled out his wallet and, from it, an old business card he'd stuffed into his wallet for the conference he was attending.

DR. LYLE MARTIN
University of California, San Francisco
Clinical Professor, Infectious Disease
M.D.; Ph.D., Immunology

Jerry glanced at it. "*Clinical* professor," he said. "Is that a real kind of professor?"

"Jerry, stop it," Eleanor said. Like *What's your deal?*

"In any case, look for tachycardia . . ." Lyle said.

"What?"

"Accelerated heart rate. Sorry, pardon the terminology." He wasn't sorry at all. It was part of his plan to sound complicated. "That could be a sign of any number of things. Should you start feeling faint, strange, any symptoms, try like hell to—"

"Hold on," Jerry said.

"I'll slow it down," Lyle said. "The point is, I think you'll be okay. Jerry, I'm sure, will have things under control in here."

Eleanor's eyes bored a hole in him and Lyle tried to remain placid and not show that he'd overplayed his hand. Then Eleanor and Jerry exchanged a look, like parents silently communicating about a child, in this case, the unruly Lyle. She nodded, almost imperceptibly, teeth clenched. She could see where this was going, didn't like it one bit, but was running out of ideas herself. And she couldn't risk leaving the plane herself and putting Jerry in charge.

"Captain," Jerry said, "maybe he's got a point."

"How's that?"

"Dr. Martin," Jerry said. "Would you be able to . . . could you diagnose the guy on the ground—could you tell us something about him?"

Lyle let the moment wash over him, a feeling of euphoria, trying to hold a poker face so as not to let them know he wanted off the plane, away from these people, all of it.

"Give us a minute," Eleanor said.

"Perfect."

"Perfect?"

"Sorry, I'll just . . ." Rather than finish the sentence, he moved a step backward while the pilot and first officer put their heads together and whispered. Alex, the fourth wheel, shuffled with him. They glanced at each other, a silent moment of recognition that they'd been sitting in the same row, now fellow travelers in a wholly different journey.

"Do you . . ." Dr. Martin said. "You have a limp."

She looked down.

"Are you hurt?" he followed up.

"No. No. It's nothing. When I was a kid, rheumatoid arthritis and it's really under control."

She said this like she wanted to move on; her clunky right knee embarrassed her. Dr. Martin honored her sensitivity but took the detail deeply inside. That was an autoimmune condition; did that have anything to do with the fact she was standing here and everyone else in the airplane was dead or sick? Might she have some internal protection?

"What do you do?" Dr. Martin said.

"Do?"

"For work."

"Technology. Engineer, on the sales side."

"Oh yeah?" He studied her. The hard eyes she tried to soften. Deferential but not really. He tried to place her demographic. Her bleach-blond hair suggested she might be part of the punk technology crowd. They could be a logical group, all about looking ahead.

"Good job these days. Was," Lyle said.

"Sorry?"

"Before the apocalypse. Was a good job." He tried to ignore the heated whispers coming from the first officer. "Please, Eleanor. Just listen . . ."

"You're a doctor?" Alex asked.

Lyle nodded.

"Are we sick?" She had her arms crossed.

"I don't . . . I don't know. Do you feel anything?"

She gritted her teeth. "I was supposed to go on a hike," she said, shaking her head. "Sponsored by the company. Get out into the air, spend some quiet time. Part of this new Stay Focused regime at work. We've got this new manager who . . ." Bitterness in her voice. Lyle stopped listening and experienced a sensation that never ceased to surprise or bother him. It was a feeling that often left him bewildered and yet he couldn't ignore. It was an awareness that he'd noticed a clue. The moment would leave him paused. From the outside, he looked stunned, like a fish that took a blow to the head. Melanie thought it a kind of mutated version of pattern recognition: he'd hear a sound or see a seemingly random piece of evidence—anything from a medical symptom to the weather at an outbreak site to the presence of a particular government official—and he'd sense it belonged to a relevant pattern. He just didn't know which pattern. Like seeing a crucial puzzle piece without knowing what picture it fit into. It would send his brain into a cascade, a kind of free-association free flow, often leaving him so inwardly focused that whomever he was talking to would wonder if he'd gone mute.

He looked outside, then at Eleanor and Jerry, back to the tech engineer, down at the door to the hold, slightly ajar, letting in air. What was it about her? Or was it this situation? Something was ringing too familiar.

He thought back to those last days, searching for some connection: the ill-fated trip to Tanzania, the whimper of an end with Melanie, ignominiously sleeping on his couch at the university, the mounting skepticism about humanity. There was a connection there somewhere, a puzzle piece that fit and he couldn't grasp it.

"Okay, Dr. Martin," he heard. "You win."

He almost smiled. All those years, he had devoted himself to ferreting out disease, often risking himself, giving obscene energy, particularly for one fundamentally introverted. But, now, he realized with stunning clarity, he really had no investment anymore in people. He just wanted to be spit out from the belly of this sarcophagus. Maybe left to die, but, at least, left to himself.

SIX

THE SOUPY EMOTIONS left Lyle in an eyeblink, and there he
stood again on the flight deck, tuned in to the voices.

"I'm prepared to allow you to go out there, Dr. Martin,"
Eleanor said. "Dr. Martin!"

"Yes, yes."

"We're going to run out of heat. We need to know if we can go
inside the terminal or inside the plane. I can't make that call without
knowing what's out there. My personal preference is for me to go but
Jerry makes a firm and fair case. So I want to ask you: Are you truly
prepared to go out there and examine that man on the ground?"

"Yes."

"You understand there could be a huge risk. We don't know what's
out there."

"Yes."

"Jerry will go with you into the hold."

"And cover you," Jerry added, meaning: with the gun.

Now Lyle thought he understood Jerry's motivations in allowing
him to go outside. The first officer wanted to *do* something. He wanted
to attack. This guy unnerved Lyle, and he'd already been in the hold,
doing who knows what.

"I don't think that will be necessary," Lyle said. "Viruses or toxins
don't respond to gunplay."

"So now this is a virus or toxin?" Eleanor said.

"I don't see blood. No obvious violence."

Eleanor handed him a yellow poncho, matching one that he noticed now that Jerry already was wearing.

"It's not much," she said.

"Good for visibility."

"You read my mind. What else would be useful?"

"Not the slicker."

"I thought you just—"

"Yes, it is good for visibility. You can see me better out there. But so could someone else, if someone is watching. Like I said, I personally doubt this is an armed attack though I'm not an expert on that front. Regardless, surely, you and Jerry talked about this and realized it is a potential suicide mission. That's why I'll be out there with the body and he'll be below with his"—he looked for the word—"weapon. In case."

She laughed bitterly. "This was your idea and don't pretend it wasn't."

Lyle smiled but the meaning was unclear. Was he saying she read his manipulations correctly or that he accidentally made this bed himself?

"So what else do you need, Dr. Martin?"

Lyle looked out the window and made a show of thinking. Truth was, he wasn't really consumed with the idea of figuring out what was going on. Most likely, these people were dead and he just wanted to get off the plane. He hadn't particularly been approaching this as doctor, so much as escapee; not that he'd just start running. He was at least curious. If something killed these people, what was it? He'd like to feel for a pulse. He just wasn't determined the way he once had been, not even close. He listed a few items: flashlight; face masks; rubber gloves from the medical kit; antiseptic wipes.

"Can we bring the defibrillator—below? Have it ready—in the hold."

Eleanor shrugged. "It's kept just beyond first class, in the overhead."

"Well, let's get to it," Lyle said. "Down through there?" He looked below the observer's seat.

Lyle nodded thoughtfully; made sense.

Lyle lifted the latch under the observer's seat.

"Whoa, there, cowboy," Eleanor said. "We have no plan."

Lyle laid out how he saw it. He and Jerry would drop into the hold. They'd close the door behind them. Jerry would help lower Lyle to the ground and then wait while Lyle checked out the body of the guy in the jumpsuit. Lyle said he would use basic hand signals. Thumbs-up, thumbs-down.

"Thumbs-down means he's dead?"

"Let's not worry about him. Thumbs-up means I'm okay and forget about thumbs-down. I'll either give a thumbs-up or ask you to join me. You can relay what I'm saying to them and we'll go from there."

Lyle didn't wait for an answer. He started down to the hatch.

Eleanor grabbed his arm. She used just enough force to turn him around and let go. She locked on to his eyes. For the slightest moment, everything around them swept away and he felt her magnetism, connection's seeds, and he blinked and looked down.

"You don't have to do this, Dr. Martin." Earnest.

He nodded.

"You need to stay low and be careful."

Lyle looked down. He couldn't handle this much sincerity, not now, and not for years. People who cared left him wondering whether or not to trust. The memories jagged in and out: Tanzania, Dean Jane Thomas, Melanie, all of it somehow leading here.

"Get a quick reading, make your best guess, and then get your ass back here," she said. "I very much appreciate this."

Lyle barely heard the last of this. He refused to let himself listen. He plopped down into the cold belly of the plane and wiped a tear from his cheek.

Cold seized him. The frigidity reminded him of when he used to walk into the refrigerated part of the lab. One time, early on in his relationship with Melanie, they stole into one of the Mortech units and tore off each other's clothes and got after it. In walked a grad student who, in fierce backpedal, spilled incubating disease in test tubes that, thankfully, weren't yet airborne. Truly, Melanie had joked, their first shared STD.

Lyle probed with his foot for a landing spot and caught the bottom rung of a rope ladder. He tested the footing, then allowed himself to rest on the rope ladder. He dipped his head into the plane's belly. He let go of the last handle in the cockpit and, presto, dropped into a new world.

"Flashlight," he yelled. He held his hand up again, waving blindly. A hand put the cylindrical light into his palm. He felt Eleanor give him a squeeze.

He heard Jerry say, "I should've gone first. This is the worst idea."

"Get down there then. Lyle, wait at the bottom for Jerry."

Lyle dropped to the floor of the hold and crouched. The light, already turned on by Eleanor, danced about, a wayward laser. Lyle steadied it dead ahead and found himself face-to-face with a crate. He listened to Jerry descend, holding a second dancing light. He dropped, scraping Lyle's leg with a loafer. Lyle could see only the crate ahead and their breath.

"Okay?" asked a muffled voice from above.

"Okay."

Jerry pointed the light to his left, revealing an opening between the crates. He walked that way and Lyle followed. He couldn't tell if the first officer's silence reflected his distaste for Lyle or a business-like approach. Seconds later, skirting crates, they arrived near the nose. Lyle flooded his light upward but felt Jerry push the tip of the light down.

"I got grounded once taking supplies into Baghdad. It was just before dawn and we had to sit for two fucking hours at the edge of this shithole village controlled by the other guys. We crouched the whole time. My point being that it's good to keep visibility low." Jerry focused his light on the floor. "Tricky latch. Can you hold the light?"

Lyle did as asked. Jerry tinkered and unlatched. Lyle noticed the frayed skin on the first officer's cuticles. Could mean nothing? When it happened to Lyle, it meant he hadn't been sleeping. A gasp of even colder air seeped out of the plane.

"We have time, Dr. Martin. There's no urgency."

Lyle responded, "I know. I appreciate it." He cleared his throat. "I honestly don't think this is all that risky. Medically speaking."

Jerry opened the hatch. Lyle pointed the light toward the ground. He could see damp tarmac, way down there, and wisps of snow in the air, and the wheel base. Big drop, leg-breaking distance. He brought the flashlight angle back inside and looked for a handhold. Next to the door, a rope handle. Lyle tested it with his right hand. Jerry took his point.

"We should look for a ladder."

"We should," Lyle said. Then he undercut his meaning by dropping from his knees to his butt, letting his rear touch the cold metal underbelly. "Let's do the old human ladder. You hold my arms and I'll drop down."

"I've never seen someone so anxious to walk into a bear cave," Jerry said. He scoped around, looking for a ladder or tool, rope, or other bit of technology to help the drop. That's when Lyle saw a box of booze. It was rectangular, with a flap open and those cheap little bottles showing. It was within arm's reach. Lyle reached. Saliva gathered on his lips. He pulled as gently as he might to keep the bottles from tumbling and getting the attention of Jerry, who was shining a light on the floor to the left, and pushing things around with his toe.

"Rope," he said.

"I'll help you," Lyle said, but only to cover the sound of him groping and succeeding. He got three little bottle necks into his hand and stuffed them into his pocket.

"I got it." Jerry turned and unfurled a rope and, with some ceremony, tied a fancy knot and flung the rope down into the breach. Jerry clearly had his attributes. He pulled the rope, testing it. "Okay."

Lyle pulled out the plastic gloves, making a show of it himself, and snapped them on. It echoed a sound he associated with "game on." The gloves always were the last thing he'd done before he walked into a disease scene. He stuffed the flashlight into his back pocket. He swung his legs into the hole. With his right hand, he grasped the rope handle the makeshift ladder was tied onto. Then he changed his mind. He reached down and felt the dangling rope with his right hand. He extended his left to Jerry. The first officer took it.

After a few seconds of wrangling, he found the position he wanted; his legs wrapped around the rope. He lowered himself, feeling with his right hand and letting Jerry hang tight to his left arm.

"Good," said Lyle.

Jerry let go.

Lyle slid down the rope. He lost his grip. The flashlight flew from his pocket. He heard it slam to the ground right before he did. Ankle, he thought, just twisted. Just twisted. He winced. He suspected it was worse than that. Nothing broken. But contusions and scrapes.

"Dr. Martin."

"I'm . . . I'm okay."

Holy shit, it was cold. And dark. The only immediate light came from above, Jerry's flashlight. Some other ambient light shone to the right, distant, a building Lyle couldn't make out. Lyle tested his left ankle. Definitely a sprain. He decided to give it a rest and sat on the ground. Frozen ground met his ass. He jammed his hand into his right pocket and pulled out a bottle. His brain crackled happily when the vodka hit the back of his throat. He wiped his mouth on his sleeve and decided not to have another one.

"Dr. Martin?"

"Just getting my bearings."

He pawed for the pieces of the flashlight. But he knew it was hopeless. Brittle plastic had collided with frozen ground. He remembered his phone and pulled it out and ignited the flashlight feature. It would drain the battery. The alternative was to ask Jerry for his flashlight and that just meant more complications.

Lit by his phone, he stood and walked toward the man in the orange jumpsuit.

SEVEN

ELEANOR AND ALEX saw edges of light peek from around Lyle as he appeared beyond the nose of the plane. The slightest phone light framed him.

"Do you think they're okay? Back home?" Alex asked. "Are they . . ."

"Hmm," Eleanor said, focused on Lyle.

"Why not use the big light?" Alex mumbled, referring to the Boeing's external lights.

"I don't want to bring attention." Eleanor clenched her teeth. She even wanted to whisper to Lyle: *Turn off the light. It brings attention.*

Lyle got within five feet of the orange lump on the ground. He turned off the light. He must've been having the same thought as Eleanor. But from the flight deck, who the hell knew what he was doing?

They could see Lyle suddenly pause. He bent at the waist, to about seventy degrees.

"What's he doing?" Alex said.

"He's looking for blood."

LYLE MARVELED AT the silence. It was so quiet as to be distracting. Just him and an unseen power, overwhelming silence as its emblem.

He waited for his eyes to adjust. Five feet away from the body, he concluded there was no bullet or shrapnel that had felled this body. That was evident from the way the man—it was a man, right?—had fallen. Not ripped from the ground, not propelled. But toppled, on his side, more or less, face flat. The man fell as Lyle had seen other bodies fall naturally. In Tanzania, one of the adolescent sons of a tribal elder had taken his last step in the direction of a water tank. His foot sunk into the soft dirt and he fell to the side, midstep, a recently deceased statue in perfect human form.

He took two steps forward and stopped again. Now he was sure it was a man, the jawline gave that away. Caucasian. Stringy long hair appeared from the edge of a wool cap. His hairstyle made Lyle think the man was youngish, twenties or early thirties, maybe someone who snowboarded, though that extraneous observation faded. The man's right arm stretched forward onto the ground. Did that mean he'd had a second to brace himself for the fall?

Lyle took two steps forward and knelt at the body.

ELEANOR TASTED BLOOD. She'd bitten her lip. She wanted to call Lyle back. Her gut told her this wasn't right. She shouldn't be sending a passenger out there, and, was that motion there, over to the right of the airplane, by the hangar? "Jerry!" she yelled.

Lyle was twenty feet, she guessed, from the tip of the plane. It was too dark to distinguish shapes. His lump of black melded into anything else. "Jerry. Get him back in here!"

CALM OVERCAME LYLE. He put his left hand on the man's cheek. It was cold. That didn't tell him a thing, and Lyle quietly cursed the lack of light and tools. That could be solved. He turned on the light on his phone. He shone it on the man's face, the left eye, the one he could see. Yes, Caucasian, and long hair. Face rosy. That was worth noting. Blood had flowed there, either recently or before death. Lyle put the light beneath the man's nose, looking for breath. If it was there, it couldn't be seen in this light or was too faint.

Lyle put his hand on the carotid artery. *Where are you, pulse?* Nothing. Lyle repositioned his hand. A blip. Was it a blip? He lost it. He repositioned again. He couldn't tell.

He scooted over and took the man's right wrist. Same thing. He thought he'd found a pulse, then it seemed he couldn't. His freezing hands weren't helping. He blew on them through the rubber gloves.

He heard a scuffling sound.

Lyle turned off the light.

He looked in the direction of the hangar. Nothing. What could he possibly see? He closed his eyes and listened. Whatever scuffling he'd heard, or imagined, was gone. He could hear the distant hum of machinery. A generator, he guessed. Otherwise, the air filled with the silence of falling snow.

Lyle turned on the light again.

He looked at the man's angular nose. A droplet of moisture hung on the right nostril. Mucus. Maybe useful. An immune response or a response to cold. In either case, the body had responded at some point, relatively recently. *Be alive,* Lyle heard himself think.

Lyle heard a sound behind him, a voice. He assumed it was Jerry looking for an update. Lyle put up his thumb without looking back.

He pulled back the light to get some context. The orange jump-suit looked puffy, indicating clothing worn underneath. *Good news,* thought Lyle; *if the man's alive, his layers may have saved him.* He was at least six feet tall, thin, sinewy with muscle. Lyle scanned upward along the body and saw the blood.

It was near the back side of the man's head. Just a trickle. Must have come when the man hit the ground, Lyle surmised. Only one way to find out.

Lyle set the phone down and slid his hands under the body. He tried to feel for heartbeat and warmth but knew he couldn't cheat this. He'd have to have the body turned over and get a good look, really confront this man. The thought jarred him. He tipped the body gently, trying not to injure a vertebrae. Gently, again, he lowered the body down.

He lifted the light. The man wore a name tag. Don.

"Hello, Don," Lyle said. "Let's see what's going on with you."

He looked at the temple where the blood originated. As Lyle had suspected, Don had scraped his head when he'd fallen. It indeed looked more like a scrape than a massive contusion. It was further evidence that the man had been able to brace himself, felt himself falling, perhaps, rather than hitting like a stone.

Lyle brushed the hair away from the man's scalp. It was time to look into the man's eyes. Peel back the eyelids and look for signs of life. He reached for his face.

Don's body jerked upright.

PART II

THREE YEARS EARLIER

EIGHT

D R. MARTIN."

"Dean Thomas, what a pleasant coincidence."

Lyle Martin nodded with a tight smile and kept up the slick steps at a trot, passing by the pantsuited woman under the umbrella.

"Dr. Martin," Dean Jane Thomas called after him. Mix of plaintive and displeased. A tone no one likes to hear but she clearly liked to use. Next to her stood a man in a purple-checked gingham shirt and a blue suit a quarter size too small, the fabric tugging at his back and shoulders. The dean, exhaling audibly, walked after Lyle. In her non-umbrella hand, a phone cocked like a weapon. "I need to talk to you."

"You know I cherish our meetings," Lyle said without turning. "I've got lecture."

"It started ten minutes ago, Dr. Martin."

Now, reaching the tall glass doors of Genentech Hall, he turned. He looked at her, then the man in the suit, seemed to consider saying something about the dean's cheap shot, half smiled, and turned back to the door. On the other side, Lyle's assistant held a gray cardboard coffee tray, watching the scene unfold. "It's cold," she said to Lyle. "They're lining up outside."

"Lyle!" Dean Thomas called.

"Emily, can you arrange for me to chat with the dean," Lyle said, taking the coffee too briskly, a wave spilling over the side and cascading onto the beach of his tan sweater. This completed the picture, the contrast between Dr. Martin, hair matted by sleep and drizzle, and the majesty of the nearly half-million square feet of marble and glass science hall at the University of California, San Francisco medical school. One of the world's gems.

"Let this be a lesson to you, Emily. If you're late for class, the dean will show up brandishing an umbrella."

"I think she's here for a different reason," the young lady said, and then, realizing that Lyle knew that, reddened, a look that measured on the dial beyond humiliation and well into schoolgirl crush.

At the door, the dean lowered her chin, shook her head.

"You warned me," said the man in the suit. His firm tone was a touch undone by the singsong of a southern Tanzanian accent, the mixed influence of Swahili, Portuguese, and military training. Hand at his side, he involuntarily made a fist and then unclenched it. "How long is this class?"

"Asshole," the dean muttered, referring to Lyle, and followed the scientist and his intern. She had given up on catching him. She turned to the man. "Michael, I think I'd like to hook you up with Dr. Sanchez instead. She's not . . ."

"An asshole?" Michael said.

The dean, in spite of herself, laughed bitterly. "Dr. Martin is not . . . He's, how do I describe it?"

"Someone who drinks himself to sleep?"

This paused the dean in her tracks. "Actually, I don't think so— the drinking part. I'm not sure where you got that information."

"In any case, my government is not negotiable on this one. He's the best and it's got to be him. And soon. How do you say it: yesterday? This can't get across the border." Michael paused. "Or into the news."

HALF A HALLWAY away, wet shoes squeaking on smudgy tile, Lyle arrived at the auditorium entrance. "Good morning," he said to the handful of students standing outside. "I'm sorry I'm late. I wrestled my alarm clock to the death, and I won."

It got an adoring laugh that Lyle didn't seem to be asking for, or even particularly notice. "Dr. Martin," called a med student in the clump, clutching a biology tome to his chest. "Will you hold office hours today?"

"He's got an hour scheduled," responded Emily.

She trailed him through the wooden doors of the spacious auditorium, clamoring with small talk, clacking of keys on gadgets, and, as Lyle made his way down the aisle, the brushing of backs on chairs. A capacity crowd filled the 268 seats, with a handful of others plopped on the ground in front of the stage. The popularity of these twice monthly lectures owed in no small part to Lyle's little rivaled capacity for mixing war story with substance. Some academics come off like orchestra conductors, prim and distant, others like the Beatles, brilliant but singular and unapproachable. Lyle more like Keith Richards, an everyman with serious licks. Or maybe a thirty something, Harrison Ford, the disheveled version, but hunting for disease and not treasure. The kind of things students loved—but some colleagues resented because it didn't fit their scholarly mold.

"If it makes them feel any better, you're totally inaccessible emotionally," Melanie had told him in the previous night's version of toe to toe.

No response from Lyle on that.

"At the risk of repeating myself, you weren't always like this, Peño." That was her nickname for Lyle, "Peño," short for Jalapeño, reflecting the sizzle nature of their relationship the first few years.

Lyle hiked the four stairs on the right side, strode to the podium, looked up and then . . . full stop. He gazed out at the audience, now come almost fully to attention, and he seemed to have lost all momentum. Many onlookers assumed he was centering himself, and the place. The ones near the front of the room, though, they wondered if it was something else. Were those tears in Lyle's eyes?

It crystallized into such a particular moment that it was impossible to ignore the pop when someone near the left side of the auditorium broke a gum bubble. This yanked Lyle back from wherever he was visiting in his mind. He cleared his throat, reached into his back pocket, and pulled out notes. Unfolded them onto the lectern.

"Where were we?" His voice projected over the microphone. A piercing screech followed from the microphone. Lyle tapped it, and the interference receded. He glanced at his notes.

From the audience, a woman shouted, "Saudi Arabia!" The voice rang just at the same moment Emily was saying the same thing—"Saudi Arabia"—from behind the curtain to Lyle's left.

"Saudi Arabia," Lyle said. "That's right. Hickam's dictum."

He looked up.

"Hickam's dictum," he repeated. "We've talked about Occam's razor."

Occam's razor, a key principle in medicine, says that when there are competing theories to explain a medical condition, the doctor should favor the simpler one. Or, as Sir Isaac Newton restated the fourteenth-century logic: "We are to admit no more causes of natural things than such as are both true and sufficient to explain their appearances."

Lyle glanced at the group. "It can be tempting to look for complex causes and diagnosis. But that often is a form of self-deception, the seeds of imagination, vain hope. Often, things are just as simple as they might appear, much as we are inclined to dupe ourselves."

Again, he paused, something odd. Where exactly was he going with this?

Dr. Martin, Emily mouthed inaudibly, wishing she could whisper in his ear.

The silent admonition seemed to make its way to him through the ether, or maybe he realized he was getting off track. "As a clinician, it is not necessary to overcomplicate things, Occam's razor. Much as we'd like to discover something extraordinary, it's usually, I'm sorry to say, just a head cold." Some laughter. "Bed rest and fluids will do the trick.

"But then, along came Dr. John Hickam. He gave us permission to get our money's worth out of medical school." Lyle explained that Hickam's principle allows that multiple symptoms often can be explained *only* by multiple diagnoses—not just a single disease or pathology but, in fact, several. This comes into play, in particular, when you have a patient with a compromised immune system.

Lyle scanned the auditorium. "There's a great phrase to describe Dr. Hickam's dictum. It goes like this: the patient may have as many diagnoses as he damn well pleases." Laughter. "Which brings us to Saudi Arabia." He told them previously that he'd done some early training in the Epidemiology Outbreak Office for the Centers for Disease Control. After doing a stint like that, the government would occasionally ask Lyle, or others in the program, to visit a place or person in need of a specialized medical consult.

"A guy in the State Department called and asked me if I'd go visit a government minister in Riyadh," Lyle told the audience. He said the State Department officer told him that the guy had MERS and wasn't responding to treatment. First class ticket, three-day turnaround, Lyle could stay at a palace.

Lyle seemed not to notice how much he had his audience rapt. He did, though, notice the dean, standing in the aisle near the back, and, more than her, he noticed the man next to her, wearing the too-tight suit. The man stood solidly, not rocking back and forth impatiently like the dean, watching Lyle, studying him.

"I'm sure you've read up on MERS," Lyle addressed the students. "But as a refresher . . ." He told them about Middle East respiratory syndrome coronavirus. It reared its head in 2012 in Saudi Arabia, thought to originate in camels. Symptoms include severe cough, gastrointestinal issues, kidney failure. It can be fatal. Lyle flew to King Khalid airport in Riyadh, got whisked past to a midlevel palace and an opulent bedroom turned medical suite with a man in his seventies prone in a gold-posted bed under a canopy. The minister.

Next to the bed stood a bodyguard in telltale fatigues, and a nurse with ice for the old man's lips and, cross-armed, his doctor, looking grave. The doctor gave Lyle an update: a CT scan showed a nodule on the lung, consistent with a MERS diagnosis, diarrhea, mostly consistent with it, and also stiff neck, light sensitivity, bouts of confusion.

"What's lesson number one?" Lyle asked his audience.

Voices from the audience in dystonic harmony: "Take a history."

So much of infectious disease diagnosis comes from taking a careful patient history. That was the thing Lyle told this class, and every class, on day one. Get a pet history, food history, sexual history, ancient history, and new history. Frontline doctors, in the emergency room or even at clinic, can see symptoms consistent with a pathology, make a fairly reached conclusion about diagnosis but one that is at odds with history.

"I pulled up a chair next to the minister. People need to feel you are the same level that they are on. Never forget the power of your white coat to unnerve; there's almost nothing you can do to diminish it. So find the humblest place you can. The less arrogance you communicate, the more likely that most patients will share a real history with you. In the case of the minister, the second that I sat down, he dismissed everyone in the room with a wave of his hand. The bodyguard didn't move and then the minister swatted him out as well." Lyle then explained that he had asked the minister basic questions to establish a baseline of communication and gauge cognition. How old was he (seventy-one); where was he born (outside Medina); what was he a minster of (domestic police); did he have a family (yes, wife, two sons, and a daughter); did he have much interaction with animals (no); what was his diet like?

"Are you a doctor?" the minister asked Lyle.

"Yes."

"Then get on with the doctoring," the man said. He had a white beard and he had been heavy once. Sleeplessness tore at his eyes and left cracked skin at each corner of his mouth. Fear and inner ugliness trickled out in his voice, the sound of a powerful person unaccustomed to feeling helpless.

"The minister's comment that I should get on with the doctoring was an important moment," Lyle explained to the students. "It told me that this might be one of those people who actually preferred me to be in a position of authority, rather than one of mere expertise. I don't want to make more of bedside style than necessary, but I also want to tell you how essential the role of listening, *really* listening, is. In this case, he was telling me I didn't need to be so humble after all." He paused. "So I could just go ahead and be the arrogant jerk my wife tells me that I am."

There was a smattering of laughter but not so much. Lyle continued with the story. Next to the minister's bed, Lyle cleared his throat.

"May I examine you?"

The man struggled to pull himself up on his bed.

"Just turn over," Lyle told him. "Please, pull off your shirt."

The minister removed the body-length nightshirt, his back exposed. Lyle ran his hand along wrinkled skin over depleted back muscles. He spent some time moving the skin around on the man's neck.

"Right-handed, played a sport. You have slightly more developed muscles and scar tissue on the right."

"Hound hunting."

"You've had some hearing loss."

"Yes."

"Did the hunting cause your hearing loss?"

"No. How can you tell about my hearing?"

"Small mark on the skin around your ear. Sometimes, that area can get itchy if the nerves get irritated from a hearing aid. Behaves like dry skin."

"My hearing loss is a state secret. I have to pretend I'm listening to the king."

"Of course. Doctor/client privilege. How long have you been married?"

"Sixty-one years." The minister was starting to relax. That was the goal. Yes, Lyle was looking for any unusual external markings, bites or lesions, signs of infection. Mostly, he was getting the man to relax. This was a veritable backrub.

"You are monogamous—with your wife?"

"The only woman for sixty-one years."

An hour later, Lyle had been over the man head to toe. He'd looked at the chart, read the CT scan. He'd looked in the man's eyes, causing the minister to recoil, confirming the light sensitivity. He cocked his head back and forth, like a metronome, lost in rhythmic thought.

Back in the auditorium at UCSF, the audience hung on his story, much like Lyle had the minister caught up in the examination. It had been an act of trust building.

"I explained to the minister that I thought we needed one more test," Lyle told his audience of med students. "Would anyone like to guess what that test was?"

Lots of looks down by students at their laps. Even in an audience this big, many students felt like they'd not like to let down Dr. Martin with a flier, a wrong guess. From the back, a hand rose.

"Yes," Lyle said. "No hands needed here. Just let 'er rip."

"An MRI of his brain," said a woman's voice. "With contrast, I'd guess."

"Very good." Lyle nodded approvingly. "Just what I told the minister. Almost my exact words."

The minister said, "Sure, yes. If you say so. What will that tell us, Dr. Martin?"

"The MRI is going to show us your brain. I suspect, strongly, it will show us a fungal infection. Crypto meningitis."

"So that's what I have? Meningitis?" The minister pushed himself up on his bed, his gown back on, his face strained with pain he struggled to hide.

"Yes and no."

"Which is it: Yes or no?"

"The fungus is a by-product."

"Of what? Of the MERS?"

Lyle felt it had gone on long enough. "I'd like to talk about your sexual history."

"I told you already. I'm married."

"And you've never been with another woman."

"You are testing me?"

"You've been with a man."

"Excuse me?"

"I believe you've got HIV, on top of MERS. It would be simple enough to give you an HIV test to prove it. But I bet your doctor wouldn't even allow himself to think about such a test. It would insult you and even be dangerous. I hear they flog people here for that sort of behavior."

"What sort of behavior."

"Homosexual."

"*I* flog people for that sort of behavior."

"Well, Minister, I think you're going to want to change your policy or your own practices."

"You're a quack!" His words exploded in a hacking cough. He doubled over.

"Minister, let me add it up for you. You haven't responded fully to MERS treatment. You've got cognition issues and light sensitivity.

Pronounced stomach issues, a lung nodule. All of that says to me that your immune system is compromised. On top of that, you sent your people out of the room when it was time to talk to me—"

"So."

"Maybe nothing. Maybe that you wanted privacy. And I can see why, given the marks."

"What marks?"

"You've got several areas of light purple skin on the back of your neck."

"I'm getting older. It's my skin."

"You know the term quack, Minister, so I'm guessing you are also familiar with the term 'hickey'?"

The minister glared at him. "This is a joke. Are you the best that the United States has to offer me?"

"I'm definitely not the best. But I have had my share of hickeys, and I've given a few too. I know what they look like. And I have seen my share of men die terrible deaths from HIV. Most of them contracted it through sex with other men."

The minister clenched his jaw, now seemingly to calculate.

Back in the auditorium, Lyle leaned on the lectern. "Nothing special about the diagnosis. In fact, I suspect his personal doctor knew what it was and was looking for someone from the outside to take the fall. In the end, they left the official diagnosis as meningitis and gave the minister an antiviral cocktail that just happened to be the same thing they give for HIV.

"The minister died nine months ago. His condition wound up being widely speculated about. He also spent the last few years of his life intensifying his attacks on homosexual behavior. His rage at his own condition, his hypocrisy, amplified. I mention this, and the story, to impart a particular idea about pathologies, diseases. They are, in their own way, straightforward. They aim to kill an otherwise healthy body. They have a deadly agenda but they don't hide it. Pathology is not duplicitous. It does not discriminate. It doesn't choose. It is pre-cisely what it represents itself to be. The same cannot always be said of people."

At the edge of the stage, Emily, Lyle's intern, tensed. Dr. Martin was out on that Dr. Martin ledge again, heading to parts unknown. In the back of the room, Dean Thomas had a similar but less generous version of the thought: *The asshole is going to get rave reviews again, and for what, storytelling?*

"Hickam's dictum," Lyle continued. "Patients can have as many diseases as they damn well please. Implicit in the phrasing is that people choose illness. This, of course, is utterly false on its face. They don't choose. But they can reveal. Even inadvertently, often, in fact, inadvertently. I urge you, when you sit at the bedside, to think about the person, the individual. Consider his or her history, habits, as well as the larger context of culture, constituency, demographic. Think about what makes a person tick. What separates a good doctor from a great doctor, in my opinion, happens outside the pages of the book."

In the back of the room, the man in the too-tight suit smiled. He thought, *Dr. Martin is brilliant, just as advertised.*

"Dr. Martin," Emily called quietly. He turned to the side. She pointed to her watch. He nodded and turned back to the stage.

"Having said all that about going beyond the book, I'd like if everyone could read the next three chapters of infectious disease prin-ciples and practices. If there are any questions, I think we've got some office hours set up in the lounge." A smattering of applause accom-panied the sound of students standing, packing up, hustling on. Lyle could feel his heart working double time with the pulse of dehydra-tion and still metabolizing sleep drugs, and from stress toxins left over from his fight with Melanie. He let his eyes wander to the dean and her guest. Whatever they wanted to talk to him about, he'd seen enough to know. Someone was dying.

NINE

DEAN THOMAS MARCHED up the aisle, looking ever the headmistress. She made a beeline for Lyle. Trailing her, a foot behind, more measured, walked Michael Swateli, a Tanzanian attaché to the CDC. Lyle ignored the both of them and followed Emily to an adjoining conference room they sometimes used for office hours. It was antiseptic, just a rectangular table made of cheap wood and, on the wall, a whiteboard. A yellow sheet of paper tacked inside the door indicated the place was not to be used for study.

Nearly two dozen students showed up. Lyle sat on the edge of the table and the students mostly stood, a few taking the nearest chairs. The dean stood near the door, resigned that Lyle appeared to be going through with his office hours. She was in a bit of a tough spot in that she had just a few weeks earlier urged him to show up for all his obligations (by which she mostly meant his faculty obligations) and couldn't now easily yank him from his scheduled office hours. Even though a foreign governmental official stood nearby with an urgent request.

"Mr. Swateli," she said in a low voice, "I do think Dr. Sanchez could be a great alternative for you."

"We had this conversation, Dean Thomas."

"She's respected without peer for her broad-based understanding of—"

"I'm happy to wait," Michael said, putting it to bed.

In pushing Dr. Sanchez, the dean was genuinely suggesting a terrific clinician. But she had a low-level ulterior motive: the dean knew such a consultation might well irk Dr. Martin. Dr. Sanchez was by the book, the sort of scholar who privately blanched at some of Lyle's more "creative" methods, and he, the dean guessed, was just as unimpressed by her. It would be nice to see something get under Dr. Martin's skin.

On the other hand, as the dean stood there, she managed a feeling of genuine pride as the students asked Lyle their questions. This group, like all the graduate students at the UCSF medical school, were not just among the best and the brightest but were arguably *the* best, a pick of the litter that matched Harvard, Stanford, and the rest. One student, seated at the table, pulled from his backpack a white mask. He described it to Lyle as a new version of an N-95 respirator, which, generically, was one of a handful of field air-purifying respirators. But the student said his version, which he'd made in his spare time, did a better job at resisting degradation from industrial oils. Would Dr. Martin take a look?

"Not exactly my expertise—product design. But I'm happy to glance," Dr. Martin said, turning the mask over in his hands. "Check with me next week. If I'm still alive, it worked." Laughs. "Okay, anything else? I can see that if I keep Dean Thomas waiting any longer, I may be killed anyway."

He looked around the room. It seemed the meeting was over when his eye fell on a student whose arm was half raised, as if she couldn't decide whether to ask a question.

"What's on your mind," he encouraged.

"What about doctor-patient privilege?" Her voice sounded familiar.

"Sorry, I'm not sure I know what you're asking," Lyle said.

"You shared the story of the minister—in Saudi Arabia. What about privacy?"

Now Lyle placed the voice's familiarity; it was the woman seated in the back of his lecture who had correctly shouted out "CT scan with contrast" in answer to a question Lyle had asked the audience: What procedure did the minister need?

Lyle studied the face belonging to the voice. Dark blue eyes and short hair, glasses with edgy frames.

"The minister is dead," Lyle said.

"Does that matter?" Her tone seemed equally curious as pointed.

Lyle took it in. "It can. Societal concerns factor in. When weighing what to describe publicly about any medical issue, I ask myself: Does the disclosure serve a larger health-related purpose? Anything else, gang? As you can see the dean awaits."

"That's what the AMA says." It was the woman's voice again.

"Pardon?"

One of the other students said, "Sheesh."

But the young lady, seeming to have found the full of her voice, continued undaunted. "The American Medical Association says doctors can disclose patient information following death if there is a societal benefit."

"Right. Okay, so we're on the same page . . ."

"Isn't there another wrinkle?"

"I'm not following, Ms. . . ."

"Obviously your work is so much about the societal good, the big picture, and it requires you in some cases to divulge personal information. Y'know, to make a larger point. To, say, prevent an outbreak. I'm just wondering if that is truly necessary or if it can be done without . . ." She paused.

"Go on."

She cleared her throat. "Bringing notoriety to yourself."

"Oh, come on," another student said.

"No, hold on. You know what?" Lyle smiled. He could feel a touch on his arm. Emily, his intern. Instinctively, she was trying to hold him back from saying something untoward. But he had no such thing in mind. "That's a damn good question, you're asking, Ms.-I-didn't-catch-your-name, and a fair one. My answer is that the patient comes first and, then, would-be patients and, in the case of the story I told you, then the doctors who would serve them. I felt it was valuable to impart the story as a way to inform the doctors of the future. I sincerely hope I've made the right call in this case but I am never beyond reproach." He had been looking around the group but, near the end of his explanation, let his eyes meet the woman's glasses-obscured gaze. She blinked, losing her nerve.

"I . . . I think you did," she stammered. "Thank you."

"Keep asking good questions," Lyle said. "You all could learn something from her."

The students quickly departed. Dean Thomas, watching them walk out, could only shake her head at how Lyle had managed to turn yet another situation in his favor. Now the students would imbue Lyle with the characteristic of humility, of all things. In her view, he was humble like frozen yogurt was nonfattening—it's what everyone let themselves believe but she knew better.

"Okay, Dean Thomas, you can see that I'm warmed up for your skewering," Lyle said, turning to her. "Emily, thank you for everything today. Let's chat over the next few days." In this way, he dismissed his intern.

The dean made sure everyone had left the room.

"Lyle, this is—"

"Michael Swateli." The man extended a beefy mitt. Lyle took it and shook. "Impressive lecture. Your reputation as a clinician proceeds you, but I had no idea about your capacities as a presenter."

Lyle studied the man's eyes, the faintly lighter skin where his sunglasses had been, a residue of brown dirt beneath his thumbnail. "You were just there. How many days ago, or was it mere hours?"

"I beg your pardon?"

"Wherever you want me to go. You were in the midst of it. You had to borrow someone's suit. A family member or someone formerly in your unit?"

Michael laughed. "Wrong about that one, Dr. Sherlock Holmes. It is mine or, rather, it was. I wore it for my own college graduation and I have since had much more food. But you are correct that I was there not very long ago. It is bad. Very bad. I only had time to race home to get this old suit and get on an airplane."

"Tanzania?"

"You've been, I think."

"Years ago with the CDC. Has high rates of albinism, twelve times greater, I think, than does virtually any other population."

"Yes, yes. My green eyes. It is in here somewhere, as you can see," Michael said. He looked down and Lyle understood why: time was wasting.

"Look, Mr. Swateli, I want to hear what's going on. I also want to let you know that it's a very busy time. Class and grant reports due and, chiefly, my wife and I have just gotten settled and—"

"Please, Dr. Martin," Michael cut him off. He reached for the inside breast pocket of his too-tight suit and pulled out several pieces of paper. "Just look." He unfolded the papers on the table. The pictures printed on them were grainy but clear enough. Bodies ravaged by disease. One showed a woman who looked like life had literally oozed out of her.

The dean cringed.

Lyle looked down and gritted his teeth. "I'm not sure that I can—"

"Dr. Martin," the dean cut him off. "How can you look at this and not say yes. What's going on with you?"

Lyle studied her. He tried to hold back his thoughts but he couldn't. "Don't pretend you give a damn, Jane. You're only here because, what, there's foreign grant money on the line, or who knows what."

"You have no right."

"Oh, Jane, you'd give your mother TB if it would lead to matching funds. Just own up to your motives for once." He said it with a shrug, making it more funny than mean. And Michael chuckled.

Across the room, through the far doorway, the slight woman who had asked the question about doctor-patient privilege—the same one who had talked during the lecture—watched rapt. Then, just as Lyle looked her direction, she spun out of view.

A few minutes later, Lyle came barreling out of the room and she stood not a few feet away, pretending to glance at a corkboard with various school announcements. She couldn't help but turn and look at him. They caught eyes. She smiled.

"Sorry you had to overhear that," Lyle said.

"I didn—"

"Anyhow, no biggie." He was talking in an offhanded way, but he looked so sad to her.

"Everything all right, Dr. Martin?"

"Fine. Thank you for asking," he said without enthusiasm. "Nice job today. You . . ." He cocked his head to the side. "Are you a med student?"

She flushed. "No." She wanted to ask how he intuited it. "I'm in tech. I work at Google. They encourage us to develop outside areas of interest so I'm auditing—"

"Well, regardless, well done. I'm not sure most med students would've been as willing as you were to put themselves out like that. Whatever you do, you've got a bright future."

He turned away, started to, when she cleared her throat.

"Do you recognize me?" She couldn't stop the words from tumbling out, though they did so at a whisper, a veritable mumble.

"Pardon?" he said.

"I said: thank you."

"Okay, great, good luck to you."

He turned and she was glad that he couldn't see her face. It was a jigsaw of embarrassment and doubt. She willed it into conviction. She had impressed a man who was an embodiment of action, who didn't shrink, and, more than any of that, a man who once had saved her life.

TEN

THE CEILINGS AT Google reached to the sky. The open-air offices and workspace of one of Silicon Valley's most respected and envied companies could feel like a military air hangar. A vast cubicle den that could fit a 747. As Jackie entered, a voice echoed through the cavern.

"Hey, this isn't gluten free. Look at this, Jackie, this isn't gluten free! How can we possibly concentrate when there are only ten free energy bars and fully 10 percent aren't gluten free? Eh, waif like you probably doesn't even eat. Oopsy, I'm gonna get sued! You won't sue me, will ya?"

Jackie Badger shook her head and half smiled at the sarcastic rant of fellow Googler Adam Stile. The geeks ran deep here, the brightest young minds in the world figuring out how to serve Internet users and make sure they stayed attuned to their screens. Some of the engineers were so geeky they redefined the concept. Adam fit the bill. If Google had a vote for most-likely-to-be-not-so-funny-as-he-thinks, he would win it.

Jackie set down her backpack in her cubicle and caught Denny's eye. He was standing a few desks away in the vast cubicle den, clearly feeling the same way about Adam. Denny Watkins ran the department. Much more than that: he ran the Basement. That's what Denny told Jackie he called it the first time he'd invited her down there, after several lunches and drinks. Just telling her about the Basement was an admission she'd been vetted. That she now knew.

Denny jerked his head to the side. She understood what it meant: *Meet me downstairs.*

Jackie sat at her desk and unzipped her backpack. She grabbed two clementines and put the tiny oranges next to a framed picture of her dog, Sadie. She reached into the backpack and started to pull out the big medical text. Then she thought better of it. Why bring any attention?

She felt a pang of frustration that the lecture had been canceled this morning. Now, they said, he was "on assignment." There was a lot of speculation about what that meant, chatter in an online group of class members. *He's battling a seventy-foot microbe with just his stethoscope and flip-flops.*

She knew better. Dr. Martin was heading to Tanzania. She'd overheard it through the doorway. Then she'd done a little harmless hacking to track his whereabouts. Greater good and all that. He'd said so himself when she'd asked about the ethics of disclosing the Saudi minister's cause of death. She couldn't wait for his next class and then his after-hours.

You've got a bright future. Clichéd, sure. But he even took time to single her out when he was fighting with that wretched dean. Jackie had risked putting herself out, asking him about patient privacy, and he'd perceived her as real, not as some showy kiss-ass med student trying to prove she was as smart as the teacher. She'd vacillated later whether she should've thanked him more clearly for what happened in Nepal and decided *that* would have come off as insincere. She'd rather be seen now as a full-bodied, able person than a self-doubting supplicant.

"I know when you're this lost in thought we might have a patent coming," said Denny, startling her. He was standing over her shoulder. "What gives, genius?"

"Wondering if we can patent your stealth gait. Who can walk that quietly?"

"You mean at two hundred thirty pounds?" Denny smiled jovially.

"Have a gluten-free bar."

Nobody else would talk to Denny like that. Everyone in the department wondered about it—how Jackie talked so casually to the big Russian bear. It was hard not to see the warmth between them, less like friends or siblings, more like doting father and precocious daughter.

"How's your audit class going? What is it again: remember-to-wash-your-hands 101?"

"It's infectious disease . . ." Of course he knew. "Jackass."

He laughed. "Can I talk with you about the protocol on that search tool?" he said.

It was thinly veiled code. Nothing specific. Just nonsense. When he said a nonsense sentence to her, it meant they were headed to the lab over at Google X. Sometimes, he said the most comically inane stuff, like *Let's optimize that engine,* or *Can I speak to you about the spreadsheet database?* This time, Jackie could see from Denny's eyes that, despite his innocuous code, he had something significant on his mind.

"Catch you in a bit," Denny said.

JACKIE SNAGGED ONE of the shared bicycles outside Lemon-Lyme, the name of the three-story glass-plated building at Planet Google where she worked. It was hard not to feel a little excited by the prospect that they had some new data. For six months she'd been going over the same incremental reports on a handful of projects, one about Internet use habits, another about reaction times of Internet users. It was also hard for her not to feel a little used. Story of her life on some level: always with the extraordinary talent and often feeling like others were using it for their ends. It took a lot for her to trust the rare individual who now made it through her screening.

One such person was Denny. At Stanford, he plucked her from an engineering class where he'd lectured a single day, and, from the back of the room, she drilled him with a question that contorted his face into wonder and then laughter. After class, he beelined for her, took her to coffee at Peet's, asked her to come work for Google. Less than a year later, he invited her to join on as a consultant for Project X, which was a catchall name for big, speculative ideas at Google that may or may not pan out, like the driverless car, clean water projects, interstellar communications technology. Her job, he told her, "was to use that overly developed antenna to ask the questions others don't think about or are too haughty to ask.

"Jackie, I like you, but that's beside the point. What's important is that you see patterns other people don't see. I'll ignore the fact you're not sure whether you like me."

Jackie liked Denny's candor and the fact that he seemed to put things in the right context. He was real. He always had food crumbs somewhere on his shirt or beard and he sometimes just stopped in the middle of a conversation and stood silently until he thought through what he wanted to say. He could live with taking his time, however awkward that might appear. It had taken her a long time to find someone she could invest in, and who she felt invested in her; three months after she joined Project X, Denny told her he trusted her enough to show her what was really going on. Not Project X, but the experiments in the Basement, the ones that didn't get discussed in the media, or anywhere. Her confidence grew, and her willingness to insert herself, like in Dr. Martin's class.

She rode her yellow bicycle off the campus sidewalk and onto the street. The move prompted her to glance in the rearview mirror, which is where she saw Adam Stile, the goofy punster from her engineering pod. He was seemingly riding in her path, following. When she glanced back, he put his head down. Then took a sharp right that landed him in a planter. Jackie, lost in the stupidity, nearly tipped over herself when slipping against a curb. She righted herself and accelerated. Something about Adam threw her off.

Or maybe, she thought, looking back, Adam, ever the gadfly, was following to see where she was going. But so what? It was no secret she worked with Denny at Project X. And there was no way Adam would get into the Project X building, let alone the lower offices. That would mean passing the human security upstairs, then taking the elevator using a key card *and* voice recognition protection to get to the floor, then the retinal scanner and the other stuff below that Denny said was "just best practices these days."

Google, she often thought, was a multibillion-dollar labyrinth, an overflowing font of money, and power. And secrecy. It was insinuated in every facet of people's lives, from work and driving, music, television, every form of communications. In the mazes of projects here, a collection of brilliant engineers who tinkered with, fine-tuned, intensified that power click by click.

She looked back. No sign of Adam. She pulled outside the Project X building and slipped the bike into an empty slot in the rack. She marveled at the line of electric cars in the lot. She had little doubt it forecast a future filled with battery-powered vehicles piloted by algorithms not humans. The line of cars reminded her of one of her prouder intellectual moments. Early on at Google, she'd suggested developing a program for Google Maps that entailed recommending driving routes to motorists that minimized the number of left turns and maximized right turns. It turns out that such a route can reduce global warming because drivers who take left turns have to wait before turning, thus burning more gas. On an individual basis, that is meaningless. In the aggregate, it adds up to tons of carbon emissions. Google eventually took up her idea, allowing drivers to opt for "eco" map mode.

At the door to the Project X building, Jackie, sensing something, turned to look behind her at the bike rack. There stood Adam wearing his yellow slicker. As soon as he saw her, he looked down. Then he peered back up and gave her a look she interpreted as a challenge of some sort. She looked one more time at Adam, found her better angels, cleared her throat, and turned inside. After passing security, she walked through the cavernous hall with scattered pods of desks and sixty-foot ceilings. It couldn't possibly feel cramped in here, even with a dozen driverless cars on mounts, their wheels spinning as engineers put them through various simulations. Easy to get lost in here, which was fine with Jackie. She walked by unnoticed, not that she really knew anyone here, then behind the well-stocked kitchen, into the foyer that protected Denny's office, where she was let through by a receptionist to the elevators. Key card, voice recognition to "B," and a retinal scan and she let herself into the "lab."

Anyone at Google who asked was told this room kept some internal servers, redundancies cooled by an alternate generator system, blah, blah, blah. Nonsense that fell on deaf ears. Not that the term "lab" was any more appropriate or accurate. The room downstairs was rectangular with built-in desk counters lined against the walls, computers at every second seat. A floor-to-ceiling screen hung on the far wall, receiving a bland Google logo from a projector mounted on the ceiling. Any accountant would be proud to work here. Denny sat in a chair at a conference table in the middle sipping tea. Jackie glanced at crumbs next to the button of his plaid shirt. She pulled out the chair where she usually sat. A blue folder sat in front of her.

"Take a look," he said. "New formatting but same idea; AI mode on the X-axis, varied by its response time, and then on the bottom are individual responses. The dotted lines map response by key word and the bars by duration of interaction."

So today they were doing the AI project. The idea was to develop and tweak new artificial intelligence modes and then map them against human response intensity and duration of interaction. They'd learned that certain words and fluidity of responses by humans could indicate the extent to which people thought the programs were "real." Over the months, Jackie had found some interesting patterns but, on the whole, she couldn't understand why this merited secrecy or was considered particularly valuable. Maybe the AI was that profound. She looked at the first piece of paper.

It caught her attention.

Could this be right?

She looked at the second, and the third. All similar results. She flipped through the pages again. Duration had spiked, the rhetorical measures were off the charts. But with some heavy zigzags. Her first thought was that something marked had changed in people's responses to the computer. She wondered whether the study subjects had, for the first time, started to really be convinced that the program was another human being, not an algorithm. But the zigzags threw her off. Maybe people felt the computer was alive, then got confused, then felt connected again. Or maybe that was how people—

Too many questions. She looked up at Denny, who was studying her. She felt a flutter of uncertainty, tinged with anger.

"What do you need me for, Denny?"

"What am I missing?" he asked.

She looked back at the pages.

"What do you see?" he asked.

It was how he always asked her about patterns. The answer hit her hard, finally. She swallowed. She put her hands underneath the table and she gripped her legs. It kept her from screaming.

She stared down at the pages. They had nothing to do with artificial intelligence or human response time and rhetorical measures. Denny had been lying to her the whole time.

What the hell was this project about?

She looked down, forced herself to count to ten and fought to find a smile. It wouldn't come. Before she knew it, her legs took over: she stood up and made for the door.

ELEVEN

"JACKIE. STOP."

She kept walking to her bike. Her stomach ached. Where had Denny appeared from? She'd seen the numbers on the paper, the bullshit diagram he'd tried to pass off as related to their artificial intelligence program. She indulged him with a few platitudes and then said that she was feeling ill, which was true but also owed entirely to the fact she was almost sure he was lying. Denny, Christ, even Denny. *No, count, Jackie.*

"Jackie," Denny said, lowering his voice, "I can tell that you know. I was hoping you'd figured it out."

She turned. "I trusted you."

The virulence in her voice caused him to step back.

"You have to come back inside. I'm not purposely . . ." He bowed his head in her direction and he spoke even more quietly. "Please, come back inside. I'm glad we're at this point." Now at a genuine whisper. "I can justify the clearances. We need you. Come inside."

She stared at him blankly. Denny assumed she was thoughtfully calculating. She felt a rush of the distrust that pervaded her thinking, her cross to bear.

Jackie first noticed it in elementary school, this pattern. At first, she got attention. *Wow, Jackie, how did you divide those numbers? Where did you learn that?* Or: *Did you see that little girl, clearing the entire memory board?* There was the time she talked two boys out of a fistfight over an orange-and-blue Nerf football by pointing out some or another common interest, and another time where she realized her little sister was in the other room eating the whole jar of Flintstones vitamins and called 911 on her own because her parents were too busy fighting to pay attention. *Nice job, young lady.* Bit by bit, she saw a different side to these remarks. They implied some responsibility. Was she supposed to be something great, or do something great? Her gifts felt like liabilities. That's what she once told her drunken father.

Impressive, Jackie, where did you learn that word?

Fuck you, Dad, you somnambulating bottom feeder.

Well, look, another pseudointellectual dipshit! Don't you ever—

Shut your mouth, Alan. She's not one of your whores! Jackie's mother had gripped a vase from the table like it was a baseball.

As years had passed, Jackie tried to stay beneath the radar. She took every effort to not be noticed so she wouldn't have to be misunderstood, underestimated, overestimated, *estimated* at all. No platitudes, and no expectations. She wore dark knit hats and baggy clothes to make herself indistinguishable. It was hard because she not only was so smart but attractive, with doll-like features. Delicate, a beautiful petite, if she'd have allowed it.

"Jackie?"

She settled on a wry smile.

She nodded. She thought about Dr. Martin, both flexible and firm, ultimately a model of how to be decisive, how to challenge, and be challenged, without being thrown off course. In Nepal, in that moment that could've gone either way, he'd saved her life, physically, even spiritually; absent his treatment, she'd not only have died, but even embraced it.

She felt light wind blowing through campus. It carried with it the feeling of uncertainty.

"Okay," she muttered.

Downstairs, he set out two cups of coffee.

"Lantern," he said.

Her small hands wrapped around the warm mug.

"Yes, another terrible code name from the company that brought you Project X," Denny said. He hoped she'd smile but she wasn't there yet.

"Bottom line, Jackie, we're studying memory."

She met his eye and saw truth there. He let her gaze at his sincerity until she looked down.

"What makes one image or memory stick? What causes it to fade? If you want to be blunt about it"—he was gaining steam—"we're trying to get people to remember better and share more of the things they see on the Internet."

"Things?"

"Advertisements. Video, banner, click-thrus, YouTube videos, et cetera. It's all about recall and sharing, whether they're taking something viral, like a song or a sell-crafted Nike ad, or remembering the narrative or image of a Lego set, car, washer and dryer. No one liked my idea of calling this project Hippocampus, and then we'd name our headquarters the Hippo Campus."

Hippocampus, the memory center of the brain.

"Lantern, Jesus." He shook his head.

Despite herself, she smiled.

"Look, Jackie, it's not *that* novel. It's a neuroscience twist on the basic Silicon Valley business model."

He stated the obvious: the entire Silicon Valley business model was built on getting people to see and respond to advertisements. Services like Google, Facebook, Instagram—go down the list. They were "free" and, in exchange, they sought attention. Fairly, this was the attention economy, the eyeball economy. And, more recently, the sharing economy; brands, whether corporate or individual, created things to be tweeted, liked, commented on, a fluid, amorphous river filled with baited fishing poles, bobs and flies and lures to be swallowed. Denny glossed over this stuff because it was simply understood.

"What's new is we figured out how to do it," he said. "Or we're figuring out how to do it."

"That's the data you've had me looking at."

"I can't say this strongly enough: I'm not sure we can do this without you. You filter information in a way other people don't, or can't. You have an unusually creative way of synthesizing data."

She studied his face for contradictions and transgressions like a child deciding whether there was still such a thing as unconditional love. She knew how Dr. Martin must have felt sometimes; used. Somehow, he seemed able to navigate it. He dug for truth on his own terms and figured out exactly the right thing to say and do. She could dig, too.

"Why didn't you tell me before?" No sooner had Jackie said it than she hated having done so; it showed her vulnerability. So she added, "I deserve a hell of a lot better than that."

"You do, Jackie. But we're playing around in a gray area of"—he looked for the word—"ethics. I didn't want to . . ." Another long pause.

"What?"

"I didn't want to compromise you or put you in a bad position, or make anyone more vulnerable than they need to be."

"I don't need your protection."

"Come to the desert," Denny said. "See for yourself."

"What's in the desert?"

"You really do have to see it to believe it. Will you just trust me?"

"Just to be clear"—she tilted her head to the side, looking virtually coquettish—"you want me to trust you, despite having lied to me, and to trust a secret project spawned by a multibillion-dollar company more powerful than the government and that only subverts its 'do no harm' motto when it suits the stock price?"

"When you put it that way," he said, smiling, "yes."

TWELVE

W HAT'LL IT BE?" a bartender at a cheesy Irish pub in JFK's international terminal asked. He had a fresh tattoo on his beefy forearm of a New York Giants helmet that looked red around the edges. Melanie put a hand on Lyle's shoulder, silently urging him not to get into the man's diabetes or possible tattoo infection. Lyle flinched.

"Patrón, double, straight," he said.

"My man," said the bartender. "Silver, okay?"

Lyle nodded absently; sure.

"Peño . . ." Melanie said.

"He's paying," Lyle responded, gesturing with a jerk of his neck to Michael, the Tanzanian representative who stood near the front of the pub looking at a menu on a stand, giving Lyle and Melanie a wide berth. Michael had thought it would be a grand gesture to invite Melanie, particularly after Lyle had said that a chief reason he didn't want to make the trip is because he'd just gotten settled in a new place with Melanie.

But the pair had been bickering since San Francisco. Michael was starting to wonder whether Dean Thomas had been right that Lyle was unstable to an extent that outweighed his tremendous value. Michael, standing at the menu, snuck a peek at the picture he'd taken to keeping in his right front slacks pocket. Even though it was a still shot, Michael could picture the man on the ground, panting, as if a dog gasping for breath.

"Make it two?" the bartender asked Melanie as he poured Lyle's drink.

"I'll have two. She's fine," Lyle said.

"What the hell has gotten into you, Peño?"

Lyle stared at his glass. Melanie exhaled. "I'll have a seltzer"—she looked at Lyle—"because I want to sleep on the plane, not because I'm taking your shit."

"Lemon?" the bartender asked.

"Sure."

The bartender sent a flash of anger at Lyle. This guy had no idea how good he had it. His wife was a knockout. Not like cheerleader knockout, which in the bartender's simplistic female taxonomy was the top of the food chain, but wife knockout. Her red hair was pulled back in a ponytail and she wore a baggy maroon V-neck sweater that, by contrast, gave her skin a pale tint. Originally, she'd purchased the sweater for Lyle but he'd shrunk it enough in the dryer that it no longer fit in the shoulders.

Lyle drained his shots in two drags. Held the glass up to the bartender.

"Are you still serving food?" Melanie asked.

The bartender pulled a menu from under the counter and slid it forward. "The au jus gets raves. Comes with fries."

"Perfect. We'll have two. I'm ravenous," she said. "Can you put them in before we have another round?" To Lyle: "Like you said, Peño; Michael's paying. We might as well have a last decent meal."

"Go home, Melanie."

"Peño! What the fuck!"

"It's not safe for you where we're going."

"So, Lyle, this is new, this is fascinating."

"What's that?"

"You've got all kinds of psychological flaws, but being bossy isn't one of them."

"There you go, that's the spirit, Melanie."

"Jesus." She'd never heard him like this, not quite. But she had felt it building. For well more than a year, he'd been changing. She just assumed it was because he'd been to one tragedy after the next, one more village, one more filthy apartment building with stricken children; such things would take their toll on anyone. She'd tried to be sympathetic. She knew in her heart what Lyle confessed to her with his eyes: love, real connection, genuine passion—it made up for everything else. Nothing could be more trite but, simply, true, this physician healed himself by feeling connected. Those weren't words he'd have used. But she knew and he knew she knew. And yet, for all her efforts, he became increasingly beyond reach. She stared at him staring at his glass. "I'd chalk this up to whatever horror is on those pictures Michael's carrying around in his jacket but you've been like this for . . . weeks."

"Is that all?"

"No. No, Lyle, you're right. For six months."

"Like what?"

"Um, reserved, distant, surly, angry, sullen, terse. Ring a bell?"

Lyle grimaced. Maybe it had been after he returned from that well poisoning in South Korea, an ugly bacteria caused by a local official who had embezzled money intended for sewage treatment and invested it into ounces of gold. A week of sullen behavior followed, then two, then halfway through the third, Melanie, sick of it, went dancing with her friends until 3 a.m. on a Thursday.

"Nice outfit," was Lyle's single rejoinder in the morning, looking at her skirt next to the bed.

"I have a right to defend myself," Melanie responded, the sympathy squeezed out of her voice.

"Against what?"

"Invasion of the body snatchers. I want to help you. I'm here to help you. But I have a life and I won't let you take my hand and yank me over a cliff."

In the months that followed, she'd vacillate between trying to reach him and making sure she continued to exist. She indulged an entrepreneurial bug and signed up for an evening class at Berkeley's Haas School of Business. Things at home didn't feel hostile, more like that proverbial frog in simmering water that would eventually boil.

Lyle looked at Melanie over his empty shot glass.

"So why are you here, Mel?"

"Because I'm looking for you."

It was a striking thing to say, especially the plaintive way she said it. He turned to her, even though doing so meant he was abandoning his stubborn self-imprisonment.

"I can't find you in our home, our bed, not in our conversations, not at the lab," Melanie said. "I'm going to see if I can find you . . . I don't know . . . in Africa, in a tent, surrounded by . . ." She had tears in her eyes. Lyle cleared his throat. She was softening him and he was fighting it.

"By . . . all that sickness." She chose the word over *disease*. "You shine there, you are magnificent, when you are called upon. I don't think you can hide from me there."

She put her hand on his knee. Lyle felt warmth course up his thigh. He looked for the bartender, a lifeline. Melanie squeezed his leg. The bartender appeared with two heaping plates of French dip and fries.

He wanted to beg her to go home. She shouldn't be going, not now, and not on this one. He looked at her, desperate to say something, and, yes, God, she was beautiful, particularly with this pink hue to her skin, and even with a slight puffiness around her blue eyes. Lyle tried to get words out—*don't go*—and instead took his last gulp of booze and felt defeat.

FOURTEEN HOURS LATER, they landed in Amsterdam for a brief lay-over before flying to Arusha. Before touchdown, Lyle had awakened with his head on Melanie's shoulder and seemed to have forgotten whatever was fueling his mood. Until he got his bearings. Then, fully awake, he withdrew from Melanie, smiled thinly, asked Michael to hand him the briefing folder. He looked at the pictures and the medical reports. He immediately homed in on the anomaly, the thing he'd noticed when Michael had first told him what was happening near the border. This wasn't ordinary, this situation. He pushed his reading glasses back on his nose and let himself dive into the folder.

And Melanie let him get away with it even though she sensed he was retreating into the work as much as embracing it. This was, she thought, a legitimate excuse, to let things settle down. Maybe she'd discover him again.

Not likely. Not with the secret he was keeping from her.

THIRTEEN

A RE THOSE TWO giraffes . . ." Melanie's voice trailed off.

"It's a wonder the first time you see it," Michael said. "Now you understand men."

They traveled south through the plains in a yellow Land Cruiser, open top, the size of a small bus. It was an angular thing, exposed metal bars, a safari vehicle but without any of the fancy signs or branding of a commercial company. Government issue. To the left, under an acacia tree, two giraffes held the bizarre pose. One had mounted the other.

"Men? They're not mating," Melanie said.

"Nope. Guess again."

She shrugged.

"The one on top just beat the other in a fight. His reward is this expression of dominance."

"Prison rules," Melanie said. "You see that, Peño?"

He sat in a seat across the aisle, reading from a file. He glanced at Melanie. "I think you should go back to the hotel."

She looked away.

"Dr. Martin. Tsetse," Michael said. Lyle didn't even notice the fly on his wide-brim beige hat gunning ultimately for his cheek. Michael stood and swatted the air, sending the fly on its way.

"Lost when he's working," Melanie said. But she was making excuses—for him, and for herself. They'd had a brief layover in the

Arusha Hotel after that exquisite landing near Kilimanjaro. Lyle had sat on the bed, eyes half closed. By that point, Melanie had given up trying to coddle him into conversation. But at one point she came out of the bathroom determined to confront him, bring her nuclear weapon and clear the air. Couldn't do it. She'd been having trouble sleeping and felt like she might be getting a cold.

The landscape was changing quickly. The dusty steppe took on high grass. Denser trees appeared. In the distance, it looked practically lush.

"We're not that far from the Selous Reserve. It's where we've set up the perimeter," Michael said to Lyle. Now Lyle looked up. A man in green fatigues stood beside a yellow police barrier. It looked like he was completely in the middle of nowhere, an oasis amid the brown grass and a felled evergreen. Hardly. Everyone in the truck knew that he was the last stop before death. The truck pulled beside him and slowed. Michael waved.

"Jambo. This is the doctor," he said. It was a formality. The man in fatigues was too young to have any say-so about anything. His mere presence intended as deterrence. Who would come out here anyway? "Have some more coffee," Michael said to the soldier as they passed.

Ahead, a small rock formation that would qualify in these parts as a landmark. Melanie watched a lizard scatter at the base of the rocks.

"It's going to sneak up on you on the other side," Michael said. He was saying: *Brace yourself.*

Lyle looked at the late-afternoon sky, pinky blue, yellows bent through the prism of wispy clouds. He scanned the rocks. Muddy water pooled at the bottom right. Maybe someone had washed there. Or people had used it for a restroom. One of the problems he often saw was that sick people did what they had to do where they had to do it—like pissing and shitting—and disease fed on it.

They rounded the corner. A small village emerged, thatched huts bisected by a footworn orange-colored dust road, more like a path. They saw the man in the middle of it. He was on all fours, crawling their direction, trying to, breathing like a dog hit by a car. An aid worker or nurse in a white suit tried to help him by the arm.

"He's the one I need to see," Lyle said.

THE STAKE IN the far right corner of the medical tent had loosened. Other than that, the setup was reasonable, nothing profound, as might be expected. Six victims in beds, four along one wall, two along another, getting saline drip. Two empty beds betrayed the fate of their most recent inhabitants; sweat and bowel stains, the bodies' last expressions. It irked Lyle that there still was insufficient manpower here six days after the first patient showed up.

Michael, an edge in his voice, said something in Swahili. A nurse who looked like a beekeeper in all his garb quickly cleaned up one of the empty beds by tossing the sheets and pillow into a plastic bag. A few minutes later, the moaning man Lyle had seen outside became the makeshift hospital's latest inhabitant.

By then, Lyle had already scrubbed in a bowl of soapy water and gloved and put on a respirator. Melanie remained in the truck. She was a nurse by training, but the risks here outweighed any help she might offer, especially before Lyle got a grasp. Besides, he'd practically begged her to stay put. In the tent, he leaned down and felt the faint pulse of a woman of truly indeterminate age; he figured her between thirty-five and sixty. Disease and sun mottled her skin, bleached her night-dark pallor near pale, obscured the truths her face might tell.

"How many days?" he asked the nurse.

"Four hours."

Lyle blanched.

A straw rested by her lips. She lacked the strength to suck or move it. A red-and-yellow scarf tied around her forehead hung damp with sweat it couldn't absorb. The Iraqw people, Lyle had read in his file, typically lived farther north. This was among their southernmost tributaries. He could see from the slightly narrowed shape of the woman's eyes the Asiatic genetics shared eons ago. Spittle on her chin suggested she'd been coughing. He picked up the chart by her bed and could make out the numbers even if he couldn't read the words. Last her temperature was taken, it had been 103.8. Another number stood out: 51. Must be her age. He patted her arm and she briefly opened her eyes and he smiled.

He stood from his bench and turned to the man from the road. He kept trying to stand up. With each tiny effort, he violently coughed. You didn't need an x-ray. Lyle could practically see the fluid in the guy's lungs. The nurse struggled with him for a second to put on a mask and the man finally succumbed, lacking the strength to fight.

The nurse said something and Michael interpreted. "The son of the local chieftain."

His smooth round head shone with perspiration. He leered at Lyle and set loose with coughing. Lyle understood. This man wasn't accustomed to being defeated. Lyle lowered his eyes and gestured to the side of the bed. *May I sit?* He took the nonanswer as an okay. He sat. He took the man's long arm and felt for a pulse at the wrist. Ordinarily, ill-advised, not a good place to test. But Lyle didn't want to reach for the man's neck. He got what he needed: 185.

"Saline, please," Lyle said to no one. He would bet that this man's pulse didn't get that high facing a mother lion. With Michael's help, he asked questions and learned the man had been sick for a day. And didn't want help. Lyle said he understood; he wanted to help the older folks, he said, and the children. He listened and watched and thought. *Not Ebola. Maybe Lassa fever.*

"You have many mice?"

"This is Africa," Michael said.

"Sir, how many dead—like you?" Lyle asked.

"Like him?" Michael asked.

"Young?"

Four. Out of a village of only sixty.

Lyle pushed the sheet up and saw the swelling in the man's legs. The man tried to withdraw but he coughed. Then he shouted, tried to, his words swallowed by coughing.

"What's he say?"

"The pure breeds did it."

"What does that mean?"

An exchange followed between Michael and the nurse. Michael explained to Lyle that a new theory had emerged among the locals that had to do, of course, with religion. The Iraqw borrowed each from Islam and Christianity. In recent months, Muslim proselytizers had visited and called them heathens, promised plague. Lyle pressed the interpreter. What had the men looked like? What had they said— exactly? These visitors called the Iraqw an abomination—*chukizo*, in Swahili. Hell's plague would befall them, *inshallah*, God willing.

Lyle saw Melanie standing in the doorway. "Go back to the truck," he said. She had tears in her eyes.

"Go back to the truck," he insisted.

"Don't tell me what to do." But she turned and left.

OUTSIDE, LYLE ASKED Michael if he had Internet. Yes. On Michael's big-screen phone, Lyle pulled up an article in *Nature*. The article was a controversial publication, to say the least. A rare piece of truth that almost didn't see the light of day; too dangerous. Before delving in, he walked the empty streets of the village. A dozen thatched huts, wood booths, empty, that must've served as some kind of market. He asked to see the well and observed it to be clean. He asked Michael about these Muslim proselytizers. Michael said it was the first he'd heard of it. When had they last come? Michael didn't know. Why?

Lyle, leaning against a hut, was too lost in the article to answer.

"Show me the man's hut, please."

There was not much to see. That was the point, Lyle said, without elaborating. A broom in the corner told Lyle much of what he needed to know. The only sign of disarray owed to a glass shattered on the ground near the bed. Where the man must've spilled it reaching in his febrile state.

"What are you thinking, Dr. Martin?"

No response.

"You're frightening me."

"Looks like Coxsackie B." True but he didn't really believe it.

They returned to the makeshift hospital hut.

"When was the last time they were here?" Lyle asked the chieftain's son. "The pure breeds?"

"What are you asking?" Michael said.

"Ask him, please."

He doesn't remember.

"A few weeks?"

"Yes."

"What did they wear?"

Lyle listened to the translation of Swahili to the Cushitic tongue and back, then to English.

"Suits, like he said."

"Dark skin?"

"Not this dark."

"Did they leave you anything? A way to get in touch."

No.

Just the warning.

"PEÑO, WHAT ARE you doing?"

"Taking a nap."

"In the truck."

"Good a place as any."

She stared at him.

"I've never in my life seen you act like this," she said.

He half smiled at her, distant. "Lyle," she said, *"say something."*

He was sitting in the last row of the safari truck. He stared at her. He shook his head, and she could tell he'd traveled to some distant place in his head. He reached behind his head and pulled out a white shirt he'd used as a pillow. He lifted it into the air, like a flag, and he waved it. Surrender.

A DAY LATER, their airplane landed from JFK. Michael had gotten off in New York hardly able to hide his frustration. Lyle had given him nothing, bubkes, well, other than his personal symptoms of emotional withdrawal. Just turned into a fucking log. Except when he shrugged and asked for a beer. Before he'd gone totally dark, he'd also told Michael, cryptically, that the villagers didn't need a doctor but a better police force.

"I'm realizing I don't speak Dr. Martin," Michael said to Melanie, trying to be as diplomatic as possible.

She didn't share Michael's sense of decorum. "I don't speak asshole, either," she said, right in front of Lyle as a taxi driver spitting chew out the window spirited them past looming Kilimanjaro in swirling winds to the airport. "If you want my interpretation, I think Lyle thinks this wasn't caused organically."

"Meaning what?"

"He thinks it's a man-made virulence. Someone poisoned these people."

It was exactly what Lyle thought. This was chemical warfare. Someone had come in here and given this tribe an intensified flu, maybe something even using CRISPR, genetically hacked viruses meant to do an end around immune systems and traditional treatments. It would explain the attack of young, strong members of the tribe, the threat by outside forces, the visitation of this virus absent any clear catalyst or patient zero and in a fairly clean community, well kept. It would explain, most of all, Lyle's gut feeling. Maybe even some government had supported this experimentation. It would be revelatory, of course, also solvable. He scribbled down several courses of action, one of which would almost surely confine this and put it to rest.

"It's absurd," Michael said before he left Melanie and Lyle in their Air France seats to take his own. "He sounds like one of those nuts in Brazil with Zika." Conspiracy theorists in Latin America had spread rumors nearly as virulent as the virus itself that the Zika-carrying mosquitoes had been planted by angry British colonialists or one-worlders. "The dean was right," Michael concluded. He didn't finish the thought but it was clear enough: he should've sought someone else's counsel. Lyle hadn't really tried; he'd mailed it. Lyle was just a good storyteller more interested in applause than answers, or maybe something more insidious than that—a malicious fraud. How had he gotten such a reputation? On the flight, Melanie willed herself to go to sleep. She talked again to Lyle when the landing gear came down to touch down in San Francisco.

"Counseling, Lyle. You're in or I'm out."

He studied her face. The water retained in her rosy cheeks.

"You're pregnant, Melanie."

"Shut up, Lyle."

He looked down so he couldn't watch the wave of revelation spread over her face. He'd suspected for a week or more. He suspected she didn't know. How could he know before her? How did he ever understand these things? It started with a sensation, like an itch, and it made its way from his body to his brain to his consciousness.

"No, Lyle, it's not . . ." She stopped and her blue eyes turned steely. "I'm pregnant? I'm pregnant!" Her utter disbelief transformed quickly into wonder. Lyle so often was right about things like this. Could he see it before she knew? "Why did you let me go?" she demanded. No words to capture her betrayal.

"Maybe the better question is why you went."

The tears leaked from her crimson-tinged eyes and one dripped off her chin. She had no strength to wipe them away.

"What's happened to you, Lyle?"

FOURTEEN

JACKIE AND DENNY hit the Nevada border just after two on a
bright Saturday afternoon in Denny's Tesla. They'd taken the
"scenic" route, Denny joked, which meant driving the flat-
lands east of the Bay Area, skirting the more populated route to the
north, and taking two-lane highways where Denny got to test out
the "autonomous driver" mode on his Tesla. The car's new software
drove itself while Denny told Jackie more about Lantern, the project they were studying in the desert. With his hands free, he could
even show her slides on the seventeen-inch touch screen in the Tesla,
which he'd hooked up to his iPad.

At the Nevada border and truck weigh station, they slowed at the
request of a soldier who waved them to the side.

"An army checkpoint?" Jackie asked.

"I assume because of what happened last month."

Three weeks earlier, the army had raided the home of a family in
the Big Smoky Valley to the east. The family's ranch was on federal
land to be used for military exercises, but the parents had refused
multiple requests and legal maneuverings to get them to move. They
holed up on the property with a veritable cache of munitions, including a grenade launcher, and declared themselves sovereign. On Instagram, they posted a sign of their twin nine-year-olds, a boy and a
girl, draped in the American flag, holding AK-47s. The army assault,

pressed by manifold interests, including concerns about the children, used nonlethal gases and took back the house.

Three days later, in retaliation, two men attacked the guard post at the military base in Hawthorne. They killed a soldier and injured three others, before they were killed.

At the border, the grim-looking soldier looked into the Tesla's trunk and waved on Denny and Jackie.

Martial law, Jackie thought. She said, "You never said why here—in Hawthorne."

He explained how Nevada was about the most business-friendly place in the world. Low taxes, lax regulations. Totally hassle free, he said, sounding mostly kidding, but not totally. "In Silicon Valley, we spend more for an hour of a lawyer's time than we do to rent an office for the month."

Jackie listened to Denny on two different levels: on one, she was getting basic information, and on the other she was assessing whether he was being straight with her, if she could still have faith in him, follow his direction. The lines beneath her eyes told how much sleep she'd lost, some nights making lists of the evidence in his favor and against. She'd let him lead her from wilderness, pull her from two decades in shadows—and what if she'd been wrong to do that all along?

"Jackie?"

"Huh?"

"You look like you've got something on your mind."

"Not really."

Another long stretch of road and silence.

"You spent much time in the hinterlands?" Denny asked.

"Did some backpacking, after college."

"Yeah."

"Nepal." She gritted her teeth. Almost didn't come back.

"You grew up in . . ."

"Ohio."

"Really?"

"No, but why'd you ask if you already knew?"

"Trying not to be presumptuous."

"Salt Lake," she said. How much did he actually know? Who was she kidding; Google knew everything.

"Family?"

"Sister."

"Oh, yeah, what's her name?"

Jackie gripped the leather seat next to her right leg. "Marissa."

"Beautiful name. What's she up—"

"I'd rather not talk about it, Denny."

He nodded. "Were you trekking—when you went to Nepal?"

She wondered if he knew about that, too.

"Finding myself, I guess."

"What did you find?"

"A near-death experience—rabies."

"Say what again."

"I got scratched by a monkey. Not that common, the monkey part. But there are lots of rabies attacks there, mostly from dogs' bites. You know much about rabies?"

"I know you don't want it."

"We've got a winner. It is a hundred percent fatal once the symptoms set in. The good news is, it's also preventable during the incubation period if you get the vaccine. The trick is getting it in time."

"Which you obviously did or you'd be salivating even more than you already are."

She laughed. "The vaccine is available there, if you get to a clinic. And I was on my way to one when there was an earthquake."

His eyebrows raised, like *Holy shit.*

"Flights canceled, trains down, chaos. Long story short, I was in deep trouble when I was essentially rescued by an American doctor who was over there dealing with a cholera outbreak. He saw me waiting at an airstrip that had ground to a halt due to the earthquake. I'd never have gotten to Kathmandu in time. If not for him, I'm not here to experience"—she focused out the window—"lovely Hawthorne."

The town now loomed, just three miles across the border. It was the kind of small highway town where the low-slung building with the red word "Motel" stood out like the Leaning Tower of Pisa. And it seemed even to lean. Another business sign read CLASSIC CAR, which probably meant "Old." And another, which made Jackie laugh, said WASH and referred to a Laundromat but the sign was encrusted in filth.

"That's a remarkable story," Denny said. "Does it explain your interest in infectious disease—that class you're taking?"

The insightful nature of the question startled her. She hadn't even told the whole of it to Denny, and how it really had been the turning point in her life. Truth is, had it not been for the heroism of Dr. Martin—Lyle—she well might've let herself just die. Sitting on the ground outside the airstrip, she had actually gotten peaceful with the idea. After so much bullshit in her life, so little faith in herself and people around her, it felt in the moment like a blessing to curl up there on the ground and let the hot wind carry her away.

"The guy who teaches it is a genius," Jackie said.

"High praise coming from you."

"I mean the real McCoy, Denny. You ever really want someone to figure something out, Dr. Lyle Martin is the guy . . ."

"I'm starting to feel jealous," Denny said, as he slowed at a stoplight. "Okay, it's decision time. I figured we'd stop at the restaurant, unless you want to go straight to the shop."

"*The* restaurant?"

"I guess there's more than one. I've never tested the theory."

They got turkey sandwiches with canned cranberry chunks on

white bread to go and Denny drove them a half mile east of town and down a dirt road. Jackie noticed the preponderance of army trucks driving both directions. The army base here was a large munitions storage facility, located outside of town, and essentially was this place's raison d'être. The Rocky Mountains loomed to the east. Two miles down a dirt road, and then a few serpentine turns later Denny parked his Tesla in front of a place that looked, appropriately, like a scientific outpost but one you might find in a frozen tundra. Two corrugated metal buildings with a generator by the side and a horizontal unit Jackie recognized as housing cooling equipment.

"Not much to look at," Jackie said.

And, simultaneously, she and Denny said, "I guess that's the idea." The idea being: don't draw attention to this operation.

Denny smiled. "Great minds . . ."

"What about that?" Jackie said. She was looking out the left side of the Tesla window, noticing that farther down the road sat another building, this one concrete, almost bunker-looking. Next to it a long stretch of paved road, like a runway. And looming over the whole thing a giant metal dish, very clearly a powerful antenna.

"Have you ever seen anything so subtle?" Denny said, and laughed. "The supersecret Google space project. Not so supersecret, right?"

It was well known that Google was playing around with low-cost ways to get into space. They weren't alone in this respect. Amazon, too, was getting into the act, and Facebook, Elon Musk, Richard Branson. The stated reason was that these companies wanted to explore the future of space travel, even for tourists. But Jackie was no dope; she and others who liked to read tea leaves suspected it had more to do with the future of much more immediate businesses, like telecommunications and even Internet commerce. If the companies could get low-cost, high-power satellites into orbit, they could become hubs to control Internet access, information, drones, who knew what else.

"Are they launching rockets?" she asked Denny.

"Satellites, I suspect," he said. "Most of that is done in Florida."

"But you're not sure."

"Yeah, I'm sure. Keep it between us. That's not my area; this is, and I try to keep my nose out of stuff that could fuck with my ability to cash in my stock options."

She felt relieved again. She'd asked about the rockets as a test, hoping he'd be frank with her. Opening the car door, she brushed bread crumbs off her lap onto the dusty ground and felt a wave of satisfaction. She was getting let into the inner sanctum at Google, though that was secondary to the bond she was solidifying with Denny.

She stepped out of the car and felt a gust of desert wind and she shivered. She hated wind. It reminded her of uncertainty, self-doubt, the feeling that little things could throw you off if you weren't anchored. She pictured an invasive memory: her mother shouting at her father, her father shouting back, the pair nose to nose on the balcony, little Jackie sitting on the couch, looking over its back, feeling the breeze through the sliding door. Marissa sucking on a bottle Jackie had made for her. Wind brought memories, guilt. Wind smelled like sweat and shampoo, it sounded like anger. Jackie put her hand to her face and wiped.

For an instant, she thought about the fateful day in Nepal, nearly dying, being saved, becoming determined to live a more directed life, to not just do the right thing but figure out how to do the right thing. She thought of these moments as the yin and yang of her life: her terror, paralysis, impotence in dealing with her parents, years of self-doubt, and then a salvation and a determination to figure it out.

"Everything okay?" Denny asked.

"Bad cranberry burp."

"Let's go inside."

Denny used a card key to gain them entrance to the larger of the two metal-framed buildings. Cool air greeted them, the refrigerated feel of a server farm. Inside, not racks of powerful computers. Just a few desks and a Ping-Pong table. A dartboard hung against a far wall. To Jackie's right, a kitchenette. An industrial-size case of Red Bull still in the Costco shrink wrap sat on top of the refrigerator. It all looked like Silicon Valley lite.

Only two of the cubicles were occupied. From one of them, a man looked up. He had a scruffy goatee poking out from his hoodie. From the other cubicle stood a petite woman in a too-tight white shirt and dark pants and short-cropped hair. She looked to Jackie like a waiter—in the marines.

"These are our two Alexes," Denny said. "Alex 1 and Alex 2, say hello to Jackie."

"Hello, Jackie," they simultaneously drawled but seemed mostly disinterested. Then the female Alex said: "And then there were three."

"That's right, three now," Denny said. "So one of you geniuses will have to figure out how to divide the Red Bulls by thirds."

"I only work with imaginary numbers," cracked the male Alex.

"You'll love it here," Denny said and took a sharp angle to the right. Jackie followed him through the building to a staircase with metal railings and cement stairs. "Where the action happens," Denny said in a low voice.

"They're really both named Alex?"

"What're the odds, but, yep."

Denny had also explained in the Tesla what happened below. Below, testing rooms where Google sought to dial in this Lantern discovery it had made. The discovery, in essence, was that Internet users experienced sharply improved rates of memory recall depending on the speed, frame rate, and also the frequency of the delivery of information.

"Like subliminal messages?" Jackie had mused. "What Alfred Hitchcock did in *Psycho*."

"Much more sophisticated and less well understood. We just know it seems to work."

He had pulled up four images on the Tesla screen of the hippocampus, a crescent-shaped part of the brain central to memory recall. The images were taken from real-time magnetic imaging scans of a twenty-two-year-old female study subject. During the tests, the woman had been using her phone or an iPad. The tests were complex because the study subject had to look at and interact with the devices while situated in an MRI machine. The images that Denny displayed in the Tesla were similar except that some images were shaded more than others. The greater the shading, Denny explained, the more of the young woman's hippocampus had been engaged at the time that the imaging had taken place. Where it was less shaded, less of the woman's brain was engaged.

Jackie could see where this was all headed. "So during some of her online interactions, she remembered more than she did in some other cases."

"That too," Denny said. The images, he explained, didn't *necessarily* mean that the subject remembered less, or more—because images can lie. But in this particular case, the images hadn't lied at all. Far from it. After the study subject was removed from the machine, she had taken tests to see how much of her online interactions she remembered. In the same conditions in which her hippocampus had lit up most, she had the strongest recall.

"Amazing, actually," Denny said. "Like she had eidetic memory."

"Photographic."

"Right."

"So what made the difference on what she remembered?"

Denny shook his head. "We're not sure. We were playing with placement of information, streams, also speeds and frame rates. We can't quite get a handle on it. Enter the inimitable Jackie Badger."

It was why they brought her here. Still, she couldn't figure out why it was such a secret. Of course, Google would be working on getting users to remember and share more information. It was in the damn annual report, their entire raison d'être, if you knew how to read the thing.

At the bottom of the stairs, Denny used his key and did a retinal scan and a door clicked open. On the other side, a long hallway, much more nicely appointed than the upstairs, even bespoke floor runners and wood trim near the bottom. *Odd,* Jackie thought. A doorway marked each side every ten feet or so with keypads beside each one. The quiet rectitude of the place reminded Jackie of the psychiatrist's offices her parents wanted her to see after she got caught hacking into the junior high school computer system to send a fake e-mail on behalf of an instructor who Jackie felt had been rude to students. It had been that confusing, interim period in Jackie's life where she was playing with boundaries: What was the right thing to do? When should she intervene or participate in the world, and how? She thought maybe she was looking for a moral compass. But, later, she discovered a different term for what she was seeking: situational awareness. It was a term of art she read about in a psychology class that applied to how people pay attention to their surroundings. Some had terrific situational awareness, like pilots. People who had to be aware, think fast, make good decisions. She still wasn't sure she had it but she was getting there.

"Individual lab areas," Denny said. He stopped midway down the hall. He kept his voice low. "I wanted you to see some of the current work. It's less focused on the imaging right now and more so on recall and behaviors. What kinds of conditions lead to more social behavior, sharing, liking, endorsing, and remembering. Basically, you'll see people using their gadgets through a two-way mirror."

"The study subjects?"

"Local folks. There's actually a pretty good pool from wives and girlfriends of military personnel, along with folks we draw from surrounding communities. Low income in Nevada, sadly, leaves us with people who will do experiments for what is pretty low pay, at least by our standards."

Jackie heard a voice behind her and the female Alex appeared with a tablet.

"Door number five, boss," she said to Denny. "Good time. We're just finishing up."

Alex led them inside the fifth doorway on the left. Behind a two-way mirror a woman sat in a comfortable office chair in the middle of a room, staring at her own tablet. Jackie watched to the point of gawking and now she, at last, understood why this project was a secret one.

The woman behind the two-way mirror looked so engrossed as to be catatonic.

For a long time, Jackie and Denny stared. Suddenly, the woman bolted upright.

PART III

STEAMBOAT

That's the word that struck Lyle. *Host.*

Was that what he was looking at?

The body had become inert again. Now Lyle wondered if he'd imagined it. He immediately dismissed the idea; for all of Lyle's flaws and quirks, he was not a sufferer of PTSD and so it didn't make sense to him that he'd had some sort of flashback or emotional break, a false memory, any of that.

Then, from the corner of his eye, Lyle caught movement. He half turned; he didn't want to look away from Don. He could see a dark shape. Jerry.

Lyle put up his hand. Stop.

"Are you okay?"

"Go back inside," Lyle said to Jerry.

"What's happening? Is he alive?"

Lyle didn't answer. Cautiously, he touched the man's neck. If there was a pulse, he couldn't feel it. But that didn't mean it wasn't there.

"Dr. Martin, is he alive?"

Lyle nodded. It was as much for himself as Jerry. Yes, he suspected, Don was alive.

And a host.

JERRY FELT THE gun in his pocket. It felt like a caged animal. He twitched. Who was Dr. Martin to put his hand up in Jerry's face? Who was he to suddenly be playing number two to Captain Hall?

There was something else bugging him. He let himself ask the question: What was an infectious disease specialist doing on a flight that hit the ground in the middle of some kind of outbreak?

Wasn't that a whole lot of coincidence?

Jerry's father had worked two jobs while his mother drank herself into a near coma. The only reason she didn't get to that point is because she fell down the stairs in a drunken mess and wound up in a

FIFTEEN

WHEN THE MAN in the orange suit shot forward, Lyle caromed backward. Two, three steps, slipped. He didn't try to break his fall. He slammed onto the ground on his ass. Of course he didn't feel it. Every ounce of him focused on the body, the baggage handler who had been comatose, or dead, just moments before. Now the body sat upright at the waist. A wonder, Lyle thought, fear giving way to curiosity. He put all his attention on the man's face, trying to discern the eyes. Were they open?

No. He inched closer. Still closed.

Lyle moved closer again, mostly just by his neck craning. He scraped for his phone. He found it and fiddled for the flashlight. He had to look down to make the phone work. *Shit,* he thought, *I've got to input my code. I've got to look down at my phone.* He wouldn't take his eyes off this man, this creature, Don, held up at the waist like a marionette.

Then, suddenly, as quickly as Don had jerked upright, he fell back again.

IN THE COCKPIT:

"Jerry! What the hell is going on?"

A muffled sound from below.

LYLE WIPED HIS mouth on his sleeve. He spit. Had he gotten the man's spittle on him? Saliva? Something from this . . . host?

wheelchair. Then Jerry got two jobs to help his dad. Jerry could see drunks a mile away. He also hated men who didn't step up and do what was necessary. Dr. Martin looked like both, a drunk and a man who didn't step up.

He felt the gun and turned back to the plane.

Then he looked back again and saw something that allowed him to give Dr. Martin a little bit of respect. Dr. Martin was crouched over the man, peeling back his eyelids, looking into his eyes with the light of his phone.

PUPIL FIXED IN the middle position. Lyle aimed the light into the man's right eye. No movement, no light reflex. That argued for brain death. But brain death didn't lead to spontaneous movement, either. Without thinking much about it, Lyle reached to the man's cheek and pinched his skin between thumb and forefinger.

Nothing.

Harder.

The face muscles tightened. Just a touch. Enough. Lyle focused on the right maxillary and pinched again, even harder. A clench.

Not dead.

Not brain-dead.

Lyle tightened his own jaw in thought. Tight muscles. He moved suddenly. He ran his hand over the man's arm, the right triceps and biceps and the muscles around the rotator cuff. Taut, tensed. No, not dead. Not rigor.

Absently, Lyle gave another thumbs-up to the plane, his way of saying: *Leave me alone.* He brushed sweat from his forehead onto his forearm. He stared at the man's mouth and considered the next, unavoidable move. Full lips, rosy with cold and pulled at the corners. Beneath the nose, that droplet of mucus had doubled into two drops, one settled into a small pool on the groove of the philtrum. Lyle held the phone with his left hand, creating a spotlight on the mouth. With his right, he reached for the lips, pausing only a millisecond before parting them with forefinger and thumb. He dove in.

He felt inside the cheeks, not for anything in particular, anything out of the ordinary. He picked up the warmth and the tightness inside the jaw. He kept a keen awareness of the teeth, ready to instantly withdraw should the man reflexively open wide enough to bite down hard.

"Sorry, Don," he said. "This next part is harder on me than you."

He opened the mouth sufficient enough to get his forefinger toward the back of the throat and lingered at the tonsillar arch. Ideally, he'd watch the pharynx to see if it elevated in a gag response, and to what extent. He'd just have to surmise. He rubbed the arch. Don, the baggage handler, spasmed. *Cough.* Spasm. Lyle pushed himself not to withdraw. He didn't want to cause a stir with Eleanor and the others in the cockpit, if they could even see him. Don calmed down again.

Lyle leaned down again and swirled his finger near the back of the throat, careful to avoid another gag. Likely only so many times he could do that and not get vomited on. As he swirled, he found what he was looking for. Mucus. Lots of it. Pooling near the edges of the throat. He tried to stir it away from the throat's entrance to keep Don from drowning. Lyle sat on his haunches.

Mucus meant the production of white blood cells. It meant the body was mounting an immune response. To what? No light reflex, tight muscles, no pupil reflex. Odd. What did it add up to?

Lyle didn't want to take his own eyes off the man. He felt he needed to. He shone his phone light on his right hand. He put his right thumb into the thumbs-up sign. Showing Eleanor in the cockpit. Showing Jerry.

Nothing, Lyle thought, could be further from the truth.

FROM THE CORNER of his eye, Lyle saw the movement again. It was to the right, in the direction of a plane hangar, unless it was used for industrial tools, like airplane steps and tractors and snowplows. Regardless, this time Lyle was sure. Movement.

He flashed another thumbs-up.

He leaned down over the body. He pushed on the belly, feeling the organs, feeling for inflammation. If it was there, it was subtle. The palpating didn't seem to bother the felled baggage handler. For a second time, Lyle put his hand on the artery coursing through the man's neck. This time, he erred on the side of believing what he suspected, a low pulse. Don was very much alive.

Lyle quickly considered, then dismissed, the idea of having Jerry bring the man inside the plane for further observation. First principle: Do no harm. Not to the people inside the plane.

Lyle considered lifting Don and carrying him to the hangar to keep him warm. That would only attract more attention from the cockpit. Mostly, Lyle just wanted to follow his muse. Or maybe he was dressing up what he wanted in fancy thoughts. He just wanted to get away, farther away. This was the principle that had replaced "do no harm." Don't be bothered. Not by a world that doesn't give a shit.

He started walking toward the hangar.

Then paused. The eyes. Jesus, why hadn't he realized it?

He practically sprinted back to Don.

"One more thing, patient zero," Lyle said. He knelt by Don's head. He focused the light on his phone on the man's eyes. He pried open an eyelid and studied the pupil again. Lyle swallowed hard.

"Jesus," he said.

He put the eyelid back in place. He stared at the hangar. Light from somewhere deep inside left a ghost impression in the doorway, a faint outline. Lyle started walking. Might as well; how long could it be before he was collapsed like Don?

He glanced at the torpid man's phone. On the screen, some comically strange YouTube video showed on the screen. It no longer played, but an image of a cat on skis was stuck there. Lyle looked back at Don. Peeled the eyelid back again. *What's going on in there, Don?*

SIXTEEN

H E CAUGHT JERRY'S approach from the corner of his eye. The first officer had his gun drawn. "Dr. Martin!"

Lyle kept walking. Most of his focus fell on the foot of pavement in front of him. Insidious black ice. Lyle's right toe caught such a patch and he carefully slid to the right.

"Dr. Martin." Jerry gained ground. Now he hit an icy patch and slipped. "Fuck!"

Lyle turned to see Jerry doing a comical man split. Lyle couldn't make out Jerry's face. That's how dark it was, even with his phone creating the slightest ambient light. Jerry's flashlight was tucked in his jacket pocket, still on, causing a little circle of light around the fabric.

"Where the hell do you think you're going?"

"I saw something."

"You saw something. Is that what you said?"

"Your hearing seems to be just fine. That's a good sign."

Jerry righted himself and closed quickly on Lyle. He was within inches. So close that Lyle thought about pickup basketball games he had been in when some numbnuts decided he wanted to start a fight. Lyle stood his ground.

"Where are you going?"

Lyle smelled breath that reminded him of hunger and thirst. *Low blood sugar,* he told himself, *a person not entirely stable even under the best circumstances.*

"Heading to hide in the hangar and have another drink, is that it, Dr. Martin?"

"I have enough for two if you're looking for a good time."

Jerry shoved his handgun right into Lyle's rib cage. He brought his lips right to Lyle's cheek. Then he pressed the gun harder. Lyle went up on his toes to get away from the barrel. He felt the pain in his ankle from having fallen getting out of the plane.

"Not much of a drinker, I take it," Lyle wheezed.

"What's the story with the guy on the ground?"

"There are ways of asking that question without the artillery."

"I'm not sure how else to get your attention, Dr. Martin. Near as I can tell, you're doing some kind of happy-go-lucky, freelance operation here. That's the nicest thing I can say about it."

"Jerry—"

Jerry interrupted him with a nudge of the gun that caused Lyle to take in his breath.

"Differential diagnosis, right? That's what you call it when you check down the list of possible illnesses. I did a little EMT training."

"Good for you."

"Yeah, good for me. So I'm doing a little one of my own."

"What's your point, Jerry?"

"The symptoms involve mood swings, a manipulative streak, intense narcissism, and a strange knack for being in suspicious circumstances."

Lyle looked confused. "Don?"

"Who? No, you," Jerry said. "You seem like you're a doctor, then not so sure of yourself, you talk about mystery symptoms. You manage to dupe Eleanor into letting you off the plane—"

"Technically, Eleanor wanted me to stay. It was you who—"

Another gun shove. "You want my diagnosis?"

"Sure, Jerry."

"You're a drunk."

"Okay."

"I'm not done. You're a drunk who says he's a doctor and happens to be in the right place at the right time for some mystery disease."

"Right place? C'mon—"

"What brings you to Steamboat?"

"A conference."

"In early November, in a tiny ski town?"

Lyle pictured the embossed invitation, remembered the gentle but persistent courtship. Expenses paid, small audience, decent honorarium, a chance to get his sea legs back. He looked at Jerry. He felt sympathy for the guy, connected to him in some way. Just as Lyle had lost faith in the world, so Jerry seemed to have no faith in Lyle, to have reverted to his own primitive state. Wasn't this what was happening everywhere? A new hyperskepticism, everything politicized, facts tossed out as partisan and any faith in humanity with it.

"Or," the first officer continued, "if you like a less conspiratorial version, then you're just a narcissistic drunk who is putting us all in danger by romping around out here. Jesus . . ." He looked off in the distance. "You really don't care, do you?"

Lyle looked Jerry straight in the eye, something approaching contrition, and gently pushed the gun down from his rib cage. Jerry allowed it to happen, indicating he'd had his say. But it was clear to Lyle this conversation wasn't over. He needed to get the hell away from this guy.

"The man over there is named Don."

"How do you know that?"

"It says so on his name tag. He's alive but he's sick."

"Yeah?" A generally skeptical tone.

"I don't have any idea with what," Lyle said, suddenly realizing his strategy. He'd pepper humility with medical talk. He just had to get away from this guy.

"His pupils are moving so rapidly that they look fixed. Fixed usually means brain-dead. But it's not that, I don't think. He's got mildly inflamed organs and heavy mucus around his pharynx, both of which indicate an immune system response. Tight muscles might mean any number of things. I can't really tell out here if he's febrile."

"Fever."

"Right." Lyle allowed himself a quiet exhale; Jerry was calming down.

"Give me the bottles," Jerry said.

"What?"

"If you think you're off the hook with me, you're wrong. First step, hand me the booze in your pockets."

Lyle felt anger's electricity. For just a moment, it was a rush to have such an unscrambled emotion. Then a major downer. Pissed off about losing his cheap swill. That was a very bad sign. Pissed off at the one guy with a gun. Maybe a worse sign. Tied for last. Lyle reached into his pocket and pulled out two bottles. Tried to look unfazed. Time to play the long game.

"My mom was a boozer."

Lyle didn't say anything as Jerry chucked the bottles into the distance where they shattered.

"So, where were we?"

"You were shoving a gun into my ribs and calling me a fraud."

"Now we understand each other better. Let's go back into the plane and you can brief us."

"Okeydokey." Lyle glanced in the direction of the hangar and the sliver of light. Then turned back to Jerry. "When we get in there, before we go up into the cockpit—"

"Flight deck."

What an asshole. *Let him think he's manned up, Lyle. Long game.* "Right, sorry, Jerry. Before we climb up there, we should disinfect. And maybe we should consider staying down in the hol—"

"Disinfect."

"Right. I touched that guy, and I got a mucus spray when I tested his gag reflex."

"Wait a second."

"I'm not saying I've got it. I'm not saying *you've* got it. Certainly, you're at least one step removed. But whatever we're dealing with is clearly highly virulent. I can't think of an analogue, not in my experience and not even in the literature."

"You've read all the literature." Jerry, with this poorly delivered snide remark, was showing his adolescent side and just exposing the breadth of his vulnerability. Then: "So we might have it?"

"I don't think you do. I'm less sure of me."

"You're bluffing."

Lyle tried to look vulnerable. "God, I hope so."

Jerry took a big step backward. "Okay, so . . ."

"One way we might increase the odds . . ." Lyle tried to look like he was thinking.

"Yeah."

"You keep your distance from me and from the guy on the ground. Get back to the cockpit, sorry, flight deck, give them an update. And I'll chase the ghost."

He had Jerry's attention.

"I saw something move in there—over there."

"I looked and I didn't—"

"Maybe it was just light, I agree. I can't be positive. But the way the shadows changed, it wasn't . . . it was herky-jerky, like a person or an animal, not like snowfall or something. Speaking of which, it's fucking cold."

"Stay on topic."

"Look, Jerry, I may have this thing. You may, too, I won't lie. But I well might, and less likely you. So better me going in the hangar and you can tell them what I saw with Don. You know as much as I do—what I told you already." Lyle thought about going on and remembered to keep it short and let Jerry reach his own conclusions.

They stood in silence as snow accumulated at their feet.

"THE TELEPHONE GAME," Eleanor muttered. Snow stuck to the window. Cold enough inside and out now that it wasn't just melting.

The pilot turned around and saw that the woman from Lyle's seat had her hand on the door. It had been a good three minutes since the two had spoken.

"I'm sorry I forgot your name."

"Alex. Telephone game?"

"The kid game, where you whispered a secret to the next person and then little by little it got completely garbled."

"Was a fan myself. It's so quiet out there. What do you think he's—"

"I mention it because that's what this feels like. It's so quiet, like everyone is whispering and then nothing makes any sense."

"Were you ever a writer?"

"What a strange question," Eleanor said. "Were you?"

"No, I . . . never mind. It is getting elliptical in here."

Both women smiled for just an instant. The outskirts of a bond. They'd have made a striking buddy team in public, Eleanor as the one who attracted the immediate attention and Alex, slighter but with a depth anyone paying close attention could pick up. And on the steering yoke. Where were Jerry and that damned doctor? Wherever they were standing, the shadows or silhouettes were outside the view from the flight deck.

Eleanor turned on the light. The man on the tarmac lay there still. Then the light flickered and failed. Eleanor slammed her hand on the steering column.

A sound came from inside the cabin.

SEVENTEEN

Y OU'RE NOT TAKING the gun."

"I wouldn't know what to do with it," Lyle said.

"You were thinking about it."

"I wasn't." Lyle, in fact, hadn't been thinking about it. But now that the idiot first officer brought it up, he wouldn't have minded having the pistol. He just wanted it out of Jerry's hands. He was more dangerous with that thing than a plane passenger with Ebola.

"You're just going to walk into the hangar."

Lyle nodded; more or less. "I'll get close enough to call out. Maybe someone else is as confused as we are."

"And they've not come out here to get our attention," Jerry thought it out aloud.

"Would you?"

Jerry thought about it.

"If it was me in that hangar," Lyle said, "and I saw some bodies and something had happened that scared the daylights out of me, I would keep glancing and trying to figure out what was going on."

"Or glancing and waiting for another target."

"Which is why you should go back into the plane."

"But you won't because you're so selfless." There it was again, Jerry's skepticism, his arrested adolescence, that's what it was.

"Jerry, listen to me."

"You're going to lecture me . . ."

"I lost my wife. She . . . we split. My family. You asked if I'm a drunk, and I don't know if I am or not. But I have had a rough last couple of years. I'm in a good place to take a chance like this. And I really am a doctor and I used to be really good at it . . . so they told me."

It sounded sincere.

"Go back and tell them to stay in the airplane, stay warm, not to touch that body, any of the bodies," Lyle said.

Jerry didn't give Lyle the courtesy of a sign-off, just turned and walked. He shrugged his shoulders, noticeably, sending a message Lyle received: *This nut can do whatever he wants.* It was passive-aggressive and way better, Lyle thought, than having a gun stuck to his viscera. Asshole.

Lyle turned to the hangar.

I'M GOING TO be the voice of reason here.

Jerry willed himself to have the walk of a calm person. He imagined for a moment that he was that actor playing the lone wolf cop in *Avalanche,* the drama set in Park City. He was glad, in a way, Lyle had asked him to return to the plane. Now he was fully the first officer, first protector, federal flight deck officer licensed to carry, navigator. Jerry took that title very seriously. He kept things balanced. *I know what Eleanor thinks of me. I know she thinks I'm neurotic. She'll see I'm the voice of reason.*

He reached the belly of the plane and looked up. Shit, the rope had fallen. Now how the hell was he going to get up there?

He heard someone yell from inside the plane.

Did he imagine it?

"Jerry!" Look. Did he hear it again? *Stay calm.*

He started running toward the downed man named Don. Jerry recalled that the luggage cart was near him. He could use the cart to climb into the plane. He shone the flashlight, made out the outlines of the luggage cart.

Noticed Don was sitting upright.

Fuck, fuck, fuck.

"JERRY!" ELEANOR YELLED into the belly of the plane. It wasn't panic but it was pointed. "Can you hear me?"

"There it is again," Alex said. A sound from the passenger cabin. Scuffling or walking, something. Eleanor fiddled with the cabin camera but it wouldn't work. The electrical system was all fucked up.

"Maybe they're—" Alex said and didn't finish the thought . . . *sitting up or coming alive like that body out there.*

"Get your jacket," Eleanor said. "I'll put on the heat in here and we'll consult with them before we do anything. . . . Are you limping?"

Alex swallowed. "I told Dr. Martin I have arthritis."

Eleanor studied Alex, wondering if she had it. "I'll lower you down—" she started to say.

Alex interrupted. "Captain. He's out there." She pointed.

Eleanor turned and looked through the window. She couldn't see details through the snow. Just silhouetted light and movement of Jerry walking toward the baggage handler.

"Captain . . ." Alex said. She cleared her throat. "How do you feel?"

"How do I feel?"

"Faint or dizzy or anything like that?"

"No. Do you?"

"A little, I'm not sure. I—" Alex didn't finish nor did she have to. She'd made her point that she didn't feel exactly right.

COUGH.

No doubt about it, Lyle thought. Someone coughed. He stood in the doorway of the hangar. He contemplated saying hello. Instead, he flicked off his phone. No need to bring attention to himself. It was an extreme version of what he told his students; the less attention you bring to yourself, the better. That helps avoid the observer effect.

Here, though, it was a different aim. What was the intuition, the feeling he was having? He strained to look into the dark. Not much to be made out. The light he'd seen earlier coming from this direction had disappeared. So had someone turned it off?

He peered into the darkness and thought, simply, *Cavernous.*

His feet felt numb. Cold coursed up his legs and back and he shivered. Untenable, this situation. He fished around in his pocket. He felt what he was looking for, a quarter. He tossed it deep into the dark cavern, giving it a three-quarters heave. It flew a long way and then clanked against something metal. A plane, Lyle surmised, or a truck or other machine.

"Hello," he finally said.

His voice echoed.

Cough.

Lyle finally realized the feeling he was experiencing. It had been a long, long time. Fear.

JERRY KEPT HIS distance, willing himself to be that sheriff. He held the gun out front, pointed at the baggage handler who was prone again. Jerry had to check himself. The guy had been sitting upright, yes? Now he was down again. Was this some sort of zombie shit? Or, Jerry wondered, maybe this was the beginning of some kind of illness, his brain hallucinating.

"Don't move," Jerry muttered. "Do. Not. Move."

No way around it, he was going to have to walk somewhat in the direction of Don if he was going to get the baggage cart. Well, unless he took a circular route. That's what he'd do. He held the flashlight and the gun on the dude on the ground and he circled to his left, walking sideways, never taking his eyes from the man covering up with falling snow.

COUGH.

There it was again.

Then another sound. A click. It didn't take a firearms expert to recognize it.

Somewhere in the darkness, someone had a gun. Lyle froze, hoping whoever was aiming at him was equally blind in this darkness.

EIGHTEEN

I DON'T THINK I should breathe on you, Captain Hall," Alex said. She held a blue-and-white scarf over her nose and mouth, blue eyes visible over the top.

Eleanor barely registered the comment. She was too busy vacillating between duty and fury. Duty told her to retreat to a triage checklist. Not that she'd ever prepped for anything exactly like this. Who could have? But she'd prepped for disaster. Fury told her she'd already failed. She'd allowed herself the ignominious thought: all her passengers were dead, and she was the only one who *hadn't* gone down with the ship. Who gave a shit if this last passenger got her sick? What was left? Not honor? Not the rest of the world?

"Jerry!" No answer. "Damn it."

Eleanor felt light-headed. She wondered when she last ate; it was the two homemade powdered-sugar-coated lemon bars she'd stuffed into her jacket pocket in the Ziploc. She turned to the slight passenger pressing her back against the flight deck wall; the captain felt like the day she lost Frank. Outside on the windshield, white flakes blotted out the coal-black night.

THE BODY WAS down again. So maybe, Jerry thought, he'd only imagined it had been sitting up. He stood ten feet away, gun out, scanning the area around him. Suddenly, he realized he was in the midst of the very fantasy he'd had a thousand times if he'd had it once; in the fantasy, for some reason set at a football stadium, militant gunmen had descended by parachutes and were killing everyone in sight until Jerry leapt on one from behind, stole his gun, started the heroic mutiny that saved the day. One of the presidential candidates in the last election had said he'd never sit around and just watch militants kill people. He'd *do* something. Jerry thought, *Damn right.* The thought of it now made him brave. With his gun, he could handle one crazy, virulent person who, anyhow, seemed paralyzed. So what, he remembered, that he'd lapsed on his gun training. At this distance, it didn't matter. He shook off the cold that was trying to nestle in the exposed areas around his neck and wrists. He allowed himself a step forward. He trapped the flashlight right next to the muzzle of the pistol. It shone on the guy being covered up with snow, who had more of the icy slivers concentrated on his legs. That suggested that, yes, he'd sat up. The snow on his torso had dropped to his legs. *Poor fucker,* Jerry thought. God, just like his mom, dying right in front of him, second by second, in her case from booze, and not a damn thing he could do about it. Just watch the silent angel.

Gun on the guy, he wound a semicircle around Don to get to the luggage rack. He kept himself facing the fallen man and pulled the cart so he'd never lose eye contact. Then he pushed the cart until he reached the plane, finding confidence with each step in the ease with which he was pushing. At the base of the plane, he let himself relax a touch. He locked the wheels of the luggage cart and stepped up to the second level, which allowed him to pop his head inside the hold.

"Eleanor!"

His voice echoed without response. *Huh.*

"Yo, Eleanor, the cavalry is back."

Again, nothing.

He bent and stuck his head out, trying to peer, neck craned low, wondering if she'd slipped out when he was getting the cart. But why wouldn't she have said something? Then he fought off a malignant thought: *What if she somehow was in cahoots with that manipulative doctor?* He saw how she looked at that cunning shit. *Stop it, Jerry. That makes no sense. C'mon, Jerry,* he told himself, *you're the guy with the gun. Eleanor needs you. You have been called.*

"Captain Hall," he said, "I'm coming up."

He pulled himself into the airplane's gelid belly.

"YOU SHOULD KNOW," Lyle said into the darkness, "that I really don't give a fuck."

He almost laughed; for whose benefit was he being so honest, cavalier, or fraudulent? Or, fairly, some combination thereof—regardless, a recipe for danger in practically any ratio. He stepped forward into the cavern. *Cough.* Then a scuffling of feet. One, two. Lyle closed his eyes. What had he always told students? Drop the textbook and use your senses. Given the blackness in here—he was essentially blind—he could toss out sight so he closed his eyes and took in the rest of it. Now, silence. A mausoleum. Then a dampened scuffling sound, echo, then nothing. Quietly as he might, Lyle reached again into his pocket and fished. Bingo, a dime. Lyle pinched the chilly coin between his thumb and forefinger and flipped it into the nothingness in the direction of the cough and other sounds. *Tink, tink,* it hit cement, then skidded— *clink*—into something metal.

Would it prompt more movement?

Quiet. Nada. That was telling. Lyle was getting a picture.

Eyes still closed, he inhaled deeply. Bacteria smelled like roadkill, decomposition. But that wasn't here. Nor anything smoky from fire or metallic that he imagined resulted from an explosion. He detected a whiff of almond, sweetened. Probably, he thought, oil and oxidation. Okay, so? *Machine shop,* Lyle told himself, and then took comfort in two things the air didn't carry: fire or blood. Fire would've meant gunpowder, ignition. Blood, that spoke for itself. Another scent then. Was that coffee? No, couldn't be.

Cough.

Cough.

Scuffle.

Aha. Lyle opened his eyes. Nearly smiled with epiphany. What he'd suspected.

"I'm Lyle Martin. I'm a doctor." Eyes now open, he walked forward. Anyhow, what difference would it make if he was wrong? So what if he was walking into his own death when he'd been as good as dead for years?

He considered turning on the light and decided against it. The closer he got to whatever light source was back there, the better he could make out the objects he passed. To his left, a forklift then an industrial tool cabinet. To his right, empty space and then, wow, the sleek nose of a small private plane that, for a second, reminded Lyle of a dolphin's snout.

Cough.

Lyle took a false sense of refuge beneath the small plane's hull. The vantage point unblocked some light, and Lyle now guessed he was looking at that kind of diffuse gleam from a field lamp. The source remained hidden by what Lyle could now see was another small jet to his left. But right behind that, the source and the sounds he'd heard. Lyle closed his eyes one more time and he pictured Melanie on the night that he found his clothes piled on the doorstep. The drought had already started but, wouldn't you know it, rain. A neighbor had craned her neck out of the house next door until she saw Lyle and withdrew. He'd won $130 playing pool and then given the entire wad to a guy outside the bar singing "American Pie."

"A long, long time ago . . ." Lyle had slurred the opening lyrics up to the window.

Melanie didn't open the window and Lyle couldn't brook another version of he-said-she-said. He picked up his favorite sweatshirt and left the rest of the clothes and decided to spend the night at his UCSF office until he could figure out a better plan. *I can still remember, how the music used to make me smile.* He had pawed at the piece of paper in his back pocket, considered slipping it under the door, and decided not to give Melanie the satisfaction.

Back at the hangar, Lyle stuffed away the image, said *fuck all of it* to himself, walking forward past the airplane to his left and toward the source of the light, and then, startled by what he saw, came to an abrupt stop.

"ELEANOR?"

"Jerry, stay where you are."

"You're okay." Jerry shoved a cargo box beneath the opening in the flight deck. "Why didn't you answer?"

"I erred on the side of caution. Wasn't sure what, or who might hear us."

"Work with me, Eleanor. I'm trying to look out for you here."

"What's your deal, Jerry? We're coming out."

A flicker of fury nicked him, like a lightning strike. Sometimes, he imagined that she thought of him like the boy in the bubble, that kid from the after-school movie who was so sick and pitiable he lived, isolated, in a biosphere. "Eleanor, I don't like your tone—"

"It's not safe in here. We're evacuating, the two of us. We're going to drop down there. I'm bringing the last medical supplies, but I don't want to bring anything else from the cabin because I don't know how it gets carried."

She held a rucksack over the opening, as if to indicate she was going to drop it, which she did. *Thud.* Supplies hit the hold floor at Jerry's feet.

"You have the gun?"

"Locked and loaded."

"Okay, Clint Eastwood. Listen, Jerry, can I get your input?"

"Of course."

"I'd like to leave the heat running. It's going to eat fuel. I . . . these people."

"Eleanor?"

"Never mind, I figured it out."

"Hey, listen, it's not your fault. You hung in there as much as you could."

"We're coming down. The passenger first."

Jerry saw a foot appear in the hole. He guided it with a hand, helping the small woman until she could stand on the crate and then dismount it. Eleanor followed. When she hit the crate, she said, "Thank you, Jerry."

"No problem, Captain." No problem at all.

She stepped off the crate. The three quickly made their way out of the hold down to the tarmac.

"Where's the doctor?" asked the captain once they were on the ground.

"He's gone over to the hangar."

"What? Why?"

Jerry sensed a moment. "I'm not sure I trust that guy."

"What happened, Jerry? Just tell me what happened."

"I can only vouch for what he told me."

Jerry recounted the story, his version of it.

The three of them—the pilot and navigator and the last surviving passenger—walked to the hangar, not sure if they should be more afraid of what they were leaving behind, or what they'd find inside the dark building.

LYLE MUMBLED, "*THE Price Is Right.*"

It's what came to mind as he looked at the scene that appeared thirty feet in front of him, illuminated by a reedy light from some-where farther back. Lyle looked at the living room set, the sort of setting that you'd see game-show contestants compete for. A couch in the middle, with a coffee table in front of it, and two end chairs. It only seemed out of place for an instant and then Lyle realized it was just a homey little construction for the workers here, an open-air rest area. What Eichler would've created if he'd decorated airplane hangars.

Lyle had a pretty good idea who used this setting to kick back. It was the guy sitting up on the couch with his head lolled on to the top of the backrest. Another body.

Lyle took a step closer. Then he remembered that a few paces earlier he'd passed a bucket with a mop sticking out of it. He retreated and took the cool wooden mop handle. Lyle marveled at the primitive nature of his instinct to take a weapon and wondered if it meant he cared, after all, if he lived.

Again, he said, "My name is Lyle Martin. I'm a doctor."

He scrutinized the shape of the man on the couch. Looking for movement, anything. The man remained static. *Static.* The word that came to Lyle's mind. He took another step forward. He felt a tickle on his upper lip. Shit. A drop of mucus. Lyle wiped it on his forearm and, without fully taking his attention from the man, glanced down at his arm. Was it bloody? Was it the beginning of an immune response? Or just his body's response to cold? Lyle inhaled the sharp, frigid air. It needled the soft, pink flesh inside his rib cage. It hurtled tiny shards of glassy air at his larynx.

Just cold, he told himself and let himself believe it.

On the table to the left of the static man stood a half-foot stack that looked to be magazines or technical manuals. Just in front of the man, a tin cylinder on an electric plate that Lyle guessed was filled with coffee or hot water. Then nearer the man on the table, some confir-mation of that: a mug overturned. A clue. Had the man been holding the cup when he was stricken, and then had an instant to put the cup down? Did he kick it over in a death throe?

Still no movement from the man. Had he been the source of the coughing? Lyle seriously doubted it. He squinted farther back, trying to discern the source of the light. It had the thin, atmospheric feel of a battery-powered lantern that you'd take on a camping trip and provided just enough light to an otherwise night-dead camping site. Lyle took purposeful steps forward, letting the man's shape crystallize. No jacket. A long-sleeved shirt covered his torso and arms, though they otherwise hung vulnerable at his sides. Faster steps from Lyle until he heard the sound of steps behind him. *Tap tap* on the cement floor.

Lyle froze. He squeezed his hands around the mop stem. He listened to the echo of footsteps.

NINETEEN

S TAY WHERE YOU are," Lyle said.

"Dr. Martin?"

"I think it's advisable that you stay there," Lyle said. He estimated they were fifty yards back.

"We need to talk to you." It was Eleanor speaking, her voice coming through the darkness from near the entrance to the hangar. Lyle, without turning his head that direction, could sense the flicker of a flashlight, presumably Jerry's.

"Can I meet you outside?" Lyle said. He directed his gaze at the right corner of the couch. Looking for movement. He heard Eleanor urge whoever was with her to stop. Lyle thought he picked up three sets of feet. Why weren't they on the plane? Who was with the passengers? He heard a scraping noise from the area of the couch, movement on the pavement. Then it abruptly stopped.

"Why can't we come that way?"

Lyle didn't answer. He didn't want to spook the person behind the couch. And a few puzzle pieces were falling into place, and he just wanted to be left alone with this patient or witness.

No such luck. He could hear the footsteps again and prepared himself for a shit show. Jerry was like the dean. A shiver seized him, warm blood fighting through cold-constricted vessels.

The steps neared and the flashlight and then they were upon him.

"What the fuck?" Jerry asked as he saw the surreal living room, and the body. Jerry directed his flashlight at the man. Lyle got his first clear look. Midthirties, beard, baseball cap crooked and nearly fallen off, windpipe and jugular exposed by the backward tilt of his head.

"Jesus," Eleanor whispered.

"It's okay," Lyle said.

"Who are you talking to?"

Lyle didn't answer.

From behind the couch, there was that distinctive click.

The hammer of a rifle being pulled into position. Then a cough.

"Get down, Captain," Jerry bellowed. He stepped in front of Eleanor and Alex.

"Come out with your hands up," Jerry barked.

"Put down your gun," Lyle said.

"Put down your gun," Jerry repeated.

"No, I'm talking to you, Jerry," Lyle said. "Lower your gun."

"What the fuck are you talking about?" Then in the direction of the couch. "Get out here, right now! Put your hands up, and get out here. I'm not going to shoot you unless I have to. You need to get your ass out here right now."

Lyle swung with the broom. He rocked Jerry's gun hand, causing the weapon to fall onto the ground.

"Are you out of your mind?" Jerry dove for the weapon. On his knees, he swung the gun at Lyle, then in the direction of the couch, then Lyle again. "Stop!" Lyle said. "It's a child."

"What?"

"Young man. I'm a doctor. I can help you and I can help your father."

"How do you . . ." Eleanor started.

From behind the couch stood a boy no more than ten, pointing a rifle square at Lyle's head.

"Lower the gun, son," Jerry said. He pulled the hammer back.

The boy held firm.

"Jerry," Eleanor said. "Jerry, listen to me. I want you to put the gun on the ground."

"Kid, I do not want to shoot you. I want you to stand down."

"Jerry . . ." Eleanor said low.

"He's been on a killing spree. This is no time to be soft. World's gone mad."

"He didn't kill anyone," Eleanor said.

The comment surprised Lyle. Of course, she was right.

"Son, is that your father?" Lyle said.

The kid didn't answer, but it sounded like he emitted a whisper.

"I'm a doctor. I can try to help him. But I can't do it if you shoot me or make me feel like you're going to shoot me. I know you're scared." Another step forward. "I was on that airplane that landed. We're here to try to help." Lyle left it deliberately vague as to whether they'd landed with the express purpose of coming to help or whether they'd just coincidentally landed. "Can I help?" Another step forward, hands up. The boy held the rifle, less steadily now, shaking.

"Put the gun down," Jerry said.

"Oh for goodness' sake, Jerry," Eleanor said. "Stop the cowboy stuff."

Jerry gritted his teeth. "Okay, kid," he said, "I'm lowering my weapon and I suggest you do the same."

The boy lowered the rifle.

"Good man," Jerry said, as if he'd saved face.

Lyle held up his hands, poised to walk forward amid a new threat: mounting tension within his own group. Jerry, Eleanor, the kid with the gun, a ticking clock they couldn't identify. It felt like they just might kill one another before this syndrome did it for them. Lyle walked again, slowing, trying to set up his examination of father and son. The nearer he got, the more things came into focus. Matching upholstered chairs, worn and fading, framed each side of the table. An area rug beneath. Someone had gone to great lengths to make this feel like a home. On the couch next to the father a sleeping bag bunched around a pillow, and a heavy wool blanket. Tears streaked the face of the boy with the rifle held in both arms over his chest, just a motion away from aiming again. He had a bowl haircut and, Lyle noticed, supreme posture. His dad, Lyle guessed, was a military guy, teaching manners and self-sufficiency.

"Your dad's the mechanic here?" Lyle asked.

The kid tried to suppress a sniffle, a whimper. Lyle took it as a yes.

From behind, Eleanor said: "Dr. Martin, may I have a word?"

Lyle forged ahead.

"What's your name?"

"Tyler."

"Okay, Tyler, I have some good news, first. Your dad is not dead."

No answer.

"Okay?"

"You don't know."

"I know." Now Lyle was at the edge of the scarred wooden coffee table and he winced; it reminded him of something and then he remembered the dream from the airplane, where a bat had risen from a bag of powder sitting on a wooden table. For a moment, Lyle swooned. Just a coincidence. "I need to examine your father. Is that okay?"

No answer.

"You were sleeping here on the couch and you got awakened by a sound."

"How does he know that?" Alex said.

"Shhh," Jerry responded. But all of that was in the background.

"Are you ten?" Lyle asked.

"Nine," Tyler said.

"Did a noise wake you up?"

The boy let out a sob. He started to cry. The walls of bravery falling, boyhood trust and yearning returned. And he said: "Can you save my dad?"

"I'm going to try," Lyle said. He clenched his teeth. The words sounded familiar—the kind of thing he used to say—but they were devoid of any emotion. Any true caring. Robotic.

"What's your father's name?"

The boy couldn't answer for the sobs. During the eruption of tears, Eleanor neared Lyle and said, "I absolutely *have* to talk to you."

Lyle didn't hear her. He reached down to feel for a pulse on the man on the couch. Abandoned the idea and looked instead at the pupils. Moving so quickly as to look still. Something very strange going on in there. He thought, *None of us is going to survive the night; I have no idea what's going on but I suspect the human body has met its match.*

TWENTY

'D URGE YOU to keep a distance," Lyle said over his shoulder. He couldn't feel a pulse, but it didn't matter. He looked at the pupils again. He could imagine a first-year medical student saying *Brain-dead*.

"Tyler," Lyle said, "your dad is going to be okay."

Tears ran down the boy's face. Talk about fixed, paralyzed; this was all just too much for him. Lyle tried to study his face without giving too much away. Was he feverish? In pain?

"Tyler, what's your dad's name?" he repeated.

"Rex."

"Okay, Tyler, I'm going to do a medical test on your dad and I don't want it to scare you. I'm going to put my fingers in his mouth and I'm going to make sure there's nothing blocking his airway." It wasn't true; he was feeling for mucus and looking for a gag response, like with the baggage handler. But he couldn't think of a good reason to explain that to the kid. "Okay, Tyler?"

A whimper of approval.

Lyle stuck his fingers in and produced the same response he'd gotten before with the baggage handler.

Behind him, the trio watched with fascination and horror. Alex looked absolutely stricken, eyes wet. Eleanor held back her own particular anguish; the incident reminded her of the story she'd been told about the death of Frank, her great love, near the peak of Annapurna.

The sherpa said he'd gotten altitude sickness at a particularly treacherous spot and fallen and the sherpa revived him, or so it seemed. Then Frank had stood up, seeming fine, and walked right into a crevasse. His oxygen-starved mind had betrayed him. Eleanor took a step backward. Jerry, feeling her need, put a hand on her back and she angrily swatted it away. She hated him, the anti-Frank. Their tension notched up.

"Dr. Martin," Eleanor said, composing herself, "I need to speak with you—privately." She knew it would drive Jerry nuts. But she needed to tell Lyle about the sound from inside the cabin, something alive in there.

Lyle, so engrossed, didn't respond.

"Tyler," he said, "is this where you were sleeping? Next to your dad?"

"Yes."

"And you woke up and he was like this?"

The kid nodded in the affirmative.

"You tried to wake him up?"

A sob of affirmation.

"What happened when you tried to wake him up?"

"He didn't. He wouldn't. I . . ." Grief paused the boy.

"Did you hear a noise?"

"What?"

"Did a noise wake you up? Did you see anybody or hear anybody?"

"I don't know. Is he okay? Why won't he wake up?"

"I'm a doctor, Tyler," Lyle said, diplomatically. He kept using the boy's name when addressing him, as Lyle encouraged students to do; use the names of patients and their families because it makes them feel like individuals. "I want to get him someplace warm. What's back there?" Lyle asked, referring to the other end of the hangar.

"An office. There's a space heater. It doesn't always work."

"Thank you, Tyler. So you didn't hear a noise when you woke up? You don't remember smelling anything?"

"No."

Lyle regretted his phrasing; too many questions, not open-ended enough. He was rusty.

"May I examine you to make sure you're okay?"

No answer from the nearly catatonic child. Lyle left the man's side and approached the boy. Then he paused, a glint on the couch catching his eye. Lyle looked down and saw a cell phone. It sat on the couch next to the man called Rex, frozen on an image. Lyle picked up the phone in his rubber-gloved hand and looked closely. A grainy image of a man sitting behind a desk that Lyle strained to recognize. It was Marlon Brando.

"Does your dad like *The Godfather*?"

"It's his favorite movie. He told me that he's seen it a hundred and four times and when I'm twelve I get to watch it with him," the boy said. He was relaxing. Lyle thought, *Okay, a step in the right direction.* He clenched his teeth; Melanie is out there somewhere with a boy just like this. Footsteps close from behind as Lyle closed in on Tyler.

"Dr. Martin, please, a word," Eleanor said.

"In a moment." He didn't want to lose the clinician's rapport. He knelt on the cement, relieving the young man of the weapon, setting it on the ground, and took him in. Levis and a striped sweater, hands balled at his sides that looked like they'd be big mitts one day, with big, booted feet to go with them. Lyle felt a pulse on the boy's wrist, a purely symbolic act of establishing intimacy, asked how Tyler felt (hot or cold; sick to his stomach). No, no, he felt fine, looked fine. Lyle palpated the belly; not swollen or tender.

Tyler's lip quivered. Alex walked forward, pulling her less agile right leg a touch behind the left. Jerry seemed poised to stop her when she knelt in front of the boy.

"I bet you could run around this building ten times you're so healthy," she said.

He looked at Dr. Martin. "Do I have to?"

"No," Lyle said, smiling. "I think she's saying that you're in good shape." He looked at Alex appreciatively. He sensed she must know something about being scared as a child, what with her early-life illness. She liked children, knew how to care for them, maybe had kids of her own, then, Lyle thought, no, a younger sibling. Lyle dismissed his wandering thoughts and said to the boy, "Would it be okay if I speak for a second to the pilot? She's the head of the rescue mission."

A moment later, Lyle stood with Eleanor and felt a pang of relief. She was okay. When their eyes met, the instant held understanding, a mutual wavelength. In a low voice, just a few steps from everyone, she told Lyle what was going on in the plane.

"I assumed they were dead," she said.

"Not quite," Lyle said. He explained what he'd seen on the bodies, the baggage handler bolting upright.

"What is this?" Eleanor asked.

Lyle shook his head. He kept his voice low so the boy wouldn't hear. "I have no idea, Captain Hall. It's something I've never seen." He paused. "Never read about." He paused again, closed his eyes in thought.

"What are you thinking?"

"I'm just puzzled," he finally said. "Obviously."

Eleanor studied his face and wondered if he was telling her everything he was thinking. She could see he was lost somewhere. "Lyle?"

He was thinking back to his neurology rotation during med school. One morning at the start of early morning rounds, the attending physician promised the handful of residents they were going to see a rarity, and an unfortunate one. The patient was an old Japanese man. He'd been delivered the night before to the hospital by his wife, who declined to explain his condition: sitting in the front seat, unable to move or speak, respiration very low, but fully conscious. Essentially catatonic but physically uninjured. The attending physician opened the door to the man's room and there sat the shriveled patient, eyes open, breathing from a respirator, wife by his side, her face buried in a handkerchief in grief. The attending saw Lyle's face, studying, assessing, calculating, and nudged him. "Lyle, please don't say anything," she said. It had become a running joke, wherein Lyle would mutter some theory during rounds, often right, about a patient's condition. It wasn't that Lyle was trying to show off, he just got lost putting the pieces together and would think aloud. Lyle stared at the old man, the liver spots on his temple, next to his frayed hair, the jaundiced skin, bone-thin shoulders beneath his gown, eyes blinking.

"She didn't mean to do it," Lyle had muttered.

The attending shot him a look. *Pipe down, Lyle.*

"I'm sorry," Lyle had said, genuinely sorry. "I didn't say he'd been poisoned."

The attending, a young-looking Indian woman with jet black hair, all but smiled. Lyle couldn't help himself, and he was right again. So she asked him what type of poison. This stumped Lyle. Another resident picked up the ball and suggested tetrodotoxin. Now the attending allowed herself an appreciative nod at this group, whip smart the lot of them. She led them through a quick physical exam and then left the woman to her husband and grief and took the group back outside and explained what they all now knew. The man had eaten puffer fish, a delicacy, but, if not prepared precisely in the correct way, leads to skeletal paralysis, eventually, likely, death.

Now it was clear what Lyle had meant by *she didn't mean to do it*. The wife, he thought, hadn't meant to poison the husband. Lyle had been right. The husband was suffering from stage four bladder cancer, spread to the lymph nodes, and, as it turned out, he'd dreamed of having puffer fish as a last delicacy. The old man darned well had known it was a win-win; if he survived dinner, it would be a great meal; if he died, a great *last* meal.

As Lyle stood in the hangar, he pictured the old man, locked in his predeath catatonia and tried in vain to remember how that toxin worked, what its physiological mechanism was. What did puffer fish do to the brain? The answer evaded him. He looked back at the mechanic on the couch and considered the eerie similarity. But there was nothing contagious or widespread about puffer fish, nothing virulent.

"Are you okay, Dr. Martin?" Eleanor said. For an instant, she wondered if the syndrome had hit him, too.

"I'm sorry," he said, and meant it this time, too. He'd long since learned to apologize after taking his mental junkets. He grimaced.

"Time to let us into your head," Eleanor said.

This further jerked Lyle back to reality. The pilot sounded like Melanie, in a good way, some appreciation in her voice that he wasn't just a lummox on a mental vacation.

"Saxitoxin," he said, with some bit of revelation.

"What's that?" The first officer suddenly was standing too close for Lyle's comfort.

"I'm thinking of various poisons, nerve agents, toxins. They can paralyze the body but leave the brain intact, more or less. I can't remember how they work."

"What's saxitoxin?"

"Nerve gas," Alex said from ten feet away, where she stood next to the boy. Her outburst surprised everyone and seemed a bit to surprise her, too. She stared at them and, nervously, down at her phone. "I'm a comic book geek. Graphic novels. When I was younger, I had a lot of time on my hands . . ." she said. "It's kind of a trope, neurotoxins used by bad guys, and saxitoxin gets regularly mentioned." After a brief pause: "But it was a real thing, not made up, that the government had."

"That's right," Lyle said, remembering. Saxitoxin, he recalled, had been used by American spies in covert operations. Great for assassinations because so little poison brought the desired result: skeletal paralysis and eventual death.

"Nixon ordered it all destroyed," Alex said. "But some survived."

Now she really had their attention.

"That's the lore, anyhow," she said. She noticed Lyle boring a stare through her, quizzical but distant. She fiddled with her inert phone.

Eleanor noticed that Lyle watched Alex like she was a painting in a museum and he was an obsessing art history student.

"Is your phone working?" Lyle asked Alex.

"No."

"I notice you keep fiddling with it."

The passenger didn't seem like she had anything to add. She, in turn, seemed struck by the way the pilot watched Lyle. Below the surface, cliques were forming, alliances, but they hadn't solidified.

"We need a plan," Jerry said.

"I'll second that motion," Lyle suddenly said and turned to the first officer. "Let's move the father into the office with the space heater and I'll go get the girl from the plane," he said.

"Say what? What girl?" Jerry turned to Eleanor.

"There's a girl on the airplane?"

"This is nuts," Jerry said. "How does he know that? Am I the only one who thinks this is nuts?"

Lyle had reverted to his old style of managing crisis, focusing on the medical issues, in effect barking orders at people with less understanding of the situation. The problem was that, unlike the old days, no one was imbuing him with omniscience or saintlike status. So, to them, he sounded like a know-it-all or, plainly, an asshole. Or a conspirator. What girl was he even talking about?

Undeterred, Lyle started walking back toward the plane.

"Freeze," Eleanor said.

He kept walking.

"Dr. Martin, I'm still the captain here."

Lyle turned around.

"A little girl is on that airplane, terrified."

"How do you know that?"

"She's immune to this," he said. "They're immune, I think."

He'd seen a little girl on the plane earlier and Eleanor said there was a noise on the plane. It must be the girl. "I'm not, and the rest of us aren't. I'm probably exposed at this point. I can't speak for you."

"Then why didn't we get it on the airplane—with the rest of them?"

"Were you in the cockpit, er, flight deck?"

Eleanor nodded.

"I don't know. Something airborne. Something . . ." He had only the vaguest ideas, not even that, just fuzzy images, not worth sharing. He could feel the shadow of gun-toting Jerry, right on his heels. Lyle shivered; this new world was feeling like a microcosm of the one left behind: growing tension, people getting their backs up, positions taken and entrenched. A gun.

Maybe there was a way to inoculate against Jerry's seeming desire to escalate, take control. Lyle looked the first officer in the eye.

"Do you have thoughts?" he asked Jerry.

"You're asking my thoughts? How gracious."

"You've been out here with me, seen the baggage guy, you can see the weather." Lyle left it open-ended, trying to draw Jerry in. "I don't know airports, airplanes, weather, any of it. I mean, should we get the bodies into the plane to keep them warm and we can see what's going on in there?" He paused.

Jerry tried to measure whether he was being baited, couldn't quite figure it out.

"It would be easier to bring the baggage guy, into the office, back here," he said.

"Smart," Lyle said as deferentially as possible.

TWENTY MINUTES LATER, Lyle had dragged the body of the mechanic by his armpits, with Jerry standing guard, into the back office, along with the bodies of the baggage handler and other workers. Now they stood under the airplane, ready to use the luggage rack as a ladder.

"You or me first?" Lyle asked.

Jerry hesitated.

"I guess I can stand guard," Lyle said. "You check the plane, which is obviously your baby, and I'll be down here if something weird goes down. But I one hundred percent defer to you."

Jerry looked over at the hangar, where Eleanor and the passenger tinkered with the cell phone and watched the child. He could see their outline in the doorway. Jerry tried to look like he was thinking hard about this, making some complex calculation. Truth was, he couldn't keep up. It was why he loved talk radio, especially Rush Limbaugh; you had to find somebody you could trust in a world where there was just too much to think about.

"I've got to overrule you on this one, Dr. Martin. You go in there and do your doctor thing and I'll keep watch if something goes down. I need to keep an eye on the women and children."

"But . . ."

"I'm decided. Let's keep the chain of command."

Perfect, Lyle thought. What he had hoped for.

Jerry hoisted him up. "Holler if you need me."

"If you don't hear from me in ten minutes," Lyle said—he paused on what to say next . . .

"I'll come rescue you."

Jesus—Lyle fought a smile—*what a prick.*

Seconds later, Lyle stood in the flight deck, now holding a Beefeater bottle that he'd snagged in the belly. The plane was just the way he'd remembered it, but darker and colder. The temperature differential between inside and out had diminished. Near freezing in here, though Lyle presumed that was because the cargo-hold door had remained ajar. The passengers, presumably, would be warmer.

The radio buzzed with static, the way Eleanor must've left it.

Lyle took a deep breath and entered the cabin. The soft ambient light would've suited a mortician, the cool air too, and, of course, the bodies. Row after row of the inert. Lyle stared at them while he guzzled the last drops from a tiny Beefeater bottle. He made it halfway through a second and stuffed it, and two Tanqueray gins, into his pocket. His senses cleared. He looked at a tall man in first class wearing headphones, head slumped to the right touching the head of the woman next to him, catatonic too. He whisked into coach. Was there a scent? Something burnt? He rubbed his fingers together to remind himself he wore the rubber gloves. He realized he'd long since abandoned his breathing mask.

He took the rows at speed, glancing, looking for anomalies. He saw a woman with a neck pillow seemingly suspended like a puppet by the weight of her chin on her chest. In her lap, her phone, attached to headphones in her ears. Lyle walked past the row and then did a full stop and backpedaled. It wasn't the woman who caught his attention but the man next to her, an older guy, nearly elderly, wispy thin hair, waxy skin, different somehow, what was it?

There, Lyle noticed, blood dried below his nose. Lyle bent down and studied, started to study. Something not right.

He heard the whimper and paused. A few rows farther down. He made his way back and found the source of the noise: a lump beneath a blanket, muffling the hysterics. The girl he'd seen earlier, clutching a stuffed bear. He steeled himself against emotion.

"I'm a doctor? I'm here to help you."

She blinked with trauma.

"What's your name?"

Whimpering, terror.

"Is this your mom? I'm going to help her."

"She . . . she won't wake up."

The girl had bangs and freckles and seemed uncertain if she were awake herself. Surely, this must be a nightmare. On the ground, he saw a piece of paper she'd drawn on and written her name.

"Andrea?"

She looked up.

"We are going to get help—for her, your mom," Lyle said. He wanted to quiz her on what had happened here but there was no sense to be discussed, the girl too far gone. He simply carried her to the front and lowered her down to Jerry. Lyle started to lower himself down and he saw the truck pulled beside the airplane, with Eleanor behind the wheel. What new plan was this?

He didn't have time to process it when he was struck by an impulse, more than that, a severe nag. Ignoring Jerry's overtures to come down, Lyle pulled himself back into the plane. He could hear Jerry say, "I think he's drunk."

Lyle cruised back into the cabin and found the older gentleman. Pulling off his plastic glove, come what may, Lyle put his hand to the man's left temple. Then felt for a pulse at the carotid. Then back to the temple. He focused on the frayed skin and couldn't deny what he was looking at: a contusion. Without an x-ray he couldn't be sure, but he'd have bet his damn booze bottles he was looking at a skull fracture.

He stood and nearly sprinted back to his row. He stared, surrounded by these near-dead creatures, inhaling whatever was in here. It hit him, right here, all of it, the weight of the last two hours. This was madness, impossible, all but a dream. He slammed his open palm against the overhead compartment to feel the pain and assure himself he wasn't asleep. Then he opened the compartment and yanked out his suitcase and tossed it on the ground and unzipped it. He rummaged. He'd managed to bring a single suit, wrinkled with folding. In an inner compartment, he felt for his itinerary. An official invitation, embossed stationery, to give a midday talk at a small infectious disease conference.

"Bullshit," he said. "Bullshit."

He'd known it, of course, on some level. He must have? An infectious disease conference, here in Steamboat, in November?

Who was he kidding?

He reached behind the itinerary and pulled out a small, framed picture in the cheap Walgreen's frame, the glass broken horizontally. Melanie smiling on a rock, an invisible bump in her belly, the last happy picture.

A sob caught in his throat.

He read the letter of invitation. He studied the stilted language, deliberately formal, an honorarium not too much or too little, a number to call, and a website to visit.

He tried to remember the seduction that got him to this putative conference—in the mountains, on this plane—the phone calls, the travel arrangements, a slow reel, patient, low pressure, persistent, striking his chords, eventually, finally pulling him out of his fetid apartment and his own stink. He must've known all along it was a setup. On some level. But what in the hell for? Who would want a washed-up infectious disease specialist? Especially one who had given up completely on humanity?

He stared at Melanie's picture and sipped more gin. He turned and threw the bottle straight down the aisle toward the back of the airplane, a perfect strike flying between the half-dead passengers. It didn't shatter, just hit with a thud against the wall of the bathroom door.

Lyle started back toward the front of the plane. But after a step, he paused. He returned to the overhead compartment. What had struck his attention? He looked at a red roller bag lodged next to where his own luggage had been. His eye stopped on a white luggage tag with green letters: "Google." He turned the tag over and saw the name: Alex. No address, or phone number.

Alex. His seatmate, the woman who had survived. Where had she said she worked? She hadn't, just that she was in technology sales. He shrugged and turned.

At the flight deck door, he stopped. Attached to the door, with adhesive, was a small gold rectangle, almost like a playing card. But it was made of metal. He pulled it off and after a brief wrangle with the powerful double-sided tape that held it, freed the unusual object. Hardly knowing what to make of it, other than its anomalous presence—had it been there before? He put it in his back pocket.

Lyle lowered himself through the bottom of the plane, hit the ground, saw the barrel of the gun.

TWENTY-ONE

G ET IN THE truck," Jerry said. He pointed his pistol at Lyle, then raised an eyebrow, like *Try me.*

Behind Jerry, Eleanor idled a heavy-load pickup truck. The back windows of the vehicle were tinted but Lyle felt he could see Alex and the two children in the backseat.

"Get that out of my face," Lyle said.

"Get in the truck." Eleanor repeated Jerry's command.

Lyle stared at her.

"Heading to town. For help and to avoid whatever is here if it's . . . contagious," she continued. "We need to get on the same page. No more renegade missions."

"This is a dead zone, a freaking patient-zero cluster fuck. We can't be around this anymore," Jerry spat. "If these kids get sick, we might need a real doctor."

Lyle ignored him and spun an instant analysis. *How best to isolate and build on the clues?*

Useful to stay at the airport?

Maybe.

"Should we make a last attempt to call out over the radio?" Lyle said.

"So now you're a doctor and a pilot," Jerry said.

Useful to see the surrounding area?

Likely.

Lyle moved around to the passenger side of the dark blue cab and felt a gentle push from behind. "You heard the captain," Jerry said. He climbed in after Lyle, sandwiching him in the middle.

The girl whimpered in the back. The cab smelled like Kentucky Fried Chicken. A driver's license hung by a clip from the visor over Eleanor. The picture on the license belonged to the mechanic.

Eleanor pulled the silver lever and put the truck in drive and it slid to a start. The girl's whimpers intensified. Eleanor turned on the radio but all that came out was static. Lyle reached up and turned it off.

"What are you doing?"

"It's best."

Eleanor shoved in a cassette tape. The voice of James Taylor filled the cab. The clock read 1:45.

Eleanor turned the truck in a tight U-turn and they headed to the edge of the terminal. They passed a movable ramp, and then an unblocked stretch of window through which they could see into the terminal, and the handful of bodies. One looked slumped on the counter. The sounds of "Sweet Baby James" filled the cab.

The tires slid on the ice as Eleanor pulled behind the right of the low-slung terminal and swung out of the airport. She reached in front of Lyle and turned up the heat. It was roaring now, actually starting to feel warm.

"The music and heat should let us talk without scaring them," she said. She turned to Lyle, briefly, then back to the road. The head-lights illuminated dancing snow. Not much beyond that. Dark ground stretched out in front of them. Then a sign emerged on the right. "Slow," Jerry said. Eleanor slowed. The sign read STEAMBOAT, 19 MILES.

"Dr. Martin, we're not going to stop until we get to town," Eleanor said and punched the accelerator.

"Sounds good to me."

"Well, look who is suddenly agreeable," Jerry said.

"Jerry, stop. Listen, Lyle, Jerry and I discussed it and agreed we've got to get these passengers somewhere safer and we've got to, in general, look for help. We need you to cooperate. It's too complicated to be divided in a crisis situation.

"But I would welcome your insights. Do you know why these children are immune?"

"I work best at gunpoint."

"Why don't you try to knock it out of my hand again?" Jerry said. Lyle stared straight ahead.

"That's what I thought," the first officer said. "Y'know, goddamn if this isn't exactly why we have a Second Amendment."

"Jerry, what are you talking about," Eleanor said and sounded like what she meant was *Stop talking*. "What's your medical opinion?" she asked Lyle.

"No, I don't know why they're immune."

"Just hold on, Eleanor," Jerry said. "We knew the shit was going to go down at some point. We have to be able to protect ourselves."

"You're gonna shoot the virus, Jerry?" Eleanor wiped the inside of the window in front of her, smudging the condensation.

"This is just one topic where we're going to have to agree to disagree, Eleanor," Jerry said. "I'm sure you'd at least agree we're lucky to have this with us right now."

"Jerry, the whole world nearly came apart the last two years. It's been a shooting gallery in this country." She paused and gritted her teeth. This couldn't be more irrelevant and she couldn't believe she was being drawn into his narrow world.

"Stop, please, the fighting," Alex said. In the backseat, she had her arm around the girl, who had her hands over her ears.

"Dr. Martin, what's your latest medical opinion?" Eleanor repeated.

Lyle shrugged, too imperceptibly for them to see. He looked out the right side of the front window at what appeared to be a barn, at least something that shape, no lights, and it quickly disappeared from view.

"What did you see in the plane?" the pilot pressed him.

"More of the same," Lyle said without elaborating. Then, "Slow down."

"We already told you, Dr. Martin, you're not giving orders," Jerry said.

"Suit yourself."

Eleanor slowed down.

"Eleanor, I thought . . ."

"Look."

She'd come nearly to a stop, and no wonder why: on the other side of the freeway, a car sat flipped on its roof. It looked to be a boxy four-door, like a Honda. The front of the car had slid off the road and tilted into a ditch.

From the backseat, the girl from the airplane let out a sob.

Eleanor put the truck in park and unlatched her belt.

"What do you think you're doing?" Jerry asked.

"Jerry . . ." she said.

"What?"

"That's the last time you're going to use that tone with me," she said.

Lyle made sure to keep his head turned forward, fearing that if he turned to see the humiliation on Jerry's face, the first officer would put a bullet in his head. Eleanor opened the vehicle's door, bringing in a rush of frigid air. Her foot crunched on the fresh snow. She walked to the overturned car.

"She's gonna get it herself," Jerry whispered, barely audible to Lyle. "Eleanor, please . . ."

The pilot leaned to the side, peered inside the car. She backpedaled.

"Shit, shit!" Jerry spat.

Eleanor turned and nearly ran back to the pickup, slipping as she reached the door, saving herself from falling only by grabbing the door handle. She climbed inside.

"Are you okay?" Jerry said. "Or do you not like that tone, either?"

Eleanor put the truck in drive and punched the accelerator. Her hands gripped the wheel and still shook. The cab felt like it might explode with tension.

"She was . . ." Eleanor started; she couldn't seem to get the words out. Her sharp exhales puffed into tiny clouds. "She was—"

"Smiling," Lyle said. "Was she smiling?"

"Yes, yes. Smiling. Upside down, blood on her face and forehead. But smiling. Jesus. How did you know?"

"I just realized. It just hit me. So were a lot of the people in the plane."

A sob came from the back. Now it was the boy.

"What, Tyler?" asked Alex. "What's the matter?"

"My dad. He was smiling." This seemed to just crush the little guy, the idea that his father could have become comatose with a smile on his face.

"This is a nightmare," Eleanor said. It wasn't anything revelatory, except the way she said it, the recognition, finally spoken aloud, that an inconceivable reality had dawned or, rather, that they'd landed inside of it.

"Not usually part of the immune response," Lyle muttered.

"Maybe they were happy to meet their maker," Jerry said. "Eleanor, do you feel okay? Seriously, any—"

"No symptoms, if that's what you mean."

On the right, they passed a green sign: STEAMBOAT SPRINGS, ELEVATION 6695. Then a yellow one advertising E.M. LIGHT & SONS. And then, a half a minute later, an isolated housing development called Heritage Park with houses set back at least a quarter mile from the road. One house had a light on and Lyle could see that Eleanor was tempted to turn down the road, but she persisted.

"Dr. Martin—" Eleanor said.

"Call me Lyle. Was the radio on?" he answered.

"Where?"

"In the car back there."

"Why do you ask?"

"I . . ." His voice tapered off. Then he reached into his back pocket and withdrew the golden-colored metallic rectangle he'd found attached to the flight deck door. "Anyone know what this is?" He held it up in front of him.

"Where did you get that?" Jerry asked.

"I found it in the plane." Lyle decided not to specify; maybe one of these people put it on the door and could explain it. "Do you know what it is?" He directed his question to Jerry.

Jerry took it in his hand. "A memory card or something like that. No idea."

"So it's not instrumental in flying?" Lyle asked.

"Was it in the flight deck?" Jerry asked.

"Near there."

They stared at it. It looked almost like it could be a mezuzah holder, the little rectangular boxes that Jews put inside their front doors. But gold colored. "A good luck charm of some kind?" Lyle muttered.

"May I see it?" Alex asked. "I do the tech thing."

Jerry shrugged and handed it back to her.

While she looked, Eleanor said, "Lyle, you keep talking about the immune system, immune response. I'm assuming you mean that the body is fighting off something. Do I have this right?"

"Are you asking me if that's what's happening now?"

"I guess."

"I'm not sure. It looks to me like these . . . bodies are fighting in the way you would if you got a virus. To answer your question more directly, the immune system, obviously, is the body's defense. It is miraculous. Within seconds, it can sense a foreign organism in a body and begin to mount a defense."

"What does this have to do with—"

"Please, Jerry, let him talk," Eleanor said. "I'm sorry, Jerry. I'm asking because I'm trying to figure out what to do when we get to town. What if we see a bunch of these people? Are we worried about infection? Can we help them?"

"After the immune system shows up, it sort of defines what sort of enemy it is up against and then starts making millions of copies of immune-system soldiers that are specifically built for this enemy. When the immune system gets overwhelmed, it can mean that the foreign organism, say, a virus, is not just powerful but novel."

He got quiet. Everyone did, even the girl in the back.

"Can't the immune system be dangerous, too?" It was Alex.

"How so, Alex?" Eleanor said.

"Crohn's disease, arthritis, and on and on. All sorts of autoimmune disorders," Lyle said, picking up Alex's thread. He seemed lost in thought. "It's a very good point. I—how do you . . ."

"When I was younger, I had arthritis," Alex said. She held the odd gold object in her hand.

"The limp," Eleanor said.

Lyle turned his neck around and was looking at Alex. With her bangs, she looked like a member of a girl punk band. She met Lyle's eyes and she tilted her head just a touch to the side.

"Did I get that right?" she said, sounding full well like she knew she had.

"It's a fair point, if likely off topic," Lyle said and turned forward again. He paused. "But not necessarily."

"Somebody explain what the hell is the point, then," Jerry blurted.

Lyle wanted to wring his neck. "You love guns, right?"

"I love the right to own a gun, my constitutional right."

"Why?"

"Get this guy. So I can defend myself, like when the shit goes down, like right now."

"Okay, so this is a way of thinking about the immune system. Guns are a defense system but also dangerous in their own way. If we run amok with guns, we destroy ourselves—"

"Pinko."

"Let him finish, please," Eleanor said. "What's that have to do with—"

"The immune system can spin out of control. That's why one of its most important features is its brake."

He explained that immune systems have two key switches, a brake and an accelerator. When the immune system is needed, neurochemicals cause the accelerator to get switched on. But when it's done, the brake starts. "The immune system must be stopped in its tracks, a fast, immediate cease-and-desist," Lyle continued. "It will consume the body faster than any foreign organi—"

Before he could finish, Eleanor slammed the truck brakes.

They were paused in front of the Sleepy Bear Mobile Home Park. It was fed by a paved road with snow-draped trees on either side. A dozen cars parked at an angle near what looked like a front office. Mostly hidden behind the trees, mobile homes jagged at various angles. A floodlight from somewhere in the middle of the camp gave more visibility than the group had had in miles.

"I saw a bear," Eleanor said. She paused. "Do you see it?" She stared in the direction of the front office.

"Can you scare it off, Jerry?"

"Why?"

"If it's in the camp, it might . . ." She didn't finish the thought.

"I don't think it'll eat people, Eleanor. It can't get into the homes."

"Right."

"Can you pull in there, anyway?" Lyle asked.

"Why?"

"I'm curious how it moves."

"To see if it's sick?"

"Just to be clear," Jerry interrupted the flow between Eleanor and Lyle, "I'm not taking any chances." Meaning: *I will shoot it.*

Eleanor exhaled with her growing loss of patience at his bravado. She did pull into the driveway. Trees loomed overhead, the most beautiful mobile home park setting they'd ever seen. Lodgepole and Ponderosa pines, Douglas firs, and the backdrop, the gray outline of mountains. The bear stood at a metal trash bin. It tried to shove a paw inside an opening too small for its arm. Lazily, it looked back at the pickup.

"Is that a bear?" said the girl. Her inner child had surfaced.

"Black, probably a mom," said the boy, perking up. "You have to bundle up your food and can't put out compost or anything like that. Sometimes, my dad . . ." He couldn't finish the sentence, the thought of his father too much to handle. Then: "He'd just shoot in the air."

"A honk should suffice," Lyle mumbled.

Eleanor honked. The bear seemed largely unfazed but put its heavy haunches on the ground and ambled away from the pickup, in the direction of the trees and two yellow mobile homes beneath them. *It moves naturally,* Lyle thought, *so very likely not sick. Anyway, why would it be? It's not like animals died off when the flu came in 1918.*

"Shit!" Jerry exclaimed. He opened the car door.

They could see why. There was a person who looked like he was sitting on the ground next to a white-and-gray mobile home. The more they looked, the more they realized the man was surely another victim who had slid to the ground with paralysis, or with whatever he was suffering. The bear walked near, sniffing the air.

"Be careful, Jerry," Eleanor said.

"Honk again."

Eleanor laid on the horn. Now, though, the bear had moved beyond twenty yards away and was half hidden by a tree. The truck horn no longer dissuaded it. It ambled forward toward the mobile home and the man slouched next to a ladder with the brand name Hitch Hiker in black letters on the top. Jerry made his way toward a lodgepole pine that was slightly to the left and between the pickup and the bear. The bear seemed to speed up. Lyle slipped to the right of the seat and out the door. Lyle shut the door to protect the people inside. It was freezing. He moved absently, curiously, almost an automaton, looking through a scientific lens. Part of him wandered, without him fully realizing it, thinking about whether the man on the ground might awaken if attacked. Part of him wondered whether the bear might ultimately ignore the man. Most animals don't eat people if they've not had the taste.

Jerry stood behind the tree and leveled his gun.

"You could hit the man," Lyle said, quickly catching up now. Snow already burned at the exposed parts of his neck and licked through his thin shoes. Jerry turned back to him and, inadvertently or not, turned the gun in Lyle's direction. "Do not tell me what to do again." He turned back to the bear. He whistled.

The bear half turned and then resumed its approach, albeit more slowly. It was ten feet from the man now and seemed as curious as hungry. Jerry pointed the gun at the ground and pulled the slide back. He looked up into the sky in the direction of a collection of trees and seemed to make a calculation. He aimed over the trees and pulled the trigger.

The bear froze.

"Scat," Jerry mumbled, as if speaking to himself, hoping.

The bear turned and looked in the direction of Jerry and Lyle. Big, not huge, 225 pounds, Lyle thought. The paws, though, that was the scary part. The big prints made gaping wounds in the snow, giant mitts with razors on the edge. The bear growled. Low.

"I don't want to shoot you," Jerry said to the bear and sounded like he very much meant it.

The bear turned back to the man felled against the mobile home.

Jerry aimed at the bear. "Please stop." The bear took another step. Jerry tipped the gun slightly at an angle, over the bear's head.

Jerry fumbled with the gun. It slipped from his hands. "Shit, shit." He dropped to his knees and he recovered it and wiped the snow off and felt it sliding, frozen, in his hands. He regripped the trigger. He looked up. The bear was practically on top of the man now.

"No choice," Lyle said.

Jerry, hand shaking, aimed at the bear's left buttocks, as far away as he might from the direction of the man. He squeezed a bit more, steadying his arm. Then he saw a flash of movement to his right.

"Easy, easy," Alex said. She stood ten feet from the bear. "My name is Alex."

The bear's ears had perked up with what could only be described as curiosity.

"Hello, bear. I have good news. I have food for you," she said as gently and calmly as if singing a lullaby. Steadily, she reached a hand into her pocket and withdrew a Cliff Bar and tore it open. She dropped the wrapper.

"She's going to get eaten herself," Jerry said.

The bear took a step in her direction. Alex held up the bar, watching as the bear sniffed the air. The animal took another step, less lazy this time, more intentional. "You can have it," Alex said. She made a show of holding the bar up into the air and then flinging it to the right in the direction of a grove of trees. The bear watched it go, sniffed the air, then walked in Alex's direction.

"It's time," Jerry said, taking aim.

"Hang on. She's slick," Lyle said.

The bear turned its angle and headed back toward the flung energy bar. One step, two, three. Still, none of the rest of them moved.

"We should go," Jerry said.

"We've still got to get this guy back inside."

"I'm not freaking touching that."

Without taking an eye off the snacking bear, Jerry and Lyle and Alex quickly convened around the man in the doorway of the mobile home. He wore a red-checked flannel shirt and jeans and a pair of brown slippers with fur on the inside of them. Clearly, he hadn't walked outside planning to be there for long. In the man's hand was a playing card, a jack of spades.

Suddenly, a blaring noise. Eleanor laid on the car horn.

"Bear's coming," Jerry said.

"Shit."

The bear had turned its attention in their direction. It sniffed the air. Then it loped forward, two big steps on its front paws, accelerating.

Alex turned the handle of the mobile home and the lot of them burst toward the door, Lyle dragging the comatose man. The bear closed in. They shut the door behind them and looked up and froze.

"Oh, Jesus," Jerry said, as Lyle dropped the man from outside with the flannel shirt and the smile on his face.

TWENTY-TWO

FOUR POKER PLAYERS sat around a table. Each of them frozen with the syndrome. One's head tilted back, exposing his neck. Another's face fell to the right, nearly to his shoulder. Two had plunged forward onto the cheap, green felt poker table. A fifth seat was empty. All were men, all, from the looks of it, at least middle-aged and two definite gray hairs. Two had puddles beneath them. The piss stench overwhelmed.

"It's in here."

Alex bent low and looked out a window to her right. "And that's right out there."

The night-lined outline of the bear moved across her view and to the door. It made a moaning noise, more foghorn than growl. A fat paw slapped at the door.

Jerry instinctively brought his shirt over his nose, wanting not to breathe in the disease or whatever it was. He took a step away from the macabre poker table to press himself against a wall. He tripped, and fell to his left, landing near another body, prone next to an ice chest. "Shit. It touched me. Shit!" He stood and scraped his hands on his chest and looked down at himself as if scouring for microscopic signs of evil. He took two more steps to the door. The bear let loose a fearsome moan.

"The window," Jerry said. "We can . . ." He paused, looked down at his hand, remembering the gun. Where was the gun? Not in his hand. They all had the same recognition: he'd dropped it in the scramble to get inside.

"You knocked it out of my hand," Jerry spat at Lyle.

Lyle appeared not to be listening, or he certainly didn't care. "Rock and a hard place," Lyle muttered—bear out there, syndrome in here. He scoped the room. Along the right wall, a stiff-looking yellow-and-brown couch beneath a window; to the left, a studio-style kitchen with faux-wood, cherry-colored paneled cabinets; directly across, an opening that led to what looked like it might be a small bedroom and bath. In the center, the poker table. Lyle walked forward. He focused on the man nearest him, head hung to the right beneath a fishing cap with a red fly-lure tucked into the brim. Spittle dripped from his lips. Lyle reached for the man's carotid artery and then suddenly withdrew with a horrifying thought: he'd reached into the mouth of the man on the tarmac and the one in the airplane hangar and that had been a terrible idea! Now he realized these people might be experiencing something akin to a seizure, a paralysis state; they could have bitten his damn hand off. *Foolish, rookie move,* he thought.

He started at the table. In front of each man, a pile of yellow, red, and blue chips, and a cell phone. The phone nearest him was facedown. Gingerly, Lyle turned it over and saw that it was powered off. He moved to the next phone and turned it over. On the screen, a screen saver image of a lake in summer.

Then, struck with yet another thought, he turned around and saw that Alex was dragging the man from outside onto the yellow couch. Why wasn't she more frightened? He caught Alex's eye and she looked quickly down as he walked over and put his hand on this man's neck. The skin was cold, unnatural.

"This one is dead," he said.

"How did you know?" Alex asked.

"I just suspected. He's been out there a long time," Lyle said. "We're running out of time."

"For what?" Jerry asked. But it was obvious. How long could some-one stay in a state like this, particularly in the snow? "Look, *Doctor*, you've seen this already. We need to get out of here."

Lyle was already walking to the back of the mobile home.

"Hey, did you hear me?" Jerry barked. "We're out of here."

They looked at him, standing there beside the felled man near the ice chest. The man lay on his left side. He wore a green fishing vest. He twitched.

Then the comatose man's arm shot up and grabbed Jerry by his left calf.

"Fuck!" Jerry shrieked. He leapt out of the grasp, smacking against the door. Behind him, the bear moaned.

"Interesting," Lyle said.

"Interesting? Interesting! What are these, freaking zombies?"

"I doubt it," Lyle said. He watched the comatose man's hand slide back down. Lyle walked around, exploring, looking. "There's got to be a comb," Lyle said.

"Are you insane?" Jerry walked over to the window, near Alex. Clearly, he was looking for an exit. He looked like he might throw up.

"A comb, and a wool jacket." They could barely hear Lyle; he stood in the tiny bathroom using moonlight to look on the edges of the sink, over the toilet, then inside the mirrored medicine cabinet. "Ah," he said, finding a comb. Lost in thought, he hustled back to the main area, where he discovered that Jerry had disappeared. Of course, he'd gone back outside.

"The bear . . ." Alex started. "It is walking to the pickup."

"Alex, is that right?"

"Yes."

"You're worried about the children."

"Yes, I mean, of course. They're terrified. They have no idea what to do."

"You have kids?"

"No."

"I'm sorry. Remind me, what brings you to Steamboat?" Lyle asked her and watched her reaction as intently as he might when taking a patient history, even as he walked to a man with a heavy coat draped over the back of his chair.

"Mountain retreat, like I said." She gave him a smile that defied interpretation. "What are you doing?"

"Testing a theory. Do you understand anything about science?"

"Took it in high school."

"You're in tech, though."

"Sales."

"Uh-huh. Big company?"

"Google, actually. I thought I mentioned it."

"They only hire the best. You must know something about electricity. You ever see the trick of rubbing a plastic comb against wool? It's like walking with your socks on the carpet. You can get a good shock."

He rubbed the black plastic comb against the wool jacket, back and forth, with increasing vigor. So much so that it threatened to tip the man out of his chair. All the while, Lyle stared at Alex. She met his gaze, then dropped it, looked up again, and there he was, still staring. His blank face gave away little of his thinking. Then he looked down at the man sitting in the chair with the jacket. This man's throat was exposed. Lyle put the comb to the side of the man's head. Nothing happened.

Lyle began rubbing the comb again, more vigorously still. Alex took two steps forward, mesmerized.

Lyle withdrew the comb from the jacket and placed it on the man's exposed neck.

The man jerked. Alex stepped backward.

"Dr. Martin, you're . . ."

He studied her face.

"You're doing it."

"Doing what?"

"You're—"

A gunshot exploded from outside the mobile home. Then—*bang bang bang*—a knock on the door. Lyle stared at the man's body, now back in its paralysis state but, clearly, something had happened. The man no longer smiled. His head lolled to the side. Some movement.

Jerry slammed the door open. "We have to go. Now!

"Hurry! Someone's alive!"

TWENTY-THREE

LYLE FELT A hand around his arm. Jerry yanked him toward the door. Lyle yielded but stared at the man at the table. The guy wasn't back to normal but he'd had a reaction. His head lolled now. Still in a state that Lyle thought of as stasis and yet not so beyond reach. Outside, the pickup had pulled as near as it could without hitting the tree line. Twenty feet to the right, the black bear sat on its haunches, growling.

"I had to shoot it," Jerry said. "I think it can live but it's pissed. We have to make a run for it."

"Why?" Alex said.

"A car just passed. Heading down the road. In the direction of town."

Jerry started running to the pickup, prompting a louder growl from the bear. Lyle followed, and so did Alex, stumbling behind. The bear started forward at them. They reached the car as the bear sped up.

"Get in, get in, get in!" Eleanor said. She laid on the horn to scare the bear.

"It's going to eat us," the girl screamed.

They slammed shut the door. The bear crashed into the driver's-side door. It rocked the cabin. The girl screamed again. Eleanor had ducked to the right and fumbled from a bent position with the controls. The bear swiped at the window, cracking it. Eleanor yanked the gear shift into reverse. Without looking, zoom, the pickup spun backward. Then with a thwacking sound, paused and spun to the right. They'd hit the KOA sign.

Eleanor put the truck in drive and pulled the wheel sharply to the left. Just before she hit the accelerator she paused and saw the bear fifteen feet away, growling and bleeding. "Sorry," Eleanor mumbled. She guided the vehicle into a sharp U-turn and back onto the main road. The truck slipped and slid and the reason was now plain to the eye: the snowfall had intensified. It wasn't quite a blizzard and also not at all a time to be out in the middle of the night. The clock said 2:45.

"There!" Jerry said.

Up ahead, quickly getting away from them, taillights. They were heading east, away from the airport and toward Steamboat proper. A stunned silence overtook the passengers of the pickup. Not even the girl made a sound. The windshield wipers thwapped and squeaked. In the back, the boy and girl sat beside each other with Alex now on the right and the three of them huddled. Eleanor leaned forward in the driver's seat. Jerry clicked the ammunition out of the handle of the gun and saw six bullets and clicked it back in and checked the safety. He stared vacantly out the window until he saw a sign and then said, "Two miles to town." The industry turned more dense: a car dealership, a veterinary hospital, a shuttered café and gas station. Signs of life but not the living. Not a soul walking or driving, other than the car they had been following and could no longer see.

Lyle stared at the electrical wires running alongside the road. Then Lyle turned his head to the back of the truck. "Hey, kiddos, I could really use your help." In his periphery, he could see the girl's face remained choked with terror and the boy stared stoically ahead. Neither acknowledged Lyle. He said: "My wife has a son."

This seemed to perk up the boy. "He died?"

"No, I just don't see him anymore. It's a long story. I'm very sad about it. I want to make sure that you guys see your parents again soon. Can I ask a question?"

It was how Lyle used to speak to patients or their families, with the human touch. Sincere in a way they might not expect from a doctor. It seemed to connect to the boy. He focused on Lyle while the snow drifted down and Eleanor followed in the direction of the ghost car.

"Do you remember when your dad got sick?"

"I was asleep and when I woke up he was . . . like that."

"Did he move?"

"Yes, they all moved!"

It was an outburst from the girl. Alex put her hand on the girl's back.

"What do you mean, Andrea?"

"They . . ." She was trying to tell them and she didn't have the words.

"Did they get mad at each other?" Lyle asked.

"What? No!"

"Did they," Lyle moved his arms around, "jerk their bodies?"

"Kind of, I don't know, maybe like they were dreaming. I don't know." She sniffled. "There was this sound. I heard this sound. It was a siren. I thought the ambulance was coming."

Lyle looked at Alex, who was staring at the girl.

"Did you hear a siren?"

Alex shook her head.

"Static, like the radio?"

"I didn't hear a thing," Eleanor said. She passed a motel with a blinking VACANCY sign, and then another mobile home park on the right. On the left, a high rock wall buffeted the highway. Trees and tufts grew nearly at right angles. The road veered to the right.

"Stop," Jerry said.

"Why?"

He was looking out the right side of the car at Elk River Guns.

Eleanor kept driving.

"Pollyanna," Jerry muttered.

Eleanor almost retorted but she was distracted by the emergence in front of them of a downtown strip. Lyle was still turned backward, talking to the children, but his eyes were elsewhere: on Alex.

"Did you feel anything in your body, Andrea?"

"My head hurt."

"Have you ever had a shock, like getting your finger stuck in a light socket?"

"No."

"I got one when I walked on the carpet in my socks," Tyler said.

"Did it feel like that?" Lyle asked.

Both children shook their head.

"Is that what it feels like?" Lyle asked Alex.

"What?"

"When you were in the airplane and all those people got stuck. Is that what it felt like?" He really was eyeing her now, with great intensity. She shrugged. Lyle kept trying to place her and her knowing look. It looked like she felt some intimacy. Was she grasping at straws and seeing him as a source of stability amid this chaos? Or was it something more?

Did she have the disease? Was this what it looked like, a kind of intensity or derangement? Maybe this was onset. But why did it take her so long to get it? Did it have to do with her limp? Something odd about that.

"Alex, do you have that thing I found in the plane, the little golden rectangle?"

"Oh, sure, right here," she said. She reached into her pocket. "Wait, I . . ." She looked around some more, in both jacket pockets, her pants pockets. "I don't know, I—"

"Did it fall out back there?" Jerry said.

"I was running, with the bear and everything," she said. "Is it important?"

Lyle was considering his answer when Eleanor suddenly hit the brakes. It prompted everyone to turn around and see what she was looking at. Ghost town. A beautiful, serene, peaceful ghost town. The main drag, Lincoln Avenue, unfolded before them for a good ten blocks, shops on each side, traffic lights overhead, most of them turned off. One, a few blocks down, blinked yellow. It had all the looks of a quiet mountain town in the middle of the night, with one exception. Two blocks down, a police car had smashed into the window of a shop. It looked like it had spun out and driven directly into the glass and then gotten stuck there, its back half sticking out into the sidewalk.

Four blocks farther ahead, the car they were giving chase to took a left-hand turn onto a side street.

"Any reason I shouldn't follow?" Eleanor said.

No one spoke.

Eleanor stepped on the gas. They all looked at the police car smashed into the front of a business advertising local art. The pilot kept going. On Seventh, she took a left turn. Now things turned residential. One- and two-story houses, some just shy of ramshackle, others not fancy but tasteful and even recently remodeled. Lots of sport utility vehicles. One house had a fence with slats made entirely of old skis. They cruised through the deadened residential area, reaching foothills just a few blocks later. They followed the car when it took a left and then wound up a hill, reached a plateau, and revealed another valley, this one dark and, evidently, not much inhabited. The car in front of them had begun descending and they followed. A half mile later, they took a left turn onto a dirt road.

"He's leading us somewhere, obviously," Eleanor said.

A minute later they drew near to a house. In front of it was parked the station wagon. In the middle of nowhere, a two-story cabin made of thick logs, looking, at least in this dim light, expertly manicured, hand-crafted. Two horizontally rectangular windows cut the top floor, suggested two bedrooms. A picture window took up the middle of the bottom floor but a curtain concealed whatever was behind it. A rocking chair sat on the narrow porch behind the front door. Parked in front, steam rising from the hood, was the station wagon but not the person who had been driving it.

"What next?" Eleanor said.

Nobody responded.

"I'm concerned this person may be violent," Lyle said.

"Ditto," said Jerry.

"Why?"

"Because that's the precautious way to think," Jerry said.

"Precautious?"

"This syndrome, it might impact how people behave. I'm not sure about that." Lyle was thinking about how the man on the airplane had been hit in the head. Someone had done that.

"What does that have to do with the radio waves?" Eleanor said. "You keep asking about them."

"I'm thinking of onset. Sorry, dumb fancy word. When this syndrome hits, what happens. Do we feel something, or react in some way? How much time do we have before . . ."

His voice trailed off.

"Maybe the guy is just as scared as we are," Eleanor said. She pulled up the pickup parallel to the station wagon, left it idling.

There was a flash of light and—*rat-tat-tat*—bullets tore through the front of the pickup.

TWENTY-FOUR

THE WORLD LURCHED forward. That's what it felt like. Bullets tore into the tires and they deflated and the pickup truck lunged with its passengers like it had fallen to its proverbial knees, sending everyone tumbling. Lyle's forehead smacked the front panel. The girl wailed from the backseat. Lyle felt the clutch of Eleanor's hand on his leg. He saw the blood on her own forehead as she bounced back. Jerry, head low, cracked the passenger's-side door.

Rat-tat-tat. Another two bullets spat at the front of the car.

Steam hissed from the engine, a spark flew, metal clanged, and then silence again. The message seemed pretty clear: *Don't move or I'll shoot.*

Without taking her hands from the steering wheel, without moving perceptibly at all, Eleanor said quietly: "He'd probably have killed us already if that's what he wanted to do."

"Sounds like a semiautomatic, at least," Jerry said with equal care. "We're outgunned. But if I can get a clean look—"

"Jerry, Jerry. Don't even think about it. If I had to guess, there's someone out there who is just as scared as we are. So let's not spook him further. Dr. Martin?"

"Sounds right to me, Captain."

"You don't think it's some half-sick madman? Like with the disease or something?" Alex said from the back. "We've got children here."

"Good point," Jerry said.

For Lyle, the world felt like it had split into two or, rather, into two screens, each showing different camera angles of the same scene. One camera focused on the house, quaint but deadly, hiding a powerful weapon and its trigger person. The other camera focused on the car, and the people in it, the formations of alliances and coalitions, primitive psychology forming. Whom to trust? Jerry was like a less-evolved animal, dangerous, impossible to communicate with but possible to manipulate and fundamentally unaware of his primitive psychology. Quite the opposite of Alex. Every time she spoke now, Lyle sensed her many layers. She stared at him almost like he was a savior or lover. Other times, as if he were a foe.

Maybe he was going nuts, he thought.

"Deep breaths," Eleanor said. "Let me tell you what I'm going to do."

She explained that she would slowly open the door, hands up, and walk in surrender toward the house and let the person understand the situation.

"No, please." It was Alex. "You're too important. I'm just a . . ." Before she finished or could say anything further, she'd opened the passenger-side back door and climbed over the boy. A bullet spat the ground in front of the truck but she stood her ground.

"Back in the truck," Eleanor said as patiently as she might, clearly about to lose her shit.

"Jerry," Alex said. "Don't let him shoot me."

"*Get back in the truck,*" Eleanor repeated.

"Keep your hands up," Jerry said. "Tell him you don't have a gun."

"Don't let him shoot me."

"Give me a sign if he's crazy," Jerry said.

"Like what? Like a little loco sign behind my back?" Alex whispered.

"Draw him out." Jerry sounded like he'd been thinking it all along.

Alex took another step forward, arms raised, and yelled toward the house: "We have children!"

She took another step. Now she was a step in front of the pickup. This time, no shots. From the backseat, the girl whimpered and now the boy choked out a sob, too. "You two, keep it down, I don't want to have to ask you again," Jerry said. "I will get you out of this."

Alex took two more steps forward. Then two more. Now she was within fifteen feet of the porch. With the headlights shot out of the pickup, she was getting less visible. Wind had joined the snow, blowing from the west. Arms over her head, Alex balled her fists for warmth.

She said something the people in the pickup couldn't hear and then the right side of the downstairs curtain moved. Not a lot, but enough to indicate the whereabouts of someone in the house.

"We have children and a doctor," Alex said. "We landed on an airplane."

Eleanor clutched Lyle's leg, and he reached over and took her hand.

From inside the house, a voice said something that sounded like: "Slowly."

"I can't hear," whispered Eleanor. "Damn it."

Alex took two more steps and stopped and raised her hands higher. She said something else.

"Channelopathy," Lyle said, almost exclaimed, with some wonder. "What?"

"Of course, ah," he said.

Alex took a step forward.

"We should stop her," Lyle said. He was emerging from a trance.

"Why? What are you talking about?"

Lyle reached over and honked the horn. *H-o-o-o-o-n-k.*

"What the hell are you doing?" Jerry pulled Lyle back. Lyle hardly seemed to notice, so lost was he in thought. "Sodium ion channels, it's got to have something to do with that."

Alex took another step forward. She was talking but they couldn't hear what was going on. Alex had lowered her hands. One of them she now held behind her back and she was twirling it in a circle, the loco sign. *This guy in here is nuts.*

"Draw him out," Jerry muttered.

"No," Lyle said. "We need him. We need—"

The front door to the house opened, slightly, and a gun barrel emerged, pointed at Alex. She made the sign behind her back again. Somewhere along the line, Jerry had opened his door and now he was moving himself outside of it. "I'm a doctor," Jerry lied, talking in the direction of the house. He had the gun pinned to his right side trying to keep it blocked from the gunman's view.

"You're going to get us all killed," Eleanor said. "Dr. Martin, why do we have to keep her out of the house?"

"I don't know. She knows something."

"You don't know? *You don't know?!*" Eleanor hissed.

"Tell him I'm a doctor," Jerry said to Alex, who stood with her hands now back in the air. She said something. The person from the house pushed the door open.

Images and thoughts were colliding inside Lyle's brain: the passenger on the tarmac, the one on the couch, their smiles, the frozen screen with *The Godfather,* an old man with his head bludgeoned, the girl clutching her head. The way the static electricity woke up that man. It would be about sodium channels and epilepsy. What was the connection there? It had to do with how the brain transferred electricity.

His mind's eye searched through his mental archives while through an actual blank stare, he watched as Jerry took another step forward in front of the pickup. His hands inside his jacket hid the gun.

"Jerry, tell her to come back," Eleanor said.

He ignored her.

Alex took another step forward, then she dropped to her knees.

"What's going on up there?" Eleanor muttered.

The front door to the house swung open and a man stood with an automatic gun slung over his shoulder. Tall and round, but sleek in his full-length leather jacket. On his woolly head, a kerchief pulled tight like you might see on a biker.

Jerry dropped to his knees and the shooting started.

TWENTY-FIVE

POP-POP-POP.

It was over in under two seconds.

The man in the doorway flopped backward, his hand making a last clutch at the door frame and then he collapsed.

"That's right. That's what I'm talking about!" Jerry exclaimed. He sounded like a high school linebacker who had just flattened a receiver.

"Jesus," Eleanor said.

Alex lay on the ground.

"You all stay right where you are," Jerry said. "We need to make sure he didn't have company."

He kept his body low and closed in on Alex. When he got to her, he gave the thumbs-up sign to indicate she wasn't hurt. Then, still crouching, he made his way to the porch. He pasted himself against the wall next to the front door.

"Crack shot," Lyle said to Eleanor.

"All clear!" Jerry said. "Let's get these kids inside where it's warm."

Eleanor grabbed Lyle by the sides of the face and turned him her direction.

"Are you seeing something here you recognize—medically? If so, I would really appreciate you communicating it to me."

He switched his gaze from Eleanor to Alex, watching how she watched him—with some fascination. He needed to talk to her.

The porch lit up, presumably from Jerry flicking a switch inside the door. Now it was clear that there was another building, to the right and set back slightly from the house. Out here it might be called a carriage house or even a barn, but in the city, another living quarters, like a cottage. Out front of it sat a sedan. It had only a dusting of snow on it. The image suggested to Lyle that people were inside the small building.

"Have you ever had a seizure?" Lyle asked Eleanor.

"Yes."

"You have?"

"Two, actually, minor, when I was young, some strange syndrome that passed."

"You remember what they were like?"

She remembered. Like her world had locked up. "These people had seizures, or are having them?"

"It's just seizures aren't viral."

"So it's not a seizure."

"I'm not sure. When you had a seizure, what do you remember about it?"

"I just told you; the world paused."

"Sorry, what did you remember about what happened beforehand, like, what were you doing when it happened?"

Eleanor processed the question. She couldn't remember a thing, that was the problem; she felt like she'd lost hours of her life, like they'd gone blank. She told Lyle. He nodded. Short-term memory loss, he said, a common side effect.

"I need you to talk to me, Dr. Martin. I'm not sure what or who to trust and I need information. I'm not trying to play captain here. I'm trying to play reasonable adult in a totally alien situation. What would we do if this were another planet?"

"I'd take you to dinner."

"What?" She laughed, seeming both slightly irritated by and appreciative of the random nature of the comment.

"It's been a long time since I met someone who welcomed my opinion in an adult conversation," he said.

"Hold it together, Dr. Martin."

"I don't know who or what to trust at this point."

"You can trust me," Eleanor said.

"Yep."

Lyle reached into the glove compartment and fumbled around. His hand returned with a pen that he used to write something on a yellow scrap of paper he'd found. He scribbled on the paper and ripped it in half. He handed half to Eleanor.

"Put this in your pocket," he said.

"What is it?"

"A note. Put it in your pocket. For later."

She looked at it quizzically.

"Trust me." He caught her eyes with his own and held the look for emphasis.

Then he stuck the other half of the scrap of paper in his back pocket. Lyle looked again at Eleanor and said, "You want to know the thing that my ex-wife hated most about me?"

"Not right now."

"The thing she hated most was that I had instincts about things that I couldn't prove, that often seemed wildly off base but that wound up being true. Like when I realized she was pregnant with someone else's child even though I had no real basis for knowing it was true."

"There are children in the car."

"This is one of those times."

"So you handed me a piece of paper with scribbles on it?"

"Something's about to happen," Lyle said. He slid out of the pickup.

He got out of the vehicle, sensing Alex and Jerry were watching his every move. He guessed that Jerry would be furious he'd had this intimate exchange with Eleanor, face-to-face.

"You gotta see something," Jerry said. "Get a load of this."

He was standing in the doorway of the house, gesturing to Lyle. Every part of Lyle wanted to ignore him.

"What are you afraid of, Lover Boy?" Jerry said.

Lyle saw that Jerry was trying to play off his lover boy comment as no big thing. He was clearly pissed while Alex's face was implacable.

"What are you afraid of?" Jerry repeated and gestured Lyle over with his gun. Lyle couldn't figure a way around it. He walked up the slick stairs onto the porch. He stared down at the body and then peeked inside the house and found himself fascinated. What was it about this place and this man that left him unharmed—well, until he was gunned down? The first thing Lyle saw was the image of the serpent. Along the far wall on the first floor, a banner hung with a picture of a snake. Lyle took a step inside. It smelled of cooking, boiled meat, Lyle guessed, coming from an open-style kitchen separated from the room where Lyle stood by a yellow linoleum countertop. The place was lit by a camping lamp. It showed a couch with a blanket folded neatly across it and a recliner. Along the wall to the right, a startling sight: stacks of canned goods—corn was the first thing that struck Lyle's eye, and peas and chili—and cases of bottled water. Someone was ready for the apocalypse. To the left, there was a trophy case made of thick glass. It was filled not with trophies but with guns, big, powerful guns, stacked horizontally.

In the middle of the room, though, were the two things that most caught Lyle's attention: a camping light that lit the cabin and a small black radio.

"What is that?" Lyle asked Jerry.

"Narrowband radio."

"Who uses it?"

"Public safety folks, hobbyists. You know what kills me?"

"What?"

"I took out one of the good guys."

"What do you mean?"

"Prepper."

Lyle took his meaning and knew it was right. This dead guy was one of those militarized citizens who was "prepping," preparing for the collapse of the government or society. Not just planning for it but hoping for it, probably. When the whole thing collapsed, the spoils would go to the ones who had stocked up on guns and food and the tools of survival.

Lyle started walking through the house taking everything in. The place was orderly to the point of being pristine. A room behind the kitchen was too dark to make out but seemed to be an office. A doorway to the right of the kitchen was padlocked. Back in the living room, he looked at the banner of the serpent: Don't Tread on Me.

Jerry was no longer in the room. Alex fiddled with her phone.

"I'm getting a signal," she said. "I think the network is back."

Lyle couldn't pinpoint what was so extraordinary about this place.

"Something's changed," Alex said. "Things are making sense to you."

He stared at her. Was she turning insane?

"I don't know you that well but you seem to be in a kind of thrall," she said.

"He doesn't have electricity," Lyle answered. "That's it. He's off the grid." He looked again at Alex. "Tell me how you're feeling? Does your head hurt?"

"Have you stopped limping?"

He stared at her leg. It no longer had that nuanced rectitude in it. He shook his head, wondering what to make of this new puzzle piece. Something about her immune system? No, it meant something else.

"You don't really care about her," Alex said, ignoring his question.

"I think you need to lie down."

"Eleanor, the captain. That was an act, wasn't it?"

Outside, the car honked. It honked again.

Alex smirked. "I've been watching you."

He stopped now and stared at her as if she were lying on the autopsy bed. Outside, the honking was going nonstop.

"Please, lie down," Lyle said. He started walking to the door. He felt his phone buzz. Then he felt Alex's hand on his arm. He turned and saw an odd look on her face, like she had grand plans.

TWENTY-SIX

THE HORN OUTSIDE the cabin continued to blare. "They're in trouble," Lyle said to Alex. It wasn't the sort of stupid obvious thing he usually said, but this woman was well more than unnerving him. What the hell was she talking about?

"It's only the beginning."

"What?"

"This is alpha, not even beta, not quite the way it should go. Give me a month to work the kinks out. You helped find them, the kinks. Of course you did, I knew you would. We needed a genius, the world did, and there you were." She paused. "I had no idea it wouldn't work on kids. I'm glad, of course. They need it so much less."

"You're crazy."

"Better days ahead."

"What did you say you do at Google?"

He looked at the door, wondering how he was going to just get past this person.

"You won't feel a thing, Dr. Martin."

Then, for some reason, he found himself staring at her hat. There was something odd about it; hadn't he thought so all along? It looked like wool, sort of, but it had these metallic strands built into it. Gold colored. Gold, right? Like that rectangle he'd found on the flight deck door.

He felt his phone buzz again. Did she say she'd gotten a signal? He pulled out his phone and thought about Melanie. She was out there, and her son. He reached the door and caught a glimpse of what was out there. Jerry lay on his back in the snow; in the pickup, Eleanor's face was buried in the steering wheel, where she must have been—

Lyle's phone buzzed. He swiped at it and saw the image of the cover of an album that he'd been listening to when he fell asleep on the plane.

Everything went black.

PART IV

NEVADA

TWENTY-SEVEN

URING THAT FIRST trip to the Nevada desert to see Lantern, Jackie spent two mornings watching study subjects interact on the computer through the thick, soundproof two-way mirror. She and Denny would be on one side and the subject on the other, using a phone or tablet, sitting at a table or a recliner, whatever felt comfortable. The instructions to the participants were open-ended and simple: visit any sites you like, however you'd spend your time on the Internet—Instagram, Twitter, YouTube, the *New York Times*.

"Porn?" asked the first morning's subject, a lanky woman who commuted a hundred miles to work at Walmart. "I'm kidding!"

Jackie felt kinship with her. Something sad in the corners of her mouth, a telltale sign of bleached short hairs over her lip. The woman loved Twitter. Her first stop that morning had been to see what was trending. A monitor in front of Jackie mirrored what the subject was doing. A second monitor showed Jackie a handful of changing external variables, including the speed of the Internet connection being fed to the study subject, frame rate of the images, the pixelation. Denny sat behind her reading a hard copy of the local newspaper. It was an uneventful ninety minutes. Nothing particularly stood out. On the memory test, the woman fared little better than a control. They broke for lunch.

Upstairs in the warehouse-like setting of Google's Lantern offices, Denny excused himself to the restroom and Jackie looked out over the office setting. It struck her as odd. The pair of Alexes was gone. Maybe it was because it was lunch. Still, the Ping-Pong table looked unused. She counted six cubicles in two pods. Only a single computer monitor gleamed with electricity. Most of the cubicles looked empty. One included a stack of manila folders. Jackie had taken a step in its direction when she heard Denny's footsteps.

They drove Denny's Tesla the few miles west to town on the empty stretch of highway to Hawthorne.

They found a booth in the back of a diner. The torn pleather upholstery scratched at Jackie's calves. They shared a tuna melt and soggy fries. Denny told her how Lantern had yielded unpredictable results. Sometimes, memory retention was through the roof, other times like it had been that morning. Denny handed her more spreadsheets. "No need to look now. Maybe tonight in the luxurious confines of the Days Inn." He paused. "You look skeptical, Jackie."

"It's a lot to take in. May I change the subject?"

"What's on your mind?"

"I realized I don't know much about your background." She already knew about it, but she wanted to hear him tell it.

Denny told her his path. Montana roots, then MIT for undergrad and a programming Ph.D. that he didn't finish. He and a classmate launched a startup doing compression software to make video delivery faster and it got acquired and "I could've retired, financially, but, emotionally, I don't know, was a lot emptier than my bank account."

Jackie looked at him over her coffee, urging him silently to continue.

"Silicon Valley's big secret," he said. "After you make money, it becomes so hollow, even insulting, and then you want legacy."

"How is Lantern legacy?"

He laughed. "Good point," then really laughed, like he was discovering the joke. "Silicon Valley's even bigger secret is that we get rich, want to create a legacy, and then get distracted on some side project that consumes us because it's almost impossible to create a legacy. So, in the end, we conflate legacy with power. Influence."

"Which is not legacy?"

"They are hard to disentangle."

Jackie smiled.

"No family?"

He shook his head. "How about you?" he asked. "Carnegie Mellon, Berkeley for a Ph.D. What about the stuff not on your résumé? Hobbies, life dreams?"

Jackie felt simultaneously nauseated and giddy. She hated this topic but she had deliberately led the conversation this direction. She suspected he knew and he would betray it.

"Just the classes."

"With the genius doctor. And family? Just you and your sister?"

He knew.

"Our grandmother raised us."

He nodded. She blinked back tears.

"Like you said the other day: you don't like to talk about it."

"Why are you asking me if you know?"

"I don't *know* know. I sense something, Jackie, I'd have to be a dim-witted asshole not to see you're lugging something around."

Jackie put her hand to her cheek. Had she imagined a gust of wind?

"We don't have to—"

"Let's get out of here," Jackie said.

"Where to?"

"I'll show you."

MOSTLY IN SILENCE, Jackie directed Denny to and up a winding dirt road to the north of town. It was the very definition of desolate. When the road started to climb, there was a lone sign: OVERLOOK. Denny snaked on the winding road. Three-quarters of a mile later, Jackie pointed to the pullover spot on the right. Jackie exited the car without speaking and walked to the edge of the brown-and-red-dusted cliff. Denny shuffled up behind her.

"How did you know this was here?"

"Fancy program called Google Maps. Very impressive, that Google." Before he could laugh, she said. "Do you trust me?"

"Jackie, of—"

"You asked about my family. It's very personal."

"We don't have to—"

"There was an incident," she interrupted him again, "and I was remanded to my grandmother. We both were."

"You and your sister?"

She nodded grimly. "Right."

"And that's off-limits?"

Jackie looked across the plain. It was a vast stretch of brown with jags of green, a blip of town at their two o'clock, some neon sign blinking red. Now Jackie was practically leaning over the side. Denny took a rapid step forward. He reached for her.

"You trust me," Jackie said, flatly. She sounded like she might be speaking to herself.

"This is weird, Jackie."

"She killed herself, my sister. Marissa."

She looked at Denny and saw that he'd blinked rapidly; whatever else he'd known about her, he hadn't known that.

"Jumped from a high place."

He nodded. She appreciated that he didn't say something stupid, like *I'm so sorry.*

"Jackie, I'm really grateful that we've found each other."

His tone startled her. He wasn't the touchy-feely type, quietly jocular at most.

"May I explain why?"

"Because I'm helping you solidify your legacy."

"Well, that." He laughed, taking the edge out of the situation.

"Because I spend most of my time in superficial relationships. Work, not at work. Don't worry, I'm not hitting on you." She thought he might laugh again to take the edge off but he remained serious. His eyes looked a touch wet, and the skin beneath them drooped slightly with age. He cleared his throat. "Anyhow . . ."

"I feel the same," she said. The truth was she wasn't sure if she did. She desperately wanted to trust Denny. Desperately. More than that, she wanted him to trust her. Much of the time, she felt he did.

"Jackie, may I ask a question?"

Her silence spoke assent.

"Do you trust yourself?"

He could see it jarred her, like she'd felt wind. She swallowed hard. "I think so."

"Why did you bring me here?"

Again, she didn't answer. Her thoughts had traveled to Dr. Martin. She thought of him as someone who knew his way, who could make hard decisions, measure cause and effect, detect the world's nuances.

"There's Lantern," she said.

"C'mon, Jackie, it's windy up here."

THAT NIGHT, SHE fell asleep in the Days Inn with the spreadsheets on her chest. She dreamed of playing chess, but the pieces were vividly colored, and they had bared teeth. In her dream, she felt a presence behind her. She turned and there stood Dr. Martin, eyeing the board. She sat up sharply in bed. It was 4 a.m. and she felt wide awake. She thought about her conversation with Denny and she was struck that, at the time, her mind had drifted to Dr. Martin. She was fascinated by him and even though she understood there was something cartoonish in that—like she had idealized him, romanticized his genius—he had played an extraordinary role in her life.

She googled the office hours for Lyle Martin and wondered if he was back from Africa. She stared at his picture and imagined that he would understand her and fantasized until she felt back asleep and dreamed of screwing him until they collapsed in exhausted satisfaction.

That next morning, the study subject looked crack addled. Lucid, cogent, but nearly toothless. Maybe he'd recovered in time. He poked the tablet, visiting poker sites, playing free hands. He knocked on the glass and asked for $100 in ante money and Denny declined, saying it would upset the experiment and the toothless guy cursed and kept on with it. At one point, Jackie looked up from the spreadsheets and she noticed a change. The man had a dumb smile on his face. His eyes had glazed.

"Denny?"

"What's up? Do you realize they're going to give that guy the death penalty?"

"What guy?"

"Who shot up the army base. We're getting to be like Mexico with the narcos, lawless, chaotic." Now Denny looked up from his newspaper at the man locked into his computer screen. "I can't help but feel like we're responsible, in part, for the violence."

"Who?" She was only half listening to Denny as she watched the toothless man become more and more entranced.

"Google, us, the tech world."

Now she looked at him. "Why?"

"The theory is nothing all that revelatory but I guess it's still heretical, at least in these parts. Thanks to the Internet, people have access to all this information but they seem to be gravitating to ideas that reinforce their worldviews. Maybe that's why we're getting more extreme, more partisan."

Denny noticed that her right fist had balled. This conversation really bugged her.

"Jackie?"

"Things are moving so fast."

"Exactly."

"Everyone getting spun up. It's really . . ."

"Dangerous. We're speaking the same language." Now he was looking again at the man behind the two-way mirror. "Anyhow . . ." He paused. "Now you see it. Look at him, he's fully in the zone."

Jackie looked at the computer monitor that showed the man was staring at Willie Mays's famous over-the-shoulder basket catch in the World Series. He watched it four times in a row. Slowly, dumbly, he clicked a button to share the image. Then he navigated "related" You-Tube videos and watched highlights from a Yogi Berra interview. He smiled and laughed quietly to himself.

"Is he drooling, Denny?"

"Hard to tell. Anything odd on the Internet speeds?"

"Similar to yesterday," Jackie said. "Mostly, maybe a half a percent here or there."

"Now watch this," Denny said. He exited the room and a few seconds later, he entered the room with the toothless subject. Denny shook him on the shoulder and the man startled back to awareness. Denny offered him some water and asked him if he'd take a test about what he'd seen. Sure, the man said. Through the two-way mirror, Jackie and Denny watched him take a test on the Internet about some of the images that had appeared on the periphery of the screen and also automatically generated questions about the subject matter of his Internet experience. What did Yogi Berra say? Then there would be multiple-choice questions about his exact wording with four different options.

The man fared okay on the memory test. Not spectacularly, but better than perhaps someone with his rotted demeanor and back-ground would suggest.

They escorted the man out.

"Are you okay to drive?" Jackie asked him.

"Of course," the man answered, seeming offended. Then he looked around, shook his head, looking confused. "Do you guys work for the VA?"

They looked at him.

"Are you okay?" Jackie repeated.

"I goddamned told you I'm okay." He seemed to get his bearings. "That was way more fun than last time."

"Last time?" Jackie asked.

"You might have us confused," Denny said.

"Whatever. Just gimme my money. I'll do that one anytime."

Denny handed him a check.

They stood in the dirt lot and watched the man drive away in a pickup. Something was bothering Jackie and she couldn't put a fine point on it.

"Jackie?"

"He looked dazed."

"One of the things we'd like to do, obviously, is minimize the intensity factor," Denny said. They walked back inside. Jackie thought the wording choice sounded unusually like corporate bullshit from Denny. "He seemed to enjoy himself."

She couldn't deny that.

"Have you considered monitoring pulse or using basic medical data, something shy of the MRI."

"Good idea," Denny said. "Hey, let's get out of here and discuss more on the road. I left some stuff downstairs. Can you hang here for a sec?"

Denny left and headed back downstairs and Jackie shuffled her feet and glanced around the top floor. But no sooner had Denny disappeared than Jackie poked her head back outside without shutting the door behind her. She realized what had been bugging her as the dazed man had driven off in his pickup. She looked in the distance toward the other Google complex, the one with the big antennae and the runway. What had gotten her attention was the fact that between that complex and the one where she was standing was a well-worn side road. It extended from the front of the building where she stood and then grooved the desert until it reached so far toward the other Google setting that she could no longer make out the rutted earth.

So what?

Jackie poked her head back inside the building and looked it over. She headed to the nearest cubicle. She passed her hand over the empty desk to see, as she suspected, not even a hint of dust or use. She went to the cubicle beside it. On this one sat a telephone but the cord wasn't plugged in. She looked around and, hearing no immediate reappearance of Denny from the back, made her way to the cubicle on which she'd earlier seen manila folders. She leafed through them. Empty. Nothing in them.

She walked to the cubicles where she'd previously seen the two workers, Alex and Alex. There were ports to plug in laptops, but neither had laptops plugged in now. So maybe this was a skeleton crew, and they were planning expansion. Maybe wasted space? That didn't seem like Google.

She bent down and looked on the floor. It was carpeted with that cheap corporate carpet, brown. That didn't interest her. She was looking for signs of life, scuffing, wrappers from energy bars, pen caps tossed and left around. There was some of that. So maybe this was just a slow day.

Still it nagged her. She glanced around the room. For a moment, she felt a light wind blow and wondered where it had come from, and she realized it was her imagination. She knew what it meant: she wasn't sure who or what to trust. All it took was a little gust to throw her off.

From the floor below, Denny stood in one of the experiment rooms looking at a computer monitor. He watched Jackie on a closed-circuit video feed and pursed his lips. Denny glanced at his phone screen. He pulled up his contacts and found Adam Stile, the goofy engineer in his group. Denny fired off a text and stuffed the phone back in his pocket.

TWENTY-EIGHT

O N THEIR RETURN from the desert, Denny dropped Jackie off at her apartment late on a Friday. Saturday, she couldn't get out of bed. That was saying something. It was not comfortable—an actual Murphy bed with a mattress that the landlord must've gotten at Goodwill. Even Google money these days couldn't buy much in San Francisco, $2,700 a month for a studio.

From the bed, she stared at the IKEA desk lodged beneath her second-story apartment window. Specifically, she looked at the router. It belonged to Comcast, her Internet provider. Lately, there had been messages on her phone telling her that she needed to replace the router. She thought about how Comcast was providing her faster Internet service, for free. Why was that? She thought about how phones had gotten bigger and pixelation denser, and how all the images were coming faster. And all of it was developed by industries built on keeping people connected ever longer. That was the business model: eyeballs. Was she sitting at the computer like that toothless old man, dumbly drooling to the digital drumbeat?

One other thing stuck in her craw. During her visit to Lantern, her phone service had been spotty and when she returned home, she'd discovered that she'd had three calls from private numbers. No voice mail. Probably robocallers. She decided to ignore them.

Jackie stretched her arms over her head and looked at the outdated "The Clash" wall calendar. The clownish look on the face of

Joe Strummer, the front man, always made her laugh and she really wanted to laugh right now. She could hear the voices over the years telling her she was too precise, too intense, too careful. How else to get to the bottom of things?

She thought about what Denny wanted from her. She was supposed to make sense of these patterns and help figure out how to maximize memory retention. She sensed strongly that was a bunch of bullshit. She needed more information. Thinking about how angry this all made her, the helplessness of it all, caused her to gnaw absently on the tip of her thumb until it bled. This was the sort of situation that always vexed her. A few times in her teens, she'd even done little pranks, minor infractions, toying around with trying to understand the right course of action, the appropriate course, the moral one. Like hacking into the computer of a teacher accused of harassment and sending an incriminating e-mail from his e-mail account. Was that right or wrong? Years earlier, she'd swiped a tip jar from a café in high school, a split-second decision that had left a school bully accused. Then she'd piled on to him by giving testimony she'd seen him do it. Who wouldn't believe the tearful recounting by the girl who had been forced to live with her grandmother after she'd witnessed that terrible thing?

Right, wrong? So nuanced. Especially when there wasn't time to think it through. The one thing that gave her solace is that, it seemed, the whole world was struggling with it. Tensions flaring all over the place, the pace speeding up, conflicts, shouts, talk shows, separatists and police, dangerous decision points, escalating forward. It felt like the wind picking up steam, a tornado coming. Instead of even trying to figure out what was right, people buried themselves in their devices. People talked to you while looking at their phones, lost in entirely different realities. It was like the world was, like her, missing situational awareness. Like a blind pilot heading into a mountain. Not seeing, not hearing, as she had not seen and heard, once that diminutive sixth grader sitting on the back of the upholstered couch, watching through the sliding glass window. The argument lived inside of her.

You're a son of a bitch, Alan. A philandering Son. Of. A. Bitch.

More like Husband of a Bitch.

You're blaming me?

Listen to you, foul-mouthed harpy. You thrive on this, crave it, invite it. Beg for it. You're a genius, all right, at creating a poisoned universe. Right in your own cackling image.

Fuck you.

I'm surprised you didn't engrave me an invitation for me to fuck her in front of you.

I've seen enough premature ejaculating from you.

I'm done, Denise. Done.

I'll tell you when we're done.

What are you doing?

Till death do us part, Alan.

What the hell are you doing?

Get up, Jackie, get up. Move. Move! Help them! Reliving the memory, blood dripped from the tip of her thumb where she counted to ten, and she breathed with each number. *Eight, nine, ten.* She sucked the blood and tasted it and spat it onto the comforter.

When Jackie finally got out of bed at nearly two in the afternoon, it was pouring. She felt overcome with loneliness and walked, drenched, to the movies and went to a romantic comedy about a loveless executive who fell for the Amazon delivery driver; Jackie abandoned the movie halfway through. That's when she saw the car. It was one of those small electric vehicles. She couldn't make out who was hunched behind the wheel. And she might not have noticed the car, or the driver at all, had it not made a mistake. While walking home, she turned onto Pine, which was a one-way street. The car turned to follow her, going the wrong direction. When Jackie heard the honks, she saw the car and realized it had been the same one she'd seen outside the movie theater, parked earlier. Just something she'd noticed, maybe having appreciated the crisp green color.

Jackie picked up her step. When she got to her apartment again, she noticed the car stopped across the street on the corner. She thought about calling 911. Was that the right move? Were her antennae lying to her?

She looked out the window and thought about the terrible movie she'd seen and about the powerful executive waiting at her front door for the Amazon delivery driver to bring her a new electric toothbrush or whatever else she'd ordered. Soon, she was ordering things just so she and this down-to-earth driver could chat. Jackie looked at her door. Then she looked out the window and saw the same car sitting there in the pouring rain. It drove away.

She closed her eyes and had a thought about what might make her feel better. It was a passing thought, and laughable at that. A few minutes later it returned to her. She let herself give life to the thought: she wanted to talk to Dr. Martin. She wanted to thank him, no, that wasn't quite right, or not all of it. She wanted to talk to this genius, listen to him, or tell him what was happening and seek his counsel.

Sitting there, no doubt deluded by darkness and the narrative afterglow of a rotten romantic comedy, she told herself that Dr. Martin—Lyle—saw things as they were, not as they were packaged or dressed up. He was someone who would meet her halfway, be un-threatened by her power, maybe truly enticed by it. She could just tell. Maybe it was fate that he'd saved her, something more than random events that had brought them together on that airstrip in Nepal.

After a bit of considering the idea, dismissing it, considering, dismissing, she called up the UCSF Internet page and looked for the class site. And she gasped. This couldn't be right.

Dr. Martin's lecture section had been canceled.

"Due to unforeseen circumstances, the lecture has been postponed indefinitely. Students will be credited with a pass."

She felt crestfallen. This wasn't right. She knew Dr. Martin had gone to Africa and that class had been off for a few weeks. This was something else. She surfed around looking for news about whether he'd gotten sick. Nothing came up. She felt agitated, surprisingly so. She considered doing some hacking into Dr. Martin's personal accounts, to snoop just a tad, thought better of it. So unfair to Dr. Martin. She went to the window and saw that car again. She came back to her computer and, unable to stop herself, decided to snoop on the UCSF servers. It was a task beyond her flavor of expertise computer-wise, but well within her grasp of social engineering. This was, after all, how most actual hacking happened, not by powerful computers breaking encryptions but by sweet-talking nerds who talked their way through dim-witted tech support people. Jackie called the UCSF after-hours computer support team, described herself as Dr. Martin's administrative assistant having problems accessing the shared calendar with a key conference coming up tomorrow, blah, blah, blah. She flirted with the guy on the other end of the phone, talked about how ditzy she could be, wound up getting the password for Dr. Martin's calendar, which in turn gave her a very good guess at Dr. Martin's e-mail address. She figured it was the same as for his calendar. She was in.

She figured she had about ten minutes to look in his system undetected but she only needed about one. She saw what she needed in the first e-mail. It was from the dean and it had come that morning. Dr. Martin hadn't seen it yet. "Dr. Martin, per my previous correspondence, you need to move your things out of the office immediately. I will give you until the middle of next week before I consider legal means. In the meantime, you may no longer sleep in the office under any circumstances. It is unbecoming and, regardless, violates our code of conduct."

Jackie scrolled back through several previous messages and could see oblique references to inappropriate behavior on the "Africa trip," and suggestions of administrative leave by the dean. Dr. Martin hadn't responded to any of them, but Jackie could see that he'd read them.

She returned to the first e-mail, the one warning Dr. Martin to vacate the premises. She looked at it for the better part of an hour. Her hands balled into fists, her jaw tight enough to prompt a headache. She felt her muscles twitch.

Finally, she hit reply and wrote:

Dean Thomas,
I am sorry that our relationship has so deteriorated. I also do not appreciate your threats. It seems odd to me that you would be so antagonistic to one of your educators. That attitude is such a far cry from your solicitous attitude toward corporate funders, including those pharmaceutical interests trying to buy access to our budding clinicians. Wearing my doctor hat, I diagnose you with a serious case of hypocrisy.

It had been no secret that the dean had been accused of fundraising with abandon, giving rise to ethical questions at the medical school. The mayor and many in the city loved the dean for having overseen the massive expansion of a high-tech campus. But many on the campus saw her for what she was, someone awaiting a CEO position at Genentech or a competitor and in line for a massive payday. The last thing she needed was an enemy like Dr. Martin. Jackie decided to make her knife thrust a tad less subtle.

Dean Thomas, I did your bidding in Africa, trying to save lives, and you repay me by stripping me of my ability to educate the doctors of the next generation. I hope you will reconsider your hasty threats or I will not hesitate to share my experiences as someone who has been thrown under the bus to serve outside interests.
Sincerely,

Jackie hit send and then deleted the initial e-mail from the dean. Dr. Martin, perhaps, would never see this correspondence. She doubted he was a dogged user of e-mail anyway. She felt euphoric. She'd gotten off her perch of indecision and given a boost to the man who had once saved her life.

Of course, she couldn't know that Dr. Martin was the one who asked in the first place for some administrative leave. She couldn't know the emotionally dark place he'd inhabited, or why. She pictured a defeated version of this great man, her distant crush and savior who, if she was honest with herself, she craved to be seen as his equal, someone who saw her, understood her, wouldn't put her into a terrible position. Now left to sleep on his couch at the office? And even that being taken from him?

She stared into the dark for a long time, pondering, exploring her feelings, taking her time with an idea, rolling it around in her brain—until she felt a surge of certainty.

She slipped out the back door of the apartment building and took an Uber in pouring rain to UCSF on Parnassus. This was the old medical-school campus in San Francisco's inner sunset neighborhood, and right near Haight and Ashbury. Much of the medical enterprise had moved down to Mission Bay, where the lecture halls were, but the main adult emergency room and hospital remained on Parnassus. So did some of the faculty and adjunct offices, infectious disease among them, and for good reason: often, when an infectious disease specialist was needed, he or she was needed in the hospital to consult with a virulent and unusual case.

Jackie took the elevator to the fifth floor in the elevator adjoining the main hospital. The setting was a far cry from the majestic new campus. This was drab and boxy, merely functional. She was looking for number 503 and figured that she'd found it when she saw from a distance down the hallway the doorway in the corner, the proverbial corner office that Lyle deserved. Colorful papers and patient reminders were carefully taped to the doorway. But that one was marked 501 and had a sign for DR. JEN SANCHEZ. The department's darling, Jackie knew. She was the one with the sweet digs.

Jackie turned to the left, and ten feet down she found 502, right beside the echoing stairwell, and clearly a little box. Jackie felt a pang for Dr. Martin at this inglorious place; he deserved so much better.

It was so much worse when she pushed open the door.

TWENTY-NINE

THE SMELL. SHE recoiled. She wondered if it was disease. Was this the odor of bacteria consuming a human body? No, she quickly realized, it was the stench of ancient pizza. From the looks of the remains in the open box on the table in the small entry room, a meat lover's special. She repressed a gag.

"Dr. Martin?"

There was just enough light from the hallway behind her, and a sliver of moon from a window across the tiny office to illuminate the mess of food remains, scattered papers, and was that a camping stove? And the light also showed the way to an opening to a second room.

She shuffled by the desk and thought, *Let him be okay.*

For all Jackie's awareness, her great skills at piecing together the world, she would not have sensed how strange it was for her to be here, how impulsive. She was grasping at straws. The Google thing, Denny, the man in the car, they'd tapped into that core part of her that was emotionally flummoxed, off balance, so much less composed than she showed the world. Now she was on the verge of coming undone altogether, torn apart with uncertainty. But that's not what she told herself. She thought, as she walked into the open doorway of the second room, *Now I know what to do. I can help this man who needs my help.*

There he was, in a heap. On the couch, an arm draped to the side with his hand near a half-empty bottle of clear alcohol and a piece of paper.

"Dr. Martin?"

"I'm retired. Call me Lyle," he muttered. He didn't bother to look up.

"Lyle?"

"Retired," he muttered again. "Honorifics no longer applicable."

She turned on the light. The office reminded her of the austere habitat of a shrink she once visited: a chair, coffee table, and the couch where Lyle was flopped facedown. On the table, several empty bottles and what appeared to be a half-eaten burrito.

"Uhhhh!" Lyle made an anguished sound like a vampire consumed by sunlight.

She turned it off. She didn't want to see him like this; he didn't deserve to be seen like this. What remained were silhouettes.

"I'll clean it myself," he said. "Please. Go away."

"I'm not the cleaning crew."

"It'll be a new career path for me."

"Let me get you some water."

She glanced around for a bottle or cup. She couldn't make out much. Some of the books on the built-in shelves had been scattered to the floor, like someone had casually pulled them off. On the table, she could make out a plastic cup. She picked it up and sniffed the contents and shivered with disgust. Cheap swill.

"Are you hungry?"

No answer. She couldn't imagine what had dragged him to this abyss. She also knew, in her gut, she *knew,* that she couldn't ask him outright. That wasn't how these things worked. Not with the proud and brilliant. She knew because she wouldn't respond to direct questions, either. She'd been low. She understood Dr. Martin, and he probably would understand her.

"May I take a liberty?" she said, and she sat.

"Have a seat." He laughed, some odd private joke because she was already sitting. He was half mad, at least half, she thought.

"You are a great man."

Lyle turned his head, slightly, curiously, like a bird hearing a sound, such that he could make out her edges through the hair. She wondered if he imagined her as an apparition or dream.

"Are you good or evil?" he asked.

"What happened in Africa?" she asked.

"Africa?"

"Tanzania?"

"How do you know about that? Am I dreaming?"

He was obviously drunk and exhausted, but she wasn't sure he could be quite that out of it to not know whether he was dreaming. His question almost sounded metaphorical, like *Is this all a dream?* She went with it. "Yes."

"To dream, the impossible dream. . . ." he sang, and then said, "Well, then let me tell a story."

"You tell beautiful stories."

"Once upon a time, there was a man who decided to be an infectious disease doctor and he had this idealistic vision that he could take on viruses and disease and find cures and then you know what would happen?"

"The world would be a better place."

"He'd get laid."

She laughed.

"Don Quixote tilting at viruses," he continued, slurring. "Holding them off from attacking all the people he was protecting, including the princess. Year after year, he tilted, and the viruses kept coming and that was interesting and good work, tilting or not. And then the young doctor, who wasn't so young anymore, heard something behind him. He turned to see all the people he arrogantly told himself he was defending from the viruses."

Lyle looked down at the bottle standing on the carpet and tipped the vodka back and forth idly. Then he picked up the piece of paper and clutched it.

"They were killing each other," he finally said. "Shooting, maiming, terrorizing, drinking and driving, stealing each other's land, finding tax loopholes and racking up speeding tickets, building narco empires, filing lawsuits and countersuits, cloaking themselves as decent and moral and, all the while, doing more damage than any virus. Just one big difference."

"Dr. Martin?"

He roared, "At least the virus declared itself: I am here to kill. I will consume you. It was forthright with its intentions. It was true. Not the people. Not the princess!"

Another long pause.

"People, they put you in the worst positions, y'know." He sighed. "Anyhow," he said, facedown, harder to hear now, "the doctor had picked the wrong side. Obviously. So he retired and decided, just now, that he might become a janitor."

With that, Dr. Martin seemed to make one last effort to raise his head. He shrugged, out of energy, nothing left to say. He fell back down and started to snore.

Jackie felt momentarily dazed and realized she'd been holding her breath. The moment had captivated her. It had, in a certain manner, seduced her. She felt such kinship and intimacy.

Whatever fantasy she'd had before that she and Dr. Martin were on the same page had now been multiplied, practically exponentially. What a man.

"Let me tell *you* a story," she whispered. He was out cold now.

"Once upon a time there was a girl. I bet you can guess, that girl was me!" She laughed slightly at her own silly little joke. Then she cleared her throat and swallowed quickly. "Her parents fought and fought and fought. Her dad drank and cheated and her mom drank and yelled and hit and probably cheated, too."

You're a son of a bitch, Alan. A philandering Son. Of. A. Bitch.
  More like Husband of a Bitch.
  You're blaming me?

"The little girl sat on the back of the couch watching through the sliding glass window. She could see it coming. But she didn't move. The little girl, me, I . . . I saw my mom take two bold steps forward. I still couldn't move. People say these things happen in slow motion, but it's not so. It's so fast that you can't stop it. It only feels like slow motion looking back on it. She shoved him just . . . just at the right angle, I guess. The wrong angle. His slipped and he fell against the glass wall. It was cheap, fractured, breaking, then broken. My dad teetered there. That was slower. I could see it. I couldn't move. She pushed him again."

Jackie had her hands balled along the sides of her cheeks. She rocked. Silence for nearly five minutes. She counted. She looked up.

"My dad was an asshole philanderer but I'm not sure he deserved to bounce off the cement from eight stories up. In fact, I can say now assuredly that my mother wasn't supposed to be judge and jury, conflict of interest and all that. The trouble is, you can't really know that in the moment. She couldn't. Maybe I should have. I had the gift to intervene and there I stood."

She was more composed now. She started talking a bit more philosophically, what it was like to walk through a world where people saw what they want to see and not what really is, people lost in their perspectives and devices, buried in their escapes and perversions, whereas a gifted few could truly see and hear. She told him about the various people who wanted to use her, had used her. She told him not to pity her.

She dropped her head. "You deserve complete honesty, Dr. Martin." She paused and swallowed. "My sister, I had a sister, her name was Marissa. Two years younger. She was there that day. We went to live with my grandmother."

Jackie explained that she and Marissa were close. Marissa went away for college, to Cornell.

"She said she couldn't be around me all the time, that I was too intense. But, obviously, she was wrestling with demons—who wouldn't, after our childhood—and she had to get away. I could take the blame. I loved her, dearly. We talked all the time," Jackie said. She swallowed. "In her sophomore year, she jumped from a bridge and killed herself."

A tear slipped from Jackie's right eye.

"I'd talked to her hours before. I knew she was in trouble. But I did nothing. I couldn't stop it." She simultaneously laughed and cried and threw up her hands. "My self-pity has grown tiresome."

When she stood, she walked over to Lyle, pulled the piece of paper from his hand, and turned him on his back. She wondered for a moment whether he might be better off dead, as she'd wondered of herself a few times in her life. She propped a pillow under his head so that he might sleep comfortably.

"I am better now, Lyle. Thanks to you. You saved me, turned my life around." She told him a story about how she'd gone to Nepal, a tattered soul with a backpack. She'd gotten the monkey scratch, and then came the earthquake. At the chaotic airstrip, she lay down and let fate take over, expecting to die in the hot wind. But fate brought her Lyle, who was in the area building a pop-up clinic to help with a cholera outbreak. That day, of course, he was dealing with chaos at the airstrip, tending to various wounded.

"I'm sure I was just another warm body to you," Jackie said. She stroked his hair. She pictured the scene, the hot air blowing dust, people running, a doctor like a superhero seemingly unfazed. He knelt beside her, examined the monkey scratch on her left forearm, asked a few questions. *I'm not worth saving,* she recalled telling him. *I'm unhinged, if you want to know the truth. Better off gone.*

"Nonsense," he had muttered. He looked up from her at a square, red-painted building with a wall curving in from earthquake damage. It stood to the right of the airstrip's "parking lot," which was a dirt area free of brush, and the so-called terminal, where Jackie sat, which consisted of a cement roof held up by pillars, without sides. The whole operation could've passed in the States for a half-built bus station.

Weakly, Jackie had watched Lyle walk to the red-painted building. As Lyle had gotten close to the building, Jackie saw him get intercepted by a uniformed man rushing by. They had a brief exchange.

"No, no. Too dangerous!" the man had said. Jackie thought she heard the word *collapse.* Then she watched Lyle ignore the man, walk to the building, open a cellar door beside the collapsing wall and descend stairs. He had returned five minutes later, covered in dust. He'd found the vaccine, administered it, told her she now had three days to get to Kathmandu for a second one, but could even make it a week. He told her she'd be fine and then went on to help someone else.

Now, back in the office, she stroked his hair again. She stared at him. "I'm so glad you did," she said.

Then she knelt beside him and she put her lips onto his lips. She felt his warmth and let her tongue slip into the crevice of his mouth and tasted his sour breath and felt sharp arousal. She pulled back.

"You are a great man. The world needs you. I need you," she repeated. "And I am here for you, as you were for me. You will rise."

Walking down the stairwell, she let herself look at the piece of paper that Lyle had been clutching. It was the result of a medical test. She took a moment to make sense of it. But then it was clear. Dr. Lyle Martin was infertile. He could never conceive a child.

THIRTY

I N THE WEEKS after Jackie returned from her first Hawthorne trip with Denny, things settled down. She took the Google bus to work, did her putative day job, met with Denny every few days to look at new data on Lantern, went home, and dug. She looked for everything she might find on Lantern, including any incorporation, mentions on the Internet, affiliates, real estate licenses or purchases in Nevada, and so on. She came up blank. But she felt such exquisite purpose.

She was careful to cover her snooping by using basic hacking techniques to bounce her inquiries from server to server. If anyone cared to be monitoring her, they'd not have been able to do it. She started to doubt anyone cared what she was doing: whoever had been following her hadn't reappeared. Maybe she'd imagined it.

She pursued a parallel path into the science of memory and its relationship to the use of technology and the Internet. There wasn't much out there. A few behavioral studies had found that the bombardment of the brain with information had an impact on memory, but it wasn't the impact that she was expecting. Memory didn't get better, as the Google tests suggested, it got worse. For instance, a study from the University of Michigan involved teaching people information and then having them go on a walk. Some study subjects took a walk in a dense urban area and a comparison group walked in a serene rural setting. The ones who walked in nature remembered information much better than those whose brains had been clouded by all the incoming stimulation from the urban setting.

A more scientific study had been done with rats at the UCSF lab. The rats were hooked up to leads that measured brain activity. Researchers found that rats who were constantly stimulated with new activities—say, presented with new challenges—did not generate as much electrical activity in the hippocampus, the brain's memory center. They were having experiences, but not generating new memories (at least that was the presumption; the rats, obviously, could not be asked their own opinion).

One Saturday, Jackie walked through Union Square. It stunned her to see the extent to which people had their faces buried in their devices. She'd always known it, of course, but as she studied the behavior, she felt like an alien landing on Earth and discovering a race of people with two arms, two legs, and a rectangular metal appendage they stared at as if it brought life. She watched a guy in a wheelchair staring at his phone lose track of his surroundings and roll down a ramp until he toppled.

As she walked, she sometimes got lost in her own virtual reality. It involved Dr. Martin. She imagined how proud he'd be of her in her investigations. She pictured them walking together, talking about how they were dissecting the world, their fingers touching lightly, a union of hearts and minds. She wanted to find him, talk to him, but she knew he needed to heal. Only at the most lucid moments did she realize she herself was unhinging. Her growing uncertainty about Denny, who had treated her like a beloved little sister, was particularly irksome. He continued to apply only the gentlest pressure to have her help him solve the Lantern problem. *You're my quarterback,* he'd say, *and my star wide receiver and my entire defense.*

It's just that things didn't quite add up.

Then one day when she was home sick with a head cold, watching *Sneaky Pete* on Amazon, her cell phone rang.

"Ms. Tether?" a man's voice said.

She almost hung up when she remembered that Tether was one of the fake surnames she'd used when calling around Hawthorne—realtors, the local tax office, et cetera—looking for indirect information about Lantern.

"Yes, it's Jennifer Tether," she said. "I hope you'll forgive my head cold."

She felt a moment's gratitude that she was sick; it always helped when massaging someone to look a tad helpless.

"I'm with the utility district; you left a message."

"Yes, thank you for calling back. I'm the administrator for Denny Watkins at Google. We're moving our payment system. I need to change the account."

"I thought that was handled out of the Intel account."

"Jesus," she said, trying to sound as exasperated as possible. "Too many damn chefs. Oh, excuse my language, it's the cold medicine."

He laughed. He gave her a name and number of his current contact; she promised him that she'd get it ironed out.

Intel?

That was just the beginning. From there, she did a reverse directory search to find the origin of the contact and phone number held for the Lantern account. She followed one digital bread crumb after the next and wound up finding that it led to a WhoIs directory—which lists the administrators of Internet domain names—for a group called TechPacAlliance, or TPA. There was an e-mail address: TPAadministrator@TPA.net, which she dared not e-mail for fear of outing herself. She could only find one other reference to the TechPacAlliance. It was from a tech policy conference brochure from three years earlier, a mention of the sponsorship by the TPA and its partners: Google, Apple, Intel, Amazon, Microsoft, IBM, HP, Verizon, AT&T, and Sony. And several international affiliates, big-name telecommunications affiliates, like China Telecom and Orange from France.

Not a mention before or since. It just disappeared, this veritable who's who of tech and telecom companies.

She clicked back and stared at the names. They were giants, obviously, competitors, direct and indirect, not all in the same businesses, not exactly. With many common interests—in everything from technical standards to the mutual value of spreading the digital culture and gospel. She lost the afternoon surfing the Internet and came out none the wiser for it.

She slept more poorly, ate little, became obsessed with understanding the game, the falsehoods. Dr. Martin had put it so well: people put you in terrible positions. More than once, thinking of Denny's sleight of hand, his failure to disclose, it was as if her mother had asked her to help push her father off the balcony.

She thought often about Dr. Martin—Lyle she called him when she had her internal conversations with him—and wished she might ask him what to do. She wouldn't be plaintive, of course, he'd hate that. She'd be his peer, with a hint of protégée, knowing that he'd been through times in his life where he'd had to buck the conventional thinking, fight through idiocy, get to the truth.

After work the next day, she felt well enough to go for a walk along the wetlands near Google's campus. It was late February and still getting dark relatively early. A half mile from campus, now well into dusk, she heard a bicycle come up behind her. She turned and saw Adam Stiles, the nerd who couldn't keep his eyes off her, despite the fact she tried to never engage.

"Hi, Jackie. It's nice out here."

He dismounted and stood beside his bike. "You want some company?"

He was so awkward.

"I'm good, Adam, thank you for the offer."

Adam swallowed hard and glanced at the surroundings.

"You think you're so special."

Her alarm bells exploded, her throat constricted, the hot blaze of terror. She thought back to a self-defense class in college and looked at Adam's windpipe.

"Adam . . ." She looked around. The spot was oddly isolated, given the otherwise wide-open terrain. They stood at the bottom of a hill, a cement retaining wall to the right and the bay on the left.

"I think you're special, too," he said.

"Okay . . ." Maybe he was just being awkward, not aggressive. What to do? What to do?

"I know you're special. I'm not talking about working with Denny, that's cool or whatever. You're *special* special. I bet you're the smartest person in the whole Googleverse."

Her heart slowed. He was confessing, that's all.

"Adam, I have a boyfriend."

"Bullshit!"

She reflexively put up her hands.

"I'm sorry," he said. "I know you don't. You think you're the only one who can snoop around."

She reached into her pocket and felt for her phone. She could hit him with that.

"Help!" she suddenly screamed. "Hel—"

"I wish you wouldn't lie to me!" Adam said. "You don't have a boyfriend. But you want a boyfriend.

"I'll be your boyfriend."

He stepped forward. It all happened so fast. Did he fall into her, or did she push him? They were entangled, falling, scrambling. He was scraping at her, or defending himself and she was doing the same thing. She pushed and hit, and Adam covered and hit or defended himself, a nerdy scuffle of confused intentions. Jackie saw a dark shape standing over Adam. Almost comically, she thought Batman and wondered if she were imagining things in her happy place. Then her vision further righted and she could see that it was Denny. He plunged his meaty fist into Adam's face. Then he put a knee onto Adam's chest.

"You're going down, you son of a bitch," Denny said.

A moment later, Jackie was sitting up, refusing to cry.

"I saw him follow you," Denny said. "Okay, okay, okay, okay," he added, looking at her terror, and reached to touch her shoulder and she let him. On his phone, he dialed 911 and told Adam not to move a goddamned muscle.

In Jackie's first act after her salvation, she took Denny's phone from him and pressed end to sever the distress call. If there was one thing she knew, it was this: she'd rather solve things herself. All of it.

A WEEK LATER, she returned to her job. Adam had been let go by the company, nothing more said about it. She had news for Denny, big news.

"I figured it out," she whispered. Then went into the Basement in the Google X building. They sat at the conference table and Jackie spread out the various data sets comparing memory retention to Internet speeds, pixelation, frame rates, and so on and so forth.

"Tell me," Denny said. He paused. "Are you getting enough sleep?"

She dismissed the question. "What's the common theme?" she asked him rhetorically.

"Was it the thing with Adam?" He ignored her question.

She grit her teeth so hard that it hurt in the back of her skull. She kept her hands in her pockets, so as not to show the little scars where she'd chewed on her fingers. No, she shook her head.

"I have your back, Jackie. Always. Adam, he was socially awkward, sure, but harmless, right? Trust me, it's taken care of."

A deep breath, *one, two, three.* She counted. She discovered herself smiling. She was so sure that Denny was full of shit now and it was nice to be sure of something.

"Of course," she said. "What's the common theme, Denny?"

He shrugged. "That's what we can't figure out."

It struck Jackie that Denny had used the pronoun "we" but she ignored it. She took a red pen and circled some of the numbers.

"It's so obvious that I'm surprised I'd not seen it earlier."

He looked blankly at her. It wasn't obvious to him.

"All the transmissions where the memory changed—they're wireless. All the ones where it didn't change, or very little, were hardwired Internet connections. Some study rooms used wireless, some wired, some either or. We didn't think it made a difference."

"But I thought it had to do with speeds or something like that?"

"Of course, so did I." She tried not to exclaim it excitedly but that's how she felt, like she really had pieced something together. "We were looking for some subtlety instead of the big fat thing under our noses."

Denny picked at his beard and looked at the pieces of paper.

"Doesn't that leave us little further along than we were before? I mean, I don't want to diminish your finding. It's great. It's just that we're still stuck not knowing what circumstances lead to what outcomes."

She didn't answer him right away. She didn't want to rebuff his silly objection; of course this was a revelation. She also wanted to keep some of her ideas to herself. If some of her budding hypotheses were right, this was explosive stuff. Something was being triggered inside the brain by the telecommunications transmissions. If she was right, it wasn't just Wi-Fi connections but, broadly, radio transmissions. When they were sent in certain bursts, certain patterns, these ubiquitous transmissions had the impact of putting people into a kind of catatonic state. It left her totally freaked out and it was also, perversely, somewhat obvious; the human brain was, fundamentally, fueled by electrical impulses. It was how cells moved information. Now, she—or the people she was working for—had muddled into a discovery about how the bombardment of the brain by certain pulses could distort neurological activity.

The more Jackie thought about it, the more it had her rethinking the entire way people were interacting with their devices. They would stare at the screen, slack-jawed. She'd just assumed that resulted from the capturing of their attention. Now she was thinking about it differently. The electrical impulses might be stuttering their brains. And when those impulses were "perfected," so to speak, when they were sent in bursts, it had the effect of capturing the brain altogether. Putting them on hold. Hijacking a moment of reality, erasing it, in a way.

"Let's keep at it," she said to Denny in as noncommittal a way as possible, declining to elaborate on her theories.

She couldn't read Denny's face. Maybe he suspected she had figured out more than she was letting on or maybe he wasn't sure to trust her just as she had no clear handle on him—this man who had hand-plucked her from a class, shown her the bowels of a secret project, saved her from a stalker, but also was not coming fully clean with her about what the hell they were doing.

She had every intention of figuring it out.

LESS THAN A week later, sitting over an uneaten frozen pizza in the middle of the night, it hit her. She understood how it all worked. Then, almost as instantly, she understood the power of it, and maybe why they'd kept it from her. This wasn't something you shared with just anyone. *Holy shit*—she stood up so quickly with revelation that she tripped over the back of her chair.

THIRTY-ONE

DENNY LIVED LIKE a tech millionaire—in a modest one-bedroom Mountain View condo sparsely appointed and littered with take-out food wrappers. Blackout shades over his bedroom window let him sleep late—engineer's hours—and helped keep out the noise from El Camino Real, a blazing thoroughfare two blocks north. This was what $1.3 million bought you in this market. His clock said 3:14 a.m., and he slept with earplugs and eyeshades in the pitch black.

Jackie sat next to the bed in a chair.

"Ahem," she said.

Denny squirmed and turned. In the red light of the clock's digital numbers, she made out the outlines of a small pill bottle. Benadryl, she surmised, the over-the-counter nightcap of champions. It was dulling Denny's senses. Jackie tapped on his bulky shoulder. He stirred, made our her foreign shape, bolted up.

"Jesus!"

"Nope, just Jackie," she said.

He swallowed, trying to make sense of it.

"Jackie of Nazareth," she said. "I like the sound of it."

"What are you—"

"Savior complex."

"Jackie, what time is it?" He knew, he could see, but he was trying to make sense of this. "Turn on the light."

"Let's leave it like this," Jackie said. "Darkens the mood."

She knew the darkness left open the possibility in his mind that she was armed or something. Clearly he wasn't all that concerned: he reached over to the nightstand and clicked on a lamp. Dim light took over the small, square room. Denny studied her. She wore a gray sweatshirt, zipped up high, and a Giants cap.

"Is everything okay, Jackie?"

"More or less. I've come to talk about Lantern."

"I don't mean to be glib but can it wait until morning?"

"It's waited long enough."

He ran his hand over his hair, pushing the sleeping mask off, then blew air out, a kind of silent concession. "I'll make us some coffee."

They sat at a dark, round wood-laminate table off the kitchen and drank from "Google" mugs. Low sounds of a melodic symphony performance leaked from the Google Home device on the near end of the kitchen counter. They sat quietly for a few minutes, Jackie happy to let Denny figure out how to express himself, content that she held a lot of cards and he knew it.

"You could've asked me during daylight hours," he finally said.

"I've asked you on multiple occasions. You've bobbed and weaved."

He sipped his coffee. "I've told you the truth."

He saw her ball her fists, open them, ball again. Anger, tension.

"Just not all of it," he conceded. "There are a bunch of different applications that we're toying with."

"Bullshit, Denny. You're holding people in a stasis state."

He let the words settle over them.

"It doesn't have to do with memory or attention, or advertising, any of our usual business," she continued.

"It does, Jackie."

"Maybe I should just tell Kara Swisher, or *Wired*."

"Jackie, I'm really not allowed—"

"What? Not allowed to tell me? Or to use me without telling me what I'm being used for? Or experiment on innocent Walmart employees trying to make an extra buck signing up for a test that freezes their brains? Lantern."

"Calm down."

She laughed.

"We're not hurting anyone, Jackie. We're exploring the idea of doing just the opposite—keeping them from getting hurt. Honestly, I've been largely frank with you but for a few details. If it's this important to you"—he saw how ticked she was starting to look and withdrew his passive-aggressive language—"I'll indulge you with the fuller theory of Lantern. But you have to bear in mind it is just a theory. It is embryonic. And it is well intended and will likely come to nothing."

He told her the story.

Several years earlier, Denny was tasked by higher-ups at Google with exploring the way in which heavy use of devices was impacting the brain. Much work was already being done at academic centers in subjects like attention and addiction. But an executive at Google became curious about the hypnotic power of the device, the way it seemed to pull people into a kind of alternative universe, essentially robbing them of the reality around them.

"I got to set up a small team and it wasn't long before I brought you on, Jackie."

"So far you've told me almost nothing I don't already know."

"I'm getting there. With your help, we discovered that certain radio waves, sent in certain combinations—staccato bursts at different frequencies—could elicit a seizurelike response. This wasn't deliberate, in the sense we didn't want to hurt anyone. It is science, though, and it does inform a"—he considered his next words—"higher purpose."

"What could be a higher purpose than giving people seizures?"

"That's neither the end, nor the point. Look, Jackie, believe it or not, Google and . . ." He paused.

"And the companies you've partnered with on Lantern, all the big boys; yes, I know about that."

Denny raised his eyebrows. She knew a lot. More than that, he noticed the twitch in her left eye. It was more than exhaustion; the twitch revealed her feeling of being betrayed, and crimson intensity, the tendency that made her valuable but also gave Denny pause.

"Jackie, it's no secret that this country, the world, stands on the brink. We're barreling into conflict and it's closer than anyone realizes." He sipped his coffee. "It's worse than anyone realizes."

"Oh yeah?"

"Look, we've analyzed a ton of data, social media, buying habits, changes to political leanings and demographics. We've looked at the patterns of explosive rhetoric on the Internet. We've seen the . . ." He wasn't sure whether to add the next phrase, then went ahead with it. "We've seen data from the military, too, about hostile communications, profoundly concerning statements from foreign leaders, militant groups, and so forth."

"This is government blessed?"

"No. Not officially, anyway. The truth is, the real truth is, I have no idea. But you're a fool if you don't think that Google, Facebook, et cetera, have very close relationships with the spy agencies. I'm not telling you anything, or alleging, anything. I just suspect data sharing is much, much closer than anyone fully knows. It's in the interest of all parties."

"But you digress."

"Maybe. You want more coffee?"

"Please. So what you're telling me is that Lantern has something to do with people being at each other's throats, a world bordering on hostilities, and . . ." Suddenly, she closed her eyes, tightened her jaw, lightly shook her head. She'd been struck by a thought, even revelation. Denny turned around from the coffeemaker.

"Things are adding up for you. Do tell," he said.

"I'd rather hear you tell it."

He topped off her coffee, put the Mr. Coffee carafe on a hot pad on the table, sat.

"You haven't made the connection between a hostile world and Lantern," she said.

"It's not that direct a connection. I'm giving you background. There's one more important piece. Look, Jackie, the tech industry is in no small part to blame for the . . . intensity in the world today. We're not idiots. We can see that the pace of media, the onslaught of conflict-centric communications, stokes the flames of hostility. Hell, we elected a demagogue last election in this country. People made some comparisons to Hitler. There are many differences. But a key one is the fact that when Hitler rose to power, there was a deep, deep economic crisis in Germany. By contrast, we've had economic challenges in this country but nothing like hyperinflation and massive unemployment. It's just the media could make it feel that way. The hammering of negative messages, sensationalism, coupled with people feeling keyed up by their interaction with devices, leads to a world fertile for conflict. Then add in a lot of high-powered, easily accessible weapons and—"

"Now you are definitely digressing."

"Probably," he said, smiling. "Look, one of the reasons why we've explored Lantern is to see if there just might be a way to . . ." He looked for the words. "Slow things down."

She thought about it. "A seizure-like state. Not just slowing things down, slowing people down," and then after another moment: "It's like a human pause button."

"What?" Now he seemed as if he were genuinely not following.

"You're putting people on pause. That's what you're talking about."

"It's just a theory, something we played with, a kind of fail-safe. What if the world started to really get out of control?"

"You're kidding me."

He put his hands up, as if to say: guilty as charged. "Yes, it sounds like a joke and that's how it probably will remain. We felt, though, it was worth exploring. Maybe, just maybe, we can use the same tools that fuel the flames to interrupt them, for just a few minutes, stop the fury from spilling over. If and when things truly come to a head, we can hit pause, as you say, reboot. We can hold people still, for a moment."

"Wow."

"Look, we still don't know how it works. Maybe what you've identified, this electrical mechanism, it's like the spinal cord acts as some kind of electrical antenna. I'm way out on a limb now. But it's not so far-fetched. The cord sends electrical impulses through the body. Hell, like I say, it's all very basic, and new. So you can see why I didn't say anything. This will likely not go far, and you're not compromised and . . ."

"No, no, no, no." She slammed a hand on the table. Coffee spilled. "No!"

"Jackie, calm down."

"First of all, I still don't believe you're telling me the full extent of it. You've got satellites out there, and a team. A small team, so you're trying to keep it on the down-low. And other companies are involved. And that's why you didn't tell me all of it, and why you've still not told me." She was shaking.

"Jackie!"

She glared at him.

"I didn't tell you because of what's happening right now," he said.

"What's happening *right now*? I'm just trying to get to the bottom—"

"You're unhinged, Jackie. You're unstable."

She blinked rapidly. She put her palm to her right eye to will it to stop twitching. She could see that Denny regretted what he'd said. He hung his head then looked up again.

"You've been like a sister . . ."

"Don't."

"You're a brilliant woman, Jackie."

"Fuck you." She stood up. She felt her hands once again involuntarily tightening into fists at her side. She flashed on the memory of her mother, little hands just like hers, shoving her father through and over the balcony. She turned the memory in another direction and saw herself, the little girl, watching, impotent.

"I trusted you," she muttered.

"What?"

"I shouldn't have. That's the worst part of this. I made yet another stupid decision. Helpless Jackie, no compass."

"I'm honestly not sure what you're talking about."

She looked down at her shoes, noticed a lace untied, tried to focus on that single image, and count. She begged herself to find control and let go of the fury. By the time she reached the number ten, she had regained herself.

"Jesus, Denny, I'm sorry. I . . . I was just so disappointed. I wanted you to trust me."

"I know, Jackie. I understood that. I could see that. I tried to tell you as much as I felt it made sense."

"I understand." It was such an about-face that Denny couldn't tell whether she meant it or not. "Maybe I just need to sleep this off," she said.

"You and me both. How about you consider tomorrow a day off."

"You mean today. Today already is tomorrow."

He laughed. But he sensed this wasn't over, not remotely. When Jackie left a few minutes later, he watched her walk down the stairs and frowned—because he could see, in the lamplight over the staircase, that she smiled.

PART V

SIX MONTHS BEFORE PRESENT DAY

THIRTY-TWO

The Met's next Live in HD presentation is Falstaff, Verdi's last opera, a comedy about the randy Sir John and his botched sexual conquests. We're at a subterranean rehearsal room three levels below the stage, where former maestro James Levin has returned to lead an early musical rehearsal with some of the principals and the cast. They're working on the second act where the scheming Falstaff gets his comeuppance by being thrown into the Thames, along with a lot of dirty laundry.

Let's listen in.

The image shifts from the woman introducing the scene to the background: a small ensemble of singers and musicians, led by the man at the front with wild hair. He waves a baton and a soprano's voice soars.

Jackie smiled.

She sat on a recliner, consumed with the digital tablet on her lap. Headphones plugged into the gadget's bottom fed her ears. A drop of drool pooled at the right corner of her mouth, lost in Lantern. This went on for more than an hour. Over and over, she saw the same video footage, her brain consumed by it.

Suddenly, she jolted. A sharp buzzing sound punctured her carefree, dull-witted isolation. The picture on her screen, and in her mind, fractured. It shattered into so many puzzle pieces. She stirred and looked up. She put a hand on the recliner chair and clung, as if steadying herself after a small earthquake or holding the railing of a boat after a swirl at sea. She blinked. *Okay,* she thought, *I'm in the testing room at Lantern.*

What am I doing here?

She pulled the headphones out and set down the tablet. Even as she surveyed the familiar scene, her mind's eye drifted to the wonderful images of the wild-haired symphony director.

Unsteadily, she made her way to the door. So that is what Lantern felt like. More like time had stood still.

She walked out of the side door and then into the observation room—on the other side of the two-way mirror.

At a table sat Denny, facedown.

"Denny?"

Her boss and mentor didn't move.

"Denny?" Now with more urgency. She hustled closer, shrugging off the disorientation. She leaned over the inert man. He stirred. She froze. "Denny?"

"Why . . ." he said.

"Denny. Are you okay?"

He tried to lift his head, but he only labored against an impossible weight. He dug for breath.

"Denny, I'll get help. Alex!"

"You . . ."

"Hold on, Denny. I'll get—"

"No!" His arm shot out and he grabbed her.

"You did this."

"What, no. I was in the—"

He interrupted her by trying to squeeze her arm and his hand fell away and through one sidelong glance from the table he fought to meet her eye. He had to tell her something.

"You have no idea how powerful it i—" he started.

"Alex!" She interrupted him. Now many thoughts flew through her brain: *What happened to Denny?* and, simultaneously, *It's a blur, all of it.*

"Shut it down, Jackie." The life seemed to be draining from him by the second.

"Why didn't you trust me?" she whispered and now she looked hurt.

He raised his head and looked suddenly revived. His eyes teared but remained steadfast on her.

"Denny!"

Jackie hurriedly turned Denny over. She frantically felt for a pulse on his neck. She laid him out on the table and she pumped at his chest.

"Alex!"

She opened the door and screamed again.

THE AMBULANCE PULLED away with Denny. Not heading to the hospital but the morgue.

Alex, the small woman who helped run Lantern, held her arms crossed around her chest.

"What happened, Jackie?"

Jackie told her: she had been in the testing room and returned and Denny was slumped, laboring for breath. He was conscious but barely. He muttered some things that didn't make sense.

"Like what?" Alex asked.

"I'm not sure." That much was true. Then she stared at Alex. Where had Alex been in all of this?

Jackie couldn't piece it together. She kept seeing these odd images, like dream moments but they were paved over with this You-Tube video of this beautiful soprano voice and the thrilling opera rehearsal. Images bubbled to the surface: Alex greeting Denny and

Jackie; Denny sipping tea; Jackie climbing into the experiment chamber. That was the one that stuck. Glorious images of the opera.

The machine, the Lantern machine she'd help perfect, had stunned her electrical system, effectively erasing her very short-term memory, the last six hours of her life, give or take, leaving her with the worst hangover of her life, not a headache, but a veritable blackout.

"I loved him," Jackie said. She wiped her face, removing a tear. "What he stood for."

"I'm not sure he told you what he stood for," Alex said.

"He did, Alex. Everything. He was like a fathe—"

"Not now. Okay." Alex turned to Jackie. "You're not going to stop this."

"Wait a second. You . . ." Jackie took a step backward, images spinning in her mind. "Did you . . . did you put me in that chamber? What did you do to me?"

"What did *I* do to *you*?"

"What did you do to Denny?" Jackie demanded. "You poisoned him."

"You're insane," Alex said.

"Don't you dare put this on me!"

"Time to put this project on hold," Alex muttered.

Jackie looked at the woman's face and couldn't tell if she saw sincerity or setup. She felt herself swimming in lost time; images and sounds of the opera. She'd been Lanterned. She had her suspicions of what had happened here today, but only glimpses in a world gone dark, bits of evidence from the hours preceding her date with Google's latest technology. What had really happened? She felt a gust of wind and ran for her car.

PRESENT DAY

THIRTY-THREE

THE RING WOKE Lyle at last.

"Dr. Martin?"

"Right."

"This is the front desk."

"Okay, got it. What time is it?"

"Eleven fifty. We rang at ten, then knocked and then finally—"

"In the what?"

"What?"

"Morning or night?" It was completely dark in the room, the curtains pulled tight.

"Morning. Are you . . . are you okay, sir?"

"Yes. Thanks for the call."

Lyle started to set the phone on the cradle. He pulled it back.

"One more question, young lady."

"Of course. We're here to help."

"Where am I?"

"Steamboat. Springs. The Sheraton. Are you sure . . ."

Lyle, the phone now nestled between his left shoulder and his chin, had stopped listening. He ran his hands over the undershirt on his chest and down over his hips, feeling for sensation. The woman on the phone had asked something about whether he wanted coffee or orange juice delivered to the room. She sounded worried about him. "Coffee," he said, and he reached over and set the phone in its cradle.

He closed his eyes and studied his dull headache. Was he sick? Maybe he'd just overslept. Maybe he'd dipped too deep this time into the over-the-counter sleeping medication. His kingdom for the prescription pad back.

Wasn't he here for a conference? He swung his legs off the side of the bed and fought a wave of nausea. It was brief. He steadied himself. He felt another symptom, a sore of some kind inside his mouth, on his tongue. He ran his finger along its right side and could feel it was raw, like he'd bitten it. He lay there, exploring these odd sensations in his body, exhaustion but it felt like more than that. Less than five minutes later, there was a knock on the door. Lyle stood and pulled open the curtains, which were vertically striped with brown and gray, and immediately regretted it. It wasn't just light but bright white, new snow white. Now he pictured arriving at the hotel, late at night, or early in the morning, in the cold. He'd gone right to bed. The small room, with quaint accents, spoke to what he figured must be precious real estate here on the edge of the ski mountain.

He opened the door to discover a woman in a smart gray pantsuit. She held a silver coffee tray in her arms but awkwardly so, and she had no name tag. At that moment, Lyle correctly deduced she wasn't a bellhop or waiter bringing room service. *She must be a manager,* Lyle thought, from the way she looked past him and into the room.

"I'm fine," he said, "much better now that I've got coffee."

"On the house," said the woman. "May I bring it inside?"

"Sure," he said. Let her knock herself out. Over the last few years, as he'd had more to drink and taken more pills to sleep, he'd grown accustomed to friends and family occasionally peeking in. It was funny, in a way, the way they'd always walk into his studio apartment on Divis and look around as if they were somehow looking around his liver for spots.

She put the tray with the coffee decanter and newspaper on the nightstand beneath a lamp with a wide-brim opaque oval shade. Lyle watched the room through her eyes as she scanned his jeans on the floor, and the suitcase left near the foot of the bed, the bedspread strewn. The woman, trying to look nonchalant, glanced at the darkened mouth of the bathroom.

"Do you need to use it?" Lyle asked.

"No, I—"

"Just kidding. May I ask, do you know which floor the I.D. conference is on?"

"Conference?"

"Sorry, infectious disease."

She straightened. "I don't think . . ." She paused. "We had an orthopedist conference last week, y'know, the guys who help the skiers and their knees, but I don't think we have anything this week. I could be wrong, or maybe the event is at a different hotel?" She ended it with a kind of question mark, as if she had somehow made a mistake.

Lyle thanked her and watched her go. He looked at his invite, which suggested he had the right place. Had he written down the date wrong or misunderstood it? That wouldn't be unlike him, he realized. He'd really sunk the last few months. That's why he'd wanted to come out here and try, at least, to restart. Maybe it just wasn't to be. How could he have made a mistake like that?

For some reason, each time he reached for an answer, he found himself humming the words from a song. It was Bruce Springsteen's "Nebraska," which talks of a man losing faith and getting up and finding "a reason to believe." In the last year, after a beer or two, Lyle would watch the video on YouTube of a concert from Germany where Springsteen had crushed it. Lyle kept the video bookmarked and now, for some reason, he couldn't get it out of his head.

He looked down at the newspaper, *Steamboat Today*. The main story had to do with a prediction that El Niño would mean a glorious wet winter for the mountain town. This qualified here for front-page news. At the bottom of the page, a teaser about a shootout in Oregon caught Lyle's attention. He turned to page 3 to read about this, yet another, tragedy: a group of separatists had killed three federal marshals before being beaten back in a massive gun exchange. Inside the group's compound, police found a cache of weapons that one official described as "rivaling that of the Portland police force." There were plans the group had tried to shred, but failed, that showed alliances with groups in two other states, Idaho and Minnesota, partly over grievances with the appointment of federal judges that group professed to dislike.

Lyle closed the paper. Maybe he was better off in retirement; the frickin' human race.

TWENTY-FOUR HOURS LATER, Lyle landed back in San Francisco. He felt for the most part bewildered. He also wondered if his use of all those sleeping pills and the recreational booze had truly begun to eat away at his cognition.

Back in his studio apartment, he listened to the sounds of twenty-somethings eating barbecue on the patio across the street and vowed he'd stop drinking for a day or two. He unpacked what little he'd taken. Put the *Nebraska* album on his old turntable and sat down on a beanbag chair, trying to shake the feeling he'd been put through the spin cycle in a dryer. It would go away in a few hours, he told himself, looking to put the whole damn failed experiment of going to Colorado behind him.

That's when he found the note in his back pocket.

THIRTY-FOUR

AT FIRST, LYLE assumed it must have been something he'd written in an altered state and decided to ignore it. After all, it made no sense. He tossed it in the tin pail he'd gotten at the garage sale where he met the last person he'd slept with. Her name was Papyrus and she was at the garage sale exploring an old fishbowl but, really, it became clear, had stopped while walking by to explore Lyle. Extremely nice, extremely sexual, woman, and young, which is how Lyle thought of anyone in their late twenties. It lasted three nights, until Lyle had, as much as he could through a sexual encounter, exorcized his fury at Melanie.

That was two years ago, give or take, and the garage sale remnant had given him a memento and symbol for his ugly existence. He was throwing his life away, everything he'd believed in or wanted. Every time he looked at that damn thing, he thought of the woman he'd slept with, nice enough for sure, but decidedly not Melanie, and his life decidedly not the one he'd invented and that he'd been driven from—mostly by himself.

Now, he realized, reclining in his aging blue beanbag chair, he again faced a fork in the road, one he felt like he'd already taken. A week ago, he set aside all his reticence and decided, finally, yes, he would attend the infectious disease conference and stick a toe into his former life. For the most part, he had told himself, it was because he needed the money. He couldn't go on forever on dwindling expenses, even in a studio where the rent didn't rise because he gave free medical counsel to the older woman who owned the building and lived on the top floor. There was more to his motivation than mere money. Little by little, he'd forgiven Melanie for having a one-night stand that, remarkably enough, produced offspring (or maybe it was more than a one-night stand but that's what she claimed). And maybe the person he was forgiving was himself for having gotten so withdrawn in the first place that Melanie had wanted to feel some control over her life and lashed out. Maybe he had been sabotaging the whole thing. Could he blame her?

He blamed humanity. Lyle had learned and studied, trained and taught, all in the name of staving off disease and infection. And humans thanked him by killing themselves off. How many patients had he seen who put themselves into perilous positions with their own behavior? Even when it wasn't his direct charge, he'd wander through the hospital and see the diabetic who had eaten himself into disease, the car wreck victim who had texted herself off the bridge, the gunshot victim who had fired first.

When he got the invite to Steamboat, he at first dismissed it. But the organization, the woman who ran it, stroked his ego and hit the right buttons. Maybe that had been a cruel joke, too. He'd have to go back and investigate and call them, find out if he fucked up the date somehow or they duped him or what. It really was strange. But, regardless, the trip, having failed, usurped by bad planning and a miasma of strange and hazy memories from a distant mountain town, put him in the position of having to get up some gumption again. If he was going to get his ass out of this dwindling situation, he was going to have to make it happen. Where was that energy going to come from?

He fell asleep in the chair and woke up in the middle of the night with a crook in his neck. He ignored it and walked over to the trash bin and pulled from the refuse the crumpled piece of paper. He recognized his own handwriting:

Beware channelopathy/seizure <u>pandemic</u>. Google? You're not imagining.

Over and over he read it. He knew it meant something, just knew, and he had no idea what.

He finally got to sleep at four in the morning and dreamed vividly of playing a game of laser tag in the snow. The dreamy sleep left Lyle feeling grateful—it had been a long time since he'd been visited by such rest, without assistance—and his exhaustion lifted. That morning, at the coffee shop around the corner from his house, he turned on his vastly outdated Mac and read the news and then succumbed to curiosity and looked up channelopathy. His research confirmed what little he remembered. Channelopathies are diseases that can lead to brief periods of paralysis and are associated with problems in the ion channels, which are gatekeepers of cells.

Already, he was baffled, partly because he'd exhausted his knowledge on the subject.

He surfed around and reminded himself that an ion is an atom or molecule that is electrically charged, either positively or negatively, depending on the mismatch inside of it between electrons and protons. Ions like sodium and potassium would flow through the openings in the cell, creating tiny but ultimately powerful electrical impulses that stimulate electrical pulses in the body to fire muscles and nerves.

Lyle looked up from his laptop and rubbed his eyes. This was mind-bending stuff, more the bailiwick of physicists than doctors. Around him, he eyed a half-dozen fellow patrons buried in their laptops and phones and then returned to his own.

As he read across various websites, feeling very much vexed, at least one thing did become clear to him: why he'd written seizure next to channelopathy. In fact, these were two very different ideas, but they both did implicate electrical pulses and both could involve temporary paralysis. Both could lead to acute memory loss. In the case of seizure, the electrical storm could complicate or even erase the memory for up to six hours prior to the event.

And neither of them, at least on its face, had anything to do with pandemic.

He did a search for "pandemic" and "channelopathy," and another using "epidemic" and then matching the various words with "seizure" and came up empty.

He combined the searches with tech, and tech-born, and empty, empty, empty.

What the hell was this note in his pocket?

He stood up to leave and was bumped into by a woman walking with a coffee in her hand and her face looking down at the cell phone in her other hand. She spilled her coffee. "I'm sorry," she said, without even fully looking up. "No problem," Lyle said, finding it mostly funny. Ever the clinician, he noticed the swelling red around her nose. She had a cold. It left him with an idea that he didn't put a fine point on until a step or two later. Absently, he sat again at a bench and fired up his laptop and confirmed what he'd been thinking: channelopathies sometimes involved an autoimmune attack. This idea, autoimmunity, was much more in Lyle's wheelhouse and he understood better what he was reading. Sometimes, the body's own defenders would attack the body itself, as in diabetes or arthritis or other autoimmune disorders, and then become more dangerous than any foreign invader.

Lyle had been out of the game a few years and knew that giant leaps were being made in the understanding of the immune system. He knew whom to ask about it, too, but the very idea gave him a stomachache. No way he was going back to Jen Sanchez. She'd had the corner office when he'd had his ignominious fall and, in passing, he knew she'd just kept climbing floors and corner offices. He sensed she'd always scorned him, maybe even conferred with Dean Thomas in their dislike of him, so no way he was going to talk to her. And then he laughed.

Talk to her?

Of course he wasn't going to talk to her.

Was he really thinking of going on a goose chase? Was he following his medical muse again?

He slammed shut his laptop so vigorously that a college student sitting next to Lyle said, "Easy there, pardner," as if Lyle had just screeched at his child in public. Lyle laughed again, this time more bitterly. He walked out of the café, backpack over his shoulder, trying to erase the gnawing of his impulses, the weird, persistent Springsteen soundtrack coming in over the top, and to just take in the world. He inhaled the dry-roasted smoked pork from the barbecue place on the corner, across from his studio, and felt a craving he hadn't felt in months. It wasn't a good use of money, not now, but, hey, maybe some mysterious pandemic is coming, he smirked to himself, so why not blow the last of the savings on barbecue.

He stood in line with the twentysomethings, listening to them roar about the latest media moment, having to do with this group of separatists in Oregon. After a few of them had been shot, a grassroots movement had started encouraging gun owners to march on Capitol Hill and make a show of The People and their right to defend themselves. A million Americans with automatic weapons, an open-carry bonanza. "A dare," was how one commentator put it. They were calling it the Million Gun March. Would the government dare to arrest or confiscate or confront tens of thousands of law-abiding citizens? That's exactly what the government said it would do "and you're goddamned right," said one of the techies standing in line for barbecue. "It's time to put this thing to rest once and for all." Meaning:

the macho gun culture. To which his girlfriend responded: "Government's thugs, too. I went to the range the other day."

Amid this intensifying talk-show moment, a minor spectacle erupted when a car without a driver circled the block.

Only of late had these bulbous Google cars started making the rounds in San Francisco. Most of the testing had been done on the roads of Mountain View, the Silicon Valley city Google called home. Now, though, the technology had come far enough that the company branched out. To mild fascination, the car passed the barbecue place and then, to whistles and cheers, executed a perfect U-turn and then an even more perfect parallel parking job. It landed right in front of Lyle's apartment. The crowd went wild, and then Lyle watched with his own fascination as everyone around him took pictures of the thing and started sending out the image to various social media. So lost was the person in front of Lyle that she didn't move forward in line and Lyle shrugged and got in front of her.

He stared at the self-driving car. Google, channelopathy, now a self-driving car in front of his house?

He ate his barbecue and returned to his apartment, overcome with malaise.

A WEEK PASSED this way, one of the strangest that Lyle could remember in his life. He felt that he was in a stupor, an almost clinical heaviness, and that, simultaneously, he was emerging from one, a long, deep emotional slumber. An impulse lingered to scrape away the dead skin that he felt like covered every inch of him. The note he'd now taped to his cheap, white refrigerator symbolized his struggle to molt. He wanted to understand it and yet the idea repelled him.

He lost himself, or tried to, reading about the so-called Million Gun March. This looked like it actually might happen: a million gun owners promising to show their solidarity through a peaceful congregation at the Washington Mall. The news sites and blogs blared and stewed with support and condemnation. Each vitriolic emotion and editorial more kindling, each more marketing. Politicians were being asked to take sides, to back gun owners or the government, as if these were somehow in opposition.

Alternately, maybe analogously, Lyle weighed his own internal conflict. What to do about this mystery? Whether to act? He vacillated, seesawed, up and back, as he read the Internet, walked the line to discovery, retreated, let ideas wash over him. Eventually, he found the e-mail invite asking him to speak in Steamboat at a conference. It was sent by a woman named Jennifer Babcock, the executive director at IDEA, which evidently stood for Infectious Disease Exploration Association. So it said at the end of the e-mail and on the group's website. Lyle e-mailed Jennifer Babcock and called a number on the website that went to her voice mail. The website gave Lyle pause. It listed membership organizations that weren't referenced elsewhere on the Internet, and IDEA itself didn't exist elsewhere on the Internet. Jennifer Babcock described herself in her initial e-mail as a Ph.D. in immunology but he couldn't find such a person online, either. She signed her e-mails J.B. Lyle gave up, irritated.

He considered calling Melanie, felt a desperation to visit her, looked her up online, and found she had moved to the East Bay, or was working there, anyway, at Alta Bates hospital. He sat on the information, letting it sink in with everything else.

Then, on the seventh day, his phone rang with an unfamiliar number. Bored, irritated with his entropy, he answered.

"Hello," a woman's voice said.

"Yes."

"Um, I'm sorry to bother you."

"I'm not interested in a time share," he said randomly and was about to hang up.

"It's about Steamboat," the woman said.

Lying there on his bed, he felt piqued enough to rise up on an elbow. He looked for words.

"Are you there?" the woman said.

"Are you the one who invited me to the conference?" Lyle asked. "I've been meaning to call. I think we had a miscommunication."

It's true, he'd wanted to get in touch but he feared he'd screwed the whole thing up or maybe he knew on some level that something more insidious was going on and he was still weighing whether and how to confront it.

"What? No. I'm not sure how to start this but please don't hang up."

A pang of vague, distant recognition struck Lyle, followed by an acute burst of adrenaline. Did he know this woman's voice?

"I'm listening," he managed.

"My name is Eleanor Hall. I'm a pilot. I found your phone number in my back pocket, with a note. I think it's important."

THIRTY-FIVE

TWO HOURS LATER, a vivid yellow winter sun fading, Lyle walked down the chipped cement steps in the stairwell of his apartment building. He'd showered, put on a decent shirt and a gray sweater, and combed his hair. To go meet a woman who claimed to be a pilot, whom he couldn't be sure he'd ever seen, let alone met, and who had a tale to tell as strange and familiar as his own.

They'd picked neutral ground, located between where each lived near Duboce Park. It was a café—known for its coffee and New York–style pizza—that each of them, coincidentally, frequented. When they'd gotten off the phone, Lyle googled Eleanor Hall and found a photo from a corporate website that indicated she was indeed a pilot. Her image gave Lyle the same feeling as her voice, that she was some-how familiar. Light hair and a trusting smile, and, if the photo was relatively recent, a few years younger than Lyle. Attractive. Maybe that was why Lyle combed his hair. But when was the last time he wanted to impress anyone?

At the bottom of the stairwell, he unchained his bike from the small storage area, tightened the leather pedal straps around his sneakers, and took off on Divisidero. He loved riding his bike, the terror of imminent death notwithstanding. San Francisco had one of the highest rates in the state of drivers killing pedestrians and bikers. No wonder, given that this city, as much as any other, mixed a driving culture with a walking one. Lyle rode and kept a keen eye.

He saw the driverless car.

It looked like the very one that had been parked outside of his house when he'd been eating barbecue. Now it crawled along, three cars behind Lyle. An empty driver's seat and the thing cruising along as if pulled by a puppeteer. These cars were becoming more common but it was still eerie, Lyle thought, and pedaled on. A few blocks later, the car seemed to get stuck in traffic as Lyle climbed up the steep part of Divisidero, right before it transforms into Castro, and took a left onto Waller. The looming California Pacific Hospital stirred a memory of doing a consult for a patient with dengue fever. It had been one of those gratifying moments when Lyle's contributions, modest though he felt them, saved a nice young man.

The autonomous vehicle crept over Waller and took a left but, this time, Lyle, lost in thought, didn't see it was continuing in his same direction.

At Duboce Park, Lyle dismounted and watched toddlers and their nannies disgorging for home. The chill had come after a drought-blessed, dry day, the sea breeze picking up and detectable even this far inland if you put your nose to the air. Lyle stopped a few blocks shy of the café to think. This putative pilot had said that she'd found a note in her back pocket with Lyle's phone number and the words: *Call Dr. Lyle Martin about Steamboat. You're not imagining.*

He might well have blown her off, at least initially, had it not been for the phrasing: *You're not imagining.* It's what he had written to himself in his own note.

On the phone, he'd started to ask her what she was imagining and she suggested they meet and she'd elaborate. He was having the same impulse and so that was that. He locked up at a bike stand on the corner and pressed himself to consider what he remembered from the flight to Steamboat. He recalled settling in, downing some Benadryl, maybe a lot of it, falling asleep. As he recounted it, he wasn't sure that's what happened.

"Dr. Martin?"

He turned to see a woman looking at him quizzically. She held car keys in her hand and had a newspaper tucked under her arm.

"Lyle," he said. "Captain Hall?"

She nodded and half smiled. "So we googled each other and we each use honorifics on first reference. Please drop mine too," she said. "Eleanor."

He wanted to look away from her, given that it was impolite to stare, but felt like he was having déjà vu. "Like we've met," she said. "Right?"

For a moment, his heart fluttered with fear and uncertainty.

"There's a table. I'll grab it."

THEY SAT BENEATH a vibrantly colored painting that looked at a distance like the state of Texas smeared by a rainbow. The uncomfortable plastic green chairs matched the yellow and green paint. The pizza slices kept this place in the game, and Lyle and Eleanor each had one, the special, prosciutto and basil. Each had professed to have been here before and Lyle wondered if that's how he knew her. He tried not to stare. She didn't touch her pizza, and he tried not to wolf his or pound his beer.

"So you're a pilot," he broke the ice.

She nodded like she was still gathering her thoughts and figuring how to express them. The voice of a popular soprano rocker came over the coffeehouse speakers. "I've been grounded, temporarily," Eleanor started and then paused. "Sorry, you'll have to forgive me; this is a little strange."

"Grounded?"

"There was a problem with the landing in Steamboat." She smiled and shook her head. "So I'm told."

"Sorry, I thought you said you were a—"

"Right, the pilot—on the flight. I was. I just can't remember much about it. Maybe this isn't such a good idea."

"Wait. I'm right there with you. The flight, I can't quite grab onto it. Small wonder, though; I slept through most of it, knowing me."

A silence descended. These were two proud people, clearly, certainly not used to having things so out of reach or feeling fundamentally helpless. Lyle guessed that Eleanor hadn't slept much lately and was surprised to also surmise that she was carrying grief.

"Can I tell you a story?" Lyle said.

"Um, sure."

"My biggest med school mistake."

It had been in his first year at Penn, he explained, a class in basic anatomy, involving the poking and probing of a cadaver. His dead body was called Ms. Phillips. "She'd been a schoolteacher, my partner and I were told." Lyle explained, "I got it into my head that she hadn't died, as we'd been told, from sudden cardiac arrest but maybe from a more chronic disease. I saw signs of malignancy. It was no big revelation but as I was pacing back and forth, lost in an internal dialogue, I was drinking coffee and I . . ."

"You spilled it into her body?"

"Poetically, at least, into the stomach."

She actually laughed, which he'd hoped for. Then she clipped it back. She was in no mood for laughing.

"That's how I feel now, like something doesn't add up and, well, at the risk of absolutely destroying the metaphor, that I'm Ms. Phillips, the dead teacher, and someone has spilled coffee inside of me."

"You're right. You absolutely destroyed the metaphor."

Now he laughed, if briefly, cleared his throat.

"Can I see your note?" he asked. "With my phone number?"

She hesitated. Was he going to take it and run? She wasn't sure why he would, it's just that it constituted concrete evidence. She pulled it from her pocket and laid it on the table, careful to keep a finger on it. Lyle nodded thoughtfully. He pulled a pen from his backpack and, on a napkin, copied the words he saw on the note.

"Same handwriting," she said.

"Looks like I did give you that, after all."

Outside, Lyle noticed a man looking in the window who looked a tad familiar, too.

"What is it?" Eleanor said.

"That guy . . ."

She turned around and followed his glance but no one was there. "What guy?"

"He was just . . ." Lyle stopped. "He's gone, I guess."

It was dusk now. This moment, and the mood, seemed to sober Eleanor, leaving her uncertain again what Lyle was about, even how sane. "So tell me your version of the story," she said.

He told her about how he was supposed to attend this conference and he woke up in Steamboat at the Sheraton and there was no conference. Besides that, his brain had gone fuzzy on him and he couldn't remember exactly how he'd gotten to the hotel, pieces missing. "Like someone slipped me a roofie."

"I had the same feeling," she said. "Almost like . . ." She paused. "It reminded me of when I'd had a seizure."

When she said it, she could see Lyle perk up.

"You find that interesting," she said.

He reached into his back pocket and felt for his own note, the one he'd written himself about seizure. But it wasn't there. He'd left it on the fridge. He explained about the note to her. He asked her what she'd meant when she said it felt like a seizure, explaining that he'd never experienced one himself.

"I haven't had one for twenty years. I do remember, because my mom told me I said it, that I felt like I lost a puzzle piece of my life."

Lyle chewed on it silently until she asked him to let her in on the secret. He smiled again. "Bad habit of mine," he said, "retreating into my brain to look for puzzle pieces myself. I'm thinking about the different kinds of seizures." He told her about the small subset of powerful seizures that involve considerable memory loss, accounting for the loss of six hours or more preceding an electrical storm. By way of an answer, her blue eyes settled on him with an arched brow communicating: *So what exactly are you saying?*

He shrugged, communicating: *Yeah, maybe what you're thinking.*

"Like I had a seizure, or we all had a seizure, and we all forgot landing in Steamboat?"

"Or flying there. Right, well, that just sounds insane. It sounds insane, right?"

"For a guy who is not a psychiatrist, you've got a pretty clear handle on the definition of insanity." She smiled and so did he. "But, yes, it sounds insane."

"What else don't you remember, Eleanor?"

"Is that a serious question?"

"In a poorly worded, roundabout way. I mean: How much is missing for you? Do you remember flying, pulling into the jetway, or whatever you normally do?"

No, she told him, for the most part, no. She felt like she had memories of all that stuff but they were tenuous.

"I recall becoming aware that I was parked at the terminal. There had been a communications glitch."

"You remember that?"

She closed her eyes as if grasping for it. "The truth is, it's what I was told."

She explained that she received a call when she had returned to San Francisco—her home base—and was told to come in for a meeting. She blinked rapidly and she held tightly to the beer mug such that Lyle wondered if she might crack the porcelain.

"You're holding something back."

She cleared her throat. "A passenger died."

He'd come to expect almost anything at this point, given what had happened the last few days. Still, this caught him off guard. Eleanor's eyes started to water and she willed away the tears.

"It's my first duty," she said.

"A passenger died?"

"I'm being officially investigated for dereliction of duty," she said. "If anyone knew I was here right now . . ."

He waved his hands. Of course he wouldn't say anything. "My word but I—"

"I can't be seen talking to you because it would look like I'm monkeying with an investigation. But I am here; you're damn right I'm here. I had nothing to do with a passenger's death."

"Someone is saying that?"

"No, not exactly. I . . . why do you keep looking over my shoulder?" She sounded exasperated.

"Sorry, rude. I'm feeling paranoid. Some guy keeps walking back and forth out there and I—"

"If you'd rather—"

"I'm sorry, go on."

She explained to him that a passenger named Milt Vener had died. He was an old guy and sometimes people died on planes. It had happened to her twice before, once owing to a stroke and another time, relatedly, to a blood clot. This time, though, blunt force trauma.

"Someone hit him in the head," she said.

Lyle felt again the ripple of familiarity like déjà vu that disappeared as quickly as it came. Then a moment of panic in which he wondered if he'd hit an old man on the head. This was all lost on Eleanor who seemed now intent on getting her story out. She said the investigators for the airline and the FAA had been very formal, giving her little information. They'd treated her in two meetings and a brief preliminary one by phone as if she hadn't been a valorous twenty-year veteran.

"The only hint I've had where they might be going with this is that they've asked a lot of pointed questions about my first officer. His name is Jerry Weathers, and they've—"

"Say it again."

"What?"

"Jimmy Weathers?"

"Jerry."

"What's he look like?"

"Why?" She studied Lyle. "Who cares?"

"I'm having one of those moments."

She nodded, and described the first officer as lanky, all elbows, full head of brown hair, a bit of buggy eyes. "Bit like a fish," he said and, just as he said it, she said the same thing.

"You know him?" she said.

"I think he's been walking around outside."

Eleanor moved so quickly that she very nearly whirled around. Her elbow hit her water glass, sending the last drops spinning. She turned back to Lyle. "Damn it, are you serious?" She quickly lowered her voice to try to limit what already was too much attention caused by her spill.

"Seems to describe the guy. He's gone, I think. I don't see why you're so—"

"Have you been listening?" She leaned in so close he could smell her soap and the touch of perspiration and tension seeping through. "I don't know what's going on and I don't know if he's playing me in some way, or what he's up to."

Lyle got it now. This first officer might be turning on her, but for the life of Lyle none of that made sense.

"I've got to go," she said.

"Please, wait."

She shook her head. She looked at the doorway to the right of the counter, the hallway to the bathroom, and a back door. Lyle felt a terrible urge to say *I can help you* but he didn't know if it might come off as patronizing when that wasn't what he meant at all. Most of all, he didn't know if he was capable of helping her when he couldn't help himself or even decide if he wanted to. He watched the pilot walk away and felt an immediate sense of loss. It was the very feeling he'd had for years crystallized into a moment—he should be doing something or saying something because life was slipping away—and being unable to do anything about it. There was nothing he could do about it now.

Outside it was fully dark. Lyle absently got on his bike and let a million questions slide around his brain without focusing on any particular one of them. With the sun down, the early evening took on a decided winter chill. He was glad he'd put on this wool sweater. He pedaled along the west side of the park on Scott, figuring he'd go left on Fell. He saw the driverless car.

It crept along behind him in modest residential traffic. At the corner of Oak, a thoroughfare with thickening traffic, Lyle thought about Occam's razor and the likelihood of the simplest explanation. Maybe there were just a lot of these cars around. He took a right onto Oak, heading east, away from home, just to test the theory. A quarter way down the block, he looked back and saw the driverless car take a right too. Okay, thought Lyle, still nothing certain, given Oak's popularity. A car horn exploded.

The driver was warning Lyle that, distracted, he'd swerved into the lane. The human driver shouted something Lyle couldn't hear. Lyle stopped along the edge of the far right lane. The fracas and pace and bouncing headlights of the cars speeding Oak disoriented Lyle. The feeling jostled him, sparked a memory of Steamboat, the cold and dark, that he couldn't quite grasp. He looked into the fray of oncoming lights and couldn't see the bubble car now. Had it disappeared?

Then, boom, there it was again, nearly on him, just a car length back. It had been hidden behind larger vehicles. The bubble neared. Fear jolted Lyle and he pedaled again.

Lyle willed himself to take a deep breath. He went right on Steiner. The traffic thinned. Lyle kept a modest pace. He craned over his right shoulder. The bubbly autonomous vehicle turned right on Steiner. So dutiful, it used its blinker and slithered onward, a perfect citizen, an innocuous robot, a guileless storm trooper. Lyle sped up. Then screeched the brakes when a car door opened. He swerved, righted himself, then at Duboce Avenue he went left and made a quick right on Sanchez Street; glancing behind him, he took another right on Fourteenth.

The driverless car went right too. There could be no doubt. This seemed to Lyle to be of zero interest to anybody but Lyle. Either these cars had become so common no one noticed, or everyone was so consumed with their own thing that they'd not have noticed a pink elephant following Lyle. He pedaled until he came to an alley and took a sharp right into it, then stopped. The car followed him. Lyle dismounted his bike.

The car slowed. It looked to Lyle like a bubble with a brain.

The car inched forward, and Lyle stepped in front of it. He scanned the attached houses across the street, a short, stark white one decorated with purple perennials attached to a taller greenish-gray house with exterior metal staircases. Was anyone in the window to bear witness? No such luck. Lyle pulled out his phone. He called up the video function and hit record.

The car had come to a complete stop ten or so feet from Lyle. He couldn't help imbue it with human characteristics. In this case, Lyle decided that *it* had made a decision. It wasn't going to run him over. He walked to the front of the car, his video still recording. Lyle, careful not to move out from the front of the car so that it might have an escape path, peered inside. He nearly laughed when he saw the cup holder. Maybe autonomous vehicles got thirsty. Other than that, the bulb of technology wanted for anything human. Sterile, beige leather seats matched either side of an instrument panel between. A trough stood in place of the dash with more gadgetry beneath it.

Lyle looked up at the black eye on the top.

The car lurched forward.

Lyle lunged out of the way. Off went the car. Just a roll of the wheel at first and then a sincere acceleration.

Lyle looked around. Did anyone see that? Did he see that? The car disappeared down Lloyd, took a right and by the time Lyle hopped on his bike again, it had disappeared. He didn't stop riding until he'd reached City Hall. He took his bicycle onto the train with him. No car would follow him here. Not that he particularly cared. He was thinking of the Google car the way he'd think of a patient's medical symptom, not as something to wish away but as a key piece of evidence. What was the car telling him?

Mostly, it was reiterating to him what his note had told him: he wasn't imagining things. Second, it was telling him that whatever strange situation he'd stumbled into involved a powerful actor, powerful enough to involve a driverless car. How powerful did that make someone?

It did give him two disparate pieces of evidence to connect, and disparate clues were of immense value to Lyle when he'd taken on medical mysteries. The more disparate the better. Someone from central California with a pronounced stiff neck and sound sensitivity could have valley fever. Talk about disparate: here was this driverless car and then there was the note on his refrigerator. The note referred to seizures and channelopathy and Lyle had trouble seeing any Venn diagram with an overlap between these disease states and a Google car.

The note mentioned Google. And now the car. What was someone trying to do?

Draw him in?

Warn him?

Taunt him?

To what end?

Lyle looked through rows of commuters at the map on the wall over the door. He knew where he was headed and hadn't fully admitted it to himself, or the reasons why. He could see the stop on the map, downtown Berkeley, Shattuck Avenue. He was going to find Melanie. His jaw tightened. The last time he saw her might've been eighteen months earlier. She'd stopped by his house with a bag of groceries. "Green things," she said, "to help your liver process." It was loving, painful, and patronizing. She'd looked around his house like a detective. "I'm here if you need me," she'd said and closed the door quietly.

The time before that had been their last screaming fight—her screaming at him to wake up and him fighting with silence. Then her acceptance had set in.

What inspired this visit?

The question slithered over and around his brain, a deadly snake in his valley of denial. He stared absently at a woman clicking on her tablet and considered the question. He was going to warn Melanie, right? Warn her about what? A note he'd written to himself? He shook his head and knew that to be too simplistic. He swiveled his head and watched the man sitting next to him pecking at a game on his phone, transfixed. *So,* Lyle thought, *maybe I'm going to ask her if she'd heard of anything like this potential pandemic; she's a nurse, and one of the most well-read and thoughtful people anywhere. If it's out there, she'll know.*

He shook his head and watched another man wearing headphones while staring at a phone he held so close to his face that it couldn't possibly have been good for his eyes. It was oddly peaceful, Lyle thought, all these people so lost in their virtual worlds that Lyle could just stare at them, lapping up and observing the world without interference or conflict. No risk of interaction. Then he had a sudden thought about what he was going to ask Melanie. The question sent a tremor through him. He tried to will the question away and it clung and festered and he knew instantly he couldn't deny it.

I'm going to ask her why I can't do it anymore.

I can't figure anything out. I don't know how to try. Then he smiled, a private smile, because he knew even that wasn't quite it. He settled back in his seat and let his shoulders relax. He was going to let the thing reveal itself to him, this powerful motivation leading him east. He looked back at the man sitting next to him lost in a game that involved shooting blocks that, when he hit them, turned into stars and soared and then turned into points.

A drip of drool gathered on the corner of the man's lip.

Lyle closed his eyes, searching broken, blurry memories from his trip to Steamboat, and disparate clues.

THIRTY-SIX

J ACKIE BADGER PULLED her rental into the dirt parking lot at Lantern outside of Hawthorne. Alarm bells went off. Why were there six other cars in the lot?

She found out when she walked in the heavy, steel door. In the middle of the room, cubicles had been pushed back to make way for a conference table. Around the table sat eight people, most of whom she recognized but only distantly. Lantern representatives from various tech companies. They'd gathered only once before, at least in her presence, just after Denny's death. They'd called it a fact-finding mission, but mostly it led to an internal, off-the-record explanation that Denny had died from a heart attack and that the Lantern program would be put on hold. Jackie had held her tongue, not sure what to say, absorbing occasional pointed looks from Alex and, at least once, giving one back. Would there be profit in accusing Alex of, what, murdering Denny? Police were not called, foul play never asserted, which Jackie rightly assumed was the product of wanting to keep this eye-popping project under wraps.

Now they'd called Jackie back to Nevada. It was early evening. The six men and two women sitting around the table were a characteristic lot of ambitious nerds. The men wore jeans and loose T-shirts and fashionable, colorful tennis shoes. Both women wore sweatshirts. In the middle of the table, a speakerphone with a green light on the side. People listening in. Jackie figured telecommunications giants. At the head sat Alex, as petite as Jackie, no less feisty.

"I should have brought donuts," Jackie said, seeking composure. She unzipped a light jacket.

"Have a seat, Jackie," said Alex.

"I left something in my car," Jackie said. "Can I go grab it?"

"Get it later," said a man she recognized as belonging to Microsoft.

Jackie had vacillated about responding to the request for her presence. In the end, she decided she held plenty of cards.

"I thought Lantern was disbanded."

Alex cleared her throat. She had evidently been christened here to take the lead. Maybe she'd always been in the lead. It looked to Jackie like an intervention.

"Jackie, we know about Steamboat."

Jackie blinked several times rapidly.

"Excuse me?"

"We know," Alex said.

"I have no idea what you're talking about."

"Damn it!" One of the men slapped the table. "We need to know what happened."

"Alex," Jackie said, glowering at Alex, "what is this? You . . . you took out Denny so that you could, what, take over?"

"Jackie, I'm not sure you realize how serious this is. You've effectively beta tested a very powerful, very dangerous system, and you've taken it over from the inside. We need you to remand control, and walk away, or . . ."

Jackie looked at the other members of the group, swerving her head.

"I have no idea what Alex—is that your name, Alex?—is talking about. Steamboat? Where is that even? Colorado, if memory serves. Something happened there?"

Alex pursed her lips.

"Jackie, this is pointless. I've prepared everyone here for your manipulations and cons. I've also prepared them for your genius, which is the better part of what is dangerous here. When I realized the system had been used, co-opted, I, *we,* did a lot of homework. It's clear that you chose a time and a place remote enough that it might not be traced through news reports. You monkeyed with flight logs—or someone did—and must've taken a dozen other steps to cover your tracks, not the least of which was deploying technology that appears to have turned to mush the memories of people on the ground there."

"My God, Alex, listen to yourself. You sound like someone with intimate knowledge of whatever it is you're accusing me of. Is anyone else hearing what I'm hearing? It sounds like an outright confession. Something very, very sinister is going on, and I'm out of here."

"Jackie, who is Dr. Lyle Martin?"

Jackie reddened, froze like a strawberry-colored ice statue.

"You're in cahoots with him somehow, right?" Alex said.

"Who is—"

"Some doctor who was on the plane, and that Jackie appears to be following, or communicating with," Alex said, then looked at Jackie. "That's right. I can do my own sleuthing."

"He's a friend. This has nothing to do with—"

"This is how this is going to go down, Jackie. You are dismissed from Google, put on notice that we will, even at the risk to this group, go public with your beta or alpha test, or whatever you want to call it, and pursue murder charges in Denny's death. Let this end here."

Faces turned to Jackie. She took a long pause.

"Before any of you reach any conclusion here, I want to offer you an alternative version of events. Alex is evidently the real genius here, and she is scapegoating me. I suspect she wrested control of this from Denny, maybe took him out. I think I know why, too."

"Jackie, I can't even get into the system. Somehow, you've locked us out."

"Lies. You know I'm on to you. You're testing, preparing. You're worried you might actually have to use Lantern. Denny explained it to me. Look at what's happening in the world; it's just as you worried: an authoritarian got elected, separatists storming Capitol Hill armed to the teeth, or a gunman indiscriminately killing toddlers at a preschool field trip— the list goes on."

She directed her voice to the speakerphone. "Overseas, too. What nation-state is safe? Right?" she said. "I'm not sure if it's altruism driving you, or the business of self-interest in keeping a relatively calm world. In any case, Alex, you've taken full advantage of your partners. What would China Telecom or Orange do if they knew you'd been toying around with their access points?"

"You're done, Jackie," Alex said. "This is not a toy. This is dangerous, even deadly, and it was in Steamboat." Alex shook her head. "Don't pretend you don't know that, Jackie."

"Wait until I go public. Wait until I tell people that we—the tech world—are responsible for the problem in the first place." Jackie suddenly stood, her voice rising.

"You're done, Jackie," Alex repeated.

Jackie refused to back down. She dug in. "Everyone in this group knows what I'm talking about, Alex. You came together initially because we felt we had a duty to deal with side effects of the digital world we've created."

"Enough!"

Jackie put up a hand. "Maybe it was more selfish than that, but that's at least partly true—an altruism, an effort to deal with the side effects of our own work, your work. Our industry, our spectacular innovation, has led us to this place, this culture of fury. With all these devices, people are gorging on ideas that reinforce their political and social views. They are getting instant reminders when someone has affronted these precious perspectives, and, all the while, they are so facedown in their gadgets, they are losing their ability to empathize, cooperate, compromise. We've created a path of least resistance for people to escape and disengage. That's precisely what Denny thought."

Alex pushed herself back from the table, an indication she'd had enough. "Regardless of the half merits to what you're saying, you're not wriggling out of this."

"You've created a fail-safe, and you evidently tested it, and you want a fall guy, or fall woman," Jackie said. "You need to get rid of me because I've put it all together. I know that you and your partners have been swapping out individual wireless routers to ones with faster speeds—ones that can send the kinds of arrhythmic radio bursts that lead to hypnotic states. You know what I'm talking about: the cable or phone company calls and offers to upgrade your model, promising faster speeds. People are gobbling up the free new modems and routers. They love faster service from upgraded radio and cell-phone towers. Oh, but do they know that Lantern will put them on hold and erase whatever grieves them?"

"This sounds a lot like a confession, Jackie."

"Hardly. I'm telling you everything I know, and that can endanger you."

Alex stood. "I have proof," she blurted. She looked solemnly at her colleagues. "I'd hoped it wouldn't come to this. It's personally very disturbing, painful.

"Let me direct your attention to my screen." The brushed silver Apple laptop had been sitting in front of Alex the entire time, top closed. She leaned over and opened the top, clicked some keys, and turned the device to face the table.

"What is this?" asked the man from Microsoft.

"It's a video taken from the day that Denny died." On the screen, Denny sat in a chair in the room downstairs, outside the testing chamber. Alex moved the cursor over the virtual play button and pressed down. The video began. Denny appeared to be reading some papers. He leafed through the papers, underlined a passage with a pen, read some more. It went on for a minute.

"What the hell?" Alex said.

"I'm not sure what this tells us," said a woman to Alex's left.

"What's going on there?" said a voice from the speaker.

"This isn't the right video," Alex said. The image remained innocuous, Denny reading away. "It must be a mix-up." Alex looked at Jackie, who shook her head and smirked. "I'll find the right one. In the meantime, I have something much better.

"I'm going to show you video of Jackie boarding a flight to Steamboat. It's taken from airport security. I was able to get ahold of it. You'll be able to see the date, and the time stamp. So this can be the end of this."

She turned her laptop around, clicked and clacked, turned it back. A grainy image appeared that showed a line of passengers lined up to board. The angle of the video suggested it was taken from a camera embedded on the large monitor behind the gate's ticket counter. Alex pressed play and the passengers started to board.

"No way," a voice said.

A petite woman walked past the counter and onto the jet bridge. Her face became unmistakable. It wasn't Jackie. It was Alex.

The room exploded into chaos.

Jackie stared at Alex and walked to the door.

"DENNY WARNED ME," Alex said. She was tapping on the window of Jackie's rental. Jackie put the car in reverse. Several of the group's members stood in the doorway, listening to Alex scream.

"When Denny brought you on, he told me he'd never met anyone like you," Alex yelled. "He said you could solve any problem. It wasn't a compliment, Jackie. It was part of a short but pointed explanation about why we needed to limit what we disclosed to you. He didn't trust you, or what you'd do if you knew everything, Jackie."

Jackie gripped the steering wheel like a mountain climber holding a rope for dear life.

"He warned me that you were unstable, possibly even insane. That's why he didn't tell you everything. He thought, he thought," Alex repeated, "that somehow he could get the benefit of your abilities without taking on the liabilities." She stared at Jackie. "It's worse than that. You're a sociopath."

Jackie cracked the window.

"Frankly, Alex, I don't care about any of your ugly business, except for one thing: You will," she hissed, "leave Dr. Martin alone."

She hit the accelerator, screaming backward, gravel crackling beneath the tires.

THIRTY-SEVEN

INUTES LATER, LYLE leaned against a worn utility pole that leaned slightly to the left. *A metaphor for Berkeley itself,* he thought, staring at a light-gray-and-white house at the corner of Milvia and Francisco. A steeply angled roof covered the small- to medium-size house with a tall red chimney pointing skyward. Lyle pictured two bedrooms upstairs, one for the boy and one for Melanie. The pockmarked lawn cracked brown with drought. Naturally, Melanie wouldn't waste water. An interior light showed the back of a couch. It suggested someone was home, a proposition reinforced by a Honda in the driveway. *Homey,* Lyle thought, and winced. The road not taken. The road sprinted away from.

He walked his bike up a concrete path to the wooden stairs to the porch. He glanced upward at a circular window on the second floor, dark inside; his eyes then diverted almost magnetically to wires that laced the space between the house and the house next to it. In a tangle, the wires connected to Melanie's house in the back corner and then to the house next door on its roof and so on throughout the block. Lyle followed the wires back to the utility pole and wondered whether these were telephone or Internet or electricity or maybe all of the above. His eyes were so heavenward that he didn't hear the front door open, nor Melanie walk down the stairs and gawk at him as he gawked at the wires.

"I know that look," she said.

The sound startled him. He looked up and saw Melanie holding a toy robot. It was in her left hand, a cavity in the red robot's belly open. In her other hand, a screwdriver.

"Peño?"

"Melanie."

A red sweater buttoned below her neck hugged her shoulders. The long, plain gray skirt told Lyle she'd probably worked that day. The moment he saw her, he ached.

"Are you okay?" she asked.

"Yes."

She dipped her chin and half smiled, eyes widening, her nonverbal way of saying *What brings you, Lyle? Say something.*

"It's a beautiful place," he said.

She laughed out loud. "Peño," she said again. It was an ice-breaking moment, part of an unspoken language in which she, just by saying his nickname, was calling out the oddity of him showing up, without explanation, and then staring at her electrical wires and commenting on her house. Perfectly Lyle.

"Is this about the text? I thought that was just spam," she said.

This shook him back to the concrete. "Text?"

Behind Melanie, a face appeared at the screen door. It was a boy, little more than a toddler. "Mommy?" Stout with bangs. Not Lyle's kid, Lyle thought, and winced. Melanie caught it. "Be right there, sweetie. Can you wash up for dinner?"

"K."

She turned around and looked for a cue from Lyle. Did he want to talk about the Elephant at the Screen Door?

"Text," he urged.

"You texted me: Kill your phone before it kills you."

"What?"

Melanie set down the robot and screwdriver and pulled her phone from her pocket. She scrolled the large-screened device and held up the phone to him.

Kill your phone before it kills you.

"You didn't send this?"

"When did it come?"

"Ten days or so ago. Middle of the night."

Lyle gritted his teeth in focus. He hadn't remembered sending it. Was that when he was in Steamboat? What did it mean?

"There's another one, shortly after. It's even weirder." She handed him the phone.

He read the text: Must find brilliant woman from last UCSF class.

He shook his head. Nonsense. But it tickled in his brain just the way random clues tickled him.

"Why are you here, Lyle?"

He met her eyes and then couldn't look at her anymore. Her tenderness overcame him. She had a hero's compassion with a survivor's backbone. How long had he been blind to this strength? He mustered the courage to say what he wanted to say. He looked down.

"Who is this woman? From your class. Were you having an aff—"

"Me. No way. You have no right—" He stopped. This wasn't why he'd come, not to fight.

The last class, he remembered, had happened prior to that fateful Africa trip. It lodged painfully in his craw. He'd put Melanie at risk by allowing her to come with him, then humiliated her on the airplane by diagnosing her pregnancy, and, as much as any of that, he well might've blown his analysis about what was ailing the small village. He'd said it was man-made. On what basis? Whimsical, cynical half-baked sophistry.

But *she'd* cheated on *him,* not the other way around.

"Are you sure you're okay, Lyle? Are you sick?"

"When did I lose it?" he blurted.

"What?"

He fought himself, his pride, his urge not to ask or delve into his own bullshit. He never tried to make it about him. It was about the patient, disease, pathology. Maybe he was those things now. He made himself ask.

"When did I give up?"

"Wow," she said, then almost immediately: "I'm sorry. I shouldn't say that. What's happened, Lyle?"

He shook his head. *I don't know.*

She looked over her shoulder, wanting to make sure they were alone.

She started to say something and then thought better of it. "Do you want to find some other time to talk?"

He looked to her in that moment like a patient who just wanted to be given a shot. *Get it over with.*

"I've thought about it a ton," she said, "when it all went to shit."

She told him about a weekend they'd had in a yurt near Santa Cruz. It had been a few weeks after Lyle had been asked to speak at the Centers for Disease Control in Atlanta. While he was there, the talk got called off because of a shooting at a nearby school. Lyle remembered that part well enough. After the shooting, he had been witness to an argument among several researchers at the CDC, one of whom had a student at the school. The kid was okay but the mom was enraged. Enraged, she'd railed against the gun culture. Another researcher took offense and railed back. They'd nearly come to blows. On the way out of the parking lot, the second researcher, giving the middle finger to the first researcher, plowed into the security hut and, while unhurt, totaled his car.

"That's when your withdrawal really intensified," Melanie said. "I'm not sure if what happened in Atlanta had anything to do with it.

That's what I thought. But then I started to wonder whether that was convenient and it might not be us—"

"But—"

"Listen, Lyle, I appreciate that you devoted your life to helping people and then found that people weren't always reciprocating, weren't always helping themselves—that they were hurting themselves." She saw that he wanted to interrupt again. She held up her hands. "You must've known that all along. It's always been a razor's-edge fight. So I suspect it was something in you, or us. Relationships live on the razor's edge, too. The great passion had subsided for us, the easy part. It was work, all of it; you got overwhelmed."

"No, I—" He stopped. He didn't have an immediate answer. Just more questions: *How do I get it back? How do I work through this soup?*

Something very bad is going to happen, Melanie. I need to figure out how to stop it. He hated those words and didn't know how to ask for help.

He couldn't get any words out.

"Maybe you should talk to someone," Melanie said.

"No—"

"Just listen. You've got this powerful brain, the most powerful brain. That power, any power, has a flip side. It might be that you've gotten off track. I think that's what happened in Africa. You said there was a conspiracy, some terrible man-made thing. But there was no conspiracy or anything like that. Just a disease that you didn't want to—"

"Something's going to happen."

Now she smiled with such love and caring that it couldn't possibly be seen as patronizing even though she was filled with pity. "Lyle . . ."

A car pulled into the driveway, crackling gravel beneath the tires as it came to a stop. Melanie stared at the car and then turned as the screen door opened behind her.

"Daddy!" the boy said.

"Sweetie, he'll be right inside. Can you go wait for us?"

The boy somehow understood she really meant this particular request. "K," he said again, and he disappeared.

From the boxy silver car stood a tall man in a T-shirt. He walked around the front of the car with a basketball under his long arm, wearing shorts.

"What happened to your eye?"

"Elbow," the man said. "I gotta take up chess." He smiled at Melanie and then offered Lyle a guileless nod. Dark stubble peppered his chin. "Eh, who am I kidding? I stink at chess."

"George," he said. "Are you a neighbor?"

"Lyle. I'm . . ."

"Oh, of course." Recognition took over his face. He nodded again, a second greeting, this one with a certain respect for the situation. "Nice to meet you, Lyle." He cleared his throat. "Don't let me interrupt, and I want to go inside and see Evan." This was guileless, too. It gave Lyle what would be his tiniest solace when he thought about this later. At least Melanie wasn't with a jerk. Now all he could think was, *Holy shit, she's got a boyfriend or husband or live-in whatever, maybe the father of her child, or not?* The screen door closed behind the man.

"Peño." She looked at him and he was impassive, that same ingrown look that had gotten them here in the first place.

"It's a beautiful family."

Tears dripped down Melanie's cheeks.

He knew what it meant. He wasn't the victim here.

A NUMB SUBWAY ride home. It wasn't that Lyle hadn't been expecting this when he went to see Melanie. He had been expecting anything, nothing. He had let himself walk into a situation unexposed. If he could have seen himself at a distance, with perspective, he might've realized how valuable that was, how necessary and, more than that, how much it was like the old version of Lyle. He walked into situations unexposed, dangerous ones, emotionally fraught ones, deadly ones, and he led with his curiosity and an essential faith things would work out. Now, on the subway, his openness left him blown apart.

"I hope they kill every one of those jerks," a woman said to another woman sitting in a seat next to and beneath where Lyle stood with his bike. She was evidently referring to the proposed show of arms on Capitol Hill.

The other woman had her arms wrapped around herself, as if cold. She squeezed her arms. "I wonder if this is what it feels like before a civil war? You don't see it and then it's all of a sudden there and people are picking sides."

The woman who had made the comment looked at her phone. Lyle glanced over her shoulder at the political website she read. He couldn't make out the particulars but could tell it was a firebrand, lamenting and attacking the other side. The woman read and clucked her tongue and muttered to herself, bemused and irritated by what she read, increasingly furious at the other side. It brought him back to Melanie and her description of the weekend in the yurt where she said he'd lost it. That was easier for Lyle to think about than the image of the boy and the man. The yurt. Lyle could only distantly recall it. When he did, he pictured himself that weekend as a lightbulb that was flickering, losing energy, petering out. Or maybe the better analogy was to a dying star; pulsing with dead energy, poised to explode into nothing.

People got on and off the train at the last stop in Oakland. The metal tube hummed and shimmied beneath the bay. Lyle held tight to his bike's handlebars. He found void and shadows when he tried to understand what had piqued him so much that weekend in the yurt. Melanie blamed it on that painful trip to the CDC in Atlanta. En route home at Hartsfield-Jackson airport, he'd waited three hours in security, which had been all backed up because of the shooting, and then missed his plane. Stuck there, he'd sat and watched the security guards and found he was imagining them as immune-system cells, carefully looking about the way b-cells and t-cells, the immune system's two power brokers, combed the body and targeted foreign invaders. What a system, arguably the most sophisticated in the body. The defenders roamed freely, instantly sensing danger and then sending waves of soldiers to attack. Not just that: the soldiers adapted. They would, at the rate of a supercomputer, try out a trillion different combinations of proteins to figure out which could kill the invader. It required a system this powerful to survive in a world with a trillion different possible invaders, from flu to cancer to random toxins. A mad scramble for survival, the immune system scrapping it out against the bacteria or virus, each desperate to survive.

Any system so powerful, though, had a dangerous side. No great survival mechanism or instinct goes without its dark sibling. Autoimmune disorders had blossomed, or, at least, we were seeing more of them. Our great defense system, the man on the wall, turning around out of control and blowing everything inside the village to shit.

At the Atlanta airport, Lyle watched the guards and thought about soldiers, police, vigilantes, armed youth, the suburban dads who, terrified, shot some kid on-site, asking questions later. On the flight, he hardly slept. He could feel a generalized fear, stoking people to defend themselves, the way that the immune system defends itself, then becoming so deadly effective, so out of control, that the mechanism turned inward.

Why had he been devoting everything to help people who were turning on one another?

Thinking back to that time, as he sat on the subway, Lyle wondered if he'd, in a way, done exactly the same thing. He'd withdrawn, protecting himself by disengaging only to discover that he'd actually destroyed the good parts of his life and himself, too. Depression, sadness, he knew the literature, they, too, were outgrowths of survival mechanisms, like the fear and anxiety that warn us of danger, remind us of situations where we've been harmed and could be so again, but toxic and even deadly when spun notches out of control. Had he protected himself and ground to a halt as a result?

Melanie had told him that intimacy and love were the true medicine. He'd never have used those words. But damn it if he didn't know she was right. The antidote in the micro, the antidote in the macro. Hard to let in when the perimeter defenses get jacked to the sky.

Lyle got off at the Civic Center and burst with energy on his ride to the apartment, not joy but grinding, an effort to exhaust himself. Lost in himself, he didn't see the driverless car tagging a few paces behind.

He considered the new piece of evidence: the text he'd sent Melanie about a brilliant student. On its face, that sounded as bizarre and vague as the pandemic thing. First of all, it was three years ago, and there were myriad brilliant students in the UCSF medical classes and he knew almost none of the ones in a giant lecture. They sat out there and he stood up there. Sometimes, one would ask a question or he'd meet a few in office hours. He couldn't remember a single student from that particular semester, well, maybe his graduate assistant. *Emily,* he thought with a last name that started with S or C. Maybe worth a contact.

Back at home, he went to the refrigerator to see what modest remains he'd left himself. He opened the creaky door and, no sooner had he done so, shut it. He stared at the front of the fridge. In the middle hung a magnet advertising a local pizza place. Last time that Lyle had seen that magnet, it held the note that he'd written himself about the pandemic.

The note was gone.

Lyle heard a gunshot and pasted himself to the ground.

THIRTY-EIGHT

I N THE TEN seconds that followed, Lyle felt a deep connection with and understanding of the veterans he had treated during his residency. That wasn't a gunshot. It had been a tire popping out his window. Yet he'd heard a gunshot, like the Vietnam vets he had seen at the VA wincing at as little as the click of an unfolding chair. What made it strange is that Lyle couldn't recall being amid gunfire.

Then he could.

He pushed himself up into a push-up position and saw bursts of gunfire. Flashes of light against the snow. He cascaded across a fleeting montage: a body in orange on a tarmac; a cavernous building echoing with footsteps; a stricken child. He tried to hold on to the images. They evaporated.

He walked to the cupboard over the dish rack and unscrewed the cap on a bottle of Black Label, mostly drained. He poured a finger, finished it, poured a second and walked to a recliner in the open area that served as a living room across from the kitchen, staring for a long time at the distant magnet on the refrigerator.

What happened to the note?

His phone buzzed. He saw a text from a number he didn't recognize. It was just a link. *Spam,* he immediately thought, and then the second message arrived from the same number. It read: We're not imagining things. I'm using a new, temporary cell phone. You can get me here. Eleanor.

The pilot. Apparently fearing some digital scrutiny. Lyle clicked on the link she'd sent him. It brought up a newspaper article. The headline read: ODD NIGHT LEAVES SGT. IN CRITICAL.

The outlet was called *Steamboat Today,* the mountain town's local newspaper. The article said that a police sergeant remained in critical condition after crashing his cruiser into Lindy's Mountain Art. The local police said they were investigating the late-night crash and stood by an officer with a spotless record.

The first big snow of the season took other casualties, including a woman whose car overturned on the highway north of Steamboat. Authorities also said they believe that may have been the night of a still-unexplained shooting involving a local hermit, Dwayne Summerset, an avid gun collector found at his secluded home. And an isolated fire broke out at the Sleepy Bear Mobile Home Park, taking the life of a resident there and may, authorities said, have been caused by a storm that appears to have caused electrical problems.

"A witching of a night," Mayor Ron McCloud said. He added that he was praying for the sergeant, eight-year-veteran Leonard "Len" Parker.

Lyle saw plainly that the unusual night being described matched the date of his landing in Steamboat. He drifted over the article again and again and kept settling on the words *electrical problems.* He felt the liquor clouding his thoughts. His head lolled with exhaustion. He fought it and scrounged for his laptop.

He looked up Dr. Jennifer Sanchez, the darling of the infectious disease department. She had moved her office from Parnassus to Mission Bay, the new UCSF research headquarters. She had taken the title of associate dean. Just days earlier, he dismissed the idea of going to talk to her and now backtracked, considered it.

He next went looking for his former assistant at UCSF. Searching through various disciplines and using Emily as a keyword, he eventually found Emily Chase. That was her, his former assistant in his lecture class. That was someone he'd have no problem talking to; she'd always seen him for what he was, guileless, rather than cunning, in his less conventional tactics. Maybe she could help guide him through the department if he needed expertise, and maybe she could make sense of this text about a student he might've made reference to.

With blurry eyes, he pulled up Eleanor's text. He put his fingers on the keyboard to respond and typed *Let's meet again* and fell asleep before he hit send.

FOR TWO DAYS, that was it. He slept and sat, and thought. Repeat. He ate there, too. He looked to be waiting. He looked in the direction of the refrigerator but his mind's eye often went to Steamboat, the little of it he could recall. Little by little, his efforts gave way to images and reflections of Melanie. He dreamed about her.

When he could no longer take the company of the stench of his dead ardor, he took a shower. Long beneath the hot water he scrubbed. He shaved away the itchy stubble. He put on khakis and a clean T-shirt.

He emerged into the kitchen, walked to the refrigerator, and stared at the magnet where the note had been. Now the magnet once again held a note. Lyle glanced around the apartment. He saw no one, heard nothing. He walked to the refrigerator and read the note. It was the same piece of paper as before, but it was turned around and a new message had been written on the side opposite.

It read:

I've got your back this time.

And there was a little red drawing of a heart.

Lyle carefully plucked the note and read it again, and again. The handwriting was neat, careful. As to meaning, Lyle couldn't make heads or tails of it. Only briefly did he wonder if the note had been written by Eleanor. No way, he dismissed the idea. Equally briefly, he wondered if he, somehow, had written the note himself. Could he be truly losing his mind—truly?

In fact, the opposite was true. Lyle was completely about his wits. Through his inaction, he had prompted the note to be written, smoked out a move by an invisible adversary. He smiled sadly. On some level, it's what he had wanted, hoped for, manipulated, even if he wasn't fully conscious of his tactics. If only subconsciously, he'd sensed a pattern that entailed a foe, an enemy—his match?—trying to get his attention, and when he lay fallow, it provoked him. A car followed him, or a note disappeared, and then reappeared. Still, this reappearing note hardly qualified as a victory because Lyle didn't exactly know what he would do with this new data point. He didn't know if he could muster the energy to pursue the answers.

He had to look at his phone to discover the date, day, and time. It was a Tuesday in early December at 10:20 in the morning.

He pulled on a leather jacket and headed down the stairwell.

THIRTY-NINE

MISSION BAY'S CAMPUS had exploded since he'd abandoned his life. High-rises had sprung up in clusters belonging to different medical specialties. A wide promenade ran to the water, bisecting the sprawling campus. Open space braced one side of the promenade and shops anchored the other. Lyle drained black coffee at a café and listened to researchers bitch and moan.

He found Dr. Sanchez's office on the eleventh floor of the new Kartling Immunology Center, a modern building that, despite its large windows and curved middle, came across as boring, lacking creativity. Dr. Sanchez wasn't in her office and Lyle didn't leave his name with her assistant. He did pick up that she'd be back in an hour.

Thirty minutes later, he found Emily Chase, his former assistant, in the Neuroscience Department, a long block away. She was a postdoc now, which entitled her to a small, shared office with desks along opposite walls. She was alone when Lyle poked his head in. She practically leapt from her chair.

"Dr. Martin!"

He looked bewildered and she laughed. "I forgot: you never grasped how appreciative your fans are."

He smiled and looked down and realized that his assistant had changed. Her tone now came across not as unctuous or adoring but, rather, as confident enough that she could speak freely and candidly. She was all grown up.

"What brings you in? Are you coming back? What are you up to, Dr. Martin? I get asked all the time."

He waved his hand and said, "Long story." Which was true. "I could use your help."

"Of course." She picked up his seriousness and adjusted. She sat in her swivel chair and gestured to a plastic black chair against the wall. "I've got a subject coming in fifteen minutes. You want to talk now or will it take longer?"

Lyle sat and explained with as little fanfare as he might that he needed to get a list of the students from his last survey class. Did she have something like that? She pursed her lips, thinking about it, and, Lyle figured, considering about whether to ask him why he needed such a thing. But, in the end, she didn't. She pulled her chair up to her computer and she clacked about on the keys.

"Something like this is probably the best I can do without working through the administrative system, and, even then . . ."

He stood so he could peer over her shoulder. Her screen showed an old e-mail that she'd dug up. It was titled: Martin, Section II; Population List.

Lyle, looking at the screen, realized he'd been copied on the e-mail. Naturally, he'd not paid attention; no point in a survey class like this and the e-mail had been little more than a formality. Emily clicked open a spreadsheet. It included names, student ID numbers, and affiliation as med student, postdoc, fellow, or audit/other. Lyle looked for a tab that might indicate there were pictures, though he was not surprised to find no such thing.

"Can you print it out?"

"Of course." She clicked the command. In the corner, a printer hummed to life.

Lyle sat back and looked glassy-eyed.

"The deep-in-thought look," Emily said. She laughed.

"Sorry. Sorry. Congratulations. Neuroscience?"

"All the rage these days," she said.

"What's your area of research?"

"Attention, prefrontal cortex, with some emphasis on the default network. Gets granular from there."

"Good for you," Lyle said and meant it. He cleared his throat. "You know much about seizures, electrical activity, ion channels?"

She studied him. "Only in passing."

The printer came to a stop. Lyle could see her desperate curiosity to understand his reappearance. There would be gossip.

He stood. "Thank you, Emily."

AT DR. SANCHEZ'S door, he didn't have a chance to consider a strategy. She'd already seen him. An instant of concern-colored surprise crossed her face as she stood beside her assistant's desk holding an opened manila folder. She snapped the folder shut and quickly reoriented as the best politicians can do.

"Look what the cat dragged in. Dr. Martin. Come in!" She pulled reading glasses from her nose and let them hang by the cord around her neck. "Ernie, hold my calls. Dr. Martin, can I get you a cup of coffee? Come in, come in."

Once a world-class cyclist, Dr. Sanchez had grown sturdier and matronly. She sat behind a thick desk and offered him the chair across from her. She smiled. It was warm but affected.

"How are you?"

He nodded, fine, fine. "I know I'm barging in."

"Not at all." She could see he had something on his mind. She was accustomed to doctors with time pressure. "What's up? What can I do for you?"

He smiled himself and touched his forehead with the folded pages of single-spaced names, signaling he wasn't sure where to begin. He exhaled.

"I'm rusty," he said.

She raised her hands as if to say: *No problem. Shoot.*

"Channelopathy."

She laughed. "That's the last thing I'd have ever guessed would come out of your mouth."

He sat there, awkwardly. "It's obviously not virulent."

"Sorry?"

"You can't catch it."

She shook her head. No, of course not. She gave the standard doctor caveat that she wasn't an expert. Some people, she said, were more susceptible than others, almost certainly on a genetic basis. She told him what he already knew about ion channels.

"What is its relationship to seizure?"

"If memory serves, they are distinctive but related. Some seizure disorders, epilepsy, are caused by channelopathy. Okay, my curiosity is piqued, Lyle. What's up?"

Her voices carried all the harmonies and dissonance of her personality: genuine interest, intensity she tried to quiet, envy that she might be missing something or that Lyle could wind up discovering or getting something she might want, however unknown or irrelevant that thing might be to her.

"I was wondering if there are any signs that we're seeing more of this. Any papers on growing incidence of electrical disorders?"

She thought about it and whether to take him at face value on such an unusual question. "Hmm."

"Maybe related to your phone or all the electromagnetic fields from cellular technology."

Now her eyes widened. It was true that there had been some talk about the potential for electromagnetic radiation, EMR, as a source of cancer. Nothing had been proven. It was more conspiracy chatter at this point than anything else. And she hadn't heard anything regarding EMR and seizure. So her eyes were wide not from curiosity or recognition but from the thought maybe Lyle had revealed himself with a kind of desperation. From her standpoint, the proper order in this room had been established.

"Are there ways to prevent or short-circuit a seizure?" Lyle asked.

"Like phenobarbital?" Her eyes went wider now as she mentioned the barbiturate. Lyle knew that some of these drugs could be used to slow or prevent seizure but that wasn't what he was asking. Of course, he wasn't thinking he'd give everyone in the world a barbiturate, if that even would work. Now he was startled by what she must be thinking: he might be trying to get drugs. Or maybe she was going to make it look that way, to herself, even others.

"Is everything okay, Lyle?" she asked.

He gritted his teeth. She wasn't going to make this easy. He felt the old irritations bubble; she was playing three-level chess—one level being gamesmanship—and he didn't want any part of it. Fatigue overtook him.

"Anyhow, thanks for your time," he said.

OUTSIDE, HE COULDN'T breathe. Forces he couldn't name grappled for control of his body and brain. He leaned against a wall with paralysis, physical, emotional, spiritual. He knew what he needed to do. He knew what he had to do. A growling sound escaped his throat. A passerby moved inches away on the sidewalk. Lyle looked at his hands white with blood loss as he held furiously to the paper with the names. It took everything not to rip it to shreds.

He put it in his pocket. He pulled out his phone.

"HELLO?"

"Hello, Melanie."

"Lyle? I'm right in the middle—"

"Please."

"Lyle, okay, hold on." He could hear Melanie cup her hand over the phone. "I need five. Can you just take ice to the guy in 210?" She withdrew her hand from the phone. "Is everything okay?"

"No." Lyle had moved himself to the backside of the building, opposite a parking structure. Were he paying attention, he could see the water and across the bay in the direction of Melanie.

"I'm in a room. I've got five minutes. What's the matter, are you sick?"

"I'm sorry."

"What?"

"Melanie, I'm sorry."

"Sorry for—"

"Everything, all of it. It is on me."

He heard first silence and then the sound of them crying for both of them. He invited the sound in. He closed his eyes. A minute passed.

"I love you, Mel. I will always love you."

Sobs overcame her.

"I'm happy for you," he said. "You have a beautiful family."

"Thank you, Peño."

AT A CAFÉ off the promenade, Lyle ignited his laptop. He pulled out the piece of paper with more than two hundred names. As the machine booted, he closed his eyes and listened to the memory of Melanie crying. He'd owed her an apology for more than three years. He probably owed her three years' worth of apology. He owed it to himself too. At some point, whoever was to blame—him—no longer mattered. He felt the poison, the toxins, release from his body. He looked at the computer screen.

He typed the first name into Google.

Two hours later, two things were clear to Lyle. This was not a smart strategy. Second and more important: he was eager to keep going. The feeling reminded him of the old days, when no clock or skeptic deterred him. His idea had been to call up the names, look at current jobs and their pictures, which almost all of them had in some form or fashion. He'd hoped that one of them might trigger recognition. Or he'd see, or intuit, a pattern. Maybe one of them worked with Google cars. Had a Steamboat connection. Involvement with seizure research. Along those lines, there had been one former student, Dr. Mischa David, who worked at the Epilepsy Center at Mount Sinai Hospital in New York. Lyle spent a few minutes poking around about her and decided nothing else about her struck him.

Another woman, Jackie Badger, was unusual in that she had not followed a medical path and had, as far as he could tell, no further medical training. She worked at Google as an engineer. There had been no other information about her and the tiniest image. So he'd moved on.

Now he was only on the H's.

He stood up and stretched. Walked outside and stared at people walking by. Most of them lost in their devices.

In the middle of a promenade stood a lone protester with a placard. It pictured a separatist with an automatic weapon. It read TURNCOAT.

"Look up!" demanded the protester as he nearly got knocked into by a student reading his device. The student bounced off like a pinball and kept on. Lyle looked at the placard and the man holding the weapon. He had a memory flash that left him wobbling. A man with such a gun, shots fired, a body in a doorway. He clung to the image, tried to. It wavered, flickered. Shifted. A woman, standing with her phone. Clicking on it. Short hair, a hat. Flicker, flicker. Then again, two children in the backseat of a car.

Flicker. Gone.

He practically ran back to his laptop. He sat and clicked away. He called up the picture of Jackie Badger. He enlarged it. He held his breath. Dark hair, a light face. He cocked his head, tried her face on with different color hair, a hat, a worried look, a smile. He was sure he didn't *know* her. Same as he didn't feel like he'd known Eleanor when he met her at a café, but, on some level he did know her.

Just like he knew this woman.

He looked around and, outside, saw a man with a fish-looking face peering at him through the window.

FORTY

OUTSIDE THE CAFÉ, the fish-faced man didn't run this time. Instead, he sat on a half wall near the bike racks, arms crossed. Lyle approached him, feeling immediate irritation. The guy wreaked of smugness and self-satisfaction. A cowboy wannabe looking for a gunfight. Not just metaphorically; the guy wore a puffy windbreaker that Lyle intuited hid a gun in a back holster. There were probably five conceal-carry permits in San Francisco, and surely this guy didn't have one. So he was some mix of stupid and dangerous and scared, or just 100 percent stupid, and yet Lyle felt undeterred.

"You're the copilot," Lyle said.

"The correct phrase is first officer, Dr. Martin."

A shiver of distant recognition braced Lyle. He knew that obnoxious tone from somewhere. The man stood nearly a half foot taller than Lyle but less than that with the hunched slant of his shoulders. His eyes bulged, red tinged.

"Good timing," Lyle said. "Is it Jeremy?"

Jerry gritted his teeth, then tried to affect a cool-guy smirk. "I'll let you figure my name out."

"Jerry," Lyle said guilelessly.

"Very good, Lyle," Jerry said. "Now what the hell is your game? You and Eleanor trying to bring me down, is that it?"

"Let's go talk about it, Jerry. And you can tell me why you're following me. Did Jackie send you?"

Lyle watched Jerry's face squeeze in irritation, like he had no clue what Lyle was talking about. *This guy is too stupid,* Lyle thought, *to fake confusion.* Stupid, and dangerous. Armed.

THEY SAT IN Jerry's red Miata on a side street and talked. The car was twenty years old, at least, and impeccable. A police scanner tucked in a compartment below the radio squawked with static and an occasional report. Lyle told much of the same story he'd told Eleanor—being on the flight, not remembering much. Jerry half listened, less interested it seemed to Lyle in figuring out what happened than in looking for flaws. Lyle patiently talked, waiting for his turn to listen, which is why he was here. Jerry didn't seem interested, though, in sharing. So Lyle had to infer Jerry's story, and his appearance outside the café, from his salty questions.

"So you were on the flight?"

"Yes, I told yo—"

"And you are friends with Captain Hall."

"No."

"But you had coffee with her."

Lyle blew air out, wordlessly conceding the complexity. He hadn't told Jerry about the note Eleanor found in her pocket with Lyle's phone number. "I think I gave her my number in Steamboat," Lyle finally said.

"You think? You *think*?" Jerry laughed condescendingly. He leaned back in the driver's seat and gripped the steering wheel of the parked car. Lyle could see it for a second from Jerry's perspective, and it looked bad.

"So how much do you remember about hacking into my e-mail?" Jerry asked.

Lyle let the question roll around in his head.

"I know who did that," he said quietly. He was speaking mostly to himself. Some things falling into place. "Can you give me a lift to my place?"

"What the hell are you talking about?"

"Tell me about the e-mails," Lyle said, feeling and sounding clinical, distant.

"Fuck you. Are you even a real doctor?"

Lyle was no longer listening to this foulmouthed pedant. He said, "I think you and Eleanor and I need to meet."

"Tell me who wrote them or I'll fucking kill you."

Lyle didn't doubt it. In fact, he flashed on an elusive memory of this faux cowboy firing his weapon at close range. Then it disappeared.

"Maybe someone named Jackie Badger," Lyle said. "Can I get a lift to my house? I'll tell you as we go."

JERRY, FEELING GOOD about being in the driver's seat—literally and, in his own mind, proverbially—softened a touch. He steered the Miata in light traffic and, through his accusatory questions, started to betray what had happened. Best as Lyle could put it together, Jerry couldn't remember what happened, either. But when he got back to San Francisco, he'd been confronted, like Eleanor, by the airlines. Unlike with Eleanor, the airline had unearthed e-mails supposedly written by Jerry that expressed nearly violent anger at his employer and saying that he would take serious measures if he wasn't treated more fairly. The e-mails had been sent to Eleanor in the days preceding the flight. The airline discovered them looking on its own server.

"Even if I was pissed at the airline, which I am not, would I send e-mails on their server? How stupid do they think I am?"

Lyle didn't take the bait on that one. Besides, he was focused on more things falling into place for him, and more certainty that a woman named Jackie Badger somehow was in the middle of this. Her LinkedIn profile said she worked at Google, which suggested computer expertise and, just maybe, gave her access to the driverless car that had followed Lyle and that was three car lengths back from the

Miata. Lyle kept one eye on the passenger-side mirror, watching the eerie bubble. He thought he knew what to do about that. It was why he was getting a ride home.

Lyle now suspected that Jackie might've had the computer skills to hack into Jerry's account. Why exactly was not clear. She was connected to Google.

Another thing, Lyle suddenly realized, Jackie Badger had the initials J.B.; same as the initials of Jennifer Babcock, the mystery woman or fictional creation that had invited him to Steamboat.

"She was on the flight," Lyle said. "I think. Maybe."

"How do you know that?"

"When we meet with Captain Hall, we'll put it together."

Outside the apartment building, they paused, caught momentarily by an urgent-sounding back-and-forth on the cop scanner. "11-54," said a woman's voice on the scanner. "City Hall."

"Suspicious vehicle," Jerry said and turned up the scanner. Then, suddenly, "11-99" and then shots. A flurry of audio traffic followed that became impossible for Lyle to follow. Jerry turned off the radio and stared at Lyle.

"What the hell do they expect to happen?" Jerry said, which also made no sense to Lyle.

"Who?"

"They're going to take our guns. But, then again, you just can't go shooting the good guys, either."

Lyle realized that Jerry sounded as contradictory and, yet, certain of himself as a two-bit radio talk-show host. Then Lyle made a random connection that nearly left him laughing. He imagined that if Jerry were a virus, he'd be the common cold; mostly harmless but impossible to avoid and, if contracted during a period of frailty or bad timing, could turn to pneumonia and kill you. A simple creature, Lyle decided, but not simply dismissed.

Jerry insisted on coming upstairs with Lyle. Inside, the flight officer made a show of checking the safety on his gun, making sure Lyle could see his nine millimeter.

Lyle pulled his phone from his pocket and plugged it in at the kitchen counter where he kept his charger. He made sure the phone was on. Then he gave it a loving pat and left it there. This all went unnoticed by Jerry, which was neither here nor there. Lyle excused himself to the bathroom. He opened the medicine cabinet and fished around among the mostly empty bottles. He found the one he was looking for. He'd saved it for a rainy day, a really bad, really rainy day. That kind of day might have arrived. He put the two little white pills in his pocket.

Absent his precious device, Lyle walked back down the stairs with Jerry behind him. Lyle led him the back way out.

"I ask only one favor, Jerry."

"You're not in a position to—"

"Go around front and get the car and pick me up here."

"I'm not leaving you." Jerry smirked.

Lyle gave the first officer his wallet and keys as collateral. "I think we're being followed," Lyle said. "Let's not take any chances."

For some reason, this conspiratorial logic appealed to Jerry. For Lyle's part, this was conspiratorial but also likely: the driverless car, he thought, was tracking him via his cell phone and, possibly, taking video of him. Who knew? Anything was possible, given the improbability of everything that had already happened.

Ten minutes later, Jerry appeared in the Miata in the alley behind Lyle's apartment. Sweat beaded his forehead.

"If anyone was following us, he's not now," Jerry said. Lyle climbed in. Jerry continued. "First in my class in evasive maneuvers in a workshop three years ago put on for gun-certified first officers."

"Would you mind turning off your phone?" Lyle asked.

"Are you kidding me? You're giving me orders?"

"Phones can be tracked. Just a precaution."

"Screw you," Jerry said. But he turned off his phone.

JERRY STOPPED IN front of a white house with a tall fence in a neighborhood Lyle couldn't recall ever seeing. Less dense houses, bigger than flats, unattached, virtually suburban. So it was in San Francisco; the neighborhoods and architectural patches like the residents themselves, all over the map. It was called Forest Hill and aptly so, with trees and hills.

Lyle got out of the car. "This one?" He gestured to the two-story white house.

"Don't pretend you don't know," Jerry said. He started walking up the hill without explanation as to why he hadn't parked in front of the house they were evidently walking to. Maybe he was testing Lyle or maybe sneaking up on Eleanor or maybe, Lyle thought bemusedly, this was some trick he learned in first-officer-gun-carrying school. Lyle followed Jerry to the house.

Lyle felt a rush of urgency. They were running out of time and he didn't even know what the stakes were. It was like he was bedside with a patient with mysterious symptoms, nothing he'd ever seen before, but who most assuredly would die in hours if Lyle didn't figure it out.

"You knock," Jerry said and nudged Lyle forward to a round-faced gray house on the corner. Stylish and deliberate, the house was not ordinary; clearly the work of someone who knew what they wanted. A window wrapped around the corner of the house, giving a glimpse inside at an equally fashionable living room. Eleanor answered the door with a mug in her hand. She blinked with surprise when she saw Lyle, but then her face took on a warm look. Then she saw Jerry. She looked alarmed.

"You've got to be kidding me. You two?"

With as much subtlety as Lyle could channel, he shook his head. *No, we're not in cahoots.*

"Hello, Eleanor," Jerry said. "Your first officer has come to the rescue."

Lyle watched Eleanor's jaw tense.

"Jerry, you're not supposed to be here."

"Then let us in already so no one sees us."

Eleanor gestured them in. As Jerry passed, she touched him gently on the shoulder. "Are you carrying, Jerry?"

"These are not ordinary times."

"Why don't you leave it in the guest room? It's down the hall."

"It's not loaded."

"It would make me feel better."

He shrugged. He took the short hallway beside a set of stairs going up. He walked into the second door on the left. Eleanor touched Lyle's elbow until he turned to face her. She mouthed, *What is going on?*

"I might actually have an idea about that," Lyle said quietly. He caught her eye and tried to reassure her. She pursed her lips.

"I'll make some coffee."

TEN MINUTES LATER, midafternoon, the three of them at the kitchen counter stared at Jackie Badger's picture on Eleanor's laptop. Lyle watched their reactions and could imagine what they were feeling. This person looked familiar to them but only in a dreamlike way. While they stared, Lyle told them his theory. He told them that he had three reasons for suspecting this woman: he'd written Melanie a text about a woman in his class and she had been in his class; he'd been followed by a Google car and she worked at Google; when he saw her picture, it sparked something inside him.

"It's pretty thin," Lyle said. "I'm not even sure this is really Jackie Badger. Maybe the picture belongs to someone else."

Eleanor had her eyes closed. She grabbed Jerry's forearm.

"She was on the deck, Jerry."

"What?" Lyle said.

"The flight deck. I remember her." Eleanor still looked at Jerry.

"You do?"

"I thought I was going to die."

She tried to describe to them what she was experiencing. She couldn't grasp most of it, and some of it she didn't want to say aloud. Eleanor could see this woman standing in her flight deck as Eleanor had had the feeling she was going to be joining Frank, her ex-boyfriend, true love, who had died years earlier. It wasn't Jackie Badger that Eleanor was remembering, not exactly. It was a powerful memory of loss and the prospect of death that Eleanor was experiencing. It was pushing through the miasma of lost memory.

"What do we do about this?" she said.

Lyle told them his plan.

FORTY-ONE

JACKIE OPENED THE door to the Lantern headquarters in Nevada. The dull hum of servers strummed through the air. Jackie held a white bag with takeout. The heavy door closed behind her. She wore a tight black cap over her short hair.

"Hello, Alex. How're things?" She stepped inside. "I know you're surprised to see me, just let me say something," Jackie said. "First, at the risk of sounding insincere, it is good to see you. Really, it is. I owe you an apology. You were right, Alex, all along. So was Denny. I wasn't being a team player. We weren't on the same page, not aligned in our mission."

It sounded clichéd, bordering on the glib.

"In my defense," Jackie said, walking forward to Alex's cubicle, "Denny never trusted me, as you rightly noted. Do you know that his distrust of me was so great, so profound, that he actually had a colleague attack me, feign an assault, a near-sexual assault. Ridiculous, right? Denny thought it would make me more beholden to him, trusting of him, so that I would follow his musty old sellout footsteps into another self-congratulatory, world-changing innovation he envisioned. Another liar, Alex, another fraud." Jackie stopped and shook her head. "I'm rambling, I know it. I just thought I owed you some explanation."

Alex sat in her cubicle. Her head hung to the left side. A dull smile held her catatonic face. Drool pooled beside her lip.

"Eh, who am I kidding," Jackie said. "I don't owe you shit."

Jackie walked beside Alex's swivel chair and kicked it a few feet to the left. The chair flew and Alex with it, eventually sliding off the edge and falling to the ground with her dumb, absent stare and pasted smile. Jackie reached into her pocket and pulled out a gray rectangular device that looked very much like a cell phone. "I think you'd be proud of me, Alex," she said. "I can now change the electrical pulses on your device with this little thing. It's a remote control—for your brain."

She stared at Alex.

"I know what you're thinking," Jackie said in a happy singsong voice. "Yes, yes, yes. I did the whole Steamboat thing, and I took over Lantern, and covered my tracks, blah, blah, blah. And yes, I hacked into your computer and changed the video so that it looked like you were getting on the plane. Do you take me for an idiot? No, of course not. You took me for a genius." She leaned over Alex. "But you treated me like I was too much of a child to trust!" She kicked the grounded woman in the ribs. Still, Alex smiled dumbly. "You took me for a weak, indecisive, helpless fool. For the last time, I might add. Jackie Badger will have plenty of time now to make smart, thoughtful decisions.

"Thanks to Lantern."

Jackie pulled a different chair to Alex's computer. She started clacking away. A few minutes later, she had three windows open. One belonged to the Lantern dashboard. A second showed a list of major telecommunications towers.

Then she pulled out her phone and pursed her lips. Someone was looking at her LinkedIn picture. From the IP address, she could tell that whoever was scrutinizing her picture was located in the house belonging to Captain Eleanor Hall.

"Wrinkle," she said. "I doubt you got there on your own."

Eleanor Hall had had nothing to connect to Jackie Badger. *Most certainly,* Jackie thought, *this is Lyle's doing.* But Lyle's phone was still at his apartment. *No, he must have left it there and he must be with her now.*

Good man, Lyle, she thought. Rising to the occasion. *Me too,* Jackie thought. *Me too.* And soon to be together. She turned to a screen that showed a map of major radio towers around the world. She enlarged the map to focus on the western United States. She hovered her cursor over Northern California until it brought up a box with information for Sutro Radio Tower. It stood tall across Twin Peaks over San Francisco. It was a radio tower, true, but many of these were in the control of Lantern partners, so she had access. Just as powerful as cell towers, but with wider distribution. She clicked to open the box and inserted a string of code from a save key.

She sipped coffee. Tedious work. She looked down at Alex, whom she'd now put into a sitting position, fixing her eyes on her phone.

"Time to get you six billion fellow travelers."

Jackie focused her attention on a small rectangular box within the larger box she'd been interacting with. She clicked onto a new window on the monitor and called up CNN. It was continuing wall-to-wall coverage of the impending Million Gun March. It was a little less than a day away. Gawkers and participants had begun gathering at the Washington Mall. So far, just one person had been seen with a gun and had been arrested by twenty members of the National Guard in a clip being shown again and again. Ominously, a growing number of mobile homes had streamed into the capital. Permitted gun owners in their "homes." Would they march?

Jackie clicked away and then returned to the small rectangular box on the Lantern dashboard, inserting her cursor on a command line. She typed: 18:00, and then hit enter.

17:59:59 it read. Seventeen hours and fifty-nine minutes.

17:59:58

One day and counting. Lots of work to do. She clicked on the

Mount Wilson radio tower in Los Angeles. The easier stuff she'd save until later, using the back door she'd created into the major telecom providers, like Verizon and Comcast, China Telecom, Vodafone, Nippon Telegraph, and on. New modems and routers for everyone or most people around the globe. All with the power to hit the human pause button.

17:59:56

17:59:55

17:59:54

FORTY-TWO

WITH JERRY BEHIND the wheel of the Miata, Eleanor in the passenger seat, and Lyle squeezed painfully into what passed for a backseat, the threesome stared at a greenish-brown-colored flat located near the western edge of San Francisco, not far from the beach. Salty wet air clung to these attached flats, the colors so worn they took on the dull flavor of the fog itself.

"You think she's in there?" Eleanor asked.

Lyle didn't answer. His eyes settled on a shaggy-looking mat lying before the front door. Something elevated the mat slightly, a box or package hidden beneath. Lyle pushed his way out of the Miata.

Jerry reached around and felt for his gun. Watching Lyle wander off without warning reminded Jerry of something, a memory he couldn't quite grasp. "I don't trust this guy for a second, Eleanor."

She exhaled loudly, a tacit agreement, but not a direct confirmation. She didn't want to give Jerry permission to do anything stupid. They watched Lyle knock on the door. Wait, knock again. Lean down and look and move the mat aside with his toe and stare at what looked to be a package. Lyle seemed satisfied and loped back to the car.

"Package postmarked a week ago," he said. "I don't think anyone is around."

"Who's the package addressed to?"

"Jackie Badger," Lyle said.

They'd found the address in minutes with the help of a friend of

Jerry's in the police department. They also discovered Jackie worked on Google's campus in Mountain View, at least that's what it said on a CV they found online. But they figured they'd never get in there and Lyle's plan had been to try to visit her place while she was gone.

Now, standing here, he thought aloud, "We could call the police, or wait until night to see if she comes back. Or . . ." He paused. "We could see about the back. There's a small yard, accessible by an alley. Looks pretty desolate back there, so if there's a back door . . ." He let it hang there, stared at the house. "In any case, it's, what, four fifteen, so we don't have long before—"

His sentence was interrupted by Jerry opening his door. He stood and straightened his dark blue windbreaker.

"I got this," he said. "You two relax."

He walked purposefully to the street corner. Lyle felt a tug of conscience and turned to see it was being beamed at him by Eleanor. She stared at Lyle and he shook his head, knowing exactly what he'd done. It wasn't quite condemnation, though.

"Let's use the powers of the gun for good," he said.

"Watch out or it will turn on you."

A FEW MINUTES later, the front door opened. Jerry beckoned them inside. Lyle looked around the street and didn't see so much as a mail truck. It was still shy of quitting time. He and Eleanor stepped out of the fog. Jerry closed the door behind them.

"What did you do?" Eleanor asked.

"Piece of cake. Some stuff I learned doing a hotshot-firefighting weekend training. I'll spare you the gory details." Lyle thought it condescending but mostly was focused on the musty smell in this classic midcentury San Francisco flat. A narrow hallway led to a bathroom and two bedrooms in the back. Halfway down the hallway, a doorway led to the kitchen and to the right of the front door, a living room and dining room with creaky wooden floors. The place looked little lived in. Lyle closed his eyes and inhaled. He took in humidity that had seeped into these walls, the low-level mold. He winced; virus could take root here. That wasn't today's business. They searched the house, first with great care, and then with more urgency when nothing of relevance, or even mild interest, revealed itself. Other than that the outdated and Spartan decor—an old futon couch in the front room, a garage-sale dining-room table, a beanbag chair, a refrigerator with a pizza magnet holding a sloppily written shopping list and little inside—reminded him very much of his own surroundings and habits. It told him that Jackie Badger focused on things inside her head, not the external. *Know your virus,* he thought, as he descended wooden stairs from the back of the kitchen to, presumably, the garage. Halfway down, he heard: "Dr. Martin . . . Lyle."

It was Eleanor, calling from the bedroom. Lyle found the airline captain looking at a photograph. Of Lyle. He was standing at the café near his house, holding his bicycle, about to mount it. It looked like the photo had been taken by a long lens.

"It was tucked in behind that picture," Eleanor said. She gestured to a picture of the Golden Gate Bridge, now hung askew after Eleanor had delved behind it. She looked at the picture. "I wonder why she's collecting photos of people who look bewildered," she teased lightly.

Jerry stood in the doorway with his arms crossed. "You've never been here?" he asked Lyle pointedly.

"Who even prints pictures anymore?"

Lyle took Eleanor's meaning: everyone keeps their photos online.

"Someone who wants you to find it," he muttered. "Everyone's phone is off, right?" he said just a touch less absently.

Lyle looked up to find Jerry staring at him. "Now why would she leave us the photo, huh? You've got a lot of strange answers, pal. Maybe you're trying to throw us off the scent."

"Jerry . . ."

The sound of their back-and-forth reminded Lyle, somehow, of Steamboat. "There's going to be more," Lyle said obliquely. He walked out of the room and into the second bedroom next door. It served as an office. Now, all tenderness or care was gone from Lyle's search. He swept things around on the desk, pulled out books from the shelf. He pawed through pockets in the two jackets hung in the closet and shuffled through plastic cartons holding files and folders. On the desk, he stared at a copy of the *San Francisco Chronicle*. It was from four days earlier. The headline on the lead story referred to the upcoming march on Washington. It was tomorrow, Lyle realized.

He stood to find Eleanor and Jerry looking at him. He closed his eyes and clenched his teeth. He thought about the note on his fridge, about how this person said she'd met her match. He brushed past them, through the linoleum and bad tile kitchen, down the stairs to a dark, damp garage. At the bottom, he found a string hanging from the low ceiling and pulled it to click on a lightbulb. It provided dim light but enough to make out a garage converted into storage space, no car, boxes, junk, a bicycle and a treadmill. Then he saw the flies. Bingo.

Lyle sidestepped crud until he got to the recycling, trash, and compost bins near the front of the garage where the bugs hovered. They told him these bins hadn't been attended recently. Then he opened the compost and saw it was more foul than he thought. Inside, a bird, half eaten away by bacteria, maggots, and flies. He withdrew from the bacteria scent and closed the green lid. The trash held similarly little interest, as he poked through what looked like the detritus of a Dustbuster, fluff and dust bunnies. He heave-dragged the blue recycling bin over the piles and stacks until he came back to the stairs and the lightbulb above. Jerry and Eleanor stood there speechlessly watching. He tipped the tall bin and dumped. Half a foot of junk mail and assorted papers slipped out. Lyle picked through it. He paused on a scrap, held it close to his face, put it on the stair for further examination. Leafed some more, tossed most of it aside. Found another small scrap and scrutinized it. Then picked up the first scrap.

He started looking again with greater intensity.

"Lyle," Eleanor said.

Lyle didn't answer and she couldn't be sure he even heard her, so lost was he.

"Hey, so-called doctor, what's the deal?" Jerry said.

Lyle now looked intently at another sheet of paper culled from the pile. He stood and whisked right between the two flummoxed pilots and up the stairs he went, into the kitchen to the fridge. He pulled off the shopping list held by the pizza magnet—a magnet that matched his own exactly—and opened the sheet of paper, which had been folded in quarters. Inside was a grainy image of a mouse. It looked to have been printed in black and white on a not-very-fancy printer. Beneath the picture, a caption that read: "The deer mouse is three to four inches long with a brown back and a white stomach."

Lyle closed his eyes and rocked on his feet, thinking. Then, suddenly, he walked purposely toward the door.

"Hey!" Jerry said.

Lyle, lost in thought, kept walking. Eleanor hustled behind him. She took his arm and gently spun him around. "Hello, Earth to Dr. Martin. What's up?"

He looked up, seeming surprised he had company.

"I know where she is."

FORTY-THREE

LYLE KEPT WALKING. Eleanor wondered if he was muttering to himself. She resisted the urge to look back at Jerry because she didn't want to encourage his skepticism. Truly, though, she felt some of it herself. She hustled up behind Lyle and walked next to him, hearing the sound behind her of Jerry shutting the door.

"You ever fly a plane, Dr. Martin?"

"What? Um, no." He kept toward the car.

"It takes all the concentration in the world. Still, though, you have to pause now and again and communicate to the passengers, y'know, explain to them what's happening."

"Uh-huh." He kept walking.

"Or they'll storm the flight deck and tear you limb from limb. Unless, of course, you've given them Wi-Fi. Then they'll be so distracted you can fly into the ocean."

Lyle laughed. "Fair enough." He opened the door and climbed into the back.

"Somebody tell me what the hell is going on," Jerry said, standing with arms crossed in irritation. "Or we're not going anywhere, capiche?"

Eleanor shot him a look.

"Give me a break and quit the lovebird crap," Jerry said.

She held her arms up, like *What the hell, where did that come from?*

"Flight plan calls for Nevada," Lyle said.

Jerry shook his head in disbelief.

"So-so start. This is the part where you need to communicate," Eleanor said.

She climbed into the passenger seat and Jerry took the wheel. He put up the top of the sports car and Lyle explained what he'd found.

In the recycling bin were several receipts that caught his eye. He fanned four of them in his hand. One was a restaurant, another for an electric-car charging station, and a third for a hotel. The fourth was for a place called "Winter Place," but left no other evidence what it was. The restaurant and charging station had come from three months earlier, well prior to the Steamboat flight. The Days Inn hotel was from the week before.

All of them had the 702 area code. The hotel had an address in "Hawthorne, Nev."

"How do you know she's there now? Why wouldn't she be at work?"

"Fair question and easy enough to check. We can call Google," Lyle said. "She won't be there. She's here," he mused, and it sounded very much like he was talking to himself or the receipts. He realized it and looked up. He explained his reasoning. The receipts were from very different time periods. That wasn't necessarily a big deal—after all, Jackie might have dumped receipts together over time and then cleaned her office and recycled them at one time. But Lyle suspected it was a clue for two reasons. One was that a bird had been left in the compost. This, Lyle thought, had been designed to draw flies and to attract their attention.

"To the compost? Give me a break," Jerry said.

"I agree it sounds thin," the pilot said.

"Or just dumb luck," Lyle said with a shrug.

"Keep going."

He showed the mouse picture and told them that the deer mouse had become a particularly nagging source of hantavirus.

"It's a symbol of sorts, something any immunologist would recognize," Lyle said. "Comes from Nevada. I think she was giving another gentle reminder, and it was held on the refrigerator with the same magnet I've got—the one where my own note disappeared." He'd already told them that story.

"You've got to be kidding me," said Jerry. "And you're telling me you've never met her."

"So, like, she's leaving clues?" Eleanor ignored Jerry. "Why in the world would she do that? Why not just leave a note saying where she is?"

Lyle looked blankly at Eleanor. He had no answer for her.

"Fair enough," Lyle said. *His logic did sound thin.* "We can call the hotel in Nevada and see if she's checked in there."

"Well now, there's a sane thought," Jerry muttered. "Except that you've made us all turn off our phones."

With about as much sense of cohesion as the United States Congress, they drove to a nearby café and Eleanor asked a man if she might borrow his phone because she'd lost hers and needed to call a friend. No biggie, the guy said. She looked at the number on the receipt for the Days Inn.

She asked for Jackie Badger's room.

"Connecting you now to 106," the woman said.

Eleanor hung up.

JACKIE'S PHONE RANG. She looked down and recognized the number.

"Ms. Badger?"

"This is she."

"Hi, it's Becky from the Days Inn."

"Hi, Becky."

"You asked me to call you if anyone called to ask for you."

"Uh-huh."

"Someone called just a few minutes ago."

"Asking for me."

"Right. I told them what you said to."

"Becky, well done. Was it a man or a woman?"

"Woman's voice."

Jackie winced and her eye twitched. "Thank you, Becky," she managed.

"You're welcome. Thank you for the new iPad and a new iPhone. I don't know what to say. I've never gotten anything like this before in my life."

"My pleasure. I take care of the people who take care of me."

"Is there anything else you need, Ms. Badger?"

"No, Becky. I'm good. Just keep me posted."

"Yes, ma'am. And, um, ma'am—"

"Jackie is fine."

"Yes, Jackie. You want me to do the other thing, too?"

"Yep, just like we talked about. Thank you, Becky." She hung up. She sighed. It had been a long time without sleep, and hard work. She'd moved her operation downstairs into one of the exam rooms they had used for study subjects. It had entailed moving a computer and two monitors. The gadgets sat on a table, Jackie in the swivel desk chair, and Alex lying on her side, dumb smile on her face. Jackie liked the idea of having her there, a mascot. Down here, at least on the scientists' side of the room, it was protected from the electromagnetic field. Not so much on the other side, where the study subjects used to sit. An empty chair was there and, as Jackie looked at it, she sure hoped she'd eventually have Lyle on her side and that she wouldn't have to put him in that chair.

She turned back to her screen. On the window, a news website showed streaming video of protesters beginning to gather for the next day's public display of citizen gun power. Mostly white men, wearing camouflage or green, milling the National Mall, looking at the National Guardsmen, stoically standing with automatic rifles strapped against their chests. The guardsmen peered back. They scanned the crowd for weapons. A policeman with a megaphone repeated that "citizens who open-carry weapons without a permit will be subject to arrest." Salivating journalists dotted the mall, setting the stage for tomorrow's possible conflagration. "Twelve hours and counting," a sideline reporter said, trying to sound concerned about this prospect: Would a protester open fire? A cop?; Would you be arrested if you had an open-carry permit from your home state?; Would it become a firefight? The reporter said: "It's a tinderbox."

"Get a load of this, Alex," Jackie said to her comatose coworker. "We could look like heroes. Shutting it all down, hitting pause, right before all hell breaks loose."

She looked at Alex and then back at the screen.

She clicked into a box reading China Telecom.

13:45:18

13:45:17

FORTY-FOUR

THE DRIVE TOOK place largely in silence, aside from the slip-stream of wind seeping into the car. The Miata was not built for road trips. It was loud and cramped. And goose chase didn't begin to capture the quixotic basis for the trip. Each, though, had motivations. Jerry, who fashioned himself as a man of action, wasn't about to sit around and let this infuriating moment pass without doing something. Plus, this Lyle guy irked the shit out of him, the more so because Jerry saw some connection between Lyle and Eleanor. *I've got your back,* he thought to himself as he watched Eleanor, *and you'll be grateful for it when the time comes.*

Eleanor had made a simple calculation that it made more sense to go than not. But it wasn't satisfying in the least because the margin of her decision was razor thin, like 51 percent to 49 percent. Or maybe her decision was more of a plurality: 50 percent go on a goose chase; 49 percent don't go; 1 percent have no freaking clue, or what's the alternative?

Two things pushed her over the top. One was that someone had died on her airplane, an old man, and she knew—absolutely knew—that she'd done nothing wrong to cause that. The second thing was that, on some basic level, she trusted this Dr. Martin. Such an odd combination of guileless and cunning. Not evil cunning, or wily, but brilliant cunning. She'd looked him up on the Internet before their first meeting. She knew what he'd been once. She was left to wonder what had caused him to come undone. It bore watching. She sat in silence in the passenger seat, trying to take in as much information as she might, watching the side of the increasingly dark road disappear in the rearview mirror.

For his part, Lyle had moved beyond thinking and into instinct. The frontal lobe of his brain, the part involved in decision making and higher-level analysis, would be surprisingly free of activity at times like these. What prevailed was free association, the appearance in his mind's eye of ideas that might be loosely described as taking the shape of puzzle pieces. He tried to link them and, sometimes, frustrated, he would emit a sound of disgust. In a couple of these moments, Eleanor would glance at Jerry, which would send her first officer into a pleasure spiral because the two of them were seeing eye-to-eye. Jerry felt the shape of his gun in his back holster and he smiled.

They pulled off at an exit just before nine o'clock looking for gas and food.

At the Chevron, Jerry fueled up and they all stared at the video monitor located on the pump. It was a split screen, one side featuring an ad with an adorable-looking cartoon car smiling because it was being filled up with Chevron gas; the other side showed marchers descending on the Washington Mall. One held a placard with an automatic weapon drawn on it. He was being confronted by a young person poking a finger in his chest.

Jerry looked at Lyle.

"What is it with you and this woman?" Jerry asked.

"I don't know. Other than . . ." Lyle's back ached from the small backseat confines. "How much do you guys know about the immune system?"

"Fights disease," Jerry said.

"Exactly. The way it does so is kind of incredible. First, it has to recognize a threat. There are trillions of possible alien threats and some of them can look a lot like normal cells. So that's no small feat. Then it has to—"

"Please tell me he's going somewhere with this," Jerry whined condescendingly to Eleanor.

"I think so."

Jerry pulled out of the gas station and into the parking lot of an In-N-Out Burger and took a spot while Lyle explained how the immune system has to look for subtle signs of a dangerous, often deadly, invader, then look for ways to attach to those cells and figure out how to produce proteins capable of attacking the offender. It is an extremely delicate task, arguably the most sophisticated cat-and-mouse game in the world.

"I think she wants to see if I can discover her and then . . ." He paused. "She's putting out these clues. She's trying to get seen, or discovered."

"Pretty damn narcissistic if you ask me," Jerry added.

Lyle pushed air out of his lips, realizing he wasn't making a lot of sense. It was the risk of putting theories out before they were fully baked. He knew there was more to this idea in his head. Something fuller was forming. He couldn't get at it.

It was totally dark now, raindrops pelting the windshield.

Lyle perked up. "What did the attendant say when you called the hotel?" he asked Eleanor. It took her a moment to orient to the question. Then she answered: "She just said she was connecting me to room 106."

"Isn't that an odd answer?" Lyle said.

"Why?"

"Because they don't give out room numbers," Jerry advanced.

"Exactly," Lyle said.

They let this tiny clue sink in.

"So what?" Jerry asked. He wasn't being an ass, just asking the legitimate follow-up question.

"Is she setting a trap? She wants us to go there," Eleanor said. Then she laughed. "Listen to me. This is nuts."

Lyle thought this over.

"Lyle," Eleanor said after a minute, "you still with us?"

"I'll get the food," Lyle said. "Least I can do." He took their orders and went inside while Jerry and Eleanor waited in the car. Inside, Lyle placed his order and thought about this clue about the room number. It was the first time he thought he might have a handle on what this disease called Jackie might be doing, and a plan took shape.

When he got back, Eleanor was stretching her legs. With Jerry out of earshot, she put a gentle hand on Lyle's arm.

"Thank you."

"I whipped you up a gourmet dinner," he said, handing her fast food.

"Hey, you two, get a goddamned room," Jerry said.

They pulled on the highway again. Trucks hummed and rattled by with decreasing frequency on the nearby highway. Lyle, chewing an In-N-Out burger, Eleanor sipping her soda, Jerry spooning hand-fuls of fries.

"Look," Eleanor said. She gestured outside the front of the car. A shooting star finished its descent and disappeared. "Remind you of anything?" she asked Jerry.

He laughed. "Atlanta."

"Jesus, if they had known . . ."

Lyle heard the friendship between them and wondered why he ever had doubted it was there. After another quiet minute, Jerry asked Eleanor: "Are you thinking of Frank?"

She shook her head. "Not really."

She turned around and glanced at Lyle. "You want to hear a funny story?"

"Absolutely."

She told Lyle about the time that she and Jerry had been at a con-tinuing education training at Delta headquarters in Atlanta. They'd been teamed up for years and just hated this nonsense. When they were live-training new landing gear, they'd been asked to pause in a holding pattern when Jerry had seen a shooting star. He pulled out this new time-lapse feature on his iPhone and they'd started playing around with it. They hadn't realized that they'd just missed altogether the second turn in the holding pattern. They looked up when the radio squawked asking what the hell they were doing flying directly at the radio tower.

In the front seat of the Miata, Jerry was laughing. "The best part was that I'd gotten the camera turned around so instead of snapping the shooting star—"

"He took a picture of me with an oh-shit-radio-tower look on my face," Eleanor completed his thought. "Or maybe the best part was when you told the guy in the radio tower that we aimed for the radio tower to punish him for putting veterans into a holding pattern." She turned to Lyle. "Gives you all the confidence in the world in your flight officers, does it not, Dr. Martin?"

Lyle smiled. His mind was half in the conversation and half in the comment Jerry had made earlier about someone named Frank. Lyle wondered if that was Eleanor's boyfriend or husband, or ex. In any case, it was someone who she'd be reminded of by a shooting star.

"Less than two hours," Jerry said.

"I'm beat," Eleanor said. She put her head on the window.

No one spoke for nearly an hour. Lyle even dozed. Jerry tuned the radio to the only station he could find in the rural track, a talk show called "The Fringe," where a guy who declared he was broadcasting from an "undisclosed basement location" speculated that the Million Gun March on Capitol Hill was easily understandable as the work of extraterrestrials. Aliens, the talk-show host said, had impregnated us with Civil War instincts so we'd wipe each other out and they'd harvest our organs.

Lyle dipped in and out of sleep. He woke up and rubbed his eyes. He listened to the radio, the voice coming in and out, static sometimes. It was telling him something. Radio, static, frequencies, epilepsy, channelopathy.

They saw the first sign of Hawthorne. It was just the other side of midnight. "Heading due east," Jerry said. "Not much of a tailwind." He sounded nervous. Eleanor was still asleep. The horizon lurked deep dark. If there was a town up ahead, it wasn't much of one. A distant, ambient light clung low to the ground, far away. Maybe some hotels or restaurants a few miles off. Then, a few miles later, something odd happened. The distant light flickered just at the moment the radio turned to static. Jerry instinctively reached for the dial and spun it, trying to regain the station, and got more static. All across the dial.

"Was that . . ." Lyle started. "That was odd, right?"

"Do you remember when we were landing?" Jerry said to Eleanor. "Hmm," she said, groggily.

"Landing?" asked Lyle.

"In Steamboat."

"Was there an electrical issue—when we landed?" Lyle asked.

"I think so," Jerry said. "I feel like . . ."

"Turn off the radio," Lyle suddenly commanded.

"Hold on, slow down there, Dr. Cowboy," Jerry said. He was back to that officious tone. But he turned off the radio. He sensed they'd been through something like this before. "Wake up, Captain," he said. "We're almost there." He shook her leg. She was way out of it. "I don't like this place. No more chickenshit stuff."

For a second, Jerry let go of the wheel and the car swerved. He twisted in the driver's seat and, with impressive flexibility, removed the nine millimeter from the holster behind him. He set the weapon in his lap. Lyle tried not to laugh. Who or what was he going to shoot? The radio?

It all struck Lyle as familiar, one of those Steamboat flashes. Jerry with a gun and this was going to end badly.

DESOLATION DEFINED THE weigh station at the Nevada border. As they approached, two eighteen-wheelers parked on the right side of the road looked all but abandoned. A toll-like plaza hung over the highway and funneled drivers into booths. All booth lanes were closed but the one on the far right where Jerry pulled the Miata. A dark figure loomed, which Lyle thought odd. Why monitor a border when there was no toll, and in the middle of the night?

"Jerry, put away the . . ." Lyle said.

It was too late. Jerry had pulled into the lane and slowed to the booth. He'd forgotten to holster or hide the semiautomatic and now it lay there in the middle compartment. The worst thing he could do now would be to draw attention to it. Wasn't this an open-carry state? In the booth, a woman wearing a hoodie, frizzy hair pouring out the sides, looked blankly at them, all bureaucrat.

"Evening," Jerry said.

Lyle noticed a small TV in front of her. "Are you watching static?" he blurted.

She looked at her TV and before she could look back, Lyle tossed a blanket over the gun.

"Somethin' weird with the signal all of a sudden," the woman said. She looked over the car again, seemed to have noticed that there was a change but couldn't place it or wasn't letting on.

"What brings you to Nevada?" she asked.

"I'm sorry," Jerry said. "Is this typical? I've never been stopped at a state border before. We're Delta pilots heading to a training."

The woman's eyes settled on Lyle's jacket covering the gun and quickly moved off them. The butt stuck out.

"Just a precaution. With all the stuff taking place in Washington and we've got a military base here, as you probably know if you're pilots," the woman said. "Where did you say you were training?"

Jerry reached for his back pocket and pulled out his wallet. He extracted a card and held it up to her. "If there's nothing else, we'll be on our way . . ." He looked at her name tag. "Marsha."

"Okay," she said. But she looked skeptical. Lyle suspected she was told to be on the lookout for anything remotely suspicious, particularly if there was a military base located here. Even setting aside whatever the hell Jackie was up to, this world seemed to be boiling with tension.

Jerry hit the accelerator. Lyle looked over his shoulder and it sure looked to him like she picked up the phone.

"What the hell were you doing?" Jerry barked at Lyle. "I have a permit. You made it look like we're doing something wrong." He didn't add the words *you idiot,* but his tone captured the sentiment. "Wake up, Captain." He shook her leg again. She was really out. Was there something wrong with her?

From the weigh station, a car pulled out, now about a hundred yards behind them. Jerry stepped on it. So did the vehicle in the rear-view mirror. In the dark, it was hard to tell if it was a cop car, though it stood to reason.

"I've never heard of a weigh station used for that purpose."

"Maybe it's Jackie Badger's doing," Lyle mused aloud.

"These are not ordinary times," Jerry said dismissively. "Assholes with guns and now the government using that as an excuse to take away our rights. Freaking liberals couldn't wait to institute martial law. Over my goddamned dead body."

"You ever notice how often you contradict yourself on this subject, Jerry."

"What's wrong with Eleanor?" Jerry spat back at Lyle. "Captain, wake up."

Behind them, red lights started spinning on the top of the cop car that was now a little more than fifty yards behind.

Ahead, in the dead of night, Hawthorne loomed. Jerry punched the accelerator.

FORTY-FIVE

HEY, JERRY . . ."

Jerry ignored Lyle and kept his foot to the floor.

"Jerry, this is no big deal. You're a first officer with a permit to carry. Just show them the permit and we'll be done with it."

"And I crossed the border from a state that's not open-carry. This all would have been easier before you put us all in harm's way."

"So just say I covered the gun by accident. I'll tell them. We really don't need to overreact to this. It'll make it worse."

Jerry ignored him and pulled a sharp right. They sped down an off ramp and fishtailed as Jerry took a ninety-degree left beneath the overpass, barely hitting the brakes. Lyle white-knuckled his pants legs. The Miata zoomed beneath the highway and emerged on the other side, the tiny town of Hawthorne suddenly looming in front of them. Jerry gunned it again on the empty, quiet, dark road that must've passed for Main Street. It cut through gas stations and fast-food joints and then modest paved tributaries.

Behind, Lyle could see the police car just getting off the highway. The cop must be taking it cautiously, he thought, recognizing there wasn't much place for Jerry to go. And, besides, a wise cop would want no one hurt. Jerry took a quick right and then another and then screeched to a stop. It was a deft move, Lyle realized; the policeman would've been unable to see which turns they'd taken. So they were, in effect, temporarily hidden.

"Go get her, Dr. Martin."

"Who?"

Lyle looked where Jerry was pointing. He had landed them in the parking lot of the Days Inn.

"Room 106," Jerry said. He shook the pilot. "Wake up, Eleanor."

Lyle took in the low-slung, low-budget motel. Or maybe it was high budget for these parts, nice as it got. A postage-stamp-size swimming pool surrounded by a metal fence took up a spot near the rooms in the center of the U-shaped complex. Not a single light shone in any room. But to the left, opposite the side of the lot where Jerry had parked, light shone from a small office. A sign blinked VACANCY.

Jerry quietly shoved an ammunition clip into the nine millimeter. He ejected it and shoved it in again, double-checking. There was no other sound. They must have lost the police car, which probably was patrolling nearby, looking down streets and alleys.

"Draw her out," Jerry said quietly. "That's the plan."

Lyle tried to hear the words and not the obnoxious tone. Did Jerry have a point? Lure Jackie from room 106 and then put a bullet in her? Of course that was too rash.

"I don't think it's going to be that simple. Let's wait another minute to make sure that cop doesn't swing by."

Jerry stared at Eleanor. A touch of drool gathered by her lips. "We need to get her to a doctor," he said. "A real doctor."

Just then, they heard a sound and a car moved on the street, slowly. A searchlight swept the lot, narrowly missing them. The car passed. Lyle pushed the seat forward to get a look at Eleanor. He shook her and she lolled a bit and moaned. Lyle stepped out of the Miata. He looked across the lot and saw inside the little office. The woman looking their direction talked on the phone and quickly looked away when she saw Lyle's gaze.

"I think you should come with me," Lyle blurted. "Let's bring her."

Jerry burst out with a bitter laugh. He caught himself for making too much noise and then just shook his head. "You think we're walking into that trap with you? Are you even paying attention to what you observed earlier? Jackie, or whatever her name is, she wants us to walk into that room. That's why she had the room number given to us."

Lyle let the words sink in. He tended to agree with Jerry. This was a trap.

"I think you should come with me," he repeated.

"Oh, okay, Dr. Martin," Jerry said as sarcastically as he could muster.

Lyle closed his eyes and looked for a reason. He said, "I'm not sure why. Just a gut feeling."

It was unfolding as he'd expected, and now he was starting to chicken out of his plan. It was such a risk. He steeled himself.

"Suit yourself," Lyle said.

"Smartest thing you've said since we met." Jerry felt the need to pile on. "I'm going to find a medical clinic. Or a diner. Captain needs a cup of coffee."

Lyle walked to the motel room door just in front of number 102. Lyle moved along the outer walkway. He could feel his cortisol levels— his fight-or-flight neurochemicals—through the roof. They kept his eyes and ears at superheightened levels. It was his hearing he found himself focused on. Something told him to prepare for a buzz or hum, a radio burst, an electrical surge.

He passed an ice and vending machine and stood in front of room 106. He knocked.

No answer.

Knock, knock.

No answer.

Lyle put his hand on the knob. He heard a screeching sound behind him. He turned to see a police car, lights spinning, pulled on to the street behind him. An officer stepped out of the car. He had his hand on his holster.

Jerry opened the driver's-side door. The officer withdrew his weapon and raised it.

"Drop the gun, Officer," Jerry said. "I've got a permit. It's okay."

"You drop the gun, sir. Right now. Put your hands in the air."

Instead of dropping the gun, Jerry crouched, putting him largely behind the Miata. Lyle could see the shattering of fragile trust, the proverbial fear of the other guy. Each side reverting to fear and aggression. He turned the knob on room 106 and pushed open the door. He blinked with surprise.

He saw the odd walls. Long metal or aluminum sheets covered them. They covered the window, hidden from view from the outside by the darkened curtains. It was like the entire inside was wallpapered in this odd metal covering.

"Put the gun down!" the officer shouted. "Step from behind the vehicle!"

Lyle stared at the metal-colored walls.

A shot rang out.

FORTY-SIX

ANOTHER SHOT. LYLE took a tentative step inside. "Down," Jerry screamed. It wasn't clear who he was talking to. Lyle stared at the room, captivated. Calculating, things falling into place. He picked up movement in his periphery. *Bang, bang,* more shots. A punctured tire hissed.

"Jerry! In here!"

Jerry said something, like, "I got this."

Lyle's head spun with information, ideas. He hardly heard the commotion now. Suddenly, he muttered, "Trap, yes a trap," Lyle muttered.

He shut himself inside, dulling the noise. He looked at the walls, and another oddity: a clock on the bedside table blinking with rapidly changing numbers. Now there was no sound from outside whatsoever.

Suddenly, a high-pitched sound pierced the air. Lyle resisted the urge to cover his ears, during the thirty seconds before the sound passed. He turned around and saw the door.

He saw the bodies.

JACKIE, TIGHT JAWED, stared at the video feed streaming on a second monitor she'd set up on her desk. The video showed a dark hotel room, number 106. Lyle stood at the doorway, back to her. She looked down at the desk. It was covered with papers and take-out food containers. It smelled. Didn't bother her at all, not when she felt such elation. He'd fallen right into it, or, more likely, he'd gotten her clue and acted on it. Either way, all according to plan. Lyle alive and well, and Hawthorne frozen around him.

She cleared her throat. There was a bit more to do before the last of the clock counted down. And she still needed Lyle to show up to celebrate with her. He'd figure it out, and be so grateful for the awakening, his rebirth. He owed it all to her. And in this new world, there would be time to think and process, slow down, take their sweet time to share the peace.

LYLE WALKED OUTSIDE and looked down at Jerry. He lay on his back, his gun hand palm up to the right, nine millimeter spilled out of it. His head tilted sideways, and on his face he wore a dumb-looking smile.

Twenty yards away, near one of the motel's metal support poles that the police officer had hidden behind, the man lay on the ground. He looked much like Jerry. Then another body near the door of the motel; it was the woman who had been behind the desk, her iPad near her feet. She must've come outside when the shooting started.

Eleanor's head lolled back in the passenger seat. Lyle cringed. "I'm sorry, Captain," he said quietly. "It's the only way."

Lyle returned to Jerry and knelt beside the fallen flight officer and felt the carotid for a pulse. He pulled back an eyelid and saw that the pupils looked, at first, to be dilated. Then Lyle really focused and noticed the pupils moving so rapidly as to appear fixed.

Just like Steamboat. The syndrome. The whole town must be like this. He carried Jerry into 106 and laid him on the bed. He did the same for Eleanor so the pair were side by side. He covered them with the flower comforter to keep them warm. He shut the door and studied the room and its oddities. First, the clock. It wasn't the usual motel room clock. It looked similar, but the numbers were going backward and rapidly so.

4:26:27

4:26:26

4:26:25

Counting down.

Until what?

He shuddered at the possibilities. The rest of the country? The world? Lyle's own fate? All of the above?

He focused his attention at the crisp green apple next to the clock. There was a bite out of the apple with a light sheen around the edges. Lip gloss, maybe. The part where the bite had been taken was turning brown. It had been here awhile.

Lyle stood and ran his hand along the metal-looking wallpaper. It was held in place by nails, closely spaced but inexpertly placed, probably with a nail gun. Someone had gone to a lot of trouble. Jackie had gone to a lot of trouble. She had protected this place from the syndrome. He circled slowly, looking in each corner, knowing he was being told something and wasn't sure what it was. How to understand Jackie Badger, this virus? He looked back at the apple.

What does an apple symbolize?

"An apple a day keeps the doctor away," he murmured. No, that was too clever by half. "Eden. The apple, the snake, Eve and Adam," he said. "Some Eden."

He scanned the room, struck by revelation. There must be a camera in here. Of course; it's how Jackie knew to trigger the syndrome outside this room. She was watching. On some level, he realized he'd known it all along. Subconsciously, it's why he set these bodies on the bed, so Jackie could see her success. Now Lyle would take further advantage of Jackie's digital presence here, her watchful eye. It was time to turn up the heat on this madwoman.

Lyle walked to the right side of the bed. He leaned close to Eleanor and he whispered, "I'm very sorry, Captain Hall. No violation intended." He leaned down and swallowed and then kissed Eleanor gently on the cheek. He held his lips there.

It might even draw her out. It was a similar analysis he felt like he'd been through before in the snowy Steamboat night.

He withdrew from Eleanor. He turned and walked from the room.

"NICELY PLAYED," JACKIE said, watching Lyle separate from Eleanor. Her words didn't match the sneer on her face. Lyle was right. She was furious. "Fucking bitch," she muttered. "Alex, that captain is a hideous siren, you know that?

"Hey, you hideous siren, how do you expect to please your man when you're locked in paralysis. You've been paused, bitch."

She took a deep breath. Okay, no biggie. Maybe Lyle was just messing with her, giving her his best match. He probably didn't care about this woman. *Remember who you're dealing with,* she told herself; it's Dr. Lyle Martin, the best of the best, her future and eternal playmate. He was just playing.

She looked at the computer windows on her monitors. They showed her that much of what had needed doing was already done. Virtually the whole world was teed up, the telecommunications infrastructure ready to send paralyzing bursts. The final commands had been keyed in. Only she knew the password to turn it off. So it was just a matter of time.

4:22:19

4:22:18

"Alex, can you hold down the fort for me? I have to grab something from the car."

Jackie pulled on a dark knit cap. It had odd-looking gold-colored lines woven into the sides. These would, in theory, protect her from any inadvertent surges in electromagnetic frequencies. There shouldn't be any. She turned it all off now that she held the town in stasis. But it never hurt to be careful. That's why she'd parked the whole operation in this room downstairs, isolated from the surges bombarding the rest of the world. It was a nice little bunker. As she shut the door, it made her a touch nervous to leave the comfort and safety of this place. But the initial surge was finished, so she should be just fine, just as she had been in Steamboat.

Besides, she was too close to starting this world over to let it be screwed up by Captain Hall. It was exhilarating, in a way, being involved in this game with Lyle. He was searching for her, not merely physically, but searching to understand her, and she was searching for him. Oh, to see and be seen.

Upstairs and outside, she let herself into her Tesla. She glanced in the glove box and withdrew mace and a Taser.

FORTY-SEVEN

LYLE SEARCHED THE motel room one last time for clues, anything at all that might tell him what to do next. He found nothing. It had been scraped clean other than the apple and countdown clock. He left the room, then carried the woman who had fallen outside to the motel office and put her on a couch. Her name tag read BECKY. Her laptop, still running, displayed a Gwen Stefani YouTube video on a loop.

Lyle looked around the office, scoured the front desk for some clue or insight. Not a ton to offer. Nothing telltale in Becky's backpack or the little zip pack on the back of her bicycle that leaned against the couch. No clue planted on the coffee table.

"Ah," Lyle said. On the tiny screen of the cordless phone, he could see the most recent calls in and out and when they'd taken place. It appeared that Becky had placed two calls right about the time that they'd first arrived at the motel. Both were to a phone number in the 415 area code. Lyle jotted down the number. He took Becky's cell phone, a spanking new iPhone. He made sure the phone was turned on.

He picked up the landline and discovered a dial tone but also static. It was half working. He dialed 911. More static. The communications system was down here.

On the counter, on a piece of scrap paper, Becky had made a doodle, a little drawing. It was quite impressive. It was a pencil sketch of a woman. It was her, Jackie.

Lyle found a phone book and the address for a medical clinic, the closest thing here to a hospital. It was only a few blocks away. A few minutes later, he'd pulled out of the Days Inn lot in the Miata. Jerry was in the backseat, covered in the flower bed comforter, so he wouldn't fall off the seat. Eleanor was belted into the front seat, a pillow behind her head.

At first blush, this town at two thirty in the morning looked no different from any other early morning at this time. Dead quiet. Behind the clinic counter, the all-night nurse, comatose, had her face planted on her iPad. Could Lyle read her mind, he'd have seen it delighted by a video of her son hitting a line drive up the middle in his recent Little League game. Inside her head, it was on constant loop.

Lyle let himself into the rooms behind the counter and found the medical supplies. He took a saline pouch and a needle kit and some first aid stuff and returned to the Miata. If need be, the hydration system could be used to sustain someone left in a stasis state. He found smelling salts. He was walking to the car when he ran back in and found the defibrillator. He stood with it staring at Jerry and Eleanor. Then he decided it would do more harm than good. He couldn't just start experimenting.

Having gotten this far, Lyle felt totally helpless. How the hell was he going to reverse this condition? How was he going to stop whatever was going to happen in four hours and change?

Jackie must have left him a clue. What was it?

He started driving, thinking he might go look for help. He wound up back at the weigh station where they'd been questioned on the way in. The woman in the booth had fallen to the side, propped up against the glass, eerily, her eyes still pointed at her phone, which sat on her open palm on the desk. On the screen, a frozen shot of a regular gag from a late-night show where an adorable animated dog spewed expletives.

Lyle wondered if it made sense to keep driving, try to get help. How long would he have to go to find someone?

"Why here? Why Hawthorne?" he asked aloud. Then he answered his question: "She's here and her operation is here. She brought us here."

Lyle reached into his back pocket and he looked at the receipts he'd pulled from Jackie's recycling bin. One was for the hotel, where they'd been. Another from a diner. Another from what looked like some outdoor store. Then a receipt for an electric-car charging station, and one from a 7-Eleven. Lyle looked at all of them. He looked at the receipts again. What was nagging at him?

The 7-Eleven receipt.

It was a receipt for a comb and steel wool.

What bell did that ring?

Steamboat again. Hadn't he tried to create static electricity using items like these?

Had this woman bought the same thing? Or was she toying with him, sending him these little in-jokes, clues. He remembered seeing the 7-Eleven not far from the motel. He gunned the Miata, muttering to himself, becoming more aware of the little signs of a world at a standstill: lights flickering, the eerie sign of a woman at a gas pump, slumped beside her car, a dog wandering the street. At the 7-Eleven, Lyle walked inside, causing a bell to jingle at the door. This did nothing to stir the attention of the guy sitting behind the counter, face-planted on his iPad. Inside his head played a highly amusing video loop of a famous actress being caught on camera stealing a purse from a major department store. The man smiled. *So hilarious.*

Lyle went to the freezer and took out some ice. He returned and laid the man on the floor, placing his jacket beneath his head and gently lifting his head to put the ice under his neck. The cold would help slow the man's metabolism and retain his brain function. Lyle walked to the section with personal supplies, like aspirin and tooth-paste and combs. He leafed through the $1.99 combs. Would Jackie be leaving him a clue? Nothing. He went to the cleaning supplies and found the steel wool. A few pieces hung next to the sponges. He leafed through them for anything unusual. Nothing. Frustrated, he threw them to the ground. He walked to the corner of the store and he looked up at the camera that scoped the inside of the place.

"What do you want, Jackie?" He spread his arms out to the sides. "Where are you?"

He couldn't be sure she was watching. He couldn't be sure she wasn't. He pulled out Becky's phone, thought about dialing the phone number he'd found in the motel office. He strongly suspected he'd get Jackie. He stared at the phone.

Then he stared at the receipts again.

He ran back to the Miata and drove two blocks away to the diner. Another all-night place. Another employee slumped on the counter. Coffee spilled everyplace, when the poor chump fell over on the shitty, ancient counter sipping coffee and watching a fishing tutorial on his phone. Lyle looked again at the receipt that had caught his attention. It said: Delivery.

Jackie had gotten delivery from this place. Lyle started pulling out drawers and looking frantically for a ledger of take-out orders, or customers. It didn't take long to find it. There were several recent delivery orders for J.B. at Google, and an address listed in scrawl. It was 85209 Deer Valley Road.

In a drawer under the register, Lyle found an old-school atlas with detailed maps of the local surroundings. It would take him fifteen minutes to find the place where Jackie Badger took food deliveries.

"JUST ABOUT READY, Alex. How do I look?" Jackie stood before her gaunt, near-death colleague, still in stasis. "I hate wearing lipstick. I think it's sexist and he shouldn't be able to expect I'm always going to dress up like this. Every once in a while, right?"

Her insanity notwithstanding, she looked stunning: a black cocktail dress, tight around her petite figure, short hair combed straight down. Taser in her hand. "Dressed to maim." She smiled. "Then lovingly heal.

"He and I can put the world on pause together, and then watch it like New Year's Eve."

She looked at the video feed from Washington, D.C.; the media was going nuts there, talking about how the Million Gun March was just a few hours away. Police had amassed in force. It looked like Tiananmen Square was about to break out. Jackie thought how proud Lyle would be after he came to his senses.

She dialed Becky's phone number.

FORTY-EIGHT

THE MIATA ZOOMED east on the highway, in the direction away from town and the weigh station, farther into Nevada. A ringing sound exploded. It came from the new iPhone Lyle had plucked from Becky the motel clerk. Lyle wasn't sure the phone would even work but he suspected it might because Jackie had done something to allow it. It rang and rang. Lyle sent the call to voice mail. Better to let Jackie stew. He needed her riled up, not thinking clearly. The phone rang again. He sent it to voice mail again.

The fifth time the phone rang, Lyle put it on speaker.

"Hello, Dr. Martin," Jackie said.

Lyle grimaced. He tried to measure her voice, figure out the best way to play her.

"This is not what Eden looks like, Jackie."

"Not yet, Dr. Martin. Lyle. I'm so delighted you got the reference. Where are you?"

"I'm sure you know that. Jackie, this needs to stop."

She just laughed, casually, like he was a husband being inadvertently annoying or naggy. "How does it feel?" she asked. "To be alive, truly awake."

"I don't know what you're talking about."

"Oh, Lyle." She chuckled.

"What do you want, Jackie?"

"What do *you* want, Lyle?" It was weirdly flirty.

"I want you to stop this, and I want you to revive Eleanor."

Silence.

"You don't give a shit about her."

"Jackie, do you remember how you stood out in my lecture class."

"Do *you* remember?"

"Let's not play games, Jackie."

"Okay, so why taunt me with this hapless pilot?"

"She's my friend, Jackie. It's beside the point, you've got to make this sto—"

"I see how you look at her and how she looks at you. Of course, she's not looking at you at all now. She's hanging in space like a macabre puppet."

"Stop this, Jackie. You have to stop this."

"I don't want to fight!" A veritable explosion. Lyle withdrew from the phone. "Sorry, Lyle. We're better than that. I think it's hard right now with all the stress. But it'll be easier when things slow down."

"Okay, Jackie, how do we make this stop?"

"Well, first, and thank you, the seduction has to be mutual."

"What seduction?"

"I'm not going to do all the work. Try harder. I'm trying to tell you what I need here." She hung up.

LYLE TOOK A right onto a dirt road. He turned off the lights. But what did it matter; she'd know he was approaching. Hell, she probably was tracking the phone. He tried to let his mind go blank. He wanted to tap into instinct. But for a moment, he could see the strange beauty that Jackie must be seeking. In the silence of a dead world, you could listen and be heard. Here she would be seen. He appreciated its seduction. And here, there was no risk of death or terrible plague because there was no life. There was no infidelity. He understood this virus called Jackie. He understood the countdown clock. She would do this to the entire world, hang it in space, free of humanity, free of menace.

The seduction has to be mutual.
Try harder.

What did she mean by that?

He let his mind go blank, trying not to overthink it.

Five minutes later, a dark shape appeared on the landscape. It was a building or huddle of them. A light hung over one of the buildings, just enough to betray the clutch. Lyle pulled into a lot beside a Tesla and he looked at the corrugated metal structure. The door was propped open, inviting him inside. He noticed a video camera—these things were everywhere—this one atop the building, scanning. Lyle pulled himself to the right to try to be as shaded as possible from the camera's view.

He fished in his pocket for a pen and paper he'd taken from the motel and scribbled a note. Then he reached below Eleanor's feet for the medical supplies he'd taken from the clinic. The defibrillator was still in the trunk. He left it there. He readied everything else. He picked up the pistol. He'd been to a shooting range once. He wasn't sure he'd be any good with this thing or if he could make himself use it. Even if he did, and he shot and killed Jackie, then what? How would he stop this thing, or reverse it?

He looked at Eleanor and Jerry.

It was time.

A MINUTE LATER, he walked to the door of Lantern. A light wind blew, chilling further a desert night. The last time he'd approached a mysterious setting, in Africa, he'd failed miserably. He'd failed the villagers, himself, Melanie. Yes, she'd failed him first, but he'd long before laid the foundation. As he walked, Lyle's mind and eyes played tricks on him. He thought for a second that he saw bodies, piles of them, then they disappeared, then scattered sufferers, and then darkness again, and then a plain full of frozen humanity, people stalled in stasis by this electrical weapon that Jackie purveyed.

He walked inside and surveyed the warehouse-size room. It was largely empty. Cubicles, a bunch of litter on the floor around one particular cubicle near the middle-center. A nondescript conference table took up the room. No sign of an operation Lyle supposed he expected to see here. What was this place? He walked in tight circles, looking, gun outstretched, sidestepping discarded candy bar wrappers and empty water bottles, a soda can. He saw dirt scuffs on the floor and followed the scuffs. They went toward the back, in the direction of a stairwell. Jackie appeared at the top of it, resplendent with formal wear and evil.

"You're not going to shoot me, are you, Lyle?" It sounded flirty. "C'mon." She gestured with her hand for him to follow. She disappeared down the stairs.

He led with the gun. Cautious steps. Down the stairs he went until he came to a bend in the well. He started to turn the corner and he saw the device in her hand. The last thing he said to himself was "Taser."

Everything went black.

FORTY-NINE

I MADE US DINNER," Jackie said. The words reached Lyle through a miasma as he was coming to.

"Have some water." Jackie held a glass to his lips and, in spite of himself, he sipped. "There you go," she said gently. "Relax, Lyle. It's over."

Jackie backed up and she sat down across from him at a square worktable. In front of each of them sat a plate with a burrito on it. Next to her plate sat a wireless keyboard. A little farther left on the table loomed two large computer monitors. One showed a live video stream, people milling about, police, a crowd of sorts. At the bottom, a caption explained the event taking place on the live stream but Lyle couldn't focus on it sufficient to read it. On the other monitor was a clock counting backward and several boxes that looked like command lines.

"I'm just kidding about making dinner," Jackie said. "Cheap microwave burritos. Not the kind of circumstances that lend themselves to cooking." She looked at him and smiled. His head still hung to his chest. He lifted it as things came into focus. She had an oddly radiant look about her, triumphant and somehow nurturing. He gently lifted his arms from the armrests and moved his legs. It surprised him that he was unfettered, not chained. Then again, the door was behind her. He realized she had a Taser and the gun tucked on her side of the table.

She followed his gaze to the computer monitor.

47:21

47:20

47:19

"You'll be out of your haze soon enough. You want more water?"

He shook his head and blinked. Could he overpower this woman?

"No, Lyle. No, you're not going to overpower me. You don't even want to, do you? Y'know what I actually think you're feeling? I think you're feeling gratitude. Certainly on some level."

"You don't have a limp," he said.

"Of course not."

He nodded. She'd faked that nicely in Steamboat.

"Maybe you don't remember how I found you, how far I've brought you," she said.

"I don't know what you're . . ."

"Shh. Listen, let me refresh your memory while you get your wits about you."

She told him the story of finding him in his office, drunk, dark, mired in self-hatred. She'd promised him, and herself, she'd figure out how to pull him out of that place. "Now you're alive again, inspired, hunting, discovering. Look at you.

"Don't get me wrong. This is not all about you," she continued. "I'd hate to start our relationship, or this stage of it, with that kind of imbalance. Leads to crazy stuff down the road."

"There's no down the road, Jackie," he managed. "There's no relationship."

Another smile from her, caring in its own way, the look of a lover who realizes her partner doesn't fully get yet what's right for him.

"On the relationship count, I can tell you one hundred percent that you're wrong. I honestly feel like no one has ever seen me as clearly as you see me."

"Is that so?"

"Fair enough. I guess we can say that point has yet to be fully determined. But my gut tells me it'll play out that way. It's rare my gut ever tells me anything I can trust this much. In any case, I feel even surer that no one has ever seen you as clearly as I can see you."

Lyle stared at this crazy person before him and considered which strategy, if any, might reorient her.

"Melanie, maybe, saw certain things about you," Jackie continued. "Eleanor may imagine she sees things in you, but now I'm digressing and that poor torpid bitch isn't really worth talking about. My point is that what we have is the very essence of a relationship."

"I do see you, Jackie."

"Thank you, Lyle."

"I don't think I like what I see."

"No, that's not what you mean." Her voice rose. "I'm sorry." She cleared her throat. "What you mean is that it's hard for you to reconcile the way I've made you feel about yourself with some of the other things you see going on."

He looked at the screen with the live TV feed. Now he could make out the words at the bottom: *National Mall; Million Gun March. Under an Hour. Will There Be Bloodshed?*

Lyle looked at the countdown clock.

38:16

38:15

"Help me reconcile it, Jackie," he said. He needed to buy time. His plan looked very much like it was not taking shape.

"Would you like some wine, Lyle?"

"Sure."

She poured him some red into a plastic cup.

"Let's talk about you first. When I found you, you were all but dead. Now you are revived. Will you grant me that?"

"It's a stretch, Jackie. I was in a bad place, and now I'm in a worse place."

She laughed gaily.

"I think we might say the same for humanity. I want you to think in a very clear-eyed way about how the world is transforming and where it finds itself. It is on the brink of coming apart. Look at them." She jutted her chin in the direction of the video screen. "It's exactly—*exactly*—what made you so angry when things collapsed with Melanie and with that ridiculous Dean Thomas and your job."

"I'm sorry, Jackie, I'm having trouble following."

"I doubt that. Maybe it's the Taser. You do realize that it was becoming very, very hard for you to defend your life choices as a doctor, to continue to get the energy to try to protect humanity. It was getting very hard to figure out what was the right thing to do. Do you remember?"

He remembered. He didn't want to admit it to her right now because his growing skepticism from three years ago bore no relation to this monster in the black dress and red lipstick.

"Suit yourself, Lyle. You know it's true, though. Of course, you were cynical. You'd fought on the side of people. But you eventually discovered that the viruses, the evil bacteria and disease, were so much more, well, frank. You knew where they were coming from. They declared their purpose. On the other hand, the people, humanity, what a disingenuous lot, right?"

"No, that's not—"

"Okay, maybe a bridge too far saying that. But confusing, at least. People are confusing, at least, sending mixed messages. People put you in a difficult position, impossible positions." She saw that he was trying to understand and she took it as encouragement. She thought of her parents, putting her in an impossible position, not knowing what to do, then her sister whom her inaction failed to save, and Denny, using her, abusing her trust. She'd had no time to figure things out, the world moving so fast. She winced and brushed away those memories. It was a new time.

"Lyle, were you supposed to treat people, help them, let them kill themselves or each other? What the hell were you supposed to do?"

Lyle felt the power of the moment. She was telling him something.

"Do people put you in a difficult position, Jackie?"

She smiled, shrugged, like *Of course, aren't we all speaking the same language here?*

"Did someone in particular put you in a difficult position, Jackie?"

She gritted her teeth. He'd not move her into those terrible memories, and, besides, this wasn't about Jackie; no, to her, this was now about everyone. Even someone as sane and wonderful as Lyle understood what it was like to be put in a terrible position, to not know what to do as violence, danger, terror loomed.

"These people, look at them"—she looked at the computer—"in Washington, at the mall, one self-righteous group of police is going to go to war with another self-righteous group of gun owners. Each certain they are saving humanity, and each about to destroy it."

Lyle tried to latch on to the change in direction, keep her going, buy time. "We're speaking about differences of opinions, the working out of ideas. That is politics, cooperation, compromise."

"No! The opposite!" She slapped the table. "We're talking about not listening. We're talking about . . ."

"What, Jackie. What are we talking about?"

"We're talking about giving people some time so that they can figure out what's right? We're slowing the world down. Don't you see how important that is?"

He pulled backward at the intensity. This was what it was all about for her, and he suddenly totally grasped that basic idea. It was all moving too fast for her. She didn't feel heard and she couldn't hear herself.

"Let's take our time with it, Jackie. I'm listening."

"I know you are. You are the first person who ever really saw me. You met me in Nepal, you . . ." She grinned, so sincerely. "You don't remember, do you? Oh, Lyle, of course you need to know this." She reminded him, seeing he had a vague recollection of helping a young backpacker. "And then, years later, in the back of class, you heard me even before you actually saw me. You *heard* me, which is even more powerful. Then when you looked at me, you understood. Just the way you diagnosed people and what ailed them. It is such a powerful gift and I want you to know that I see you, too; I hear you. I heard you calling and I came."

On the live video stream, there was a flash of light.

"It's starting," she said.

"You did that?" he asked.

"No. No. I mean that one of the nut cases on one side or another has started the violence. Honestly, I can't tell which is the immune system anymore and which the disease—whether we're defending or attacking ourselves. I guess maybe that's how you felt when you got depressed. But the thing is, Lyle, the thing that I think you'll be most proud of is that I figured out a painless way to stop things." Before she could elaborate, the pair of them looked at the screen and the scrambling of footage as reporters and cameras jogged around. Several shots rang out loud enough to overcome the extremely low volume on the TV.

"How does it work?" Lyle asked.

"Quite effectively. Before you know it, everyone at the mall, everyone in the world, will be on pause. No more violence, no more"—she looked for the words—"crimes of passion." She paused. "Then when they come out of it, *if* they come out of it, they'll have forgotten what got them so incensed in the first place. Think of it, Lyle! A reboot for humanity." She knew that wasn't the question he was asking. "We've got a few minutes. I'll bring you up to speed on the process."

From the way they were talking, Lyle couldn't tell if she felt he was softening to her, or whether she thought he remained her sworn foe. In any case, she was still keeping him in a physically inferior position. She wasn't going to give him a chance to extricate himself or stop her, if he could even figure out how to do that. He tried to think about what he would do if she were a deadly virus. In such a case, he'd try everything to hold the disease at bay—through fluids and managing infection spread—until the body came and healed itself or he could figure out another solution, a medical miracle. His original plan looked like it was going to fail, miserably. She was going to destroy the entire planet. He could imagine her hitting the proverbial green button and everyone heading into some strange seizure and crashing their cars, falling down and splitting open their skulls, failing to turn off their ovens and having fires burn down the world.

18:16

18:15

18:14

"Is it a channelopathy?" he said. "Or more seizure?"

She perked up at the question. She loved his engagement with her, as peers, as equals.

"Physiologically, you're probably better equipped to analyze the mechanism. But, to answer your question, somewhere between the two, seizure and channelopathy, but with much longer lasting effects. Indefinite, as far as I can tell."

"It's why I saw an immune response in Steamboat."

"Right. That was so exciting to watch. Your gift emerging again. Anyhow, yes, to stay on point: the electrical signals evidently stimulate an immune response, the body recognizing something alien."

She pointed over Lyle's shoulder and he looked into a room that he hadn't even realized was behind him. It was on the other side of a two-way mirror. And there sat a woman slumped in a chair. "Lyle, meet Alex. Alex has been rather unresponsive for days."

Lyle grimaced and turned back. "Let me help her."

Jackie just laughed again, as if to say *Give me a break, Lyle.*

"If you ask me, and you did, I think that all our heavy use of devices is predisposing us to this seizure state, this syndrome. It'll be interesting to see when I flip the giant switch in the sky, whether everyone succumbs or just big groups of people. You can't really know until you try."

"Big switch?"

"Proverbial. I've already programmed it to push the algorithm through to every major transmitter in . . ." She looked at the countdown clock. "Fifteen minutes or so. No switch that needs flipping. I can't believe it's really here."

"You said they might come out of it."

She shook her head, not understanding his comment.

"Earlier, you said they would come out of it, *if* they come out of it. Will they come out of it?"

"If I reverse the frequency process. I did it in Steamboat. No harm no foul."

"After people crashed their cars and died and who knows what else."

"Small price to pay to save the world from itself."

"How do we stop it, Jackie?"

She just shook her head. "I'd hate to discover you were someone who wanted to fight, not listen."

Her eyes were wet.

"No more time. You have to decide now, Lyle. Save 'em or join 'em."

SHE CLICKED ALONG on the wireless keyboard and a second window opened on the monitor with the countdown clock. Lyle recognized Jackie's intensity as the sort that might overtake him when he was in the midst of discovery. He didn't feel seen by her, as she insisted, but he could acknowledge distant similarities. Not sufficient to have him accede to whatever she was asking him to decide in her favor. He was waiting to find out what that might be.

The clock said eight minutes and thirty seconds.

In the second window, an image appeared. It was a green field with a path cut through it leading to a mountain where aspen trees grew. It dissolved and there was an image of Melanie climbing into bed with the father of her child. It was on video feed. Lyle was watching his ex-wife climb into bed with the man she'd cheated with.

"Stop it, Jackie."

"Fair enough, I'll spare you the gory details."

She closed the window. "Which world do you want to live in, sweetheart?"

He didn't speak.

"The one where we must constantly fight to curtail the worst parts of humanity, or the one less traveled? I'm not so stupid, so naive, as to think a world on pause is a perfect world. I'm not insane, not *that* insane." She laughed. She didn't think herself nuts at all. "It's just a world we haven't tried yet. A world of two, for the time being at least.

"Will you join me?"

She held out her hand. It struck Lyle he might grab and yank it.

"I made this world for you, Lyle. To awaken you, and then to take away all the pain of indecision: What's right? What's wrong? Are people good or bad? They're on hold, at least until we can figure out what we want to do."

"I have a question first."

6:56

6:55

"If I join you, if we take the road less traveled, and it doesn't work, will you wake everyone up? Can we return to the way it was?" Lyle asked.

She shrugged. "It's a relationship. We'll work it out." A nonanswer.

"How would we do that?"

"Work it out? We'd talk and we'd listen."

"No, how would we return it to the way it was, the way it is?"

She smiled. "Are you really still trying to figure out how to reverse this?"

"I'm a doctor, Jackie. I never quit trying to figure out how to kill the disease."

"You *are* a doctor, Lyle. You never stopped being one. I know that. I love that about you. So I'll answer, in general terms. It's a password, of course, that I've no need to tell you about at this point. So, what's it going to be?"

5:27

"You know I can't do this, Jackie."

She looked at him, curious, shaking her head.

"It's a chance to make something beautiful and pure."

"You're on your own, Jackie. I'll go down with the ship."

"I'm so disappointed to hear that."

"How does that work? Do I go outside?"

"Yes, that's one way. But I prefer something more intimate," she said, tears in her eyes. "I'll need you to go into that room there, behind you. It will get the signal. I will be spared it in here. You can sit, and I can watch as you fall into a stasis state. I hope the bears don't eat you."

"What?"

"Kidding, Lyle. If I let bears eat you, then how would I be able to enjoy looking at you now and again."

4:47

It's not working, he thought, *the plan has fallen apart.*

"Up you go," she said.

Lyle stood. He looked at the woman on the other side of the mirror, her body inert, as Lyle's was soon to be. He turned back to his captor.

"Jackie, would you offer me any final thoughts?"

She smiled.

"Hickam had it right."

Now he smiled sadly, recalling his own lecture on Hickam's dictum. It must have had an impact on her. "Patients can have as many diseases as they damn well please," Lyle muttered.

"So true, right. It's sheer and utter chaos, nothing so obvious and simple as Occam's razor. What is doing us in? Everything. What can we do about it?" Then she looked at the monitor of the live feed from the National Mall, as if the image of people about to kill one another off made her point. "Hit pause. Anyhow, off you go."

3:22

3:21

Lyle smiled grimly and let himself into the adjoining room. He stood with his arms crossed beside the chair with Alex. She did not smell good. Lyle couldn't help but flash for a moment on his own hubris. He'd given himself too much credit. He supposed he'd prided himself in the past on the opposite. He'd tried to be humble and listen. He watched the clock count down.

When it was at two minutes, Lyle saw a hint of movement behind Jackie. It was the door to the research room. It jostled. Lyle banged on the mirror. "Jackie," he said. "Jackie." He waved, trying to distract her. She looked at him and walked to the window.

"It's too late to change your mind," she said.

"I need to talk to you, Jackie!"

"Do you mean it?" she asked, plaintive, hopeful.

1:30

Lyle put his hands on the window, as if urging her to put her hands against his. She did it.

The research room door burst open.

Jackie spun around. There stood Eleanor. She had a device in her hands, the defibrillator. She bulled forward. She crashed into Jackie. *Boom!* She zapped Jackie with major hits of electricity. The woman fell to the ground, seizing. Lyle exploded out of the room on the other side of the mirror.

"Lyle, are you okay? Where are we? How did you—"

"We're almost out of time." He ran to the keyboard.

:57

:56

Lyle had been studying the screen before and figured he had one shot to get it right, to stop this thing. On the top, he clicked on an icon that said program. Menu items materialized. He clicked on Fail-Safe.

A single word appeared.

Password.

:42

:41

"Lyle?"

Lyle froze over the keyboard. What if he got it wrong?

He started to type.

:29

:28

A few more letters. He held his finger over the enter key.

:18

:17

"Ahhhh!" It was Jackie. She'd somehow shaken off the electrical surge. She sprang forward, lurched past Eleanor, and knocked Lyle backward.

:12

:11

:10

She punched at him and kicked, spasmodic. Lyle threw her off.

Sharply. She thudded to the side. Eleanor took the paddle to her again. *Zap.* Jackie seized, shivering with electricity.

:4

:3

Lyle scrambled to his feet. He put his hand over the keyboard.

:2

:1

Lyle hit the enter button.

EPILOGUE

A NYONE EVER TELL you not to fondle the pilot, Dr. Martin?"

"I'm just saying, there is no substitute for a careful, hands-on examination."

The prop plane circled the southern edge of the Canadian Rockies. Eleanor Hall had the helm. Lyle sat in the bucket seat beside her, hand on her knee.

"Gorgeous. Not a soul out here for miles." Eleanor caught herself after she said it and looked at him and smiled. "Not that I'm calling for wiping the planet clean of other human beings. Just a nice, quiet afternoon."

"I could do without a newspaper for a few days."

Three months later, the fallout from the Million Gun March had moved from the front pages. An explosive end had been averted, by the protesters themselves, after one among their ranks began discharging bullets at an empty police van. For a moment, the world watching, the fates swirled with indecision. Then a handful of other gun-toting protesters walked up to the shooter and convinced him to put down the gun. They turned him over to the cops. Silence swept over the Washington Mall.

The protesters raised their guns over their heads. In their ability to control their own, they had proclaimed their power. The next morning, they disbanded, claiming victory.

Each side returned to a stasis state, not the kind that Jackie had envisioned, not a dead one, but a living one. Ever threatening, sometimes exploding, often just on the edge. Cat and mouse, disease and immune system, the difference razor thin.

Lyle felt great relief, obviously, but little triumph in his role at stopping Jackie. Though if he'd allowed himself to admit it, his plan had been ingenious.

He'd realized that Jackie wanted him to go into the motel room to spare him the syndrome. He'd also figured out there was another way to protect someone from seizing: the use of the barbiturate phenobarbital. So he'd secretly slipped some of the drug into the soda he bought for Eleanor at In-N-Out Burger. It's why she'd been knocked out. But it protected the pilot's system when the electrical surge happened. When the syndrome hit Hawthorne, Eleanor had been saved.

Jackie didn't know that. All she'd seen on camera was a comatose Eleanor. That was part of Lyle's plan.

Lyle had left a note for Eleanor in the Miata, given her smelling salts before he'd gone into Lantern and hoped she'd revive in time to read the note, get the defibrillator, and take Jackie by surprise. Mission accomplished, with seconds to spare.

Then it had come down to figuring out the password.

Lyle always told his students: ask for a patient's history and then really listen. When he'd asked Jackie for her final thoughts, he figured she'd tell him what was most important to her.

Hickam's dictum.

Jackie couldn't live in a world with myriad threats. To her, life and death struggled all the time, and she felt caught in between. Lyle understood it. For now, he could live with it just fine.

"How about there?" Eleanor asked. Up ahead a field that looked like it had been struck by fire a few years back. Little brush, no trees.

"Nice."

"Can you turn the yellow knob there, Dr. Martin, helps lock the speed."

"I'm not a pilot, Captain Hall. I just play one on TV."

"Have you at least got the picnic basket?"

"Affirmative."

She turned to Lyle and met his smile.

She guided the airplane with a soft bump into the open field, a grove of trees up ahead.

ACKNOWLEDGMENTS

M
Y DEEP THANKS to my editor and friend, Peter Hubbard, and to my agent and sister-from-another-mother, Laurie Liss.

Thank you to Liate Stehlik, publisher at William Morrow, an authentic friend of writers, and leader of a group of like-minded and gracious editors, marketers, cover illustrators, publicists, and salespeople. Big fat thanks to Nick Amphlett.

I once again received terrific insight from The Council, the tight-knit group from the Stanford Medical School class of 1983 that includes my talented and beautiful wife, Dr. Meredith Jewel Barad. A special shout-out to Dr. Jen Babik, a brilliant infectious-disease specialist and the best shortstop I have a privilege to know personally.

Over the years, as I've sunk my 10,000-hours-plus into learning to write, I've been supported through advice and deed by some of the world's best thriller writers. It is a collection of people who matches talent with generosity and class. You've taught me to pay it forward.

As always, my love to Meredith, Milo, and Mirabel, and to my parents, who generously support and encourage creative flights.